THE MOON IS NOT HAUNTED

THE MOON IS NOT HAUNTED

J. R. CYGAL

Library of Congress Control Number (LCCN): 2023901551

Publisher's Cataloging-in-Publication Data
provided by Five Rainbows Cataloging Services

Names: Cygal, J. R., author.
Title: The moon is not haunted / J. R. Cygal.
Description: Seattle : J. R. Cygal Publishing, 2023.
Identifiers: LCCN 2023901551 (print) | ISBN 979-8-9876915-4-0
    (hardback) | ISBN 979-8-9876915-0-2 (paperback) | ISBN
    979-8-9876915-1-9 (ebook)
Subjects: LCSH: Astronauts--Fiction. | Lunar mining--Fiction. |
    Space race--Fiction. | Conspiracies--Fiction. | Mental
    illness--Fiction. | Thrillers (Fiction) | Science fiction. |
    BISAC: FICTION / Science Fiction / Space Exploration. |
    FICTION / Thrillers / Technological. | FICTION / Science
    Fiction / General. | FICTION / Psychological. | GSAFD:
    Science fiction.
Classification: LCC PS3603.Y53 M66 2023 (print) | LCC
    PS3603.Y53 (ebook) | DDC 813/.6--dc23.

J. R. Cygal Publishing
https://www.jrcygal.com/
Editing Services by Emily Poole at Midnight Owls Editors
Book Design by Jonathan J. Reed
Book Cover Art by Rose Miller

Published in Seattle, WA in the United States of America.
10 9 8 7 6 5 4 3 2

This book is dedicated to the countless engineers,
technicians, scientists, and mathematicians who work
tirelessly for our future.

THE MOON IS NOT HAUNTED

"The sunlights differ, but there is only one darkness."
- Ursula K. Le Guin

PROLOGUE

Apollo 17, the last time we touched the Moon, was the first and only time a working scientist traveled beyond low Earth orbit, outpaced the torment of its gravity, and challenged the tyranny of our traditions: the frontier is still there. In the spirit of us, the consciousness of this new land has not yet been shaped. Since reaching that symbolic precipice in 1972, our species has been stagnant on this romantic and necessary front of human exploration. The expansion of knowledge, the boundary of experience, the appreciation and art of the universe—it's in our DNA to be drawn to the frontier. People want to be part of the adventure, the growth, the sacrifice, the extension of awareness. We need it.

At the antiquated lunar training facility in northern Iceland, on the edge of the world, the sun long set behind the sharp chill of the Arctic Sea, the Northern Lights bring vague color back from the pitch dark of a perpetual night. The retexturing of the sky humbles the modern-day astronaut trainees with the terrifying reality of being disconnected—untethered, ambitious, alone. But in the most isolated region on Earth, looking out across the black sea and up to the green and purple sky, the hearts of those still at home touch them. Those on the edge are still threaded to the rest of us.

How far can they ascend beyond our boundaries? Who in the future will surpass where they stopped, extending the periphery of what is known and can be touched? Have they even been born yet? These questions pass through isolated persons over millennia but connect them regardless of time or location.

Standing on this ancient Norse frontier, the purpose of space exploration and human space flight becomes self-evident. It is every part of our identity. Our history, science, mathematics, endurance, philosophy, tragedy, triumph. Our unknown.

Looking back toward the cratered ground, one of them wonders. Will we eventually be the ghosts of some new frontier? Centuries from now, who will share our thoughts?

CHAPTER 1

Darkness. A confined cell.

I have no idea what to do next, Samuel "Scorcher" Robertson thinks to himself. *And everyone else is just full of shit, especially the ones in the Technical Fellowship. They're only proficient at writing conference papers and promoting their own tacky websites. But when it comes to real engineering problems, they can't be bothered.*

The urge to not be idle overcomes him even though he's constricted and can't see. *Should I kick it till it starts working again?* He attempts a light kick to test the stiffness of his spacesuit. *I swear, the more I see in the field, the less I understand—the less these guys seem to understand, which means we're all screwed.*

He wonders if his disdain of everyone isn't just from his own arrogance—or fear. He knows he can be overly confident sometimes. He admits it. But isn't he justified? He can simply look at a jet engine and know exactly where it'll fail in sonic fatigue. Glance at a gear and spline design and know it'll lock up after a thousand cycles.

His overthinking nature continues to eat itself. *No. We're all just full of shit, including me. Especially me. All talk. Somehow our species has made it this far. Apes on a rocket, funded by a dotcom to mine moons. Are we really moving all the polluting industries off Earth, or are we just extending the damage to other planets now? If I'm doing the wrong thing, does any of it really matter?*

The lights are back on. Floating in the airlock, the visual cues reappear before his eyes and snap his consciousness back to reality. He's no longer alone. He's looking at his colleague, who goes by her callsign Space-Bee, and who is now peering back at him through the observer's window, hair standing vertical in the microgravity.

Which way is vertical?

The clanging of the metal tools attached to Scorcher's belt is louder than expected, echoing through the whole ship even though he's sealed off. A first-time astronaut, he squirms around, awkward and stiff. In space, legs are useless.

How does Space-Bee move with so much finesse when she does spacewalks?

As the pressure drops to a complete vacuum, the tool clanging gets quieter until it goes silent. Everything looks the same to the observer, but now the volume of the natural universe is unnaturally muted. For some reason, this gets Scorcher's adrenaline rushing. This is real. He knows he's where no human should ever be. He was brought to this environment, though not by natural selection or biological evolution. Scorcher knows that the laws of the universe won't submit to persistence alone; one miscalculation and the space game ends in an instant, like you were never there.

Unlike in the movies where astronauts can hear themselves breathe and see their face shields fog up, real-life space is loud, uncomfortable, mechanical, and unnatural. Humans don't belong here. There is no music, but there is a rhythm as fans and pumps circulate air and liquid coolant through the spacesuit. The white noise of systems operating to temporarily sustain life in an astronautical diving bell being ballooned apart by a vacuum. All spacesuits are deafening without headsets, which, for safety reasons, can't cancel the white noise.

Over the intercom, he hears, "Space-Bee to Scorcher. We are GO from Seattle to egress the airlock and hold. Attach the tether externally but hold at the hatch."

"Copy. Exit airlock, hold position at latch until your call. Don't leave me hanging there too long."

"Copy 'don't leave me hanging.'" The tiny window can't obstruct how hyper focused Space-Bee is. Normally all the audio between Seattle and the ship's COMM is heard in the spacesuit headset, but their ship is running on the backups of the backups—ergo the impromptu spacewalk. All communication to Seattle is non-audio.

The QEC—quantum entanglement communicator—is the second-tier failsafe for interfacing with Seattle Ground Station. It is the only true encrypted communication technology. In fact, calling it encrypted is an understatement. It is completely invisible and undetectable. Invisible to the universe except for a pair of entangled photons which communicate via "spooky" physics, as Einstein declared years before the phenomenon was proven to exist. "Teleportation," as it is called by news media, even though it's no more teleportation than a voice over a phone call. "Dodgy and unreliable," Scorcher calls it.

Space-Bee mumbles something inaudible back to her crewmate manning the adjacent engineering station. He clearly shares her frustration and is probably groggy from lack of sleep. All crew members, both permanent flight crew and engineers en route to Central Lunar Mining, are attacking the current crisis. The en route engineers and technicians are often hazed for being glorified passengers, though no one gets an idle post through cislunar space. And in a crisis of this magnitude, it's all hands on deck.

"Of course the QEC wouldn't work," Scorcher says in a scratchy voice, not worried about whether he is complaining to another person or running commentary to himself.

Scorcher floats, staring at the black, lifeless ocean with no waves, no texture, no life. Annoyed by Seattle's delays, he turns around and focuses his sight away from his ferry ride, the *Space Clipper Vegvisir*, heroically named after the Icelandic symbol for way-finder. He assumes it's because of the Company's close connection with the lunar mining training facility in northern Iceland. To Scorcher, the name is a bit nerdy, but the Founder's ambitions are anything but timid. The *Vegvisir* is intended for a much larger mission than its currently scheduled use. It is oversized for the role of simple space taxi and was engineered by the Founder for a broader purpose. But as massive as the *Vegvisir* is, built out of aluminum, titanium, carbon fiber laminate, and nickel superalloy, to Scorcher it yields the confidence of a dinghy when among the stars.

He floats in an iceless freezing sea with a permanent sun, no horizon to orient the frigid pitch-black sky. A sky with no edge or profile, it steals heat just to disperse it as infrared radiation, out to nothingness, lost forever from the law of entropy. Inside the ship, it's so cold and metallic that the spacesuit is half a relief.

Ultimately, what has struck him on his first spacewalk is how many contradictions exist in this nothingness. How can nothingness contain so much? Unlike his occasional ocean travels on Earth, there's no salty spray, no odors. Monsters are not lurking below as they do in the real ocean, shrieking in the night only to disappear, untraceable in the relative peace of daylight. The monster here is permanent and infinite. It's nothing and cannot be touched. It kills but doesn't exist.

His tinted visor is no match for the singular and blinding light source. It's like a black room with a single spotlight an astronomical unit away. The sky is so black and starless, he can almost touch its texture. Nothingness — even simulated, he wonders — always evolves into human sensation, one way or another.

With his focus dangerously lost from Seattle's delay, he wonders if anyone else ever thought this was what escape velocity would feel like. He tries to pretend he's moving fast but gets distracted from the discomfort of idleness and shifts again. An almost unbearable burning heat is on the sunny side of his knees, the cold of Dante's hell on the opposite. This temperature gradient is infinitely more extreme than the sun-versus-shade of any Earth-side desert in high summer.

"Space-Bee, can you confirm that no ice is visible on my suit?" he requests.

"Copy 'check for ice', Scorcher. No problem. Rotate around." Space-Bee peers through the airlock window. It's difficult for her to get a thorough visual over the acreage of spacesuit. Mobility is limited, but she searches with a studied intensity. Her black irises are piercing, and the contours of her sharp eyes trend upward and move outward to blend with the structure of her high Eurasian cheekbones. At her detailed inspection of his body, covered though it is by the suit, Scorcher feels vulnerable in a way he's never before experienced.

Scorcher mentally shakes it off and notes she's neglected the COMM station for too long. Her strength in focusing is countered by her weakness in multitasking. So far on their short voyage together, he's noticed that she'll become one with the object or task that has her attention. It's intimidating but intriguing to him at the same time. He wonders if he's stronger at focusing or multitasking—probably neither.

"Looks good. No ice is visible." She returns to the COMM and gives an excited thumbs up. "The life vest is a GO."

"Copy."

The life vest is a mini backup jetpack powered by compressed nitrogen jets, used only in case the astronaut accidentally starts to float away because their safety tether gets unlatched.

To save from having to do two spacewalks, Scorcher lugs around more tools than he needs. Not his idea—or first choice—but Space-Bee's, though he didn't have a good argument against it.

But before doing a spacewalk outside of the ship—which engineers verbosely call an Extra-Vehicular Activity, or EVA—an astronaut needs two hours of physical preparation before even donning a spacesuit. It starts with breathing pure oxygen via a gas mask and a series of vigorous exercises meant to cleanse the nitrogen out of the blood, a practice adopted from twentieth century astronauts and cosmonauts. The air pressure in the spacesuit is far enough below the *Vegvisir's* cabin pressure that insufficiently acclimated spacewalkers risk decompression sickness.

The spacesuit's mechanical functions and bearings can only work reliably when the air pressure in the suit is dangerously low. This is complicated further by the uneven thermal expansion caused by the four-hundred-degree difference between sun and shade. Astronaut training includes extensive physical conditioning to handle heavy labor in air as thin as at the summit of Mt. Everest. To help the astronaut's lungs compensate for the thinness of the air, the spacesuit maintains one-hundred-percent pure oxygen—an extreme fire hazard.

There's a click in his headset. "Scorcher. We can start the visual assessment of the damage. Proceed to the first foot restraint."

"Copy."

He proceeds.

The foot restraint is missing. He reports it to Space-Bee and continues. Part of the area being surveyed is close to the airlock exit hatch.

The first objective of the EVA is to visually assess and document whatever damage may exist. The space vessel is obviously prone to hypervelocity impacts, so protective shields made from aluminum and Nextel–Kevlar are used. They provide a sort of raincoat where the wearer can still get a little wet, though these "raindrops" strike at much higher speeds—about 210 times the speed of sound. At these velocities, a grain of sand striking the surface of a spaceship forms sonic waves traveling and ricocheting within the metal framing, causing micro-cracking in parts of the structure that aren't inspectable and make no sound detectable to human ears. Somehow Scorcher still manages to sleep a third of the time he's supposed to.

"Rocko" Rodriquez, at the ENG station next to Space-Bee, chimes in. "Well, we definitely didn't get hit by a satellite. I mean, we ain't dead," he cringes. "And it's just our primary and secondary radios not working. We have no air leaks. I'll be curious to see what Scorcher finds. Seems unusual that both systems went out. But this is space. Weird things happen."

Just then, Scorcher reports over the headset, "I'm not

seeing any deflagration or vaporific flashes."

Space-Bee acknowledges.

She responds back to Rocko. "The damage could have been done when we went through a radiation hot spot in the outer Van Allen belt when we passed 60,000 km. Seattle Trajectory hasn't been putting any effort into helping us dodge the radiation hot spots in the belts. Fuel is expensive, apparently, even if we mine it ourselves from the Moon."

The Van Allen radiation belts are the natural occurring force fields held in place by Earth's magnetic field. These belts primarily trap solar radiation from both the sun itself and from supernovae of other stars, preventing the quick annihilation of the Earth's biomes.

And each time astronauts travel between the Earth and the Moon, they must pass through these collection points, high-density concentrations of dangerously charged particles.

"Doesn't matter with our radiation-eating fungi," Rocko laughs. "Courtesy of Chernobyl. Our sweet lady has been upgraded with fungi that metabolize radiation." Rocko starts to pet the outer hull of the ship, knowing that all that protects them from space is a couple millimeters of aluminum sheet and a plastic honeycomb panel housing filled with genetically modified fungus. The fungus was first discovered by scientists studying the impact on life around the nuclear fallout at Chernobyl. The fungi evolved to use radiosynthesis to metabolize and eat the radiation. "In the Ukraine, fungus isn't just good on pizza."

"It's just Ukraine, not 'the' Ukraine. No definite article," Space-Bee says pedantically. "Most of the radio hardware is externally exposed. The fungal panels don't cover the whole ship, just places where we are, assuming it even works." If it didn't work, then the crew would be experiencing a lethal dose of radiation equivalent to dozens of CT scans, not a level of exposure a person's cells could handle regularly.

"Stay on task."

"Aye," they both reply to the Flight Commander holding silently and studiously behind them. Commander Lucy "Siren" Ōtsuka has a well-defined glare, though empathetic, a motherly look superimposed over that of a seasoned military commander. Her long, straight brunette hair is tied back taut, a contrast against the others who allow theirs to float wildly. She's a veteran of space operations in general and the *Vegvisir* in particular and has been doing supply runs between low Earth orbit (LEO) and the distant outpost of Central Lunar Mining at the Moon's South Pole. She is a master at adjusting leadership techniques as needed, switching compassion on or off, and adapting to the color of any crisis like a chameleon. The current predicament, just as unique as anyone could expect, is her cup of tea.

Primary and secondary communication is inoperative. Overall electrical failure, along with the crash of the vessel's computer operating systems. The main power supply was terminated via the automatic reaction of the onboard computers. And only minimal life support systems are running alongside backup lighting.

The crew are pacing themselves while following checklists to reanimate the components of this complex machine, in parallel to a complicated and exhaustive process of diagnostic checks along the way. The *Vegvisir* is an orchestra coming to life: first the strings, then the woodwinds, followed by the brass, and lastly the percussion. Then halted all at once by the maestro after careful tuning and warm-up. Silence.

The fans briefly stop, the lights flicker, then everything

awakens all at once to the natural hum of the ship. Life is back to the vessel! The music is playing in harmony — or it should be. But something is not quite right.

CHAPTER 2

Ten months earlier.

As reported by the Wall Street Journal, rare earths are a group of seventeen elements valued for their magnetic and conductive properties. They are used to manufacture a range of crucial technologies such as components in electric cars, smartphone touch screens, and missile defense systems...

"Why are you seeking this job transfer? What do you hope to gain from it? And how do you hope to contribute?"

"Well, I've seen how things have been going so far from our perspective on Earth. There seem to be a lot of inefficiencies with our mining operations on the Moon, even with respect to the day-to-day facilities operations." He smiles and nods slightly when he sees the interviewer, whom he's never met, nodding in affirmation at his comments, as though they have a common understanding of the gross inefficiencies at Central Lunar Mining. "It'd be nice for the technicians to just be able to focus on the mining part of the job, without having to worry about tasks related to survival. I'd love to be able to help with that—maintenance of life-support systems, management and troubleshooting of system failures. It's super exciting for me. What a unique challenge and opportunity to contribute to something important. Like that one issue with the SAE power cables—"

The woman waves her hand to stop him before he starts sharing technical details. "Why would you be good at that?" she pursues.

Scorcher thinks for a moment while staring at the wrinkles above the woman's upper lip, clearly caused by years of smoking. "I like to take complex problems and break them down into simple, easy-to-follow steps that any technician can follow. My skillset can be useful in an off-Earth setting, helping advance technologies by managing and maintaining support systems. I want to be the arrowhead of the human journey." He hopes that isn't too tacky, but her eye contact and relaxed grin reassure him. "Also, I've heard rumors that CLM is not just a mining operation. That the Company is going to expand to commercial research. And you're looking to test out some technologies and infrastructure for a future on Mars. I'd love to position myself for that future growth by proving myself at CLM." He wonders if this is the time to throw in the word "synergy" to bait the MBA.

The woman reacts warmly to the career-centric theme. The man isn't being fully honest with his optimism about terraforming Mars. It's already a disaster of a program tainted by a bunch of tenured and stuffy bureaucratic engineers just milking the Founder for a paycheck. But CLM and the Moon seem different to the interviewee, and he passionately believes he can make it work as part of a small team.

He continues, "I'm absolutely humbled you would even consider me to go on a three-year tour at Central Lunar Mining. I think my mechanical engineering background qualifies me to help turn things around, especially with fluid systems—"

"Excellent," she interrupts with a real estate agent grin,

looking back at her notes with a sudden change in manner. "With your engineering background, Mr. Robertson, we can rush the EVA and spacesuit safety training and skip over some of the training that's just busy work. We can cut the zero gravity EVA training since you'll be on the Moon full time. What are the odds you'll have to do a spacewalk en route on the *Vegvisir* anyways? So that's a huge plus for schedule." She taps her nails on the desk. "Can you please give an example of a difficult person you've had to deal with, what the problem was, what your solution was for dealing with the conflict, and if your solution in handling the dispute worked? The CLM residents have a reputation for being eccentric. It just kind of worked out that way," she says, taking a deep breath while tightly gripping her pen. "They have their own strong subculture. Is that something you can handle?"

"Sure. I'm really good at not being a troublemaker, which I know management is always nervous about." He says this after the briefest flashback to his old colleagues accusing him otherwise—falsely, in his view. "I'm fairly non-confrontational and try to use an empathetic approach of trying to understand everyone's perspective," he replies, thinking of a self-help communication book he recently read.

"Oh? What's an example?"

"Sure. There was a time when I was a technical lead engineer for a team of eight people—"

"Oh, well actually, before we get into that...sorry to skip around," she interrupts, scribbling notes. "I need to ask about your essay," she says, referring to the two-hundred-word essay about human spaceflight, a requirement for every job applicant.

Scorcher despised the idea of writing a cliché essay about

growing up as a kid looking up toward the stars and being inspired, which was almost always a lie, in his view. So he took a risk and wrote something honest, not that he felt he had any other option.

She reads a few lines from it, "*The Founder speaks of the Moon as our frontier. To me, the frontier is a place beyond the tyranny of our traditions, beyond the ghosts from our pasts. I want to go to the Moon because I know it is not haunted...*" She pauses without finishing. "Different, for sure. Maybe a little too personal. Everyone else just writes about being a kid looking up at stars and building model rockets." She rests her pen to sidetrack further. "But I have to ask, what do you mean?"

CHAPTER 3

Scorcher proceeds with the inspections. Step by step. Move by move. Action by action. He does everything with intention, plans every activity mentally before executing, always thinking five steps ahead. His abbreviated lunar-only EVA training didn't teach him all the tricks he needs for microgravity ops, but Space-Bee sees this right away and chimes in as needed. Commander Ōtsuka wants her skills at the engineering station and decided to take the risk with Scorcher.

If I step here like that, how will I rotate? Will the inertia of the tools swing me back slamming into the spaceship? Or will I simply lose my grip? My legs feel so useless.

There is nothing under his feet pressing into the soles, and he feels the lack of having something firm, measurable beneath him. The depth is unmeasurable. Or is it?

"Space-Bee, what's our current altitude?"

"Huh? What's that?" she asks.

"How far are we from Earth?"

"About 320,000 km. That doesn't matter, though. We're in the sphere of influence of the Moon now. The Moon's gravity should be stronger than the Earth's at this point."

"Just curious," says Scorcher. "I guess if I fall, I will become a meteorite on the Moon and not the Earth."

"Right. Copy 'meteorite on the Moon.'"

He continues making his way along the semi-planned route while being monitored closely by Space-Bee and Rocko. "The damage is not from physical debris impact." Based on the discoloration, mimicking a burn that would occur in an atmosphere, it appears to have been something else. Precise, in fact.

Scorcher discusses his findings with the *Vegvisir* crew, followed by hours exhaustively spent removing and replacing the secondary antenna and some of the electrical components. Good thing astronauts wear diapers.

Access constraints limit what's accessible from inside the pressurized, environmentally controlled portion of the ship. Many systems are only accessible via external non-pressurized access panels. And now with his initial assessments complete, like exploratory surgery involving a team of experts working in synchrony and consultation, his next objective is to get radio communication back online and reestablish a digital data link to the mining complex on the Moon.

Before Scorcher can finish replacing the hatch, dampness soaks his skull cap and trickles down his back. *Is there a cracked egg on my head?* He calls to Space-Bee, "I must really be sweating here. I'm feeling soaked." He continues, "I'm having difficulty reattaching the access panel."

"Be sure to manage your exertion level. I don't want you overtaxing the spacesuit's environmental control system with too much carbon dioxide or heat." Even NASA's and ESA's latest suits have their limits.

"Copy. I just don't want to leave any unfinished work when I egress," Scorcher replies.

Space-Bee acknowledges, "Understood. But remember, if you damage the suit, the repairs come out of your paycheck."

Scorcher snorts.

Commander "Siren" Ōtsuka, who has been tirelessly monitoring the progress while floating behind Space-Bee and Rocko, chimes in. "Double check his vitals."

"Looks fine," Rocko informs her. "Nothing out of the ordinary."

"What's this here?" Space-Bee is looking over.

"What's what?" Rocko asks.

"No, on the video screen. That doesn't look like sweat," Space-Bee observes. They visually inspect the visor on the helmet through the live video feed. "Scorcher, can you face aft? Towards the narrow angle camera?"

He breaks his concentration to obey. As he turns around, Commander Ōtsuka calmly grabs Rocko's headset microphone, "You're looking pretty soaked in there, Scorcher. What's your status?"

"It's getting quite wet in my helmet." He shakes his head violently to knock a drop off.

A couple droplets float in front of his face. "It feels a lot like water, not sweat." He reaches out with his tongue. "Oh gross, very metallic tasting. Definitely not my drinking water from the CamelBak. Must be the coolant water."

"That's concerning," Rocko says to the two next to him. "You definitely don't want any liquid build up." He checks the systems readouts for the suit. "I'm not showing anything outside of tolerance. Everything looks nominal. The pumps are still pumping." He pulls up the time history to see if there are any degrading trends, even if within the tolerance bands.

Ōtsuka gives the order. "Abort the EVA and get back to the airlock."

Scorcher acknowledges, "Copy." He knows not to question an abort call, regardless of his perspective. "I'm climbing my way back now. I guess I can just bring the panel back in with me." The thought of tossing it like a frisbee out into space crosses his mind. "Should I try to reattach the panel quickly, just tether it, or bring it back?"

Space-Bee replies, "Abort, Scorcher. Leave it tethered."

"Copy. Leave it tethered."

They're all studying him now: visually and numerically. Attempting to combine instinct with data.

Another of the en route engineers to the Moon, who has been busy re-connecting to CLM, glides over to attend the commotion. The most trivial thing, like a failed circuit board cooling fan, can lead to a fire in microgravity. A pinpoint-sized grain of pencil lead can short circuit a switch.

Scorcher's head is getting wetter with accumulation creeping down his forehead. Things don't always go exactly as planned while suited up. Something pinches in a weird way or the thermal long underwear, interwoven with micro-plumbing for coolant, doesn't fit right after a few hours.

"I'm still at a loss as to what's leaking," says Rocko.

As Scorcher mentally plans his path back, he recalls everything he is and is not allowed to use as a handhold. Many components are fragile or have delicate surface treatments and coatings. Space-Bee is guiding him verbally along his route.

The mystery liquid shorts out Scorcher's mic: verbal communication is lost. Assuming he can still hear the instructions, Space-Bee continues giving verbal cues. Scorcher is unaware of it at first until his inquiries stop being answered. He methodically rotates his posture to briefly wave back toward the camera again.

"Does that mean he can't hear us?" Rocko asks. "What camera is he looking at?"

"I don't think so. The liquid has blobbed down to cover his eyes and nose. He's breathing through his mouth now," Space-Bee observes.

Blinded and suffocating, Scorcher struggles to turn back around and reorient himself.

Ōtsuka turns to her team, "Keep an eye on his vitals. Space-Bee, keep talking him through this in case he can still hear us."

"Aye," she replies.

The spacewalker is carefully reaching forward, taking cues based on touch and resistance of his suit from physical contact with the space vessel. Blinded, desperately trying to blink off the stifling liquid, he says a quick prayer and unlatches his tether. He estimates he needs to rush his movement.

"Jesus," says Ōtsuka.

Scorcher slowly slides around circumferentially to traverse the tube-shaped section of the spacecraft, then re-attaches the tether. Ōtsuka asks aloud, "Why'd he do that?"

"I guess he's going the long way to avoid the data link hardware he just repaired?" Rocko ponders. "Probably doesn't want to do it a second time."

"He's not hearing me. He grabbed something he wasn't supposed to," says Space-Bee. "Scorcher, wave if you can hear me."

No response.

"Now he's breaking new things. Why is he avoiding that handrail?" the Commander asks.

Space-Bee replies, "He knows it has micrometeoroid pitting on it. The damaged metal can tear his gloves." She notices the Commander tightening her face. "Though that's obviously the least of our worries right now." The spacesuit can handle minor cuts without a rapid decompression event.

"Understood."

They notice Scorcher second-guessing in rash, stiff gestures. He's starting to move more quickly than they would normally have liked under "routine" circumstances.

"He's veering off course—I think."

Rocko interjects. "I'll suit up."

"I need you onboard to receive him and we need that airlock kept vacant. There isn't time for you to suit up. Standby at the airlock," Ōtsuka orders. "We just need him to roll in and we can get him."

Space-Bee starts working out a plan in her head. "I think he's trying to slosh around his head to keep the liquid from accumulating over his mouth."

Scorcher has a plan. If the water starts blocking his mouth while he's in the airlock—if he makes it to the airlock—he's going to open a purge valve in his helmet to suction out the liquid. He knows he'll pass out for a few minutes as the airlock repressurizes, but it might be his best chance of not drowning or getting toxic coolant in his lungs.

He continues speaking and providing status—just in case. "Which is worse, hypoxia or drowning? I know my vote."

He grabs a solar panel that shouldn't be there. Which really means *he* shouldn't be there. "Goddamn it," he swears, trying to keep his tension and exertion levels down. He juts out his lower lip to blow upward over his upper lip, trying to push the contaminant back.

At this point, it's hopeless to try to get the water off his eyes. He has repeatedly tried blowing his nose, but it's not until someone is in microgravity that they realize just how sticky water is.

"CO2 rising," Rocko observes. "The spacesuit's fighting

back even with the heavy exertion, though."

Scorcher debates whether to ditch the tools he's flopping around. He can only imagine how many times they've banged against the hull over the past few minutes. But even that delays him. He blindly tries to get his bearings by moving his glove along a systems tunnel—a duct which houses cables—that runs longitudinally along the spacecraft around the propellant tanks. It runs along the exterior of the ship to avoid having systems going through the center of the cryogenic propellant tanks, minimizing the potential for explosions like on Apollo 13. And this external duct runs straight back to the airlock. He does a mental coin flip.

"I have no idea where he's headed," Rocko states aloud.

Metallic impacts are heard traveling along the length of the spacecraft. The crew instinctively looks toward the noise from Scorcher. The en route engineer, a silent observer until now, finally speaks up in an Irish accent. "Apparently, he's studied the systems well enough to know the ship blind. I had a feeling he would. That's why I told Seattle I had to have him on the Moon."

CHAPTER 4

Scorcher carefully guides himself into the airlock, trying to not trigger the pond of coolant in his helmet by either collision or direction change. No matter how he turns, each action makes it worse, submerging his face even further.

He shuts the hatch and starts breathing heavily, unintentionally inhaling the liquid and choking. He leverages his training not to panic from the subtle wet strangling, consciously not submitting to the burning sensation in his lungs from holding his breath. He knows he needs to prevent the coolant from penetrating too deeply into his sinuses. If he can't hold out, the only alternative will be to break open the helmet's purge vent to evacuate the coolant, but at the risk of the low air pressure boiling his blood.

The crew watches helplessly through the glass, though they remain externally stoic. Space-Bee initiates the emergency rapid re-pressurization, setting off audible alarms.

Meanwhile, the spacewalker weighs his best course of action.

His ears pop, telling him he's almost returned to normal pressure. What he first mistakes as his heartbeat he eventually recognizes as the deep thump of a siren coming from inside the *Vegvisir*, growing louder with every pulse.

He imagines he can hear the crew hastily debating the risks of removing his helmet prematurely. It may rupture his ear drums and pop the blood vessels in his eyes, but it could save his life.

As the tight chamber is repressurizing, the crew see a thumbs up from Scorcher. Rocko smiles to himself, then refocuses stoically, reserving relief until Scorcher is back onboard and alive.

A new squealing alarm goes off, and Space-Bee silences it with the push of a button. Typing. Stopping. Studying. More typing. It goes off again, and she smacks it off once more. She says, without shifting her focus, "Just a barotrauma warning because of the rapid pressure increase—we're riding on the edge. I had to trick the software to ignore that there is a human occupant. Hang in there, please." The swinging tools become audible again, starting as light clicks and then evolving to loud metallic bangs as more air is pumped into the airlock. The noise indicates to the crew his transition back to their universe.

Green light. Green light. Green light. Computer: *Pressure stable 101.3 kPa and 21% oxygen.* Latch unlocks. Interior airlock hatch slams open. Four hands pull him through. Helmet off. Sticky water everywhere.

"Welcome back. Glad to see you're conscious," Ōtsuka says.

Scorcher attempts a joke but starts choking.

Rocko smirks. "I wouldn't go that far, brother."

Rocko won't wait to start inspecting the suit piece by piece as they take it off Scorcher's body. About one liter of coolant needs to be contained and properly recycled.

"Hey, bud, you scraped the shit out of the solar panels as you came pummeling back. And now there's a tear in the glove," Rocko says.

"I hadn't noticed," Scorcher coughs. "What else do you expect from a future Moon monkey?"

"It's stuck now and won't come off," Rocko grunts as he struggles to remove the damaged glove from the suit. "I don't want to damage it any further."

Space-Bee grabs the glove from Rocko's grip and studies it, giving a slight nod like she's seen this before. She full-arm swings one of the hammers from Scorcher's tool set, mimicking half a jumping jack, and strikes right into the sweet spot on the steel bracelet lock around the glove's wrist. It breaks free without harm, other than giving Scorcher another coughing attack from the sudden action. If her aim had been only a few millimeters off either way, it would have been his arm or hand that broke free. Or worse yet, more damage to the spacesuit.

Scorcher spends an hour recovering himself, draining his sinuses, and having his vitals checked by Rocko while the rest of the crew re-establishes the data links and other communication before he can finally discuss his findings.

His thought process is interrupted by speculation that this could be sabotage or an attack, but that suggestion seems wild to him. He realizes that, in many ways, the crew is disconnected from the reality of what's happening on Earth. Their speculations of what's going on in other regions of cislunar space do not match the tamer versions he's used to reading from LinkedIn articles.

*　　*　　*

The next day, after the commander's daily briefing, they take a group coffee break. A debate about the previous days' events steals its way in, interrupting the white noise. The surly Irishman throws in that it's sabotage from a foreign state, but no one else is buying it, and Ōtsuka withholds any opinions on these distractions. She instead floats away with the pride of not being a daydreamer, always staying industrious. After she leaves, the scuttlebutt boils down to taking jabs at who are the real players, trying to lay claims to space real estate, versus the "wannabees." But they all agree it's the overconfident wannabees who can be the most belligerent.

According to the ancient 1967 United Nations Outer Space Treaty, no nation can claim ownership of the Moon. However, the purview of these restrictions on claims does not apply to private industry—or at least that's how it's currently interpreted. Thus, the modern Moon cold-war for resources. The gray area of state-run businesses, such as from China and Russia, politicizes the debate but hasn't slowed their actions. The Moon has water, vital for life and rocket fuel. Helium-3, vital for nuclear fusion. And other rare earth metals—fifteen lanthanides, scandium, and yttrium. Until the mid-twenty-first century, China was producing 90% of the rare earth metals, but easy access to these resources has been diminishing for decades and has nearly evaporated, driving cutthroat efforts to fight increasing costs and adjusting to the economic strain of silicon chip shortages.

Tens of thousands of micro-satellites, some capable of malintent, have been launched over the last few decades. Scorcher reads about it all the time in *Aviation Week*. At this point, the governments of Earth have been prioritizing non-confrontation and non-involvement with this private economic expansion into space. But this doesn't prevent government-sponsored companies from existing. Or rogue hacker attacks, and these hackers aren't just playing to annoy.

"Who really is rogue, though? Who doesn't have a boss? Humans are wired for domination. It's in our DNA."

"That was a really existential comment, Scorcher," Ōtsuka says while passing by, making a rare jest. Apparently she was listening. "Are you always like this after a near-fatal mishap?"

"You know I didn't mean rogue in that way," Rocko adds defensively in response to Scorcher. "Of course, if it was a laser attack from a satellite—"

"'Satellite' implies orbit."

"—okay, 'space vessel' thingy, there would have to be a group of people involved. With the path our L.L.C. is on, we're already disrupting the East Asian suppliers, possibly pushing them out of the market."

Scorcher: "Don't forget to mention synergy." Everyone ignores him.

"Why would 'they' target our communication? And is it really escalating to the point that they would kill us?" Space-Bee asks, unconvinced.

"Maybe so we're forced to camp in parking orbit around the Moon until help is sent. Just a delay tactic," Ōtsuka adds, though she sounds unconvinced herself. Scorcher concludes she can't help but think strategically, even if the conversation annoys her. "Keep it low profile."

"We don't have enough supplies to last that long, if we were to get stuck in orbit," Space-Bee interjects, always a planner and never waiting to cross that bridge. "We're packed in pretty tightly."

"This could just be general harassment. Or a power move," Rocko continues.

"Maybe it was someone rogue. They launch a tiny probe, not fast enough to escape orbit, but definitely make it up high enough, on a single stage rocket. Clear the atmosphere and take a shot."

Scorcher isn't buying it. "No way someone could target

us with that level of precision. At this distance, it takes light one second to travel that far, so you'd have to lead the moving target and know enough of our trajectory to know how far ahead of us you should aim."

Everyone seems to collectively pause and blink at the realization that light moves slowly on this scale. The speed of light is actually slow enough to miss its target.

He continues. "You know how unlikely it would be to precisely take out a ship's antenna? Something doesn't make sense. And I'm not saying it was gremlins, but an attack doesn't seem plausible."

"It is possible, though." Rocko waves his hand. "Maybe we passed something that attacked us. Maybe someone invented a stealth space-mine device."

"How would they do that? It would have to be in orbit on a set path and velocity. Even something tiny would have been identified by some tracking station. Stealth doesn't exist in space," Scorcher counters.

"Except for all the meteors we miss until they're in between Earth and the Moon or already past us. Those are even larger objects than a microsatellite," Rocko replies.

"I'm not buying the space ninja theory."

Ōtsuka chimes in, "Rockets don't launch stealthily. Someone's always watching and recording. Nothing ever enters or leaves Earth's atmosphere without every major player seeing it."

Finally joining the conversation is Sean "Four-Leaf" O'Conner. As he's floating over, he looks around wildly. "Think this was a laser, Rocko? Why a laser? The whole computer was bloody shot, this was electromagnetic. No doubt from the sun. What's the solar weather report?"

Space-Bee checks. "Clear. No activity."

Scorcher considers it. "You could have a KP of zero on

Earth, and still see the Aurora Borealis. I've seen that happen once while on a boat out of Alaska. Solar reports don't always indicate what's really out there."

Four-Leaf then states what everyone has missed. "You all are so focused on lasers and satellites and conspiracy theories. Could be much worse. This could have come from the Moon. And if it was a directed microwave attack, it would be barely provable. You're looking the wrong way. Look out there, mates." He points to the Moon that fills the windows, a Cheshire Cat smile appearing in the black nothingness speckled with stars. The gibbous Moon of the start of their journey is now transitioning to new as the black circle lights on one crisp, cold edge, sharp enough to cut the ship in two.

Scorcher considers it as he's getting his first glimpses of Four-Leaf, the onsite representative from Seattle who provides technical oversight to everything Moon-side. He's assigned there indefinitely. "If you're right, this is opening a can of worms."

"We're the worms in the can," Four-Leaf clarifies. "What's your hypothesis on the missing foot restraint?"

"Gremlins."

"Ha!"

Commander Ōtsuka stops them. "Time to get back into action. Right now, we're showing nominal on the arrival hyperbolic trajectory. In four hours, we start the timeline for perilune thrust arc configuration to get us in lunar capture orbit. Let's get some needed rest so we don't make any mistakes out there."

Scorcher leaves to try to get some sleep, realizing that his exhaustion will probably keep him from getting any meaningful rest. *Oh, the irony*, he thinks.

He tries anyway. He goes into the closet-sized dormitory

and straps himself into his cot after the normal toiletries. The wonderful thing about sleeping in microgravity is you'll never sleep any better or more naturally, at least in his opinion. No tossing or turning needed. He wonders if it's even better than the slight rocking of a boat moored in a calm harbor. On Earth, at least, nothing is better than sleeping on placid water. The cold crisp cool air, the slight rolling motion of the boat. Scorcher often wonders if he should have stayed on Earth to do marine engineering. But that wasn't a frontier enough for him. He needed to escape Earth, his life, his divorce, his habits, his sidetracks. His whole life since his teenage years has been a perpetual midlife crisis.

He begins dozing off, but his mind is still going, the gears turning, though not steadily like a clock. More like gears tumbling in a laundry machine. He can feel the strain of exhaustion in his eyelids. Maybe sleeping in space doesn't work.

Every life choice is reevaluated. Fate decided long ago that grunt engineering work was his true calling, not something ambitious like scientific discovery and research. Though when he starts to feel sorry for himself, shame blankets him for complaining or feeling lost. He doesn't have time for that. There's no idle time to simply enjoy life. Scorcher's life isn't one for comfort. His sense of purpose is stronger than his aptitude for happiness, so he's either tirelessly working on some new job or obsession, or he's idly sitting in dark depression. It's borderline black and white for him, but to him there's nothing extreme about this.

I'm just too good at what I do to be able to switch to a different field. Dumbed-down applied physics is where I exist. Structural engineering. Newton's second law superimposed with energy theories. It would be starting over to switch to something more ambitious. I should stop phrasing things like "more ambitious." "Should" is a violent term…

His mind keeps rambling, competing brain lobes arguing amongst themselves, fighting for dominance within the bounds of his skull.

His wish for his brain to take a break and go blank is finally fulfilled. Coherency dissolves. In sleep paralysis, he opens his eyes slightly and doesn't know if it's a dream. He's alone, in darkness.

CHAPTER 5

The crew is present, but everything is different. Scorcher can't get a sense of whether time is running forward, drawing backward, or splitting in two.

He can't make out their faces, but he knows who they are through a vague kind of intuition. There is gravity on the *Vegvisir*, but he doesn't take notice of the strangeness of that. Nor does it seem weird that the compartments are reorganized and that there are extra rooms along a length of hallway kilometers long. There are windows with blinds tilted down to block an early sun, outside of which is the front lawn of his uncle's house a mere stroll from the ocean, with short putting green-length grass and Pacific morning dew. Everyone is arguing over something, but the words and language are unfamiliar. There is a common frustration, but no panic.

As he walks up to the commotion, he notices the faceless bodies discussing a mini-USB drive plugged into the console. Oddly comforting. Like someone returning home after many years, only to find that nothing has changed and their long dead parents are there with smiles, looking happy and strong, uneaten by cancer.

He hasn't seen a physical memory stick like this since he was a child. He goes to reach for it…

Now he's back in time after slipping back to fifteen

minutes earlier. He's with the rest of the crew who somehow have their faces back. The gravity is gone, he's just floating.

He sees an old man enter from an unknown doorway and walk, as though in normal gravity, down the length of the *Space Clipper Vegvisir*. No one recognizes him. He is tall, has a brimmed hat, and is wearing a long coat. He is missing one eye.

As he approaches, he observes everyone very closely, though without making direct eye contact. Scorcher doesn't approach him; he doesn't need to. The old man stops and melds into the shadows…

Scorcher is now back with his crew. He senses the old man staring at him. Scorcher turns around and watches the old man walk through the crowd of four floating astronauts, and he inserts a memory stick into the computer console next to a keyboard, into a place where no USB port existed before. The old man turns towards everyone and firmly states that there is an unfamiliar weapon now inserted into their computer, and only one person is meant to decipher its purpose.

The old man walks away.

Everyone tries tirelessly to extract the USB stick drive. But no one can remove it. Nor can they discern its purpose. With unrestrained effort and leverage and trial, no one can remove it, smartly or brutely, or see what it is doing, or know its purpose. Now it's his turn to have a go. Scorcher pulls himself forward with his left hand, stretches his right arm and hand, away from his torso. He pinches the object between his thumb and index, and the stick slides out without effort, spraying silvery mining-machine lubricant. Was it even plugged into anything? Everyone stares at him in awe, then with disgust. The digital data is absorbed by

Scorcher. A burnt man hides inside the drive, screaming for help.

The object bites Scorcher quickly and violently, hard enough to slash his wrist. Though when he looks down to check his wound, he notices that his wrist is unharmed but covered in someone else's mercury-colored blood.

CHAPTER 6

The *Vegvisir* is in contact with the Moon tracking station and is sending telemetry to Central Lunar Mining, which has the only space dock on the lunar surface that can handle the size of this ship. Strapped into his cot, Scorcher struggles to move his arms due to an extreme absence of energy, as though all his electrolytes have been siphoned.

Lying there, delirious, with his eyes closed, he wonders: *Am I a ghost? Is this what it's like?* No weight. No substance. No life force.

More noise in the background. This time, it's clearer. It reminds him of waking near the end of a flight as the flight attendants noisily bustle about with their final crosschecks. Scorcher's self-awareness of his physical location and position starts to become less cloudy. He's in outer space, for some reason.

"Scorcher."

"Uh, yes? Commander?" Scorcher asks, unsure who he is talking to.

Ōtsuka continues, "We're exiting the capture orbit and initiating the phase-two burn in 20 minutes for parking orbit intercept. We're going to skip the third phase burn and instead just get us direct to the nominal 110 km circular. Then we'll be landing at the Homestead."

"I'm sorry, the Homestead?" Scorcher is further

disoriented as he opens his eyes to see that Commander Ōtsuka is standing, or floating, upside down while speaking to him. Or has his vision flipped?

She smiles asymmetrically. "It's what the locals used to call it before Seattle rebranded the place and told them to clean up. It's more often called the main campus of Central Lunar Mining. Or simply CLM. Or the hamster maze—though that might be an insult. I wouldn't know." Her smile drops. "Your new home."

"Hmm. How long have I been asleep?" Scorcher asks out loud towards the bulkhead.

"That's not my job to know. But we've completed one LLO which takes about two hours. Hope that's enough for you. You got a full day ahead."

Four-Leaf floats in as Ōtsuka leaves. "We're doing orientation together once we land."

"Makes sense, since you're the technical fellow and Seattle's representative, and it's your third time here," Scorcher replies.

"Fourth, mate." He smiles and holds up four digits with some of the tips missing—one nail is only ten percent what it should be. "There's plenty we haven't told you yet. You have no idea what you've gotten yourself into."

"Grand," Scorcher replies passively, unintentionally mimicking the Irish accent. He shakes his head clear of the surprisingly vivid dream. "I haven't had time to prepare."

"You'll never have time. But I can help soften the blow," Four-Leaf offers, but not so much from sympathy. He presses against the bulkhead to give himself extra height over Scorcher. "As the site operations engineer, you'll be expected to perform all the same duties as the four mining technicians, in addition to attending to your full-time job as lead engineer. You get to set the priorities of the whole team going forward and be responsible, keeping the team on schedule."

Scorcher likes the way that sounds: the freedom to get the job done his way, for once. Exactly what he is looking for. No bureaucratic webs or political trenches to navigate, all that corporate B.S. left back on Earth.

He makes his way to the jump seat for landing preparations, where he notices Space-Bee and Rocko arguing about the telemetric readings from the lunar surface. He's too red-eyed to care right now.

"I need coffee," he says.

Space-Bee breaks her focus for a moment. Apparently, she does multitask on occasion, or at least her hearing does. "I'll need one, too, once we lock it up after landing."

She snaps her attention back and continues verifying the waypoints for apolune and perilune, which are off by more than her liking. Rocko is more of a cowboy and dismisses it as not being a big deal since they can easily compensate when downrange with fuel to spare, even though doing so takes far more propellant.

"You know I'm a perfectionist, Rocko. I need to know what went wrong."

Rocko answers back quickly. "Wrong? Seriously?" He then ignores her suggestion, contrary to his extensive crew resource management training.

Because of the relatively low gravity, any imperfection in the mass or shape of the Moon is sufficient to throw the orbit off course. In some cases, changes in the shape of the moon are caused by heavy meteorites whose concentrated broken fragments have significant enough density and gravitational pull to nudge a satellite off course. A deep crater or an extinct volcano reaching up could also pull the *Vegvisir* off course. NASA engineers like to say the Moon is "gravitationally lumpy." This makes LLO—low lunar orbit—much more difficult to maintain than low Earth orbit, where the effect of gravity from individual mountain peaks is small compared to the total gravity of the Earth. As a result, only four specific orbital inclinations around the Moon—flight paths—are considered stable for long term orbits lasting more than a week—also known as "frozen orbits." Due to the location of the landing site, they are not in one of those preferred stable LLO orbits and need constant steering adjustments.

Four-Leaf straps in next to Scorcher and decides to get chatty. "Farthest you've ever been from home?"

Scorcher catches himself staring at a nasty scar on the side of Four-Leaf's jaw for far too long, so he quickly focuses on his nose as a neutral point, but then realizes the bent nose points back toward the scar.

He gives a delayed laugh back. "You mean like the far side of the Moon? You can say that again. It's amazing how the sky explodes with stars once the sun and Earth are blocked. And crazy how many more craters there are on the far side."

"It is," Four-Leaf agrees. "Wait till you see Aitken Basin. Unreal."

Both are staring off to the side, focusing their sight through a small porthole window. At this point in the flight, they're just dead weight and should probably behave as such, quietly. This is Rocko, Space-Bee, and Ōtsuka's time to shine.

"What could go wrong?" Four-Leaf grins.

Rocko announces, "We're T-plus 2 minutes 45 seconds from apolune. We're a little late. Navigation GO for burn."

Space-Bee: "Systems GO."

Ōtsuka commands, "Initiate auto-vector burn when

ready."

"Aye," Space-Bee answers.

The *Vegvisir* does a three-second burn to change the direction of the orbit. Doing so at the apolune, the highest and slowest part of the orbit around the Moon, is the most energy efficient time for correcting flight path direction.

"Turn left at the McDonald's," Rocko jokes.

Space-Bee doesn't laugh.

They're now laser-pointed to Aitken Basin near the South Pole, where Central Lunar Mining and its countless outposts are entrenched, burrowed, and expanding. Aitken Basin is one of the largest and oldest impact craters not just on the Moon but in the entire Solar System. At thirteen kilometers deep, it's implausible for Scorcher to try to comprehend his destination, like trying to imagine the Arctic Ocean drained, except with a range of elevation nearly twice as extreme as the Himalayas. An ancient lunar basin full of valuable rare elements.

When the Chinese sent the first ever successful lunar lander to the far side of the Moon years ago in 2019, it landed specifically in this region. The Aitken Basin contains a plethora of geologically distinct rare elements, and it's the only location on the Moon where water exists. This water is a sustaining source for drinking, oxygen for breathing, and hydrogen for rocket fuel.

"Protein bars and coffee. You'll learn to love it, mate," Four-Leaf says.

"I'm sure I will," Scorcher concedes, craving volumes of coffee after intensifying the habit at the Icelandic training facility.

Commander Ōtsuka speaks over them to address Space-Bee and Rocko, signaling for the pair of soon-to-be lunar locals to stop the small talk. "Nicely done. Initiate landing procedures per four-decimal-one-five. We're no longer in Seattle's realm. We're on our own," she says, turning towards Scorcher. "Sterile cockpit till we land."

"Understood," Scorcher replies.

The Earth is gone.

Ōtsuka continues. "All crew prepare for lunar landing." Four-Leaf and Scorcher immediately double-check their restraint belts. "*Vegvisir* crew, perform crosscheck."

"Aye," respond Rocko and Space-Bee in unison.

Space-Bee speaks over the radio. "Central Lunar Mining. This is the *Vegvisir*. Please relay to Seattle that timeline for lunar landing initiated at T-plus 3 days, 23 hours, 14 minutes, 18 seconds."

Five seconds pass on the COMM. "Copy all. We're tracking your trajectory. Coordinates are soft-wired and linked. Looks like you're following procedure three-decimal-five. Over."

"Negative, four-decimal-one-five, not our normal approach," says Space-Bee.

"Copy four-decimal-one-five. Good luck, *Vegvisir*. I'll have Norman meet you at the dock with the snake."

"Thanks, Ed. We'll see you once we land?" Space-Bee asks.

"Negative. Once we latch you down, I'm heading out immediately to one of the ancillary sites we've lost communication with. I'll wave at you through the windowpane."

Space-Bee smiles. "G'day. Out."

The deceleration uniformly compresses Scorcher into his seat, a fun sensation after a few days of microgravity. It's also much smoother than the dragon ride he experienced when leaving Earth and intercepting the *Vegvisir* with Four-Leaf practically sitting on his lap and the rest of the volume filled up with personal cargo and bags of coffee.

When they took off from Launch Site One on the Pacific coast, it took mere minutes to leave the Earth's atmosphere but another thirty-six hours of waiting in intercept orbit to finally meet the *Vegvisir*. Four-Leaf used the time attacking emails, while Scorcher spent it sleeping and reading as much as he could about mining.

During his reading, something that particularly piqued his interest was the grander mission of the Highway to Space initiative, similar to the Chinese equivalent, the Silkroad to Space. Central Lunar Mining is far ahead of its competition. The *Vegvisir* itself, not a simple steppingstone or taxi service, is evidence of formidable ambition. The spaceship is exceedingly overdesigned, oversized, and over-crewed for a task like transporting Scorcher and coffee to the South Pole of the Moon. It's designed for a much grander role. It supports the Highway to Space initiative in its infant stages and is a cog critical to the Founder's overall ambition to win the billionaire space race.

The key obstacle with expanding industry away from Earth is that gravity is too strong there. This means that with the best technology available, rockets can just barely escape Earth's overpowering and oppressive gravity. Over ninety percent of the weight of any rocket is fuel, and the theoretical limits defined by the laws of physics and chemistry say it is impossible to do much better, not without magic. That means only tiny payloads can be launched, and only from certain locations on Earth during very specific time windows. This makes it expensive, economically impractical, and politically costly, given the red herrings of humanity's woes and distractions on Earth.

Part of the expense not commonly discussed is that to fall into the correct orbit, a satellite or spaceship must be launched at just the right moment and location on Earth. The closer to the equator, the better, because the rotation of the Earth itself gives a boost in velocity. The Earth's surface is moving at a higher speed at the equator than the poles. If launching from Alaska, an equatorial orbit with a meaningful payload is impossible to achieve because of Earth's tyrannical gravity and the disadvantage of being near the stationary North Pole.

To allow heavier payloads and more cost-effective access to space, the *Vegvisir* is envisioned to decouple launch windows and ground operations on Earth from the logistics of space operations while in orbit. If the *Vegvisir* could act as a middleman and provide support for orbital transfers, electrical power, communication relays, and other logistics, that would allow for much heavier payloads to be launched without restrictions on launch time or launch location. The possibilities of economic expansion into space would no longer be affected by so many variables. No more limitations on tight launch windows. No more payload weight being sacrificed on communications and data relay hardware. Even a small country with limited resources, far away from the equator, like Namibia, could afford general access to orbital space and its economic frontier. Just as the internet, once expensive and impractical, now reaches even those who couldn't independently support it otherwise.

The *Vegvisir* is designed to support low Earth orbit, geosynchronous orbit, low lunar orbit, lunar mining, research labs, orbital industry parks, tourism, art galleries, cities, and whatever else the imagination can invent for humanity. The ship was intended to be so much more than just a spacefaring clipper.

The Founder named the *Vegvisir* after the Icelandic symbol for wayfinder. It is a circular symbol mimicking a compass with its four cardinal and four intermediate directions and runic imagery. The holder of this symbol will never lose their way. In the modern case, the symbol, in both word and physical imagery painted on the exterior hull of the spaceship, christens today's wayfinder.

* * *

After a gentler landing than Scorcher anticipated, the *Vegvisir* is latched down to the tarmac via massive steel clips which lock through a half-dozen machined lugs around the periphery of the spaceship's aft end. One of the umbilical doors opens to "safe" the vehicle.

A person in a spacesuit drags a small, flexible, giant slinky-looking tube and attaches it to the ship to pressurize to one atmosphere of pressure, matching CLM. The process is precarious, even with the assistance of one of the ground service crew hopping around. Scorcher and Four-Leaf are meant to disembark using this method. "It looks like a glorified rubber hose," Scorcher says. "It's bright green, too."

There's a spray-painted message on the closest building: "Welcome to the Far Side's Bottom!" Scorcher accepts that the south pole must be the bottom. Some additional welcoming graffiti is written below it, but the lighting makes it too difficult to read due to the absolute darkness of the shadows.

"Nothing glorified about it. We call it the snake. It takes donkey's years to pull yourself and all your gear through," says Four-Leaf. "Ah, look at good ol' Minister hopping around like a crippled rabbit. A mean bastard, he is, a little eccentric. You should definitely meet up with him some time, though. Very knowledgeable. He's been around longer than smart phones. I'll give him a wave since it always seems to sour his mood."

Spying through the porthole, Scorcher thinks he sees the Minister mouthing Four-Leaf to "piss off" but isn't completely sure.

"Ah, there's so much to tell you, mate, but first I want to get settled and send a note to a lady friend. How 'bout ye meet up with Space-Bee for a coffee after we drop off your gear in the dormitory quarters and do an abbreviated tour to get you set up. I remember her mentioning she wants a coffee." Four-Leaf continues and winks. "I got to check something quick."

"Um, sure."

Scorcher does just that and arranges with Space-Bee to meet for coffee at the small dining hall, which is partially visible from the tarmac and the only part of the living quarters of CLM which sticks out above ground level, providing a viewing window onto the lunar landscape.

Four-Leaf has made a head start without him. Through the window, Scorcher sees the green snake slowly digesting what looks like a hearty meal.

CHAPTER 7

Scorcher approaches Space-Bee, who is already seated at the café informally named "Café at the End of the Universe," according to a sticky note on the wall. He ponders ordering the "Buzz Latte" with powdered milk.

She has a stone-cold face.

Is she angry? Nervous? Either way, this is a little awkward.

Scorcher greets her with a genuine smile. "Hi! Fancy seeing a lady like you in a place like this."

"Not that we have any other option."

"True. No one told me this place has the only Tully's Coffee on the Moon," he attempts.

"I don't think you have any idea what you got yourself into." She pops a couple of pills and swallows.

"What's that for?"

"Just general nausea. The whole crew on the *Vegvisir* is experiencing it. It's been getting worse for everyone over time. Probably from long term exposure to microgravity. Though our symptoms are more intense than what they experience on LEO space stations. Maybe it's some mysterious illness," she jokes.

Her face relaxes around her eyes, but her jaw is still tight. "How long are you stationed here?"

"The standard three years. Three whole years of not seeing Earth, not even up in the sky. Kind of crazy. But anyways, I took this opportunity when I had the chance. Figured I was a prime candidate for site operations engineer. Nothing keeps me rooted back home after the divorce, and I was sick of the normal grind. I was looking for something less compartmentalized, like what you see working for the government or a large bureaucratic behemoth like Boeing. Though it's a little outside my traditional background, which is structural engineering. My job will be to cover CLM non-mining operations support, but occasionally going out to the field, too. Basically, I'm not a full-time miner. So, I'm more for the factory day-to-day industrial operations and maintenance itself." He keeps chatting to avoid silence, like someone failing an interview. "Either way, I got my EVA and maintenance certifications, Class 3, and now I'm here. Probably one of the few mechanics with an advanced engineering degree." He smiles and winks. *Since when do I wink?*

"Neat," she says with an aspirated 't.'

Silence.

"Oh, you already got your coffee?" he asks unsurely.

"Yeah, I'm letting it cool down. Figured by the time it cooled down enough you would have grabbed yours," she explains.

"I'll go get mine, then." Scorcher decides to simply go with the flow without reading too much into it.

He walks up to an elaborate coffee vending machine offering a half-dozen different varieties of essentially the same option. He has a flashback to Tokyo. "Do robot baristas have to pass a drug test before they're hired?" He says it loud enough for Space-Bee's benefit.

The vending machine towers over him with no reply.

"Obviously no personality test to work here."

With his back still turned, Space-Bee takes off her boot

and throws it upward, slamming it loudly into the ceiling.

Scorcher jolts and twirls around, "Jesus Christ, are loud noises your thing or something?"

"There was a bug. We have strict orders to kill anything organic since it's a safety risk. Your training should have mentioned that."

He decides there is something odd but interesting about her.

He comes back with his coffee, amazed he hasn't spilled it. She re-boots herself.

"I think Four-Leaf has got me all set-up now, at least enough to be dangerous." He sits, then continues, "Apparently, there is a shoebox-sized robot vacuum making the rounds. They call it Stabby because there's a knife bolted to its head, like a knight's jousting pole. I guess it's up to me to figure out where Stabby takes his coffee breaks on my own time. And not touch his knife. He didn't explain why, though," he adds, hoping for clarification.

Space-Bee laughs, relaxing more face muscles but not erasing a sadness in her black irises contrasted by her colorless skin. "Oh, yeah, good ol' Stabby. Watch your ankles."

Scorcher starts to ask for elaboration, but she continues before he can get the words out. "So, anyways, how do you like your new partner? Or is it 'boss'? It's hard to tell."

"You mean Four-Leaf? Um. I don't really have an opinion yet, I suppose. It isn't super clear, it's kind of a gray area. I'm the lead engineer, but he provides technical oversight on behalf of Seattle. I guess that's what all tech fellows do on behalf of management. The org chart is a little vague, as always. What are your thoughts? You've ridden along with him for a few trips now."

Space-Bee thinks for a moment, tilting her head. "There

have been quite a few times when he's gotten into a sticky spot or near disaster, but he somehow manages to make it through not dead. I think he's from Northern Ireland, and his wiki page says he worked his way 'across the pond, to space, and beyond,' which is kind of a weird thing to write. No, wait, I lied. He didn't write that. People say that to rattle his cage. Anyways, he can be charming in an unexpected way, and seems to have a level of optimism that would impress even Arthur Dent, my hero from Hitchhiker's Guide."

"Yeah." Scorcher nods, with only slight interest in talking about the technical fellow. But he really wants to use his limited time to learn more about Space-Bee and what's behind her intimidating manner. "So, what's your real name? You know, the one you use on Earth," he asks.

"What? I have a name?" she asks dryly but looks genuinely confused.

"Yeah?" Scorcher replies, not playing along smoothly.

"No. Samantha. I'm just not used to hearing my name anymore."

"So, we're both Sam!" He laughs out loud. He reaches out to shake her hand.

Space-Bee replies, "Oh, I hate 'Sam.' You can take that one."

"Well, legally I go by Samuel Robertson, at least according to my life insurance policy. But I guess Scorcher because even though I have dark hair, my beard is red when I don't shave."

"'Calico' would have been better," Space-Bee says. "Samantha Drake."

"You mean 'drake' like a male duck?"

She babble-mumbles like a duck. "I'm really good at making animal noises." Then she giggles to herself but stares past Scorcher, lost in a moment of internal distraction.

Scorcher starts up the conversation again to bring her back after they both take a moment to stare out of the only windows. "It's amazing to look out and see an infinite spectrum of gray, and still find it so beautiful. It's just a big desert out here. Not much different from Iceland or Nevada, really. Did you know the Van Allen belts were discovered from the first scientific measurements collected by a satellite?"

Space-Bee shrugs. "I did not. From Sputnik?"

"No, that was just an orbiting basketball that beeped. It was from America's first satellite—"

"Called?" Space-Bee asks.

"I can't remember," Scorcher admits. "Explorer? But anyways, they just threw on a Geiger counter to see what would happen. And they accidently discovered what protects all life on Earth from the black death of space."

Space-Bee rolls her eyes. Scorcher still can't read her confidently. She says, "Oh, I just realized you didn't say Van Halen. You're saying Van Allen." She laughs at her own statement.

"You laugh a lot at your own jokes."

Her face turns serious again, "Of course I do! It's hilarious! Why would you not laugh at your own jokes?"

Scorcher submits but then relaxes when he thinks it's safe to.

He notices the faded freckles on her nose. "So, what got you working on a supply ship, running back and forth?"

"Workaholic. I always have been. Working fourteen-hour days has been normal for me since I was twelve. My doctor got mad at me and said I need to stop walking so many miles a day when I was back on Earth, but I can't help it. I'm always moving."

"How many miles?" Scorcher asks.

"Well, about twenty-five thousand steps per day. However many miles that is," Space-Bee says while turning towards Scorcher. He notices that she's actually making eye contact.

"Holy shit. That's a lot of steps."

"Yeah, my joints were killing me, and I always have an electric pain running through my legs," she explains.

Scorcher studies her. "That's not good."

"I know." She squints her eyelids and grinds her jaw after speaking.

Is she stressed? Distracted? In pain? Her smiles contradict the messages from her face she can't conceal.

Though now she smiles with her eyes, staring back at him. She relaxes and lifts her brows, almost imperceptibly.

Scorcher asks, half-grinning, nearly blithe, "So working in space is better?"

"Probably not. Who knows?" Space-Bee responds with a subtle apathy. "What about you? Are you going to be Four-Leaf's shadow and obedient servant, like everyone else?"

The wording of the question catches him off guard, and he shifts awkwardly. "Well, there's me as the main point of contact onsite to manage the day-to-day stuff like life support, systems, blah blah blah, while everyone else is assigned to specific field mining tasks. I can technically pull a miner from the field to help out. I just don't get into the details of where to mine, the geological stuff, nor figuring out what gets shipped back to Earth. Unless they need me to." Scorcher is repeating this out loud mostly to reassure himself. "The miners will be overseeing the processing of the raw ore and precious metals at Central Lunar Mining prior to shipment back to West Texas. But I'm solely responsible for converting Moon ice into rocket fuel, oxidizer, drinkable water, and breathable O2."

"Have you met your mining technicians yet? Ed, Ayubu, Keystone, the Minister?"

"Just in email," he admits. "Though from what I understand, the Minister just hangs out more in the hangar and machine shop next to the underground CLM. The Minister is less of a field tech than a pitman to load the ore when it's ready for shipment. Among other things, I guess. Speaking of sending processed ore back to Earth, what about you?"

"That's a funny way of putting it."

"Oh, I didn't mean you—"

"I know," she laughs. "Yeah, our ship won't be bringing the ore back anymore. Too inefficient, lugging needy humans back and forth. Seattle wants to go back to using single-use mini rocket pods for shipping all that valuable stuff you guys dig up. And maybe pull us back full time to low Earth orbit ops and help with some other ambitions kept hush-hush."

Scorcher steers the conversation back to his original inquiry. "So what's the story behind your callsign?"

"No story, really. My father was a U.S. Navy Seabee working as a builder alongside Marines, who don't have their own combat engineers, so they use the Navy. Putting up bridges, making bases, pouring concrete, digging ditches. All while getting shot at. There's an old John Wayne movie, quite horrible actually, that my dad made me watch about the Seabees. How contractors in World War II kept getting killed on the front lines so they invented Seabees and handed them guns and tool belts. Even though their logo is a bumble bee with machine guns, the name Seabee comes from the letters C.B., construction battalion."

Scorcher interrupts to ask, "Who's John Wayne?"

Space-Bee takes the question with raised, disapproving eyebrows. "Are you serious? Anyway, what really happened is my dad didn't make it through BUDS training to be a SEAL but had a passion for making stuff work and a tolerance for hard labor, so he became a Seabee. I have the same passion to solve problems using whatever junk is laying around. That's how it is in the military. You never have what you need to get the job done, but you figure it out anyway. I love that." Her posture relaxes. "And I love that in the space environment, we're out here all on our own. So, Dad started calling me his Space-Bee. And when someone else heard, the name stuck."

Her intimidating façade disappears for a second—like it fell into a hole in her heart—as she says "his Space-Bee."

Reflecting on what Space-Bee just said, Scorcher adds, "I guess that's how it is with you, your father, and everyone else not living a cushy life. You, on the other hand, have to make things work with what you got."

"It's like that for everyone, Scorcher, whether you're pouring concrete or sitting at a desk," she counters. "For me, it's like that. Every morning, I wake up and wonder what's the point of it all. I just put myself together with whatever I've got. Sometimes I'm not equipped with what I need, and it feels impossible, but I do it anyway." She stops and leans away, just staring. She's not turning away to avoid his gaze. She's disappearing more.

Scorcher wasn't expecting the mood to go back to being serious so quickly. It might have to do less with her trusting him and more that she is stuck in her own head—probably often. He asks, "Have you ever tried anything to stop the thoughts and voices in your head?"

"Oh, wow, the way you ask questions," she says, chuckling while cringing.

Scorcher fumbles his words. "Ah, I didn't mean that. Just—"

"No worries, it's just an odd way to ask. I mean, in high school I smoked pot, but no, nothing serious," she responds honestly. "Maybe occasionally something more serious to escape. But that's my problem, no one else's."

"We don't have to talk about it," Scorcher says. "I mean, we all have our vices. I'm not sure what mine are."

"I've been through a lot of shit in my life, going back to my earliest, extremely vivid memories. But some years are totally black. I can't remember first and second grade at all—not the teachers, the classroom, Christmas, nothing," Space-Bee says. "It's just so odd."

She suddenly derails the moment while looking through the window to the Moon's surface. "I didn't know it snowed on the Moon," she states weakly. "Is that dust kicked up from the sheep?"

Scorcher quickly turns around and stares intently for a short moment, "No. That's ammonia." Underneath his glare, a rectangular robot slowly tracks by beyond the window. His eye catches a crude caveman-like painting of a sheep on its side.

"Oh, you're right," she says, slapping Scorcher on the arm.

He studies the snow for a couple seconds more, "That's not good. Where's that falling from?" With the limited field of view, it isn't obvious. "Coolant leak somewhere. Looks like a large one, too." They both instinctively exit the café to get some attention on it. "Looks like our conversation is cut short for now. I'll have to try to get a SNIFFER robot to find the source. I'd better get Four-Leaf's attention."

"Good luck with that. I'm gonna check to make sure it's not coming from the *Vegvisir*. I'll catch you later. I need to get back anyways. I've got to prep for the mission back to LEO. I'm sure at least a couple glitches will pop up, given my luck." She spies a quick glance at Scorcher and runs off.

In midturn, he stops when he realizes he doesn't know where he should go.

What's my game plan?

He hopes this is just a "milk run" and nothing too serious.

CHAPTER 8

Three hours pass after the café with Space-Bee. Scorcher walks briskly down to a lower level of the hamster maze while still getting accustomed to the lower gravity. Going downstairs takes longer because there's less force to pull him downward. Being in a hurry, this gradual sinking creates a new kind of anxiety for him. He recalls how sci-fi author Arthur C. Clark described the extreme challenge of walking on the Moon: a person has less gravity but the same mass and momentum, meaning that quickly turning a corner is more challenging because the gravity is too low to create good traction on their feet. He runs down to the end of a long hall, trying not to launch himself into the ceiling by stepping too hard, then slides his fingers on the wall to help stop.

He's in the wrong hall. Time's ticking.

"Where the hell is the 3-D printer?"

He radios Four-Leaf and gets directions for the opposite end of the ant farm. He imagines his path as one of those cartoon pirate treasure maps with a dotted serpentine line going in many loops just to end up back in the same corner of the page where he started.

Arriving, he checks the status of the machine, an additive manufacturing printer, more colloquially called a 3-D printer. It allows for any number of cogs or widgets to be printed in the absence of a factory full of expensive tooling operated by skilled machinist labor. It uses a tray of aluminum powder and an electron-beam welder to melt and fuse the powder to a solid component, all done in a vacuum so oxygen doesn't embed itself and embrittle the alloy. The new metallic fitting creeping upward out of the powder a millimeter per minute is the replacement part to fix the ammonia leak—the leak that's still spraying. He reluctantly decided against turning off the flow, but it's a gamble either way.

This same pipeline feeds another critical system which can't afford to be turned off for more than a few minutes without causing a domino effect of disruptions that will take a few days to reset. Scorcher thinks the design engineers should have known better, but maybe he shouldn't judge too harshly.

Alarms and notifications on his smartphone keep distracting him.

"Yeah, I know, I got it," he responds impatiently.

The machine stops.

"What happened now? You shouldn't be done yet."

He gets a message on the machine's screen that the wrong build file—the digital instructions that tell the machine what to print—was sent over by their valve sub-supplier.

If I had a nickel…

His phone gets an email that an invalid build file was sent. He gets an SMS that an invalid build file was sent.

Christ.

Click, click, click.

The lunar snowfall is still in his mind's eye.

The part geometry is correct, but the build orientation of the part was sideways. This seemingly trivial mistake results in micro-cracking from unwanted porosity, similar to a bad weld. The part would not have thermally cooled uniformly or at the correct cooling rate. These sensitivities make Scorcher wary of 3-D printing. He prefers traditional casting. Though he gets that a 3-D printer is infinitely more pragmatic than a casting house or full machine shop on the Moon, even given the unavoidable metallurgical quality issues with using 3-D printers.

With plastic gloves on, he grabs the partially built cog for it to be recycled, careful not to contaminate the aluminum powder with dust, oxygen, or any infinitesimal amount of water vapor. He tosses it into a large bin for aluminum scrap in the corner of the room. It lightly bounces off the sides of the bin and settles on the other waste.

He loads the newer, correct version of the build file software and lets it run. In the meantime, he drafts up the repair procedures and gets Seattle's sign-off.

*   *   *

Scorcher is back in the spacesuit locker and EVA preparations room. He jumps onto the stationary exercise bike and puts on the oxygen mask, set to one-hundred percent pure oxygen. He starts pedaling the nitrogen out of his blood.

Normally, one of the four mining technicians would accompany him on a repair like this since the extent of the damage is not known and an extra set of hands might be needed. But the urgency of the ammonia leak leaves it to Four-Leaf to assist, which Scorcher is fine with.

Before such operations take place, it typically needs to be communicated back to Seattle for EVA mission planning review and approval. But as Four-Leaf explains to the rookie, through his muffled oxygen mask after jumping on the bike next to him, the approval from Seattle can be waived at any time by the on-site tech fellow (meaning Four-Leaf), who waives this requirement without a second thought.

The Minister is not immediately available since he's made a home for himself in the hangar, a permanent above-ground structure housing cargo containers, rockets, and other equipment adjacent to—but not environmentally connected to—the Central Lunar Mining habitat and ore processing facilities.

The other three lunar laborers—Ed, Ayubu, and Keystone—are scattered around at remote mini outposts that have been constructed and jury-rigged into temporary human habitats. They're treated as permanent structures in practice but are considered "temporary" in terms of leveraging less stringent safety requirements. Being partially subterranean, these remote outposts appear like mud-constructed turf houses with a door and a couple of portholes poking out. These, of course, were designed by Seattle for transient human occupancy as a last resort. They were never intended for storage of long-term life support items such as food, water, toiletry, cots, and people.

As the scope of operations around CLM has grown aggressively outward over the past few years, it has become impractical in some respects to keep everyone stationed at the dormitories near the ore processing plant and hangar. The original architects laid out the central facility and its distant surrounding ancillary structures into a hub-and-spoke system. But when Seattle sent Four-Leaf, he intervened by dispersing everyone to the far reaches to keep their bodies in the field and their heads on the mining. He wanted to plant people directly to those areas where the mining prospects seemed hot. No need to have workers "commute" every day when they could just live out there.

Though Scorcher's first impression questions the practicality of having everyone split up—it requires redundancy in logistics, it seems unsafe, and it must by psychologically taxing to be isolated. But this is the way Four-Leaf demands it on behalf of Seattle. Scorcher was previously warned by a colleague that Four-Leaf's mind cannot be persuaded otherwise and that if challenged, Four-Leaf aspires to confrontation and has the stamina to wear out any challenger. But Scorcher hasn't put much thought into it.

He asks Four-Leaf, "Why isn't the Minister joining us for this one? If anything, I'd expect another tech to be joining before you jump in. He's not that far away."

"You're right. But the Minister is on his lunch break and couldn't be bothered by anything short of a direct meteorite impact."

This seems like an odd, insufficient answer, but he dismisses his curiosity as a distraction. This leaves only Scorcher and Four-Leaf in the vicinity of CLM. The other techs are a long drive away.

Four-Leaf explains, "The Minister used to reside here but moved his stuff to the hangar to stop from being distracted. You'll notice that he's also very picky about what happens to his herd of worker-bot sheep, his tools, and other such gadgetry in 'his' hangar." He uses his fingers as quotes. Four-Leaf leans forward and takes his mask off to whisper, as though he and Scorcher aren't currently the most isolated pair of humans in existence. "There is a rumor that every morning, he starts off by urinating in each corner of his hangar to claim it as his territory. No interfering with his business there. Doesn't take kindly to pranks."

"Noted," Scorcher acknowledges.

Four-Leaf shrugs his shoulders and adds, "He also

despises Stabby." He takes the lead and jumps off the bike sooner than Scorcher thinks is sufficient.

As they are suiting up, Four-Leaf keeps getting sidetracked from the EVA checklist. "You're pretty lucky, mate, that we're keeping you at the CLM and not out in one of the Annies."

Scorcher responds as he locks his boots, "So 'Annie' is what everyone calls the temporary remote outpost?"

"Yes. All the Ancillary Outposts for kilometers around are nicknamed Annies. Temporary or not, that's a different debate. We're all temporary in the end."

Scorcher nods. "I see." He thinks about nitrogen. "So CLM is kept at sea-level pressure, but are the Annies?"

"No. Unlike CLM, they're kept at one-third atmosphere with 100% pure oxygen. That way, they can quickly jump into their spacesuits on demand without needing to exercise. But at CLM, it's natural air for us, obviously, with our workout closet next to the airlock."

One-third atmospheric pressure can't be easy on the human body after a few months, Scorcher thinks. "Yeah, I remember that from training. I just don't recall anything on Annies."

Four-Leaf doesn't respond.

"Is it factory outgassing creating that smell? It smells like a firecracker went off," Scorcher says.

Four-Leaf replies, "Buzz Aldrin apparently said the exact same thing, mate. It's not an industrial smell. That wet ash or gunpowder smell is the natural scent of Moon dust reacting to oxygen for the first time in billions of years. Nothing harmful."

They go back to the checklist.

"Just remember, mate, you follow my lead. You might be the site operations engineer, but I make the final calls while I'm on the Moon." He looks Scorcher in the eyes and tightens his lips to grin without actually smiling.

*   *   *

It's no longer snowing; the repair's done.

Scorcher is exhausted and dragging during the repair debriefing with Seattle. It was hours of knuckle-breaking work, meaning the EVA suits need to be repaired, and was more seat-of-your-pants than he ever could have expected. And after all that, it still feels like very little got accomplished for all the effort. When the debriefing concludes, Four-Leaf starts chatting as Scorcher walks his way back to the dormitory section where his cot and toiletries are.

From this conversation, Scorcher learns that one of the unusual customs here is to refer to the dozens of robots roaming the horizon near and far as "sheep." The sheep are all the same cookie cutter cubic design, with tracks instead of wheels, and appear as though a miniature sized forklift and a tractor had a child together. Most of these worker cubes are currently herding around the polar region of the Moon while "eating" the regolith—Moon dirt—in search of desired minerals. Samples are sorted and brought back to the humans for further analysis if needed. The results are mapped out and reviewed by geologists back at Seattle. Satellite imagery alone is not sufficient for making the final call on pursuing mining in a particular hectare. When a place is chosen, however, the sheep are reconfigured to heavy-duty mode to lug the ore back to processing. Light-duty mode is for quick scouting and other odd jobs.

The sheep are perceived by the miners as being most fundamental to the way of life here on the Moon, spiritually akin to a pagan's connection between livestock and Mother Nature. The sheep are closely tended to and cared for and are necessary for not just doing a good day's work, but also survival. A favored sheep is often selected by a technician and modified for special tasks—and even for personal use—by those residing in the lonely Annies.

As interesting, and maybe disturbing, as this all is to Scorcher, he needs sleep and shamelessly cuts the conversation short, forgetting to take off the thermal underwear used for spacewalks, and passes out in his cot, face down, into a deep and dreamless sleep. Residual coolant fluid drips out of the tubes sewn into his space underwear, about one drop per minute, playing water torture on his dusty boots.

CHAPTER 9

The next day, Scorcher takes the initiative to apply lessons learned from the repair and composes new required inspections that everyone should be performing from this point forward. The inspections involve many tedious steps and a new method of bolting together fluid pipes that are "separation critical," a technical designation given to bolted flanges where if the pipe deflects enough to cause the seals to gap, things start leaking and blowing up. Classic rocket science problem that no one seems to have mastered, even after a century. But at least ESA and NASA are aware they haven't. And undoubtedly the Chinese and Russians, too, he considers. In his experience, even if all the part numbers are identical, switching approved suppliers for something as trivial as nuts can have unexpected—and dangerous—consequences.

On the first Space Shuttle flight immediately after the Columbia disaster killed seven astronauts, a similar outcome was averted by pure chance: nuts were bought from a different supplier (same part number) and torqued as per specifications, only for engineers to accidentally discover the night before the launch that the bolt clamp load holding some joints together was at half the needed value, even though the installation steps hadn't changed. A third Space Shuttle crash, two of them on consecutive missions, would have been devastating to the space program.

With this nightmare in mind, Scorcher spends the entire shift in solitude and with coffee, working out all the details of problems he sees around CLM as low hanging fruit, ripe for improvement. First, he makes an improved build file of the 3-D printed part he had trouble with the day before: that's a hit out of the park. Secondly, he creates some homework for his mining technicians to inspect other similar part details that risk springing a leak: he figures they can squeeze that somewhere into their schedules. The Company publicly touts that safety is the priority. Thirdly, but not lastly, he details new required inspections for all the spacesuits to ensure the experience he had nearly drowning inside his helmet on the *Vegvisir* will not occur on the Moon. He takes a blind stab at this problem since it's inconclusive how his spacesuit failed, but he figures it's worth the effort for safety.

Fueled by an eagerness to make a positive impact, he continues to append more improvements to the list. Each one down feels natural and powerful, like the perfect feel of hitting a ball with the sweet spot of a baseball bat.

After exhaustive re-reading, walking away, coming back, and re-editing his emails, work instructions, and memos, he sends his new protocols out to the four mining technicians and takes a sigh of relief from the climax of anxiety. He hasn't even met everyone yet, so he wants to be careful how he comes across. He wonders if he's overstepping his bounds or jumping the gun but decides he's not. It's up to them to recognize that he's a go-getter who takes the initiative and does what's right, and if they have a problem with that, it's on them. At least that's what he tries to convince himself. Even so, the hypothetical of having just embarrassed himself in front of his new colleagues makes it hard to breathe. Without thinking, he goes to shake it off.

Space-Bee is a good distraction. His fingers start with the email subject "Waz up gurl?" then stop typing. Embarrassment floods back. He's trying too hard.

Uncertainty transforms into a brief urge in his hands, and he rashly flips over the keyboard with his fingertips, fueled by something invisible to him. It smacks loudly against the computer monitor, making a noise that is inexplicably satisfying, tempting him to flip it again.

He slowly pulls the keyboard back upright and stares at the keys. He centers it nicely but then can't decide if it should center with the computer monitor or his chest. He scooches his chair over.

He fantasizes about being congratulated by his new teammates for his meaningful contributions and saving the day. He'll be the new go-to guy that everyone can rely on. Everyone will praise him and respect him. In the cramped spaces on the Moon, he already feels strangely unconfined knowing he'll no longer be bullied by corporate bureaucracy. The countless annoyances from project managers and the Technical Fellowship engineers are literally a world away now. He'll finally be able to stand on firm ground built by a reputation he can mold by his own design, not on the weak shoulders of those in the good ol' boys club back home.

He looks up from his keyboard and realigns it neatly a second time, to the center of the computer monitor. He uses his sleeve to dust off the top of the monitor and clean fingerprints off the screen. Order out of the chaos of dust, one speck at a time.

Nothing can be more satisfying in the short term than creating order out of chaos. What else is there to life? What else is there to his mission here? It's relevant on every scale.

He thinks back to a particular time during college, when he was stuck in one of the valleys between the peaks, when his father had told him that he just needed to stay busy. *That's your problem*, his father explained. *Too much idle time.*

A notification ding flicks him back to reality. He opens his email and reads it with confusion at first. Then the confusion is followed by something else.

Apparently, the only technical fellow and authority in his immediate realm has demoted his entire list of safety protocols. Four-Leaf didn't even list them as "Mission Critical," which is one step down from "Safety Critical," but to the lowest priority level, "Trivial." He's deprioritized all Scorcher's solutions to the infinite backlog of hundreds of tasks that will never get reviewed or worked on. Scorcher's heart sinks under the weight of the hours spent. Four-Leaf, one by one, replies to all his emails and says these updates have not been reviewed by him and aren't deemed reasonable. Scorcher gets the message, loud and clear: he has overstepped his bounds.

Amorphous embarrassment bobs in his chest and works its way upward toward his windpipe.

Four-Leaf sends out a follow-up email—no, wait— multiple emails, widely distributed. One email per each of the three main "Safety Critical" issues, each including the same copy-pasted statements: "This is not a Safety Critical issue requiring immediate attention. This has not been technically reviewed by leadership or put on our agenda for the next semi-annual review board, so it'll have to wait till the next agenda—"

What the hell? What semi-annual agenda? These are obvious and immediate safety issues. And it's fresh in everyone's minds. Why wait until we forget about it? My helmet tried to murder me.

He deletes his lame flirty email to Space-Bee and takes a walk. Walking always clears his mind. So does speaking out loud. Walking and speaking out loud feel like a marble rolling stably and securely in a groove.

He hops and skips down a long hall in order to move quickly. He hates that this cheerful-looking action is out of sync with his frustration, but at least no one can see him.

On his way to get coffee, he turns the corner and trips over Stabby, falling in ridiculously slow motion in the Moon's weak gravity. He drops his phone like an awkward teenager, and the vacuum races up to it to capture it, for God knows what reason.

Scorcher reaches down quickly and gets his phone off the ground before the tip of the blade can impale his hand like a medieval joust.

Stabby's modus operandi is the continuous cleaning of all surfaces and removal of the Moon dust which irritates everyone's skin and eyes, an annoyance since the first Apollo landing.

He scolds Stabby. "You naughty boy. Why does everyone like you? You won't be around for long if you destroy my phone." Scorcher stops himself, recognizing in his own voice the old-fashioned tone of his grandfather scolding him when he was a boy caught playing with dolls. Not to mention he hates when people talk to pets or inanimate objects like they're important.

The vacuum's sucking noise halts. It's a face off.

"Hmm." He checks over his shoulder instinctively, reassuring himself that no ghost is behind him, then he turns back at Stabby.

Stabby blinks a red light, on and off and on, repeatedly, like a failing circuit.

Scorcher stares at the tiny light bulb on top of the

vacuum.

The red-light flashing begins again and then it momentarily stops, on and off and on, in an incoherent random sequence.

"Are you dying?" Scorcher asks, fighting his urge to smile at the stupidity of this situation. "Are you cussing me out? Do I need to put you back on your charger?"

Silence.

After a few moments of the red-light blinking, the light show ceases, the vacuum cleaner fan turns back on, the spinner initiates sweeping, and Stabby turns away, rolling about his business.

CHAPTER 10

Scorcher wakes abruptly to the sound of Four-Leaf greeting him. "Hello, mate."

He jolts, rubbing his eyes, irritated by the fine, intrusive particles of regolith. It must be the next day.

"You'll get used to it in time, mate. Or maybe you won't," Four-Leaf adds, seeing that the fine Moon dust is particularly irritating to Scorcher's body. "It's a good thing regolith doesn't cause lung cancer or black lung disease. Between that and radiation…well…hope you're not hoping to have kids when you get back—"

"I'm not," Scorcher finally adds, irritated as much by Four-Leaf's foreign accent as his disregard for personal space.

"Anyways, we should chat. I'll meet you in the café after you wake."

"I'm awake. I'll see you there in a minute."

"Grand."

Four-Leaf vanishes while Scorcher shakes his head to wake himself. He debates whether Four-Leaf was actually there or if he hallucinated him.

After doing his toiletries, Scorcher arrives to see that Four-Leaf already has his coffee. *This scenario is seemingly familiar*, he thinks to himself.

The conversation starts off with the normal greetings, the

rubbish vestige of civility. Scorcher isn't paying full attention since it's all superfluous speech, just filler so people don't feel uncomfortable when not looking at their smartphone.

After this verbal prologue and with coffees in hand, Four-Leaf explains to Scorcher that the tag-up has two purposes. Four-Leaf's boss in Seattle and thus, by association, Scorcher's boss, is requesting that Scorcher create a schedule for the backlog of tasks, such as process improvements, systems upgrades, and other such things. Four-Leaf is late in creating this schedule. It's being delegated to Scorcher to track the technical fellow on a full-time basis.

Scorcher's mind blanks at the idea of being someone else's scheduler and babysitter. He attempts to reset by sipping caffeine. If there is one thing he despises, it's project engineering and scheduling, especially when the schedules are a meaningless façade. He knows he'll just get yelled at for proposing a schedule that takes too long, then be shamed for not meeting an unrealistic revised schedule that he told everyone he couldn't meet in the first place.

Four-Leaf, studying Scorcher's reaction to this, talks neutrally and calmly, then he leans forward in a more engaged fashion to transition to a more urgent topic.

"I want to make it clear that everything needs my oversight review before proceeding. Even though you're the lead engineer. This includes memos, technical instructions for maintenance manuals, operations tasks for the technicians, pretty much everything going on here."

"I see," Scorcher replies. He takes a moment to think. "That seems fair," he concludes out loud, shrugging his shoulders, knowing that since he's the new guy, he shouldn't disrupt the established order too much. The technical fellow's tone reassures Scorcher's unspoken hope and assumption that this is only temporary and for mentoring.

Four-Leaf doesn't seem very satisfied with his response. "I just want to make sure we're on the same page as far as what our roles and responsibilities are. Ultimately, it's up to you, mate, to set the agenda for the entire team and get things done, like a sergeant for the Company. I'm just overseeing to make sure nothing critical is missed. But you're the leader here. And as such, it's up to you ultimately to determine what improvements the team needs to enact to get this operation profitable. As you already know, the Founder in Seattle isn't too happy, and his ambitions will eventually go somewhere else if we don't get our act together. It's a target-rich environment, mate. You can score big here."

Scorcher likes the sound of that; it might actually work out. After the regolith settles and he learns the lay of the Moon, he'll be able to take his training wheels off and start getting stuff done. Little accomplishments are a huge but short-lived boost in confidence and morale for Scorcher. Long term goals are important, but breaking those up into more palatable ones is what drives him. "Personally, I hate things dragging on. I say spend time on getting shit done, and get it done quickly."

Four-Leaf gives a careful response after assessing Scorcher, "Getting stuff done is important."

"Yep."

"So, about that," Four-Leaf continues by tilting his head, leaning forward even farther into Scorcher's personal space, but talking to his hands on the table, "About earlier. I'm sure you noticed I intervened, and not just because it's an oversight thing as part of my job. Marking something Safety

Critical and making too big of a deal about a small thing can be career ending, especially if it is not true. If you pursue it that way, you'd better be damned right. There's a lot of politics around Seattle."

A flashback of confrontation replays over Scorcher's mind with a reminder of the moral and political war he had at his previous employer. He spent eight years working on an all-electric commercial airliner which ultimately had a design flaw, discovered early on but acknowledged too late—a flaw that was very fixable if industry best practices were used—that resulted in 346 fatalities and two crashes prior to the fleet being grounded and the commercial aircraft manufacturer going bankrupt. The anxiety of standing up to the chief engineer, program executives, and federal regulators, just to be shot down and demonized, still haunts Scorcher. Even at the time, he hated confrontation, but now he has this trauma to accompany it. When he was hired onto this new company, he of course never mentioned his issues with his previous employer. Four-Leaf, on the other hand, according to conversations Scorcher has had with others, thrives off confrontation, and even seems calmed by it. Scorcher is still seeing how true that is, though, and has actively told himself to keep an open mind because people can make random accusations in high stress environments.

"I agree, mate, that"—he looks at his hand again as he holds up three fingers and feigns counting them—"the spacesuit, the 3-D printer build file, and the new mandatory inspections you wanted for, oh I don't know, some three thousand common installed parts of bolted joints for pressurized pipes around the campus—these things are important. But we can't shut down for them. That's just not practical."

"What about the spacesuit?"

"We haven't had issues up until this point. First figure out what happened, then make a fuss about it. If you identify a problem, it's best to also give a solution. You know that."

"What if someone is killed?" Scorcher asks.

Four-Leaf takes a measured breath and shakes his head. "Seattle will argue it's less likely since we're not in microgravity. And I agree with that. Your boots will fill up with liquid, not your helmet."

Unconvinced that he's wrong, Scorcher pleads, "We still need to get to the bottom of this." He neglects to point out that a spacesuit failure is still a risk for the *Vegvisir* crew.

"I know, mate," Four-Leaf nods in agreement. "I'll take a look at what you have by the end of shift."

Scorcher submits and believes him. "Is that all, then?"

"In a hurry?" Four-Leaf smirks, leans back, and broadens his shoulders.

"Well, I like to keep busy and get stuff done. Just so you know, I'm very goal oriented. Even with long-term multi-year projects, I need to meet goals along the way," Scorcher adds, taking pride in his approach. Stay busy and be praised often.

Four-Leaf responds, "Instead of checking things off without any standards or quality, I prefer a team where only the best comes out of it. Not partial solutions in the interim. The technicians already come up with those on their own. They don't need your name or mine on that. It's best if you don't end up with your foot in your mouth." He pauses for about fifteen seconds. "Ultimately, it's up to you, mate." He smiles.

Scorcher is a little confused at where he stands or what's expected of him in terms of leading the team. "As a leader,

I'm not really into the whole hierarchy and control thing. I view myself as empowering and serving others and making sure to remove any obstacles in their way."

"Like iron meteorite boulders?"

"What?"

"Just joking. Interesting. Well, ultimately people are paid to do a job, and they just need to follow instructions," Four-Leaf states. "It's always a battle, mate—with people, that is. Don't ever expect any less."

Scorcher instinctively pulls back. "Well, I'll just ask you if I have any questions. I guess I'll put together a priority list—"

"Sounds grand, mate. You'll do just fine." Four-Leaf gets up and exits without waiting for Scorcher to finish, leaving him sitting with both coffees.

CHAPTER 11

Two weeks pass.

Scorcher learns that to promote morale, Four-Leaf holds a regular and informal monthly get-together—called Stammtisch—either at CLM or at one of the remote Annies. Why the meetup has a German name, no one tells. They are held once every synodic month, or about twenty-nine solar Earth days, to keep everyone's travels sunny. A day on the Moon, starting with a sunrise and ending with the next sunrise, lasts about seven-hundred hours instead of the more natural twenty-four hours on Earth. No point traveling while on the dark side of the Moon. Though at the South Pole, certain craters have "permanently shadowed regions" which never know the sun, nourishing the highest ice density. However, these ice reservoirs, which are required to sustain life on the Moon, are extremely dangerous. Tapping the ice wells is one of the most technically challenging tasks, and as far as Scorcher knows, CLM has only used specially fitted sheep, many of which get fried by lightning released from the ice.

During astronaut training, Scorcher learned that since CLM is located at the South Pole of the Moon, and the sun's light, affectionately called "solar wind" by scientists, skims nearly horizontally across the ground. This solar wind is made up of negatively charged electrons and positively charged ions. The invisible electrons, which are about one-thousand times smaller than the ions, easily swoop down and collect en masse in the pitch-black craters. This build-up creates about half-a-million volts of static electricity. If the sun shines on the crater again, the direct sunlight destroys almost all the static electricity, so for the Apollo astronauts near the Moon's equator, it was just a nuisance, like rubbing feet on a carpet and touching a metal doorknob. However, in these permanently shadowed icy polar regions of the Moon, the static electricity stubbornly sticks around, meaning the ice needs to be discharged before it can be tapped. Before heading out to Stammtisch, Four-Leaf has Scorcher memorize the locations of these high voltage "No Go Zones."

Though this meet-up isn't officially required, Scorcher sees that the miners' routines are hell-or-high-water immutable. The gathering usually progresses over coffee, dinner, then coffee, a few hours of conversation, debate, gossip and speculation, followed by more coffee. More than anything else—even greater in magnitude than the advancement of technology and the species, the seeding of democratic or authoritarian ideas, or the growth of an empire—this face-to-face, day-to-day need to shoot the shit is what humans are really spreading through the universe. The perforation through any frontier may be driven by the spear of ambition or conquest, the arrowhead the brim of brute force and pride, but the person driving the spear lives in a different reality than what they write in their journals. Which is partially why Scorcher doesn't even bother keeping one. The reality is excessive boredom, routine, and spiritual fatigue: the daily emotional ups and downs, fallacies and weaknesses, the human experience. On a fundamental daily level, this is what the miners live for and enjoy: a cup of coffee and a little drama to keep themselves connected by discussing and obsessing on the brief moments of terror that break up their otherwise meaningless existence.

They've brought to the Moon this complex social system that keeps humans mentally sane. Sanity is not something that a person in solitude can perpetuate or invent. A person's psyche needs another person for reference. The facts of the universe must be agreed upon by the group, otherwise the individual will continue to drift until they are no longer human. And out here, the emotional support system needed to maintain an individual's sanity is even more scant than in any desert on Earth. The instinctive habits currently on the Moon are the same as those from Ice Age caves. The DNA is shared.

After the meetup has run its course and invisible purpose, it is followed by everyone's long journeys back to their respective lonely residences.

To break Scorcher in to his new macrocosm, Four-Leaf suggests, without opposition, that this month's meetup should be at the most distant Annie, which also happens to be in rugged terrain on the boundary of the Aitken Basin.

Though two heavy-duty lunar rovers exist, looking like stripped-down Ford F-350 pickup trucks with wire mesh wheels, the chosen means of getting around are modified sheep. The human passengers simply hop onto the sheep, whether onto the sheep's forklift feature or some other jury-rigged seats placed on top, to get ferried across the lunar desert. To Scorcher, it looks sketchy in function, practicality, and safety.

Four-Leaf explains to him why he enjoys the exposure of sheep transport. "It's sort of like the difference between driving a car and riding a motorcycle. In a car, you're just an observer of the environment, like looking at a painting. On a motorcycle, you're in the painting itself, part of the action, not just a bystander."

"I don't think I'm certified to drive a sheep," Scorcher replies, finding himself a pimply faced freshman again. He imagines his space helmet cracked over a boulder, his brain broken over it like a yolk cooking in the 250-degree sun. His intuition mentally estimates how top-heavy the setup is and the likelihood of tipping with the slightest miscalculation.

"Well, it doesn't matter anyway, mate, since you haven't had time to fix one up for yourself. There is a broken sheep that I'm sure you've noticed needs some love and attention. You can maybe get that going for next time. Today, we'll take the lunar rover since three of us can't fit on a sheep. Norman removed the seats and wired up some extra batteries to give us the juice for a long drive. He's picking us up."

"The Minister?" Scorcher double checks.

"That's right," Four-Leaf answers. "He drives slow like an old man, but it'll give you time to enjoy the scenery of the mountain ranges. It's grand."

"I'm sure it is, in its own way," says Scorcher.

"In every way, mate," Four-Leaf replies. "Norman would probably disagree with me, but he gets bored easily. Just like with women."

"That's probably not a problem here," Scorcher observes. "You have a theory on why women are not actually stationed out here? I mean, our competitor's two space stations in LEO are majority women."

Four-Leaf laughs. "Too smart for it. As you know, NASA, ESA, and the orbital business parks—where the *Vegvisir* isn't allowed—don't have the diversity issue," he huffs ironically. "But as far as being out here, I think they just know better than to join outcasts like us. Women aren't into macho lifestyles to prove themselves, nor chasing paychecks over prestige. I hope that's not what you came looking for, mate," Four-Leaf jokes. "Well, I guess we'll see if 'The Minister'"—he says the title with a sense of mild mockery and air of superiority—"is in a mood for conversation along the ride."

They wait outside in their spacesuits as though waiting for a taxi. Within a minute, the Minister slowly drives up. Scorcher can see Four-Leaf impatiently twitching even through the bulky spacesuit.

An audible ding alerts that all three headsets are Bluetooth linked now for communication. "Ah, here's the extra body. Well, I guess we've met now, Mr. Robertson. Jump aboard, lad, and don't expect a smooth ride. No shock absorbers."

Scorcher's difficulty in understanding what he assumes is a Scottish accent from the Minister embarrasses him too much to ask about it. "At least we're not sacrificing torque, then," Scorcher replies, noting the lack of shocks.

No one responds to him as the three get situated. The rover has a removable module for a pressurized cabin, but it only fits two people and is not currently installed, giving the vehicle the appearance of a dune buggy.

Scorcher is facing backwards and tries his best not to grip the power cables.

The vehicle accelerates, and its bumpy ride blurs the surroundings. Nevertheless, it is overwhelmingly humbling for Scorcher to be out here. It still feels like his first day here. He starts laughing to himself, not believing where he is.

"Everyone does that the first ride out, mate, except for Norm, of course," says Four-Leaf, clearly hoping to egg on the Minister. "You know, mate, if you can solve some of the problems here, you can easily make tech fellow and either have a cozy job back on Earth, or who knows, maybe even Mars."

Scorcher has mixed feelings about the technical fellow career path. Most of them are grumpy old men who struggle with Microsoft Outlook. What happens to the human brain at middle age that causes that? Four-Leaf continues to mention that this job can lead to getting the venerable technical fellow title if Scorcher can hold course.

"You think so?"

"Of course, mate. Maybe after we expand beyond mining, you can switch over to a chief scientist role and manage a research team."

Scorcher senses that Four-Leaf's attention on him right now is for testing the waters.

"Yer arse and parsley. Why are you always chatting?" shoots back the driver. "Let the boy alone for five minutes. You never shut up."

And that is the end of conversation for the ride, except for one more snide comment from Four-Leaf. "I could get us there in thirty minutes, tops. If you're not full-throttle or braking, you're only sleepin'."

Scorcher assumes that to mean it would be an even bumpier ride if the thrill-seeking Four-Leaf were driving. He then tilts his head back to look at constellations and southern stars he doesn't know well, specifically, the Southern Cross, which he can just barely make out due to the brightness of the Moon's reflective surface. He only sees it fully when The Minister drives through a shadow. Maybe this counts as finally crossing the equator.

Along their route, even on this well-traveled trail, the vehicle must sometimes come to a complete stop as the driver judges the terrain and determines the best path to take. Even with the telemetry sensors helping with collision avoidance, this can be very tedious and time consuming. For the visual astronaut, it is particularly difficult to judge size or distance with no trees, buildings, or other size references, and maybe most importantly no atmosphere to disperse the light and add depth. What may look like a two-meter-wide rock is in fact a giant hill half a kilometer away. A shallow ditch may quickly reveal itself as a dangerously steep and deep gorge after it is too late to recover. Crater walls tend to be sheer cliffs but look like bunny hill slopes.

On one such ridge where size is imperceptible to Scorcher, the vehicle is stopped for longer than he expects. After some time passes, he turns to see the Minister out of the vehicle placing a helmet-sized stone on a location of no prominence or distinction other than a pile of rocks, possibly stacked artificially, about one meter tall. He then returns to the truck, and they continue in rough silence for the remaining forty-five minutes.

*   *   *

As they arrive, the technical fellow's propositions about advancing to a chief scientist role are swirling through Scorcher's mind. He's always obsessed about being an "actual" scientist, breaking some barrier or leading some push into a new intellectual frontier. Making a name for himself in history. When he was in primary school, he would ride his bike to the public library and check out books on the planets and the cosmos; his parents were restrictive on internet screen time. But at the university, he never did well with research and academia, being better on the practical side.

His father was a leading scientist but was emotionally and physically abusive until estrangement, so he wasn't exactly a role model except via inherited genes. Scorcher's mother has since denied him any support for things that resemble the man she despises. For any similarity in ambitions, personality, or philosophy between Scorcher and his father, regardless of merit, he knows he needs to hide it to protect her (and himself). So far, being on the Moon hasn't felt any more isolating.

Gazing at a place lonelier than what he has been capable of appreciating until now, he notices a mismatch of various structures compacted together. It vaguely reminds him of the slums of a developing country, where houses are built one room atop the next with no resources for long-term forethought. Then he looks over to the actual habitat. This is it: his first visit to an Annie.

It appears, in terms of size, layout, appearance, and soul, as one of the Icelandic or Faroese turf houses which were used up until the mid-twentieth century. Essentially a mound of Moon dirt, acting as a radiation shield, with windows poking through and an obligatory front door. Though instead of square windows cut through mud, the lunar version has circular port holes, and in lieu of a wooden plank door, a metallic pressure hatch with an extremely tight airlock pressure chamber as the mud room. The door looks like it could fit on a child's playhouse.

They disembark the transport vehicle and literally hop on over. Scorcher is proud he doesn't fall.

With good fortune, not everyone arrives at the exact same time, since the airlock operates slowly. Albeit there is still a slight traffic jam when Scorcher arrives, which gives him time to connect Bluetooth headsets and meet some of the others. This is where he is introduced to all the outcasts of the Moon. Scorcher looks down as best he can and steps upon a low-quality concrete pad. It appears to be made of rock aggregate, too coarse and not enough cement matrix.

Ed is struggling with the airlock as his headset connects and dings with the headsets for the rest of the CLM crew. They hear the impatient mumbling of Ed, who evidently has a reputation for always struggling with electronics. Somewhat ironic for an engineering technician, unless you know one.

"I *hate* this thing. Who coded this?"

"It's not that complicated, Ed," interjects Four-Leaf, who impatiently hops over to take control of the situation.

Scorcher butts in awkwardly. "Hello, Ed. I'm Samuel Robertson. Callsign Scorcher."

"Yeah," Ed responds. "We've met before."

"Oh. Of course," Scorcher lies. He doesn't think this is true since he has a particularly good memory for people. Usually, it's the other way around and he himself is the one forgotten by others.

"Two can fit. Jump in, Scorcher," orders Four-Leaf.

"I'm not going in there at the same time as you," the Minister firmly informs Four-Leaf.

"I wouldn't ask you to." Suppressed vexation.

Scorcher squeezes himself in. Four-Leaf adds, "What could go wrong?" as he slams the hatch. The thump is received by their feet but not their ears.

The outer latch is locked. Pressurization initiates. He and Ed wait patiently, pushed up against each other like Moon-crossed lovers while making unintended intimate eye contact in silence. Scorcher closes his eyes and pretends his limbs are not shoved into an awkward location on Ed's body.

Any minute now…

The inner latch opens and Ed—through his inherent daftness—loses his balance and slowly floats to the ground, bounces, then pops back up and is caught by Ayubu, who isn't wearing a spacesuit and greets him with a large friendly smile. He pats Ed on the shoulder and coughs from all the dust; the airlock didn't do its job at sucking out the contaminants. A whiff of gunpowder odor instantly invades Scorcher's nose after he removes his helmet, even though he's already grown numb to the Moon dust scent at CLM.

Scorcher doesn't believe he's ever seen a smile so sincere. He notices the host wearing a cleanly pressed white African Space Agency polo shirt tucked into black Adidas gym shorts. His shirt contrasts with his dark skin. Scorcher wonders to himself how he isn't too tall for Moon duty. The max permitted height is something like 190 cm, and Ayubu clearly exceeds that. Maybe the lack of gravity caused his spine to decompress?

"Hello, my friend," Ayubu says to Scorcher in a Kenyan accent and gives him a hand at de-suiting.

"Thanks! Nice to meet you!" *Was that too enthusiastic?* The energy from his friendliness is overwhelming, and Scorcher instinctively throws it back. He takes a risk, "Hu—dyam—uh," stuttering at all the wrong times, but finally gets it. "Hujambo?"

"Aha! Shikamoo. Unafahamu kiswahili bwana?" asks Ayubu in Swahili.

"Um, that's all I know," Scorcher laughs nervously and feels stupid, not realizing he unintentionally answered the question sufficiently.

"That is fine, friend. Ninafuraha kukutana na Wewe. It is nice to meet you," he replies.

Scorcher asks himself if he's sounding too much like an awkward stereotypical colonial. Being unsure, he feels like he needs to keep talking, "Did he work with any of these people back on Earth?"

"No. But I crossed paths with Mr. Four-Leaf in South Africa once. He worked there briefly, at a mine."

"Oh, really? Interesting."

Scorcher realizes his headphones are still on when he hears the Minister bickering and threatening to go back home to his hangar, refusing to go into the airlock ahead of Four-Leaf. Scorcher missed the reason and points to them with his thumb as though asking Ayubu what the deal is, but he just shrugs, nods, and smiles at Scorcher to non-verbally acknowledge the absurdity of their cohorts.

As they are waiting for Four-Leaf, Scorcher trips over Keystone—the only person he has yet to be introduced to—sitting quietly on Ayubu's cot. He has lanky arms, no chin, very long sideburns, and is generally not very attractive by any standards. Scorcher goes to shake his hand, and Keystone timidly reciprocates. After speaking with him briefly, it becomes clear that Keystone is a quiet and quirky fellow. He laughs with a dramatic swinging of the head but is noiseless and mimics being out of breath.

"So where are you from, Keystone?"

"Oh, a small farm outside Westmoreland, Pennsylvania." The intonation at the end of his sentences always falls on a down note, which makes him sound sad when he's really not. It's the peculiar verbal rising and falling cadence used by those from rural Western Pennsylvania. It really strikes Scorcher as awkward, like he's supposed to feel guilty for something, but others tell him they don't notice it.

"Were you at NASA before this?" Ayubu asks.

"No. Before this Moon gig, I spent some time on offshore oil rigs," Keystone says, "and then briefly on a whaling ship before they got outlawed."

"Hasn't that been outlawed for a few decades now?" Scorcher asks.

Keystone laughs to answer Scorcher's question. "Just don't tell the environmentalists."

"Um. OK."

Now with Four-Leaf de-suiting and becoming comfortable, the Minister is taking his time to go through the airlock pressurization procedure, being sure that no one misses a single injustice that he experiences, cursing under his breath at every little thing. Offensive mumbling clogs Scorcher's earpiece like a mosquito in his ear.

After everyone is settled, the conversation starts off by everyone congratulating Scorcher for being lucky enough to have the Stabby to vacuum up all the regolith. It's a constant battle in the Annies, and the dust tends to evade the elaborate vacuum sequence during the airlock's pressurization routine. Scorcher doesn't ask why there's a knife attached to Stabby, though his ankles might have wanted explanation. The residents of these remote Annies have all fitted out one of their sheep to continuously vacuum up the dust in the living quarters. But it frankly doesn't work as well as Stabby for the nooks and crannies.

For those who have been on the Moon the longest, like Four-Leaf and the Minister, the Moon eyes are permanent, and the technicians collectively suspect that they will never go away. Like Arctic fishermen who have spent their lives at sea but who now are retired on the shore, their seaman eyes are constantly filling with tears, not because they are crying, but because the salt-burn is perpetual at the tear ducts.

Scorcher confuses the group and inspires some intrigue, if not fear, when he tells of his brief confrontation when Stabby stopped vacuuming for a moment and performed an unexpected light show. "Does he need to be put on his charger if he starts blinking red—?"

"So, you claim he was trying to talk to you?" Keystone asks immediately. "I used to spend a bunch of time with Stabby. He only blinks green."

Scorcher sees Four-Leaf roll his eyes and get up for more coffee. The Minister blesses himself. Ayubu closes his eyes as though to meditate and escape an uncomfortable situation.

"Stabby only blinks green," repeats Keystone.

"OK," responds Scorcher.

Ed speaks up. "Aren't all of our backup LED lights multicolored? If you've replaced them at some point, it is possible they could change to be any color."

Scorcher is puzzled about where this conversation is going but plays along anyway. "Maybe it wasn't red. It might have been green, or blue—"

"*Blue?*"

"—I probably don't really remember then, but it was interesting that it—or he—sat there just blinking. I haven't really put much more thought into it. Other than to ask if I'm supposed to do something."

"Ed, I know that the light can turn red. Of course it can. Only one time before have I seen him blink red," says Keystone.

Scorcher laughs because he doesn't know how else to respond. Keystone's seriousness is absurd, and Scorcher just assumes it's an innocent result of cabin fever on the Moon. It doesn't take much time for him to see he's the only one laughing, though. He stops.

Ed is sitting there deep in thought, looking at the floor, "I think I saw Stabby flash red once."

"Oh, come on, Ed," scolds Four-Leaf, returning with his

coffee. "Scorcher, the reason they're making a big deal about this, if you remember your training, is that we have a strict protocol on light colors." Keystone directs a furrowed brow toward Four-Leaf like he needs to interrupt. "For instance, a red flashing light on a control panel is always a bad thing and needs immediate attention. Like if there is a life support failure or a fire. That's why the smartphone we issued you doesn't display anything red unless it's an emergency."

"Oh. Oh, I see, of course," replies Scorcher, satisfied with that answer. He looks over at Keystone and sees that he has turned completely pale. *Is he shaking?*

"Mr. Stabby never blinks red. It would be a distraction to our well-trained eyes," finishes Four-Leaf. Scorcher thinks the technical fellow's eyes have a warning glint, but it's difficult to tell. Then the Irishman redirects the room's attention by introducing Scorcher officially, talks a little about his biography, getting some of the details wrong, and then everyone takes a turn introducing themselves again. Scorcher tries to pay attention to what everyone is saying but uncharacteristically forgets the details from being put on the spot. And after they've been all the way around the room, the Minister comes out with sugar and cream for the coffee, a luxury only for special occasions. Scorcher remembers that dairy products are strictly prohibited as child-like excitement blooms on every face.

Over abhorrent amounts of coffee, most of the conversation ends up being about the sheep: how to care for them, how to treat "ailments," how to get the most productivity out of them, how to keep them happy. Much of this is based not on scientific process or rigor, but the aggregate of adage, lunar legend, folklore, and rumor, all held together by a matrix of stubbornness and strong opinions. At some points, Scorcher thinks a fistfight might break out. But it never does, the gathering just calms down and stays on course.

Officially, all the employees up here work on commission for what the sheep can map out and exploit as future business opportunities. Though other state and corporate entities have been mapping out the Moon from low lunar orbits, the Founder took the approach of getting dirty and intimate, taking big financial risks, and thriving on simplicity both in philosophy and logistics. Instead of worrying about being right, the goal was to be the first: make mistakes and learn quickly, assuming the money is in the long term, not quarterly profits. Hence, the sheep are designed to be simple, rugged machines and are mostly autonomous. If one of them becomes damaged, they are easy to recover and repair. If needed, they can be customized to do any odd job.

Occasionally sheep need to be herded or straight up hunted down if attempting "escape," wandering off into parts unknown. Scorcher takes this as tongue-in-cheek since the sheep don't actually use artificial intelligence and thus don't have desires like wanting to escape. Though based on the smiles Scorcher sees on their faces when talking about it, the miners have an unspoken love of the occasional distraction of chasing down and reuniting with a lost sheep, the closest thing to fun and sport they will ever come across. Even the grumpy Minister joyfully tells a story of how one of his sheep he'd modified for steep climbing ran off and was found on top a boulder shaped like a vertical column, and it took days to figure out how to rescue it. Scorcher decides this isn't something he should ruin with a software patch.

Unofficially, the sheep have been rigged by the miners to

do some off-the-clock panning of minerals by sifting through the surface dust during the process of mapping out the Moon. Hence the "eating" and retaining of the precious regolith. Though insignificant in the grander scheme, this black market opens the opportunity to make some side cash tax-free. Everyone gets personal luggage and shipments, albeit small, going to and from Earth, free from Customs inspections. For now, the Founder turns a blind eye because he ultimately benefits from the incentive of keeping the sheep fully operational and constantly on the move.

Scorcher is still stuck thinking about the superstitious vibes he's getting from these otherwise hyper-practical people and can't help himself from interrupting with questions about Stabby's backstory.

Keystone replies, "The knife is there to keep the halls safe."

Scorcher: "Oh? From what, exactly? What's a little knife going to do?"

Keystone sits up and broadens his shoulders. "What makes you think you're more powerful than that knife in *this* environment? Do you even know where you are? Stabby keeps the halls safe, he keeps everyone safe, even out here. Man's best friend. The knife is at the right height and length for the job—"

"You mean my newly scabbed ankles?" Scorcher asks, trying to keep it lighthearted but conflicted in annoyance.

"—and when that light blinks red, it's not a false alarm. You wake the f—"

Four-Leaf takes Scorcher aside and distracts him with some shop talk and other unrelated anecdotes. They get on the topic of Four-Leaf's ex-wife after Scorcher admits he's recently divorced and wants to get away from relationships and family for a couple years. Scorcher surprises himself when he blurts out that he's tired of being a failure in his personal life and successful but bored in his professional life. Is there something in the coffee?

With the eyes of empathy, Four-Leaf tells his own crazy stories. Like how his ex-mother-in-law backed up her car once over a stray pet that was sleeping behind the tire, then just drove off after telling him to clean up the mess, annoyed at the inconvenience on her way to the market. It reminded Scorcher of how he had been run over by a car as a kid but never told anyone in fear of being punished and slapped by his father for being a "dumb fuck." After hearing some other stories, Scorcher is surprised that the technical fellow has such an insane personal life and somehow hasn't ended up dead for having the wrong accent in a Northern Ireland pub.

On that sobering note, they turn their attention back to the main crowd, where they notice the Minister is actually participating and not just grumbling in the corner. He tells the story of his super-climber sheep for the third time, then switches to stories about his kids.

The Kenyan man with a jovial smile exclaims to the Minister, "Wow, you have been married for forty years!"

"Yes," he replies.

"And you still like her?" follows up Ayubu.

"She's good around the house."

"Ah," responds Ayubu.

"Anything that moves, right, mate?" jabs Four-Leaf.

The Minister replies, "Anything that's still warm. And you judge me for being with my old lady and tell me you don't know how I still poke her. But here's some advice to you: don't stare at the mantel when you're poking the fire." The crudeness was lost on the Kenyan because of the Minister's strong accent. But Scorcher is keeping up, and he's not surprised the Minister, a married man, has been away from home for so long.

The Minister pokes his finger right at Four-Leaf, "And what did I tell you? Snip, snip," making a scissor action with his finger. "You don't date someone younger than your sister. I warned you! Now you're broke and stuck here!"

"At least I date," comes Four-Leaf's lame response. He squints, his face wrinkled with years of bad decisions. He takes his thermal skull cap off and brushes out his shoulder-length red hair, shot through with gray. When he turns to reach for his coffee, the untied hair poofs up like a lion's mane, comically large above his body. When the hair is tied back and the skull cap replaced, he transforms back into what a macho astronaut miner should look like. This is a curiosity to Scorcher since his mind can't decide which persona to identify with Four-Leaf. "So, Scorcher, lad, why is a good looking fellow like you out in a place like this?"

Feeling like a broken record, Scorcher opens up to them but provides an abbreviated version. Though he does admit that he didn't want to be like most men and get married on the rebound. Scorcher thinks he hears Four-Leaf grumble and the Minister laughing disdainfully at him like there's drama more to the backstory. He also explains that he gets bored with the monotonous analytical tasks of a day-to-day engineer and needs to have some creative outlet. He jokes he's not a good painter. No one laughs, but Ayubu smiles. And he also goes down the tangent of wanting to promote science on the frontier. He admires the classical aristocratic intellectuals of a few centuries ago who were well-rounded masters of science, math, logic, art, poetry, and religion instead of specialists in more narrow fields.

Ed tells him there was no glamor in the Wild West, but good luck here anyways.

Do they really just think I'm a wannabe cowboy? Scorcher wonders. He doesn't know why he admitted so much when he was uncomfortable doing so. Maybe he felt pressured somehow to be social, but like always, he doesn't know how to be casual about it.

Scorcher closes off when everyone loses interest in his story and gets reabsorbed into his internal thoughts. On the quiet drive back, he can't recall the rest of the meetup.

CHAPTER 12

With both the brief and infinite on a single thread, seven months pass.

Scorcher has fully learned the day-to-day oddities that are the people of the Moon and the monotony of their existence. He himself, however, does not fully assimilate to this adventurous and novel lifestyle without falling into the same old pattern of boredom and vexation with his work.

The name "Founder" is a proper noun in addition to being a descriptor—such as God versus a god. He had another name while making his fortune as a social media Khanate, but when his power turned to conquering extraterrestrial market share, his cult-like followers turned his title into a proper noun. Scorcher has always felt uneasy about the psychology behind it, that and how in his formal memos tech writers always correct his language to read "the Founder" and "the Company." Nonetheless, the mission itself is too enticing to resist for space enthusiasts. For engineers in particular, it's a lot more exciting than designing aircraft lavatories, even though it's the exact same physics and engineering practices (*so don't get too cocky,* Scorcher thinks, but only when he's already in a slump). The engineers and technicians working for the Founder clearly feel empowered by the bragging rights of space, but the business operations leaders and MBAs are entranced by the outer-worldly potential of monetary returns and growing an economic empire beyond the constraints of Earth. The latter disgusts Scorcher, so he ignores it: the counterculture beliefs of *Star Trek* economics can never be a reality.

To Scorcher's relief, his impression is that the understaffed crew on the Moon are largely apolitical, not really picking sides. He actually kind of forgets the Founder even exists even though he's the face of the Moon back home. This industrial mining monolith, away from culture and life, away from genuine existence, is too far gone even to be considered the frontier, but a parallel universe. Cold, hot, bright, dark: a universe of contradictions, extremes, and yet consisting of a terrible homogeneity in the most severe sense. Cruel to both the mind and soul, even the most emotionally robust are challenged, and anyone lesser is worn to regolith.

Even in these tight quarters, little face-to-face interaction occurs between the skilled workers. Even when they do make it back to the main campus where Scorcher is residing. A people with cult-like beliefs but lacking a cult. Scorcher previously hoped that there would have been some sort of camaraderie and closeness, but he has felt nothing. The work is virtually endless: people exhaust themselves at distant firefights across the lunar polar region, the economic and schedule pressures from Earth eliminating the possibility of downtime. In fact, lunar mining for rare elements is not readily profitable or practical, and every part of the operation needs to be leaner. Like rolling dough as thin as paper, they stand there watching helplessly as the efforts either spring back or tear. The volume just isn't there to support mining long term, and the rocket technology was over promised.

To make it worthwhile, the Earth-to-orbit rockets and

their motors need to be reusable for at least seventy-five flights. At best, the technology allows for six launches before the vehicle must be retired. The design of the systems and primary rocket structures were so rushed and disorganized, going back to make improvements for weight savings or structural integrity is nearly as costly as starting from a blank slate. For rockets, intense vibration and extreme temperatures overwhelm the structure. But many overly optimistic engineering judgments were leveraged which backed many design configurations into a corner: no easy path forward towards improvement. The only path, over and again, is to start over again.

The access to water on the Moon to make propellants—hydrogen fuel and oxidizer from ice—ended up being more challenging and costly than anticipated. NASA's Artemis missions, which brought the first woman to the Moon, failed to maintain government funding and public support long enough to perfect ice mining; people were too concerned with the ice issues on Earth. Engineering best practices were not used in the facility designs of CLM. Lightweight but brittle titanium bolts were used in lieu of heavy nickel alloy bolts for cryogenic applications, thus resulting in cracked and failed fasteners. The -253°C thermal environment makes engineering materials quite brittle, like glass. Life on the Moon mimics this fragility, and the psyche of these astronautical frontiersmen is equally brittle despite their strength.

Scorcher finds it difficult to accept the corporate culture of entangled and unsolvable problems, from engineering failures to crew resource management to a lack of standardized processes. Sometimes he wonders if he made the right decision, coming here. Is it worth this frustration? The isolation? But who has time to ask philosophical questions when trying not to perish?

In another aspect, though lacking process, there is a tyrant who forces a certain order by restricting change and progress. Scorcher has been waiting for weeks now for Four-Leaf to approve his process improvements, which could help reduce significant waste and make the business profitable. But Four-Leaf keeps delaying, mocking agreement while speaking to Scorcher in person, then throwing Scorcher under the bus during teleconference meetings when the topics arise in front of their teammates on Earth. This is usually followed up by Four-Leaf feigning shock and responding to Scorcher with something like, "This is really what you propose? We need to chat offline in private, mate." All to Scorcher's embarrassment in front of those watching.

On the other extreme end, though, Four-Leaf is impressed with some of Scorcher's work. There have been very few instances when that's been explicitly acknowledged, though. In fact, as though in rebuttal to himself, he tells Seattle that Scorcher is the man he needs. And to Scorcher, it seems true that Four-Leaf couldn't survive without him. How did he do it before?

Four-Leaf has been working on his own ideas for facility and operational improvements, like acid showers to clean spacesuits or pressurized long underwear to maintain blood pressure which would allow for the ambient facility atmospheric pressures to be lower. But these random ideas seem way too risky to be practical, at least in Scorcher's mind. Scorcher attempts to talk about his concerns to Four-Leaf, including the fact that this all just seems like a science project with no real practical application. But in front of their colleagues back in Seattle, Scorcher gives in and decides it's not worth fighting in circles anymore. "Oh, don't give up so easily," Four-Leaf says with a sly smirk. Scorcher gets the creepy feeling that Four-Leaf enjoys this power game.

A few weeks ago, Scorcher and Four-Leaf firmly met head-to-head. It started during a meeting with the Seattle team when there was some disagreement on the definition of a technical term. Something minor that normal humans wouldn't fret over, but a small few in this industry would stake their reputations on these technical or regulatory definitions. Scorcher corrected Four-Leaf on the video call in front of the Founder, which thoroughly infuriated the technical fellow, like he felt his image had been tattered and challenged publicly. Personally, Scorcher just wants to have the most correct information to ensure clear communication, and if it comes from someone else's better insight or experience, so be it. He couldn't care less about the hierarchy. In his mind, there is no judgment for being "wrong," just for denying the truth.

This was followed up a couple weeks later by Four-Leaf publicly, in front of the Founder, trying to shame Scorcher for being "incorrect." Scorcher, motivated by having the right information he needed to do his job, stuck to the facts and tried to answer as objectively as possible. With each response, however, a quicker responding Four-Leaf countered. He started writing down everything Scorcher was saying. Scorcher was too nervous to do the same, so he wrote down Four-Leaf's words in private after the fact, but then threw it out.

Later, things subsided, and Scorcher bitterly conceded by not having the last word and allowing for ambiguity so Four-Leaf could save face. In his view, no one in Seattle was paying attention anyway, and conflict in general causes undue anxiety.

He starts disclosing his discomfort in more detail to Space-Bee during their video chats that have become routine over the past six months. Though, to Scorcher's disappointment, when Space-Bee is "in port" at Central Lunar Mining, she never finds time to have a simple coffee again. She avoids actual in-person interactions at all costs.

"You think it could be you and not Four-Leaf?" asks Space-Bee innocently. "Maybe you're the problem."

"Excuse me?" This strikes Scorcher as a personal attack. "I've spent the past half-year just randomly working these side projects which have no point. I don't even understand the purpose of half of what that leprechaun wants me to do. Like, the other day he had me make a new shade of damned blue paint, just to see if it could be done, and then that was it. I never used the blue paint. Or he'll redline my emails back and forth over endless iterations. Then he'll get pissed that I wrote something a certain way, even though they were really his words—"

"Just playing devil's advocate. Are you sure—"

"Four-Leaf is the devil. Are you his advocate?"

Space-Bee sighs. "Do you have an issue with authority? You mentioned earlier about how tech fellows only care about their career scorecards. I think you might have an issue getting along with people. Like anti-social or something. Have you spoken to a therapist about it?"

"I don't have an issue with authority, if they earn it." Scorcher defends himself as though he's guilty of having authority issues and then becomes even more defensive because he knows that authority has nothing to do with his head-butting with the Irishman.

"Didn't he, though? He has a pretty tough job, you gotta give him that," Space-Bee says.

"I'm not saying whether he earned his job, that's not the

damn point." Scorcher stops his words to take a breath. He sees that Space-Bee is fidgety on screen.

"You're still new there. Just give it some time. If Seattle trusts him, I think we can, too." She changes the topic in what sounds like a hope to salvage the conversation. "I don't think you listen to enough music."

"What's that again?"

"You've never mentioned what sort of music you listen to, and it doesn't ever come up," she says.

Scorcher asks, "What are you listening to?"

She replies, "Tribal music. You should listen to some."

Scorcher laughs. "I can't really relate. I feel like an outsider."

"Don't be ridiculous. It's just music. You're overthinking it," she says.

"I'm not, I just don't want to be one of those douchebags with dreads."

Space-Bee: "What the hell does that mean? Are you a racist?"

His chest and arms tighten, and he ends the call. "I have to go. I'll talk to you later." He abruptly logs out and goes to walk aimlessly around the halls to burn off steam.

As he attempts to pace down the hall without unintentionally hopping, he thinks about how the one thing that he used to do when he was frustrated was go on long neighborhood walks. It is one of the few things that seems to work for him, and the stupidity of not considering that habitual need before taking this job tears at him. The hallways all looking the same around every corner compresses him even more.

CHAPTER 13

Scorcher's negative energy rolls down the hallway. He craves coffee despite his animation. He discovers CLM is out of coffee. Completely. He must wait a couple days until the *Vegvisir* resupply ship makes its way back to the lunar dock. Desperation drives him to consider saddling up a sheep to visit Ayubu in person. He knows he can take advantage of his kindness to get some grounds.

Instead, he drinks some water recycled from urine and paces around the underground halls. As he struts around, he passes Stabby multiple times but takes no conscious notice of him.

More walking. Walking helps stop his brain from exploding.

He stops the moment he sees the pattern.

"What the hell are you doing loitering there? You know you make no sense sometimes, right?"

It's a stare-off with Stabby. Scorcher approaches, but the machine immediately responds by wiggling back and forth, waving his knife at him. Scorcher pauses mid-stride and takes a step back. This is enough to appease the bot, who reacts by halting his knife-waving. The Space Roomba pauses his vacuuming each time Scorcher passes and then rotates to stay pointed towards him as he passes. Scorcher realizes now that this is what's been happening the whole time. He considers that he might be misinterpreting malintent, that it's possible Stabby just wants to get his attention for something. "Is this the vacuum equivalent of staring at me and giving me puppy dog eyes? What if I just take that knife out and stab you with it?"

The Roomba rolls back a couple inches, then remains completely still.

Scorcher feels empowered now but is then flooded with guilt at picking on this machine. "Who programmed you? It was Keystone, wasn't it? Is this his redneck Pennsylvania version of artificial intelligence?" Scorcher imagines Space-Bee telling him to not be so horrible, so he stops. He sounds too much like his father, which he regrets. "OK, buddy. What do you want?"

Stabby lights up, this time his bulbs flashing yellow, turns, and then leads Scorcher down the hall. Scorcher knows instinctively that he's supposed to follow.

They continue traveling for a while. To take the stairs, Stabby has a little zipline that lowers him to the next level and a mini-crane that lifts him back up. When they arrive, it's broken.

"Is that it, then? You just need a lift? I can do that, I suppose." Scorcher picks him up, resisting the urge to be affectionate, and carries him down the stairs. "All right, now. Carry on."

Scorcher walks back up the stairs and then suddenly stops. The hall lights have turned off, and all he sees is a dim red flashing. Or is that just his eyes adjusting? He turns around and sees that it's coming from Stabby. Or maybe it's…

He slowly navigates down the stairs in the dark, and the hall lights turn back on. "That was weird. Did the lights going out scare you, too? Is that what caused you to blink red?" Scorcher pulls out his smartphone to do a systems check on facility lighting and power while he's standing midway down the stairs. But he's interrupted by the sound of Stabby repeatedly rotating clockwise, then counterclockwise, quickly back and forth, waving his knife. Scorcher puts his cellular device in its holster. Stabby halts and stares at Scorcher, proceeding towards him again.

Stabby turns around and starts driving off with his lights flashing yellow, mimicking a construction zone. He follows.

The hallway lights turn off, then back on again. "What the—" Scorcher pulls out his phone. Stabby stops as soon as Scorcher stops, turns back around to face him, and does the whole knife waving routine again. "All right, fine, I'll follow you." Scorcher pockets his smartphone.

He has an idea. "How about I figure out how to attach a flashlight to you?"

Stabby stops, twirls a couple revolutions while flashing green, then turns back to race down the hall, flashing yellow.

"I guess that means affirmative."

After a moment of walking, they arrive at a closed hatch to a storage room. Stabby stops, with his knife pointed at the door, and starts blinking red. Scorcher verifies via a small access panel that the room is pressurized to one atmosphere, then opens the hatch and looks into the storage room of spare sheep, sheep parts, and salvaged electrical components. At this point, he's lost as to what to do.

"Why did you bring me to the barn, Stab-meister? Looking for a new place to take out my ankles?" On the far side of the "barn" is a short pressure lock that allows sheep to drive back and forth between the maintenance facility and the lunar surface as needed.

Scorcher walks around to investigate and sees sheep that

are neatly lined up but with the power units removed, plus plenty of other spare parts and virgin metallic powder for 3-D printers in hermetically sealed containers. He recognizes the metallic powder containers from the trip out on the *Vegvisir* and recalls Space-Bee lugging it around effortlessly, even though on Earth it's a two-person lift. The 3-D printer that was giving him issues the first day he was here is also sitting there, idle but ready, its flashing red light indicating standby mode.

"I thought red lights were for emergencies only," he snarks.

Scorcher turns around to see the Roomba flashing red in the pressurized hatch way. Then the little vacuum starts to chirp, indicating that it needs to return to a charging station.

"Are you kidding me? Why'd you bring me here? You're seriously just going to ditch me?" he asks. Stabby drives away and disappears around the corner.

Seeing everything in order, Scorcher walks back towards the hallway, exits the barn, and closes its pressure-tight hatch. Looking all the way down the hall back toward the stairs, he is caught off guard when he thinks he spots Four-Leaf but dismisses it as Stabby's overly bright LEDs leaving temporary blotches in his vision. He should be the only person at CLM right now.

CHAPTER 14

Scorcher is no longer surprised by the general lack of automation, even for sending digital data back to Seattle. His latest soul-numbing tasks include transmitting data on energized solar particle radiation, galactic cosmic radiation, temperature fluctuations, humidity, power grid usage, water usage, plumbing, human waste, water conversion to oxygen and hydrogen, recycling, how much regolith Stabby sucks up, and suggestions on improving team morale. Data scientists galore in Seattle sift through the data, make interpretations, and then nothing comes out of it, at least from what Scorcher has seen. Four-Leaf keeps telling him that his efforts in data collection are futile. However, making use of this data would require planning, implementation, and execution, none of which is possible if Scorcher's token technical fellow just keeps giving him the runaround.

"God, this pisses me off," Scorcher says out loud to his dry coffee cup. "He's always firefighting but never clears the brush to stop it from happening in the first place. It's almost like he enjoys the repeated flare-ups. He's one step short of an arsonist." Scorcher stops to think about it further, wondering if Four-Leaf isn't the source of the chaos. Or if he isn't just a well-composed emotional mess with his knee jerk reactions. Shocking, for as chaotic and seemingly impractical as he is, he's quite predictable.

"Maybe I'm spending too much time armchair psychoanalyzing him," he thinks out loud, "I don't really know what I'm talking about anyway." He notices he's also talking to himself out loud quite a bit. "Where are you, Stabby? Maybe I'm not a lunatic if I'm at least talking to *you* out loud?" He laughs. "Lunatics. Good thing there aren't luna-ticks. Speaking of which, what kind of bug, exactly, was it that Space-Bee crushed with her projectile boot months ago?"

His mind jumps to a time once while showering when he found a tick near his groin and lived in complete anxiety and disgust for nearly a week until it naturally fell off.

He goes back to his desk and recalls his weird interactions with Space-Bee. Why is she so awkward? After dropping off the much-needed coffee—and everything else, secondary—she just went right back to her docked ship. Constantly sending text messages to Scorcher before Moon docking, saying basically nothing while she was here, then flooding his email after she got back on the *Vegvisir*. It's almost like her friendship with him is most natural when he's digital, but in person they don't know how to act around each other.

He decides to ask her directly over instant messenger, forgetting about their previous argument: *Why do you chat with me so much online? Not that I mind, I love it, you're like the only person I can freely vent to without holding back. I'm just curious. Not trying to be weird.*

She writes back: *I don't know. You just seem easy to complain to, even though you're a weirdo.*

He writes back, playfully irritating her: *What about Rocko? You two seem to get along. Did you hear he was a sponsored roller skater back in the day?*

She responds: *He's like the most annoying person ever. You know I can't stand him. And everyone else is just so stuffy or creepy. Who else could I talk to? Don't let it go to your head.*

He laughs.

Aren't I supposed to avoid women anyway? he asks himself. He then starts fantasizing about what must be going on behind her intense eyes.

An unexpected call comes in from Seattle.

"Hello? You need me to resend radiation data…It's slightly corrupted…No worries. Thanks…Thanks, yep. Thanks." *Click.*

One of Scorcher's tasks is to relay back to the Seattle Medical team all the radiation measurement data. It's transmitted monthly alongside astronaut basic vital signs and noted health irregularities. Some of this checkup is done via a quick phone interview. Radiation is done separately, however, since the individual astronauts are not directly involved in collecting their own personalized data. Various sensors, including particle detectors, collect measurements at the Moon docking station at Central Lunar Mining, at one of the remote Annies with Ayubu, and through bulky radiation sensors on the spaceship *Vegvisir* with Commander "Siren" Ōtsuka, Rocko, and Space-Bee. Solar radiation exposure is about twenty to thirty times greater on the Moon than what people experience at a sunny beach on Earth, and this excludes galactic cosmic particle beta-radiation. Scorcher knows that the risk from the latter is that the very high energy impact from beta radiation will ionize the atoms in DNA, causing cancer. It makes sense to Scorcher that this is something they don't take lightly. He checks the files he sent and sees that they are corrupted and not readable.

Maybe due to radiation? he asks ironically.

He checks on the local servers for the same data files, and they, too, seem to be corrupted. He then goes to the digital database with all the raw data and tries to figure out what went wrong. After digging through the code for three hours—he sees what output format it's supposed to be in but for some reason the code isn't working—he decides to just write his own computer script to extract the data. Then he'll send it over afterwards.

Forty-five minutes later, he's done and, out of pure curiosity, starts looking at everyone's calculated radiation exposure versus their allowance. Scorcher has a tendency to redo analysis so that he learns it better—something to break up the monotony and frustration, and at the same time feed his curiosity. He's far from being an expert in medicine and radiation, but his background in engineering—essentially, applied Newtonian physics—has taught him to critically analyze scientific data. In secondary school, Scorcher was drawn to engineering and Newtonian and Hookean physics since they're intuitive and based on peoples' innate understanding of how the universe should behave. The Hamiltonian physics he learned later, based on the axiom that God would create the most efficient universe possible, is a parallel mathematical approach which gives you identical predictions as Newton.

But after all the fancy differential equations and calculus, it comes down to something as simple as axioms like this: doubling the weight of a truck on a bridge will cause the bridge to deflect downward twice as much. As one of his professors repeatedly explained, engineers love to make things as overly complicated as possible in order to simplify everything back down to something that can actually make sense. Scorcher could never figure out if some engineers do this to rank themselves intellectually above others on university campuses, or if they're just sadomasochists.

Well, he mused, *there's nothing like doing everything as right as possible just to watch it blow up anyway on the launch pad.*

After doing the basic calculation, he sees that the *Vegvisir* crew, particularly Space-Bee, have been *significantly* over-exposed. He suspects he's screwed up. He goes through all the algebra again.

Goddamn it, he thinks. *Why can't he just get the numbers right? Is it a stupid minus sign error? At this rate, Space-Bee should be suffering from radiation sickness and probably have cancer already.*

Then he remembers that the radiation on the *Vegvisir* is collected at two locations on the spaceship. One is external to the protective radiation blanket attached to the ship's hull, and the other is internal to measure the actual amount being received by the crew. He considers he's using the wrong data.

Scorcher recalls Rocko talking about the lush "fungal lawn" that is housed in 3-D-printed polyethylene honeycomb panels attached directly to the inside of the spaceship's hull. The fungi are radiotrophic, meaning that they consume radiation and metabolize it as energy. These particular radiotrophic fungi use melanin combined with radiation to perform radiosynthesis. Radiosynthesis is thought to be a similar process to the anaerobic pathway that occurs when oxygen is not present. In short, these fungi eat dangerous radiation for breakfast.

To the risk of the crew onboard, there are still some unknowns in the reliability of this approach to shield the astronauts from radiation. It is still not fully understood how, or if, multi-step processes such as photosynthesis or chemosynthesis are used in radiosynthesis. This means the long-term viability of using fungi is untested and unknown.

It was something first experimented on the International Space Station years ago after fungi were extracted from Chernobyl, Ukraine—the site of a major nuclear disaster from the last century. It seemed successful then on a small scale but was then implemented on the *Vegvisir* with the risk that it could always randomly fail, as new tech often does outside a tightly controlled lab environment. They would have to put the entire Moon enterprise on hold for a couple more years to be properly "risk-managed."

Scorcher recalculates—again—the data from the *Vegvisir* crew using both spaceship sensors, internal and external of the radiation shield. He finds the sign error, but Space-Bee is still coming up unrealistically and dangerously high in her total radiation exposure.

Wait, the total count is cumulative over many months. Right? Or is this count per day? Am I doing this wrong? "This can't be right."

Scorcher goes to walk around for five minutes to give his brain a break. If he becomes too frustrated, which happens often recently, he can't focus on basic analytical tasks like adding and subtracting. But at the same time, he gets too obsessed with figuring this type of stuff out.

As he is walking around, he begins to calm down and reset his brain. That's when his anxiety strikes tenfold and he begins to feel sick in his gut, nauseous even. The thought of Space-Bee getting radiation poisoning…he chokes on anger.

She isn't a random statistic or an employee badge number. This is real. The potential destruction of someone's life through a horrible, agonizing death is very real. He debates to himself about even bringing it up to her. He's too flustered. He doesn't want to create a panic over nothing.

"Isn't this Seattle's job?" he asks Stabby. "This wouldn't

be the first time I stuck my nose into something and looked stupid." Scorcher convinces himself he needs more caffeine. His body is craving it. He needs it. Destruction and productivity—both—are fueled by it.

CHAPTER 15

"Hello, my friend!" Ayubu says over the phone. Hearing his voice always seems to make Scorcher forget that he's on the Moon, as though he exists in some normal location with other humans doing normal people things. Whereas getting a message from Space-Bee is more like a comforting fog to a nebulophile that returns the same time each day.

"Hey, Ayubu. I just wanted to touch base with you," Scorcher says. "How are things up there? Did everything work out?"

"Ah, yes. The sheep are grazing for now. Those 3-D printed filter pans work great. Your design is much simpler to install. Thank you, friend!"

Scorcher smiles. "No problem. I'm glad. Let me know if you need anything else. See you at the three o'clock." Scorcher takes his cell phone off his ear to disconnect. He's a little nervous that Four-Leaf might interfere and give the runaround, so he keeps a lot of these small projects on the downlow.

He goes back to thinking about Space-Bee. He is anxious to see her in person and is finally able to convince her to stop by during her next docking and get another coffee. Scorcher doesn't like keeping secrets and wants to tell Space-Bee his concerns about her radiation overexposure. But at the same time, the drive to avoid confrontation conflicts with his desire to help and bullies him into avoiding awkwardness. He has this fear of accidentally yelling out the truth. But maybe it's all a conspiracy theory and he just needs to have faith in people. There's no way such a large operation doesn't have checks and balances. But then he starts thinking about the airline crashes at his previous employer, where 15,000 employees and federal regulators, at some level or another, were all involved and allowed disaster to occur.

Scorcher waves as he sees her walking over, staring at the floor. He smiles anyway. "How's my little busy bee?"

She looks up and blushes. "Shut up."

They both have their coffees in hand. "How are things?" he asks.

She replies, "Well, you know, I just texted you about it. Commander and Rocko are both feeling nauseous, so Seattle Medical is trying to figure out a remedy. All our vitals look fine, of course. Oxygen levels, radiation levels, diet, stool samples, urine chemistry: the whole deal looks good. Nothing like having to record every single bite of food and ounce of fluid in and out. Must be nice down here, not having to archive your stool samples."

"As long as you don't check your stool in the coffee shop and promise to wash your hands, I think I'll be fine," he says.

Space-Bee is unresponsive and neutral. She gets up to walk to the window, takes a pill out of her pocket, and chases it with coffee after swallowing it.

Scorcher tries another witticism, "Don't you get enough of the view?"

"It's actually quite nice, being close to it. The Moon, I mean. It almost doesn't seem real, though, even this close," she says.

Scorcher follows her lead. "Personally I like having a constant temperature and not having to deal with rain or pesky wind. I probably should have worked on a submarine."

"Oh, I love the wind," she says softly. "Or that feeling in the Midwest on a hot sticky day, standing on the edge of a field, looking out. Dark clouds rolling in and you can see the edge of the breeze, the front of the storm, pushing across the grass and racing towards you. Then instantly, the cool breeze hits you and you almost fall back, the drop in temperature making you shiver, but now the suffocating humid air is pushed away behind you. Like you're rushing forward but standing still at the same time, to enjoy the moment. You can take a cool, deep breath as you watch the storm thundering closer and closer."

"That's amazing," Scorcher says softly. Though he can't fully relate to what she is saying, being from Southern California where interesting weather doesn't exist. He tries to contribute. "I like storms. Definitely miss those. So that's what you miss the most?"

She thinks for a moment, looking down at the lifeless dirt. "On the Moon it's not called soil, because soil is alive and composed of organic material. Maybe that's why it looks fake. We're all fake here. What I miss most about Earth is being back home—like 'home' home—sitting outside, at night by myself. And in the middle of the night hearing a far-off train horn in the distance."

"Sounds sentimental and melancholy."

"No," she says, "neither of those. It's like hearing someone far off crying for help."

"Like, in the distance?" asks Scorcher.

"Yes. Like, I need to go out there and save them," she replies, gripping her coffee hard enough to make her knuckles white.

"Save them from what?" he asks while turning to study her face.

"I don't know. Anything? It's not about something specific. I just need to save them."

Scorcher tries to relate. "Almost like in *The Catcher in the Rye?*"

"What's that? Oh. Yes. Maybe. Like, I get that feeling, like an emotional response to some kinds of music. It brings up a heavy, sad feeling, and I feel I need to go out and save them." She tilts her head up to stare at the horizon.

He studies her profile for a while, at a loss for words. It's like he's not even there.

"Yeah, that's interesting. Lots of people have strong emotions associated with songs." He doesn't know what else to say.

"Yeah, I have that, too. But it's different. For me, it's the sound itself. Different from a song with lyrics. It's sort of like with violin music. Not like a fiddle playing something quick. But like Amadeus's father."

Scorcher wants to understand, but he doesn't, so he follows up. "Do you play the violin?"

"I own one, but no. Back on Earth, I mean. Always wanted to, though," she replies.

"Maybe I can 3-D print one," Scorcher jokes.

She's silent for a moment, then snaps back to the present. He has said something, and she should react. "Ha! Yeah, maybe." She turns around, and her demeanor becomes more like a friend hanging out. "I'm always swollen with this microgravity stuff. Even the Moon doesn't help."

"Sorry about that," Scorcher says.

"It's not your fault, you didn't do it. Just another thing for my body to deal with."

He wants to tell Space-Bee about his radiation exposure concerns but holds his breath. He figures if it was an issue, someone in Seattle would have caught it. Plus, he doesn't want to make an awkward lane change in the middle of their conversation. He'd rather keep talking about non-work-related topics and figure it out later.

They stay sitting in silence for five minutes, stuck in their own thoughts.

Space-Bee finally says, "Unlike you, I actually get to see Earth through the windscreen. I see it often, and you never see it. You're lucky, Scorcher. It's so much worse than not seeing it at all. It's better to let your memory go complacent and forget it even exists. Just like death. Sometimes it's better to let the memory fade like it never existed."

"Do you really believe that?" he asks.

She doesn't respond.

"Are there any people you miss from home? You never talk about anyone," he says.

"Neither do you," she says.

"I don't mean to prod…"

For the first time ever, she deliberately turns to look right at him, making direct eye contact in a way she's never done before. It makes Scorcher want to back up and lean forward at the same time. She looks sad, which is new and intriguing to him. But from that excitement, he feels inexplicably ashamed for wanting to connect with someone after seeing their sadness.

"I've been on shore leave two times, Scorcher, and each damned time I head back home, only like one person comes out to see me. Not even my family. And both times it was the same person, and she just had this look of pity, like she felt sorry for lonely me with no friends or family. Someone I've casually known since kindergarten. Not even a close friend, really. But still a sweetheart. She is so kind to me. Everyone else I knew growing up and spent so much time with has always given excuses for not seeing me, like work or co-parenting step-kids at soccer games, or some other bullshit reason. What the hell? I traveled all the way back from outer-frickin-space and they can't travel five minutes to see me? And I've helped a lot of these people out when they needed money, or an extra hand moving apartments, or dog-sitting. Am I nothing?"

As she's explaining this, Scorcher is acutely aware that his heart is drawn toward her in this vulnerable state. There's a weird magnetism that pulls him towards her for being an emotional outcast, and he hates it. He doesn't like her suffering and feels he's wrongly benefiting from it somehow. The idea of being her only close friend is overwhelmingly validating, but at the same time terrifying and draining. It's the same cycle each time: he's instantly attracted to a woman who is highly intelligent but who struggles to make connections with other people and simply can't fit in with anyone. He needs to be that hero who sets her free and gives her happiness. And somehow that will make him happy, too. But he also knows he doesn't have the ability to do that, and his heart's ambition is wrong, as history and a failed marriage have proven. He knows he's letting himself go toward a trap with Space-Bee, but he doesn't resist.

Nor does she.

CHAPTER 16

Scorcher is dreaming that he's suffocating. He sees a dark shadow sitting on his chest pouring blood on his head from a teacup. The viscosity of the fluid…

He can finally catch his breath: he isn't dreaming.

Lying on the floor, his tendon indicates a shoulder impingement which feels like an elephant stepping on his arm. He rolls slightly to relieve it. There is a high-pitched ringing in his ears, like they've been blown out by an explosion.

Have they?

Red lights flashing—bright, dark, bright, dark—his eyes aren't adjusted.

"Where the fuck am I?"

He sits up from the freezing metallic floor to access his pants pocket, but it doesn't work, his hand can't get in. He lies back down to reattempt to reach into his pants pocket, and this time, it works. His hand is in. Wrong bloody pocket. Everything is so confusing. He lies back down to relieve the pain in his shoulders.

How did the ringing not wake him sooner?

He rolls over to his side, exerting through all his tolerance, and sees Stabby's shadowy outline. The robot holds its ground with each red flash then quickly disappears again; he's guarding the smartphone with his knife.

Scorcher reaches for it quickly and takes it. "You bugger," he barely hears himself say that, so he checks again, "Blah, blah, blah. Nope, can't hear myself." He shrugs pathetically.

The pressure hatches in the hallway are shut, behind him and in front. Sitting up now, he hears—no, feels— a small explosion through vibrations in his bottom. He wonders if this isn't at least the second explosion he's felt in the last few minutes, and not dozens he missed. Sirens start blasting now.

"Ay, God!" Scorcher flinches and squeezes his eyes shut for a moment.

He uses the wall to get up like a fallen geriatric. He hears a large screech like a locomotive's brakes, starting at one far end of the hallway from behind the aft pressure hatch, then scraping quickly towards him, flying past overhead, only to quickly end up rocketing toward the distance behind the opposite pressure hatch. His ears pop. The railroad screeching strikes Scorcher, "I don't wanna die, I don't wanna die, I don't wanna die—" He hugs himself as tightly as possible to stop the panic, then releases after a few deep breaths.

He wipes blood from his forehead with his arm, briefly verifying its color on his wrist. The blood looks falsely metallic in the dreamlike red light.

The siren ceases. Scorcher pauses for a moment. "Check the systems," he orders himself. He can't think clearly so he starts screaming out loud, which helps for some reason, "OK, there must have been an explosion. What was my training? Check life support first, got it. Do I need oxygen? Pressure and O2 are..." He doesn't know where he is. "Well, I'm obviously breathing." He lowers the volume of his voice after getting quickly exhausted. There is a glow-in-the-dark painted numeric code on the bulkhead telling him his location. "So, I'm on the bottom level. Check. Life support running on backup battery power, the main hydrogen-fuel electric power generator has starved and turned off. Can I get to a pressure suit?"

Pressure suits, for emergencies just like this, are supposed to be available in every pressure zone. The construction of Central Lunar Mining includes multiple pressure hatches throughout the hallways and for each room entrance which can be locked, either manually or, as in this case, automatically. These maintain habitable pockets in case of a chemical leak, a meteorite strike, explosion, or other traumatic event. Just so that no one gets trapped inadvertently, a pressure suit—only meant for temporary indoor operations—should be available in each pressure zone. This requirement was waived and ignored since pressure suits are expensive and need continuous testing and qualification. Instead, it's just Scorcher, alone, and he could be left trapped to suffocate if he's cut off and pressure is lost behind the doors.

"How are the other zones looking? It will be so stupid if I die this way," he says with forced sarcastic intonation.

"Pressure is only lost in the hydrogen power plant high bay. Everything else seems stable." Scorcher tries to call Four-Leaf. No one picks up. Then he tries the Minister but is unable to reach him either. He checks that the Wi-Fi phone service is working.

Scorcher manages to turn off the alarms and stop the annoying flashing red lights. Dim and sparsely spaced white halogen lights illuminate the hall, giving it the feeling of a parking garage. "It blows my mind that not all these lights are LED. Idiots."

Scorcher manages to reach one of the mining technicians. "Hello, Ed."

The phone answers back on speaker. "Hey, Scorcher. Burning the place down yet?"

"Well, maybe. There's been an explosion, I think."

"Oh, you really are burning down the place." Ed becomes more serious.

"Standby, I'm going to get others on the call." Scorcher manages to reach Keystone, the superstitious Pennsylvania farm boy. Lastly, Ayubu, their rotation engineer from the African Space Agency. The four of them start discussing what happened.

Keystone says, "Is Stabby with you?"

"Um, oddly enough, yes. Though I can't remember why or if it's just a coincidence."

Ed replies, "It's no coincidence."

"That's why you ain't dead," interjects Keystone.

"We programmed him to go to the nearest human after an emergency," says Ed.

This jolts Scorcher. "He what? How does he get through the doors? What if there is a pressure leak—"

Keystone interrupts. "It's for your own safety. Don't worry, I did the coding. It won't put you in danger. If the hatches are still connected to the network, then Stabby can open them. Ed double checked it."

Scorcher thinks to himself: *Good God, my life is in dipshit Ed's hands.* "Did you even do regression testing on this? Forget it. We'll talk about the Stabby issue later. I need everyone to plan on coming back here to CLM. As I've said, there has been an explosion, and I have no idea what caused it at this time—"

"Stay at your posts for now, do not come back yet. I'm not sure if we've got sufficient life support at this time, mates," says the technical fellow over the phone. This surprises Scorcher since he thought Four-Leaf hadn't picked up. "Scorcher, can you agree with that until you and I get a handle on what happened? Come upstairs."

The lights quit and the Wi-Fi network goes down. "If you can hear me, yes, I agree Four-Leaf, I'll head up to the top deck," Scorcher replies, even though he knows the connection has been lost. The halogen lights turn back on, providing dim ambience.

Ironic, Scorcher thinks, *since LED lights use less power than halogen.*

Scorcher walks up to the hatchway and grabs the lever. He is unable to push the door open. He then remembers to open the tiny pressure-equalizer door first. He does this and his ears pop, which he feels more than he hears, then the hatch opens. There's a stab at his ankle, like his skin got caught on a hook, but without any pain. He looks down and sees that Stabby—either accidentally or purposely—cleanly sliced him near the ankle, right through the boot. Scorcher turns around and viciously kicks Stabby multiple times, with blood squirting from his boot each time. Stabby starts blinking red and rolls away to escape, much more quickly than Scorcher thought possible. A shame synonymous to striking a child weakens him.

"God, this place," Scorcher sighs.

He hops around as Stabby opens the pressure hatch in the opposite direction, supposedly out of precaution to avoid killing Scorcher with hypoxia via the vacuum of space, then closes it behind him.

Scorcher reaches the pressure hatch to the control room to find Four-Leaf. He's unable to open it, then decides to simply knock. Four-Leaf opens the hatch to let Scorcher in.

"Your name is living up to itself," says the technical

fellow.

Scorcher is dazed. "I didn't do this, did I?" He hopes not; he hasn't even considered that he could have caused whatever this is.

Four-Leaf is extraordinarily calm in his eyes, mannerisms, and spoken tone. He says to Scorcher, "This is what my panic face looks like. I'm panicked. You see?" He smoothly turns back around. Scorcher can feel it in his gut, but the visual cues don't make sense. Is he panicked? "You're bleeding on the floor, mate." He throws his junior man a greasy rag, probably contaminated with some toxic chemicals. "Based on what I can deduce, there was an explosion along pipeline 15F heading into the hydrogen-fuel power plant. I'm not really sure how, but it must have happened in a pressurized zone. Life support is running off batteries, which are currently being charged with solar panels, so we're doing quite well on facilities and life support."

They hear a loud pop.

Scorcher: "What was that?"

Another loud pop. Then another. A siren goes off.

"Shit," exclaims Four-Leaf. "That's a pressure differential alarm on one of the N2 tanks."

They both run to the tank. When they get to the 20,000 liter tank, the walls are caving in like a beer can.

"A pump must be running still and creating a vacuum in the pressure vessel. We need to unlock the valve before it implodes the tank and tears apart half of CLM."

Scorcher interrogates Four-Leaf, "Why is the valve not working?"

"Lord knows."

"I can manually cut out the intake pipe to allow air to vent in while you disconnect the power on the pump.

Hopefully it's enough to equalize the pressure in time."

Four-Leaf stands impressed by what Scorcher is proposing to do. "I'll pull the plug manually, mate. Good luck on the suicide run." He smiles and bails on Scorcher.

He must be enjoying this in a sick way, Scorcher considers.

The tank is in a separate room above ground. If it implodes, the shock could be massive enough to disable CLM, making it uninhabitable and inoperative indefinitely. The only way to the tank from this room, without having to traverse multiple hallways, is through a smaller access duct via a ladder. Scorcher makes the climb after grabbing whatever hand tools he can: a random screwdriver and a couple wrenches. Once he reaches the room through a pressure-tight manhole cover, he rushes to the tank. He crawls underneath the tank to the intake pipe, nearly impossible to reach. The tank's wall dimples further inward, giving him more room to wriggle in. Using the screwdriver, he stabs the sheet metal without second thoughts to create crude vents. The massive aluminum tank whistles and suddenly pops back to its original not-collapsed shape.

Scorcher is pounded back down to the floor under the tank and is compressed to the point of crushing to death. His ribs will give way at any second.

I'm gonna fucking die here.

With pressure on his chest and his head tilted at an almost unbearable angle, Stabby rolls up out of the darkness and stops short of stabbing him in the eye.

"How'd the fuck you even get in here?" he grunts, half towards Stabby and half towards his own fate.

Scorcher's hand slides on the smooth metallic surfaces, unable to realize traction; his body is pinned at the lowest point of the cylindrical tank, and he just needs to get his breastplate past this tight point. He feels the intercostal flesh straining between his ribs like hot needles. The stars forming in his vision further distract his attempts, until he changes tactics. He drags in Stabby by his knife blade, ignoring the cut it makes on his hand. He then wraps his arm around him and wedges the robot under the cylindrical tank as well. This is enough for Scorcher to use Stabby to pull himself out. He manages to leverage his body feet first from under the tank but struggles to get the vacuum out. Still on the floor, he kicks Stabby out with his shin—what is pain at this point anyways, he just needs to be fast—and right after breaking him free, he hears the motor from the cryogenic pump cease. He didn't realize how noisy the room had been till now.

Scorcher shakily gets onto all fours and pets the bot. "Your timing is too interesting. Maybe I won't toss you into some random crater the next time you tick me off."

He inspects his hand. "Well, liquid stitches it is, then. Hopefully you don't have tetanus and only came here because you didn't want me to die too quickly."

When he makes it back to Four-Leaf, he explains what happened. The best he can tell, Four-Leaf appears to have a new respect for him. "I'll keep it our little secret, mate, that you broke protocol to climb inside of a collapsing structure. You almost became a hero in there." He slaps Scorcher on the back while laughing—the only time he's ever heard him laugh.

Scorcher drinks some water and sits for a few minutes to examine his bruised ribs and bad life choices before going back to his engineering crisis assessments.

After his recess is over, he jumps right back into action. "It looks like the only thing completely shut down right now is industrial operations, like Moon ice propellant and oxidizer conversion and mine ore refinement. So the factory part of the operation is down—"

Four-Leaf interrupts. "Correct, the business is shut down, but our bio dome is solid. No need to hold your breath, at least for now. Seattle is going to be angry about this one. Let's get everyone to come back here to square things away and clean up the mess. We need to inspect damage everywhere and do extensive diagnostics checks. The sooner the better, before Seattle gets knee-deep in our business. I want Seattle to see that everything is in order, then I never want to hear from them ever again about this."

"OK," Scorcher says, "I'll get assignments divided out among Ed, Keystone, and Ayubu once they arrive. I'll let them know to come back. I'll first do some additional verifications and tests of the life support systems before they start—"

"Call them back now since it'll take them a while to arrive," says Four-Leaf.

"Got it," Scorcher replies and follows orders without challenging them. His head is starting to throb now that his adrenaline is normalizing.

Both men start making lists of what's showing as inoperative on the hydrogen generator used to power the ore processing. It's damned near everything.

*   *   *

Twenty-four hours later, the site is deemed secure enough to operate at a less restricted safety level with the damage being contained and superficially understood. It's all extensively noted from the computer diagnostics as a first pass. However, before all the mining technicians start inspecting things hands on, Scorcher demands extra safety precautions until further notice. Four-Leaf goes with it, giving Scorcher a slight bit of hope. The industrial operations should be down for about a month before everything is fully assessed, repaired, and once again operational. Seattle insists they reduce that to three days.

Exactly thirty-two hours earlier, there was a liquid hydrogen leak from a cryogenic pipe for about one-tenth of a second, as far as Scorcher can tell. It was at this moment that the hydrogen ignited from an unknown static electricity source and an explosion occurred. The way the pipe blew apart seems to indicate that a bolted splice joint in the pipe itself gaped to a level where the seal was no longer effective at holding in the hydrogen. The actual cause of the seal gaping apart is unknown. The time-history data for the system indicates that this might be due to a valve failure somewhere else in the system which caused a very temporary over-pressurization event. The over-pressurization caused a "water hammer" effect in the pipe, similar to a knocking pipe in an old house. But since the valve didn't stay stuck, they don't know which valve out of dozens had temporarily failed.

There was supposed to be a pressure regulator that would protect against such a valve failure, but it was never spliced in for installation. In fact, it was never even fabricated with the 3-D printer. Contrary to this point of blame, however, the peak pressure spike should not have actually caused the bolted joint to gap enough for the seal to leak—but it did leak. This is all very disturbing to Scorcher. He has Ayubu perform some inspections, looking for possible cracks in the pipe section that had been removed, postmortem. But the fractures that exist are very rough and jagged, as opposed to smooth.

According to Ayubu, if the crack surface was smooth, with microscopic striations pointing to a nucleation site, that would have indicated a material flaw as the source of the failure. However, it wasn't a material flaw or initial crack caused by a manufacturing defect or damage that led to failure. The metallurgical analysis indicates it was an overload event that caused instant ductile fracture in a perfectly good pipe. The defect in the pipe itself wasn't the cause of failure.

So was the seal bad? Or was it the bolts themselves? Or was the strength analysis wrong? Scorcher wonders. *Is this whole place a ticking time bomb just waiting to blow at a moment's notice because of some random failure of a two-hundred-dollar valve?*

This is right in Scorcher and Four-Leaf's domain of responsibility, and it terrifies Scorcher to the point that he is too paranoid to sleep for more than an hour at a time or ingest anything more than coffee and ibuprofen.

CHAPTER 17

This infinitesimal group of miners—all of Moon's humanity—are united to solve what happened at CLM. Ayubu's background in structural failure and fracture analysis from his university's laboratory continues to be invaluable. Even the Minister has been coming out of his hole to help, surprising all. Four-Leaf, coincidentally enough, gets preoccupied with other things whenever the Minister is around.

Scorcher sets up a meeting to discuss Ayubu's findings to leverage whatever knowledge and insight he can share. Hours later, Scorcher is sitting silently with the Minister and Four-Leaf in the Café at the End of the Universe. He is amazed that the two can to sit next to each other without open combat as they wait for Ayubu, who is always late. Space-Bee informed Scorcher earlier that the two Celts used to be close friends when she first met them, but the Minister most likely ruined that. Although, Four-Leaf does seem to antagonize as much as the former.

Scorcher stops picking at the bandage on his head for a moment and looks out of the large café window, wondering if Keystone has in fact properly inspected the stretched-acrylic window to ensure there is no detrimental damage or delamination from the hydrogen explosion. Surely a good portion of the entire South Pole region shook and rattled that day. He still has no recollection of the initial blast. He pokes at his bandage again, then stops.

During his job interview centuries ago, Scorcher mentioned that he wanted to be the "arrowhead of the human journey," which seems shamefully tacky to him now, something he would say during one of his optimistic phases and then later be sickened by during one of his pessimistic freefalls back into "reality."

He turns back to look at the two men sitting quietly at the table and wonders who they are and how they got here. Every time he asks one of his colleagues for a cup of coffee or tries to find time just to chat, they always respond—all the mining technicians, that is—that they are insanely busy. It's as though taking a Sunday off from a schedule of sixteen-hour shifts would be cheating in some sense. Amongst themselves, it seems like a valid response, but Scorcher, he fails to understand. Now with everyone crowding around, awkward unease is mixed with the excitement for human interaction. It tragically takes disaster to unite people. It took a near loss of Central Lunar Mining to get to the point where he can share a coffee with someone other than the vending machine.

"How'd I get here to be with this odd lot?" he accidentally says aloud. Both the Minister and Four-Leaf turn their heads toward him. Scorcher realizes his accident. "Oh, I mean Stabby and the sheep." He tries to recover.

Four-Leaf laughs. "You insult the sheep in front of this old fart? The sheep are everything to him."

The Minister grumbles and curses under his breath.

Ayubu interrupts as he enters. "Sorry, friends, I am late."

"No worries," Four-Leaf sighs, without making eye contact.

Scorcher begins, sipping his caffeine. "What did you

find?"

Ayubu explains excitedly, "I think this gaping issue is caused by the titanium bolts and the lightweight aluminum nuts. The funny thing about these nuts is that they might be underrated in strength because of our environment."

"I don't believe so," Four-Leaf says. "I crunched the numbers and did the stress analysis myself a while back. I signed off on it, mate. It's all per NASA standards."

"I did, too," Scorcher replies. "But yeah, that is a good point, so we have very high-strength titanium bolts with these very weak nuts holding them on? Even though the joint is in tension trying to pry off the nuts?"

The Minister sits up. "Ayubu, you're telling me that for a tension joint application, for a joint that is separation-critical—meaning if it gaps, we all blow up—we're using aluminum 2024-T6 nuts which have virtually no strength?"

Four-Leaf shrinks back a bit.

"Yes, friend. They have less than half the rated tensile strength as the bolt," Ayubu explains. "But these are rated to 3000 pounds-force ultimate load—"

The Minister slaps that table. "How do none of you idiots know that it's bad design practice to install nuts that are less than half the strength of the bolt? The nut should always be at least as strong as the bolt and never the weak link—"

Four-Leaf explains. "It doesn't matter mate, I ran these numbers—"

"And you did it wrong, you fraud! These things are really complicated. You can't just run the numbers and call it good. These nuts are over-torqued to prevent gaping. That means the bolt preload from over-torquing the nut eats up all the tension capability. So these nuts don't fail at 3000 pounds applied load per bolt, they rupture *before* separating, meaning it'll only take about 250 pounds to fail, not 3000! Don't you idiots know how to do anything per NASA-STD-5020?"

Ayubu apparently also doesn't like confrontation, like Scorcher, and is merely silent. Four-Leaf doesn't back down, "Look, mate, this joint gaped, which means they didn't fail at 250 pounds per nut. The joint preload from over-torquing can be ignored in the analysis and didn't play a role. I can show you the NASA tech memo on preload effects."

Scorcher thinks for a moment, struggling to follow the logic. "So if the joint is designed specifically to rupture or fail before the seal is able to gap, that means you can't ignore bolt preload from over-torquing in your analysis. Over-torquing effectively lowers the rated strength capability. But we didn't account for the knockdown in strength. And the seal looks per spec. So does that mean the nuts just simply broke off? Everything holding these pressurized pipes might just blow at any moment?" Scorcher thinks to go back and check the over-pressurization event. Maybe it wasn't a stuck value, just normal operating pressure that caused the pipe to blow.

Four-Leaf defends himself. "These aluminum nuts are labeled as 'tension' nuts, so obviously they're good for our tension application. The bolted joints are fine. We just need to install the pressure regulators to avoid this in the future. These things are used all over aerospace. The service history rates it 'Good.'"

Scorcher is having trouble keeping up.

The Minister: "All you've done your whole life is write design manuals and run mechanical testing. You don't have any real-world experience! There are two obvious design flaws: one, the use of titanium fasteners in a cryogenic operation, which even though their strength goes up, titanium becomes intolerant of the slightest defect and can't handle any imperfection or damage from installation. This is the rocket industry, Four-Leaf, not bloody business jets. On airplanes operating near room temperature, crack defects will grow slowly, that's why it's not a problem you've seen before. Two! Ordering lightweight, quick-install aluminum nuts instead of using steel nuts essentially invalidates the rated capability of your joint. You're wrong!"

Four-Leaf looks at the Minister suspiciously. Scorcher has a flashback to his parents fighting. He doesn't know if he should feel lost or impressed that the Minister so quickly figured out the problem.

The Minister gets up. "I'm going to where I know I won't blow up. You"—he points to Ayubu and Scorcher—"run the numbers properly, accounting for over-torquing the nuts. You'll see." He gets up and leaves. "I hope this place waits till I leave before it blows again."

Four-Leaf turns to the remaining two. "Service experience shows all of this as good. We haven't done anything NASA or anyone else wouldn't do. By the way, steel is three times heavier than aluminum, so good luck trying to convince Seattle to launch boxes of steel—essentially dead weight—up to orbit. Maybe you're right, Scorcher, and in normal circumstances, we should be using steel or nickel alloy bolts, not titanium." This last sentence shocks Scorcher because Four-Leaf rarely concedes, even slightly. Then he says something inaudible about the titanium bolts as he leaves the room.

Scorcher and Ayubu sit silently, trying to absorb all the scattered information that has been thrown at them: engineering analysis assumptions, service experience, logistics, egos, personality disorders.

*　　*　　*

After a couple days of working around the clock doing inspections, systems diagnostics, and repairs, checking for defects in bolts and nuts, Scorcher is still unresolved about the points of the meeting.

Scorcher catches Space-Bee on instant messenger and decides to give her a voice call.

"Hey," she says.

"Hey," he says back. He explains to Space-Bee the situation, but a couple of the details come across as contradictory. "I know I should get this, but I don't. Why are titanium fasteners bad at cryogenic temperatures? Don't they get stronger as they get colder?"

"Yeah, so they do get stronger, but they are also more brittle." He pauses for a moment. "Think of it this way, like if you're a Viking blacksmith."

She laughs, "All right, I'll go along I guess."

"The Norse learned that as you make a sword and work it over the fire, to make the sword stronger, you have to let the iron absorb the smoke. Essentially adding carbon to the iron—"

"To turn the iron into steel, of course, got it," she replies quickly.

Scorcher continues, "But what they also learned is that the more smoke it absorbs, the stronger the sword gets. But there's a practical limit. At some point, it gets so strong that it also becomes brittle, like glass. Meaning that any tiny imperfection, nick or ding in the sword, will cause it to crack instead of dent."

"Right," she replies, following along while making noise over the phone, caused by her attempts at multitasking.

"So, the trick is to have the sword not be *too* brittle. Or in otherwards it has to be ductile enough to take a little damage without shattering. It's a careful balance. Another analogy," he says without noticing Space-Bee getting distracted, "is a Pyrex glass bowl versus a wooden bowl. The Pyrex is much stronger and fully resists my fingernail pushing into it. But with a wooden bowl, I can indent it with my fingernail. However, if I drop both bowls off the roof of a building onto concrete, the Pyrex will shatter, but the wood will just take the abuse with a slight scuffing." He stops to think further about yet another example of the fragility of strength, mostly for his own benefit since he's never thought about it in practical terms like this before. Academic engineering training is so focused on mathematical derivations that professors and professionals alike tend to forget what it means off the chalkboard.

"You boys are silly," Space-Bee interrupts, turning full attention back to the conversation. An obvious point is clearly missed.

"Huh?"

"You can extract iron from regolith and meteorites, right? I mean, you have a big ol' fancy factory already doing mineral extraction from ore. Why not just make your own steel fasteners? And then *I* don't have to haul all that aluminum and titanium dead weight to you. More room for coffee?"

Scorcher thinks for a second, and without realizing it, he picks up the tone of some of his colleagues, "Well, aerospace fasteners require very strict and repeatable processing controls. These aren't like what you buy at Home Depot. They are super strong, lightweight, and have tight geometric tolerances."

She doesn't respond.

"We're definitely not experts on making aerospace fasteners." Without forethought, he uses a phrase he's been told himself many times. "It's more complicated than what you think."

"Oh, really?" she replies shortly.

"I didn't mean it like that. I'm just saying that we're not that smart up here." He tries to recover. "*I'm* not that smart. It'd require more precision than just chemically extracting ore like what we currently do."

"Why don't you just *make* it work? That's what I have to do in orbit. Does it need to be that precise? Just account for it in your design. Like, maybe use twenty bolts instead of ten, for example."

Scorcher thinks back to how the Germans in WWII would size aircraft structures assuming that only sub-standard materials were available, something that was obviously inefficient but kept them fighting longer than expected. "That's a good point, actually. Maybe that could work, even if it'd get pushback at first."

"Thanks."

"We don't need anything optimized for weight. We could just make things bulky, like what civil engineers do for bridges and buildings. And maybe we can just proof-test everything to eliminate the need for overkill with the process specs and equipment qualifications. We can do proof-testing instead of the relying on more rigorous process controls they do back on Earth." Scorcher hates to admit it, but maybe they should have had civil engineers instead of aerospace engineers do the factory design. Aerospace structural engineers make things lightweight, sleek, and fast; civil structural engineers make things rugged, ugly, and reliable. That divergence in mentality goes back even to undergrad…

"Too bad you guys didn't think about that before you built a Moon base," Space-Bee says.

He considers that. It might have just come down to

schedule: be the first to claim squatters rights on the Moon and get that ore flowing. Immediate quarterly profits are too attractive not to sway long-term strategy, typical for twenty-first century American aerospace. But in the case of the Founder, his motivation was probably just to be first since there might not be a second place.

"Can we switch to IM? I'm getting distracted," she says.

"Uh, sure," he replies and disconnects. He agrees with Space-Bee that they should have been smart instead of fast. But everyone seems to fight him on that, even now.

He proceeds to tell Space-Bee that aside from all that, he doesn't trust Four-Leaf and is going to go behind Four-Leaf's back to talk to the Minister.

She writes, *Do you think that's a good idea?*

Scorcher responds, *Why, because I'm doing my job?*

He sees her start to type, then stop and log off.

CHAPTER 18

As Scorcher enters the hangar to find the Minister, he casually checks for corrosion in the corners of the building. He notes to himself that there is in fact corrosion and a slight smell. "Ammonia?" Scorcher asks himself aloud. Though there are no ammonia sources nearby.

To his immediate problem, he needs to know where to begin to investigate why the titanium-bolted joints failed and caused an explosive liquid hydrogen leak. In the back of his mind is also the radiation issue and Space-Bee's worsening health. He's not very good at dealing with multiple problems at once. Four-Leaf is unable, or unwilling, to help and only provides vague political answers to all these random issues, and Scorcher is overwhelmed.

"Of course that lavvy heid can't help you, he's a fraud and doesn't know what he's doing," says the Minister. "Typical these days. A bunch of career-driven toss pots only focused on meaningless job creation and trying to look good on paper." Scorcher doesn't know whether to take him literally or not. "No ethos for these morons. You can fire half of them and be better off. Why do we even need one with us on this rock?" He throws something across the room, maybe a pen, but Scorcher misses what, exactly.

"I see," Scorcher says, consciously replying in a way that

doesn't take a stance. When the Minister tends towards phrases of discouragement like, "That'll never work," or more blatantly, "That's stupid," it's best not to fuel him.

"You think you can come here because I'm the only person on the Moon with alcohol? Well, you're mistaken, you brat. You won't find any poison here."

"I'm sorry, there must have been a misunderstanding—" Scorcher tries to say, nervously, like a child wrongly suspected of lacking social propriety, but made to feel guilty nonetheless due to circumstance.

"Oh, I'll have none of that. There's no hope for me. I'm dying, you see. Terminal." He pulls out a traditional blue and gold Polish ceramic tea set.

"Dying?" asks Scorcher in alarm, caught off-guard.

"Well, I'm not diagnosed, of course. It's much too serious for Seattle's idiot wet nurse Amy to be able to get her mind around it."

"You mean *Doctor* Yang?" Scorcher verbally ameliorates as someone offended on her behalf.

"Precisely! Another Yang. And don't correct me," the Minister yells back at him, pointing at Scorcher with his empty cup. Scorcher submits and sits in silence. He knows his place and needs the Minister's help.

The Minister opens a makeshift drawer and pulls out a bottle of whiskey. Scorcher pretends not to see it, reminding himself not to be too rash. He's better traveled than that. Then the Minister pours thick black coffee into both cups.

"Is that Italian coffee?" asks Scorcher, shocked, but accidentally sounding like he's pleading.

"Yes, and don't interrupt with any more questions, I get lost bloody easy on tangents," he says, digging around for something unknown to the visitor.

Scorcher notes to himself that they were both sitting in

silence, and he didn't really interrupt him, for the record.

The Minister continues. "I hope you turn out better than that last guy: Edward Jones. It really goes to show you that former NASA astronauts are not always the brightest. 'Braindead Ed,' I call him, in keeping with tradition. He got the nickname from NASA's Houston engineers while working on the International Space Station, before it retired into the ocean and space stations all went private with companies like Terra Origin and Space-Y. Even the simplest tasks, he screws up, no matter how much hand holding nor how thorough a checklist. Of course, like all people like him, he just sticks around somehow and will make a fortune out of coming here for a couple years, costing more in resources than he contributed, that's for damned sure. He'll probably go back to be a NASA chief scientist now. Can't stop someone with a resume like that. He's just too damned good on paper, or electrons, I suppose. No one has paper resumes anymore..."

This is going to be one of those lengthy one-way conversations with an old-timer, Scorcher thinks to himself. But he's too curious, "What are you dying from again?"

"Oh—" The old man pours the whiskey into both cups of the Italian black coffee and puts away the bottle. He downs it in a single gulp and signals for Scorcher to do the same. Scorcher takes the hint and downs his as well, trying not to choke. Three different kinds of fire just went down his throat: burning whiskey, scorching coffee, and something else which can't be identified by science or religion, but Scorcher knows it's there.

The Minister brings out the whiskey again. "A good friend of mine from Karelia once told me that the first two must never be separated far apart."

"First two what?" Scorcher asks, trying to keep his

composure.

"The first two drinks, of course. You know, lad. Coffee," replies the Minister.

They down another cup each, and he pours a third round.

"Now, don't get anxious and drink so quickly. It's not good for you," the Minister instructs the younger man, who is relieved at the order just given to him. The Minister continues the discourse, now accompanied by minor gesticulation. "I don't see myself ever making it back to Earth. No. I see this place being the end for me. Just like Shigley, who is buried on the ridge."

Scorcher isn't following.

"Shigley was a miner who died in a 'mysterious mishap.'" He quotes with his fingers and sounds mostly ironic, but his eyes are clouded. "There is no video evidence of what happened, and the computer logs were taken off the network by Seattle, kept totally inaccessible, but his suit appeared to have depressurized. His blood boiled, and then he froze solid. And that was that. Everything you worked for your whole life, just gone in a few seconds." The Minister blesses himself with his left hand, then catches his mistake and does it again but with his right. "Well, anyway, I'm not totally surprised. This is space, by the way. But people started talking about the Factor…er, you know, a ghost in a sense—"

"A ghost?" Scorcher asks incredulously, with the same shock as someone hearing about elves on the Moon.

"Third Man Factor is what it's called. Very common in traumatic experiences or for those who are serious adventurers." The Minister leans forward, like one educating a child, with great empathy, understanding, and patience, all of a sudden.

What a strange change in manner, thinks Scorcher.

"Famous cases, like those traversing an ice sheet in the Antarctic, or crossing the Sahara Desert, or a pair of climbers reporting the presence of the third person. A spirit of some kind. Though maybe not just a spirit or a ghost, but someone who is actually there to help them through the ordeal. Or sometimes not help at all, I suppose. But who is there, nonetheless. Let's not argue about it. It is what it is."

"Interesting," Scorcher says.

"Yes. A man by the name, I think, of Steve Wilkes was hiking Mt. Everest by himself, or trying to be the first, and that's when the Third Man Factor hit him. Though in his case, I guess it's Second Man. Anyway, at one point, when he was only 300 meters from the top, he actually tried feeding his imaginary friend biscuits. Quite interesting, that is." The Minister pauses for a moment to drink more coffee. "It might even happen to you at some point. Just remember that. Well, anyway, per the request of Shigley's will, his body is laid to rest on the northern ridge line overlooking us now. As you pass, you should make a prayer and stack a rock on his grave, otherwise only the worst luck will happen to you and the sheep."

"That sounds ridiculous," says Scorcher who is emboldened by the whiskey now thick in his veins. "Who says that again?"

"Everyone says that! And so do I! Goddamn it! Goddamn this bloody place!" The Minister leans back again to calm himself before continuing. He catches himself out of his element, resets, and addresses Scorcher, who is now questioning the veteran's stability with all seriousness. "Scorcher? That's what you go by, right?"

"Yes, sir," Scorcher replies.

"Okay. Very well. I'm a busy man, but I'll help you. Just

send me the trouble reports from the sheep, and I'll give you the solution. But after that, don't expect me to help you. I'm very busy, you see. Lots of responsibility. Without me, this whole place would go under, and I can't be distracted any more than I already have been."

"I appreciate it, thank you, sir," Scorcher says, neglecting the real reason he came here. He gets up and nearly tumbles; he could be just getting used to the gravity.

"How about you stay a minute and finish your coffee first? It's a very valuable thing up here. I know you're used to being a wasteful person, but we can't tolerate that here," the Minister says.

Scorcher sits back down to finish his coffee in silence as the Minister pours himself some more.

"He's buried there on that ridge, you know," the Minister repeats.

"I see."

"It's pagan, that is," he says solemnly. "I understand that—I appreciate, I mean—well—" He stutters and can't find his words. "I know Shigley requested to be laid to rest wherever he had fallen from life. He believed that the Moon was consecrated dirt just by the nature of it being closer to the heavens, being in heaven itself, nearly. But I think that's rubbish. This place isn't holy, just the opposite. Proof that hell…"

Scorcher sits silently, unable to make out what the Minister is mumbling.

A few moments pass, and the Minister gets up to relieve himself in the toilet which is in between where the two are sitting. Scorcher waits silently and turns his nose away.

"Four-Leaf was the one who sent a sheep to retrieve his body. Apparently, his suit depressurized when he was out in the field." the Minister repeats himself without realizing it. "No one ever figured out what happened. I can only presume he buried the body properly. Not sure where his personal belongings went." The Minister goes back to criticizing Four-Leaf about his meaningless side projects. "You know those spineless MBA executives let this bastard run around wasting time on anything. Do you know his first role up here?"

Scorcher is clueless. "Um, no. Was he a technician?"

"No! Of course not. He couldn't change the oil of a petrol engine. He was originally the automation engineer. I told him it'd never work, but it is because of him I work up here. I'm not sure why I got myself involved in all this mess." The Minister leans over to admit something and does so more quietly. "I can't leave this place on my own. Someone will have to do it for me."

Scorcher assumes this means the ancient man lacks the resolve to pull the trigger on retiring.

"Anyway, our former automation engineer—meaning *your* current tech fellow, I refuse to claim him as mine—sold the idea to the mining investors and executives of being the first to get people dirty on the Moon. As of now, there is always a human somewhere in the process. Total automation, the approach that all our competitors are taking, would have taken too many more years to reach fruition. And the competition is intense. Too many. Time was running out! Or so they thought. So, instead of getting it right on Earth, our beloved"—the Minister smacks his lips—"ambitious billionaire decided to throw bodies at the problem and get people working out the kinks as an afterthought. Right here! Directly in the Moon environment. And who planted that seed? Your mate. The way that nincompoop sold it—"

The Minister pauses for a moment.

Almost too long of a moment, Scorcher thinks.

But before Scorcher says anything, the Minister starts back up. "He sold them by telling them there was no point in trying to dream up every hypothetical problem that could occur when you could just come here to figure it out firsthand. Then, full automation would occur naturally. That dunce, I told him this would never work. And then the humans could go back home to Earth. However, that isn't what happened. You're here and shouldn't be! There has been virtually no advancement on removing humans from the Moon mining equation. I think you're meant to fix that."

"I am?" Scorcher asks. He's not sure what to think about it.

"Well, you won't, of course. You're going to go crazy first. It'll be a failure. You just don't know it yet. See our centipede Founder—I mean centibillionaire Founder—has gotten distracted with other ventures on Earth, the real money makers who are funding us on charity at the moment. But I bet he's starting to put his attention back on us to figure out why things are not progressing. You might be the first step in 'cleaning house' here and bringing in all new people. And then towards Mars without people, only robots."

Scorcher digests that for a moment. This is a perspective he has not at all considered, if it's even true. But he's going to need time to think about it. "Hmm." Scorcher is cynical enough—or is it realistic enough?—to think he's a pawn. He hopes he's not *the* pawn, is he? "So, you're saying the long-term vision is actually—"

The Minister continues as though he doesn't hear Scorcher begin to talk. "I know why you really came here. Because you can't wrap your head around the bolted joints and the hydrogen explosion. I'll send you the NASA and university references warning against using titanium bolts. It goes back to a memo written in 2003. ULA had some titanium bolt failures just from parts sitting in the shop in Colorado, causing months of program delays. The cold working of titanium bolts during the manufacturing process, in order to get them the same high strength as steel bolts but at half the weight, makes them too brittle for cryogenic environments. This is why we don't use them for cryogenic plumbing. They're meant for joints like on sheet metal aircraft. But apparently, I'm the only one left who knows anything. All the good engineers are either senile or dead."

CHAPTER 19

Sipping coffee. Sitting silently. Staring. *Who was Shigley and how did his spacesuit just randomly depressurize for no reason? Does Four-Leaf really not know what happened to him even after retrieving the body? Was his death someone else's fault? Why is there no training on this mishap to prevent it from happening again?*

Rocko walks into the room. "Hey, what's up brother? You look so serious." He pops a couple of anti-nausea pills.

"Oh, hey," replies Scorcher. He's thrown off because he was expecting Space-Bee, and frankly he kind of forgot that Rocko even existed because he rarely gets off the ship when they're in port.

Rocko burps. "Ah, that's nice, it's been a while. Microgravity makes it impossible to burp without some food coming up as well."

Yet another totally random thing that Scorcher never thought about before. "Why's that?" he asks. "Because the air bubbles need gravity to collect at the top of your stomach?"

"And *your* stomach." He belches again and grins like a boy on his birthday. "Figured I'd get off the ship for once, get out of my comfort zone, you know? It also feels good walking. I was kind of hoping it would help with our mysterious 'lunarnaut syndrome,'" he jokes. "Plus, I don't

150

really jive with some of the people here. But you're here. Nothing personal against them, though. They just seem kind of weird. Always spooked me out," Rocko explains.

Scorcher wonders if there is anyone who wouldn't be spooked out living in solitary confinement like this: nothing but sheep, repetitive muscle memory, and trying not to die. "Well, good timing Rocko. What are the odds of us almost blowing up twice in the same month?" Scorcher replies sarcastically.

Rocko claps his hands once. "Ha! No kidding man. Don't forget, bro, things happen in threes. How's *that* shitshow going?"

"Well, I think it's just a bad design, bottom line. It's kind of hard to pinpoint. Which means it's hard to fix and prevent from recurring. But Seattle is pushing us hard. We can't just start from scratch, and we have limited resources, so before we change anything, we have to know for sure exactly what happened. Otherwise, if there's half a dozen things that *could* have gone wrong, it's impossible to change all of them."

Rocko asks, turning his head to the side to scratch it, "So you have no idea, then? Maybe I *should* bail." Rocko laughs again while faking running away.

"I wouldn't blame you," Scorcher says.

Rocko heads over to the far side of the room to get a coffee.

Scorcher asks, "Do you know anything about Shigley? What happened to him?"

Rocko looks over his shoulder, then turns his head back forward, facing away from Scorcher. The change in mood is instant.

After a moment he turns back around and returns to sit next to Scorcher. His speech is intentionally muffled now.

"You mean Four-Leaf's former mentor? I don't know all the details, to be honest, man. As far as I know, there was some sort of accident. I heard a couple conspiracy theories about there being a confrontation with Chinese scientists. You should talk with some of these cool cats hanging out in the, uh, what do you call them again?"

"The Annies?" Scorcher helps.

"Yeah, the Annies. But if I were to guess, the simplest explanation is the most likely."

"Occam's Razor."

"Right. Something went wrong with his suit, and that was it: he died. No need to overcomplicate things. And now he's buried out there, apparently, according to his wishes."

Scorcher nods. "I see. Strange I haven't heard more about it."

"Yeah, man," Rocko acknowledges, "very much on the downlow."

Scorcher asks, "So there was no accident report or lessons learned presented to everyone? Something I can check out myself? You know, so we don't die the same way he did?"

"That's a good question, man. I don't know. As you know, we're a different business unit from you since we're supposedly set up to deliver supplies to the other space agency bases and space stations and stuff. But still working for the Founder. So we don't always keep up with what you mine rats are doing." He slaps Scorcher on the shoulder and grins when he says "mine rats."

"You're the second person to mention 'his wishes.' Is that the company's response? No one's ever seen the body?" he inquires.

Rocko has to think about it. "Maybe there was some memo or email about it. I can't remember."

Seems like something that someone wouldn't forget, but Scorcher decides to drop it.

Rocko winks at Scorcher, "So you looking for your space lady?"

High school just came back to Scorcher with Rocko's joking. Nice to not be someone on the Moon for once. He laughs awkwardly and sees that Rocko finds it amusing, "Well, yeah. Someone to chat with, of course."

"Hey, I get it man. I get it. It's crazy the places we end up. I don't know how you do it. You're a real hero." Rocko stretches out his arm and twists it to check if something is on the back of his sleeve. "I can tell you one thing. It's crazy that someone like Shigley, who was a workaholic like all of us out here—no avoiding that—was just gone. Just like that. Bet he had months of paid time off built up, too."

"I'd like to figure out what happened," Scorcher says. He looks at Rocko's face and sees he wants to say something but doesn't.

As Rocko and Scorcher are parting ways from the break room, they both run into Space-Bee.

Rocko mimics firing a finger gun at Scorcher. "See ya later, bro. Take it easy. Don't work too hard!" And he hops away in the low gravity.

That always looks so stupid, Scorcher thinks to himself.

Space-Bee and Scorcher greet each other with the normal niceties and dive into meaningless small talk while standing in the entryway, something they both despise. Then the conversation goes deeper into Scorcher's findings about the cause of the explosion. He also talks about how he thinks Four-Leaf might be to blame and how the Minister gave some good background.

"You'd better be careful about throwing your tech fellow under the bus. He might not like that," she advises.

"Well, I'm trying to be careful, but also objective and non-judgmental. Very scientific like," Scorcher says, trying to sound lighthearted in this horrible predicament.

Space-Bee sighs. "Good luck to you, then."

"What could go wrong?" Scorcher jokes, realizing he has just used a catch phrase that Four-Leaf says all too often.

CHAPTER 20

Scorcher unheedingly places blame directly on Four-Leaf and his negligence. He uses the NASA and technical references that the Minister provided to come up with new design guidance, concluding that the best approach going forward would be to use steel or nickel alloy bolts and nuts, and do away with the titanium and aluminum lightweight bolt-nut combination. This should be sufficient to handle any pressure spikes that the non-existent pressure regulator would have caught, if it had been installed. It seems like the best approach going forward. However, after starting to learn the politics around here, he knows that recommending the replacement of thousands of bolts and nuts will not be a very popular request. Especially since these can't be fabricated on the Moon. It requires a direct shipment from Earth, and a very costly one at that.

He also throws in there that the fasteners weren't procured per NASA-STD-8739.14, but only as a passive-aggressive jab at Four-Leaf because the Company waived those quality requirements anyway.

Scorcher puts his recommendations together, placing blame on the design decisions that Four-Leaf made, but without calling out Four-Leaf explicitly, though it is clearly implied. He includes it in a formal memorandum to everyone on the Moon and key leadership back in Seattle.

Scorcher is nervous about using Four-Leaf's big concession—that they should *never* have been using titanium bolts—but feels slightly empowered since Four-Leaf admitted it himself. This is how Scorcher justifies it in his head that he is in the right for pushing forward with these conclusions and further justifies to himself that sticking to objectivity is the way to go.

Before he pushes the "send" button on the email, however, Scorcher goes for a walk. Not just any walk through the halls or to the sad, lonely coffeeshop that he's starting to despise for its irony at having two dozen chairs, but for a non-work-related spacewalk around the facility. He justifies it in the worklogs as being pre-planned facilities-related routine maintenance, and thus pre-approved by Seattle, but in reality, he just needs to distance himself from this compound to inspect what can't be seen.

Maybe this is what Shigley was doing when he perished.

As he's suiting up, he sees the token dust buster come rolling in. "Hello again, bot. I'd take you along, but I don't have a leash." Stabby ignores him and keeps making the endless rounds on the floor.

Scorcher notices something that he hasn't noticed before, even though someone has already explained it to him. Maybe he hasn't acknowledged it until now because the floor is more reflective in this room. There is a purplish ultraviolet light that temporarily turns on whenever Stabby takes a second pass at brushing up Moon dust. This reminds Scorcher of some cars he has seen with aftermarket LED under-glow lights, though he knows this isn't Stabby trying to "pimp his ride," to use an adage his grandparents would have said. The bristles on Stabby's spinning brush contain electrodes that attract statically charged lunar dust particles, but not all particles are sufficiently statically charged. So the ultraviolet light charges those remaining particles—just enough—to be bristled and sucked up during a second pass. Scorcher stops for a moment to think of how impossible it is to have this mining post out here, with endless people who have contributed to the intricate details of making such an endeavor possible. And in the end, he still has to argue about bolts and nuts and other trivial nonsense.

Maybe this is just how life is. Is this really what life's all about?

Scorcher moves his leg to avoid being slowly jabbed in the ankle. "Let's finish suiting up." Which he does, going through the safety checklists through the airlock, then out onto the lunar surface, alone—something he definitely wouldn't have done during the first few months out here.

As Scorcher is hopping along, contaminating his suit with new dust, his chest feels empty. Almost like a bittersweet sentimental feeling, like he's been here before. Not physically, of course, but mentally and emotionally: traveling alone for a walk, like he would have through a downtown urban area, with aimless wandering, or through a park with ill-defined paths. He decides to go clockwise and take a step back to look at his little existence here. He can see the main body of Central Lunar Mining with the pressure locks and the storage rooms, the docking station for the *Vegvisir* or other spaceships that might land here. He notices the colorless industrial facility not too far off from his area, where the Minister has chosen to spend his remaining bitter days. The mineral processing plant, hydrogen power plant, the container warehouse which packages up the rare metals and prepares them for transport back to Earth. Scorcher realizes he hasn't spent much time on that task himself since the Minister prefers to be the pseudo postal worker, sort of like how the least social workers at a grocery store tend to be the stockers.

Scorcher turns to continue the lap, checks his suit settings and oxygen levels, and hops along his way to clear his mind. He starts thinking about his family, particularly his mother. How she told him once that she can "never watch the Blue Angels perform" because he wasn't one of them. This was right after the military medically disqualified him from any possibility of a pilot slot, so he never served. She had always wanted him to be a pilot, for one reason or another, which was never totally clear to him. It's just something ingrained deeply in her mind for reasons she could never reflect on to understand. He also thinks about how every time he helped around the house, she would chastise him for doing it wrong or carelessly, even though he tried his best to impress her. She seemed to pride herself on telling her children they always fall short and should have done better. To this day, he sees this attribute in every woman.

He picks a rock up and attempts to throw it over the horizon, imagining Newton being struck on the head. He admires those Renaissance-era intellectuals: their pursuit of science, mathematics, art, literature, religion, language, logic, all as subsets of philosophy, but all interrelated. He wishes he could have studied more at the university before they basically became extended daycares. It amazes him how two totally different philosophies or two completely different mathematical derivations can still converge, after enough rigor, to a single common answer. Sometimes there *is* just one truth. Sometimes.

This is so unlike today, when everyone is so specialized, bragging about how they can't do math or how they can't spell, or how they don't get art or don't get religion. Scorcher doesn't feel he fits into modern society's compartmentalization of intellectualism. But this is also where Scorcher knows in his heart he falls short.

So then why try at all? he asks himself. *Does it even matter if I die out here? Won't I just be buried in the ground as Shigley was, hushed away and forgotten?*

With these questions, he stops for a bit and just stares upward at the black sky, so black that it feels like it's approaching him, like a falling blanket. Leaning back farther, he reaches his hand up to see for himself, but nothing. Just nothingness for infinity.

*　　　*　　　*

Scorcher arrives back at the pressure lock in a sullen mood after an otherwise uneventful stroll, returning with no questions or thoughts in mind, just emotion and exhaustion. Loneliness.

He tries to shake himself out of it. "Time to get back to business," he says aloud in his suit as the pressure lock is repressurizing. He wishes that he wouldn't be like this. Like if he tried hard enough, he wouldn't become so melancholic and hopeless. It's like being hopeless about something undefined, so how does someone address it, or even begin to understand or fix it?

But something he does understand is that he needs to just suck it up, be an adult, and send his technical findings and recommendations up the chain. What Scorcher wants is a complete shipment of new bolts and nuts, and he suggests that engineers back in Seattle help determine what bolted joints need to be prioritized for rework. Which is not a trivial task in any sense, especially since this basically means shutting down Central Lunar Mining for weeks, if not months. And after things are shut down, problems always arise turning them back on.

He hits the "send" button on the email with the memorandum attached, then goes to take a shower. Even though water resources are tightly regulated, he breaks the rules that he normally enforces on himself and takes a long shower, thoughts of Space-Bee in his head.

After he gets out of the shower, he sees that his phone is already blinking from lack of attention. He has already gotten an email response back from a company executive in Seattle. *Don't these people have lives?*

He reads out loud the one sentence rebuttal against him, that was written by an individual who ironically happens to be the Executive Sponsor of workplace safety: "Wrong answer."

CHAPTER 21

Scorcher's heart drops as he reads the brief email reply to his memorandum. He knows this will be even more awkward the next time he sees Four-Leaf, which frankly can be at any moment because last Scorcher knew, he was returning to Central Lunar Mining after a two-day trip to help Keystone with a couple sheep he had trouble reconfiguring for heavy-duty mode.

As Scorcher sits at his desk, he hears a brief siren, and all the pressure hatches lock. It's a new automated process he implemented every time the pressure lock engages or some other external hatch to the vacuum in space is being accessed. He knows Four-Leaf is here. Scorcher gets up from his desk and kills time by walking around. His mind is not able to focus.

Minutes later, after all the hatches open themselves back up, Four-Leaf comes around the corner. "We gotta chat, mate." He's still wearing his spacesuit underwear with coolant system hoses flailing.

"Yeah, we probably should," Scorcher says, trying to sound calm but also assertive and in mock control. He sits down behind the safety of his desk. Right now, he's hating himself for the involuntary adrenaline rush he's feeling. Scorcher looks down and notices Stabby—who he didn't even realize was there—looking to escape as though it has emotional intuition.

"I told Seattle you are wrong about the titanium bolts to calm them down a bit. You should already know better about the NASA procurement standard waiver. I also told them that you hadn't discussed any of this with me or anyone else on the team ahead of time. They understand you were just over-reacting from the stress."

"Of course, I spoke to you about it, though," Scorcher responds angrily. "We *did* talk about it as a team. And I'm just stating facts." Scorcher goes a bit further. "You contradicted me and said I was wrong."

Four-Leaf is silent for a moment, sits down, and pulls out a notepad to start taking notes across from Scorcher. "You know, mate, I thought we were friends, that we could trust each other. I told you about my ex-wife, my family, my estranged son. I convinced management to bring you here to help square things up."

Scorcher just nods but doesn't see the relevance to any of this. "You said, yourself, that we 'shouldn't have been using titanium bolts.' Then you throw me under the bus and say we didn't even talk about it."

Four-Leaf is caught off guard by the precise accusation and lifts his eyebrows. "Well, I was really just criticizing myself, not you." He writes something down on his notepad.

Scorcher doesn't see the logic in that statement, and it pisses him off even more.

"It seems you are really trying to undermine me, mate. You didn't see me end your career by telling Seattle about your safety protocol violation."

"The hell are you talking about?"

"Remember when you played hero with the crippling N2 tank? And you manually busted the valves open with a homemade pitchfork?"

"I saved the CLM," Scorcher declares incredulously.

"It's debatable on that front. But certain that you didn't follow protocol. Going forward, everything you do will need to be technically reviewed by myself. An oversight review." He takes down more notes. "Speaking of not following protocol, I also know about your scheme with Ayubu."

"Our scheme?"

"He had you use a 3-D printer to make a new part for his coffee machine. That's against company policy since it's for personal use. But I won't ruin your career over it."

What other pointless and arbitrary things can he throw at me? Scorcher thinks. "That's a *lot* cheaper than flying a coffee part to the Moon. But regardless, you've told me multiple times that the direction of the team is up to me, that I have a huge responsibility in setting the long-term strategy of how to make this place actually work."

"Well, you *do*, mate," Four-Leaf says in an encouraging and friendly tone. "And you're almost there. You're *so* close."

"How close?" Scorcher asks, skeptical.

Four-Leaf is looking down at his notes and doesn't answer.

What the hell is he writing? Scorcher asks himself. "So what's the path forward? What do we do now? Just sit on it?"

"No, we're not going to sit on it. I'm going to go through the details of your technical findings and combine it with my notes. I'll get back to you by the end of the day. I want to be direct with you, contrary to how you are with others. I know that you like doing things your way without taking direction. But I need to stay in the loop."

As a roadblock, Scorcher thinks. "I just want to focus on the mission and not worry about politics."

"Politics?"

Scorcher isn't sure what to say now, and Four-Leaf is staring silently at him.

"Right," Four-Leaf says. "Well, let's follow this process that we agreed to—you do agree to this, correct?" Four-Leaf asks firmly, and Scorcher nods out of obedience. "I'll be the technical reviewer on any findings, process improvements, memos, and once you get more on your feet, I'll delegate more of the authority to you. In the meantime, you have to be a team player. I already communicated all this to Seattle, and they agree."

"What about the spacesuit improvements? Or the 3-D printer build file? Or the half-dozen other things?" Scorcher asks raising his voice.

Four-Leaf sighs. "Right. I'll get back to you on that by the end of today as well." He takes a few more notes. "Well, I'd better get going. Do you have anything else?"

Scorcher shakes his head no.

"Very well, mate." Four-Leaf stands and goes off to do whatever it is he does.

"Wait, wait," Scorcher, still sitting, yells out to Four-Leaf as he leaves.

He turns around in the doorway, unamused. "Yes?"

"So are we at least replacing the aluminum nuts with higher strength steel nuts?" Scorcher asks, trying to get some sort of resolution with something he loses sleep over.

"It might be best just to splice in a pressure regulator. Actually, Scorcher, if you can come up with a software patch to help regulate the pressure spikes, that would be a good solution in the interim so we can at least turn the second power plant back on."

"A software solution," Scorcher questions, not believing what he's hearing.

"Well, we got to get this place going again. Of course, only after I do my safety review signoff. Seattle is going to be livid if you don't get this thing up and running this week. Also, I just remembered I need you to put together a schedule for getting things operating at full capacity. A Gantt chart would be a nice touch. No need to run it past me first. Just send it to Seattle and CC me. Anything else?"

"I guess I'll let you know, I still feel kind of unresolved about this," Scorcher admits.

"Still unresolved?" Four-Leaf asks, sounding confused. "Clear as mud, eh? Don't worry, mate. What could go wrong?" He turns for a second time to leave.

Did you also turn your back like that on your former mentor and supervisor before you took his job? How could you have never mentioned him? Were you his "friend?"

CHAPTER 22

Two weeks later, Four-Leaf still has not gotten back to Scorcher. Nonetheless, Seattle is hammering him for the continued delays. "This is completely hopeless," he says to Stabby, who is rolling past to get under his cot but keeps getting trapped on trivial obstacles like boots. "How are you so advanced but struggle with the simplest things?" he asks Stabby. Then he looks at himself in the small shaving mirror over the sink next to his bunk, and his posture slumps slightly.

For distraction, he runs through the numbers of Space-Bee's radiation poisoning. He doesn't consider that he's thinking mostly of her over the other crewmembers. During every coffee break and other idle moments, his heart races and obsesses on thoughts of Shigley and Space-Bee. He imagines their organs being cooked from radiation. He hates these thoughts, but the more he tries to stop them, the more often they invade his mind, and with more power. Coffee drinking dwarfs in comparison to the frequency.

"*Potential* radiation poisoning," he reminds himself, argumentatively. He's been obsessing about this unmeasurably in the back of his mind when he sleeps at night—so about two hours per "day." But when he's out of bed, he gets so distracted reacting to all the landmines he doesn't have time to consider it further. So the emotions build up behind the dam and drown his dreams later.

He previously wrote to Space-Bee: *There is almost no point in trying to be proactive or have initiative. Once again, I've fallen into the slump of being reactionary and getting punished for even attempting to do the right thing. And on top of that, I'm supposed to make meaningless schedules and define long-term team goals.* The emotional battle—continuous confrontation and fighting—paralyzes him. Disdain knots his stomach for submitting to authority all the time, like a coward.

The sunny side of this obsession is that Scorcher doesn't wake up in the morning wondering why he shouldn't exist. Suicidal thoughts usually hide in the shadows of his bouts of feeling worthless, as he learned from half-listening to his previous therapists. When there is no distraction, no panic, no suffering, no purpose, he slumps to self-pity and nihilism. Powerlessness tortures him for being aware of this fact, this cycle of emotional struggle he has ridden since a teenager. He wonders if he isn't just inventing drama for the purpose of having a purpose—more overthinking. Is his mind just looking for a way to preserve itself? Is this the only method of motivation for living?

While in the trough, he often reflects on the few times in his life when he was content, when he was successfully creating order from chaos—that's why he took this job! (He hates that an image of his industrious father often appears when he thinks about this.) And by creating order from chaos, he nurtures purpose and meaning. But everything Four-Leaf does…

Scorcher asks himself if evil people don't actually exist, but then reminds himself that he doesn't fancy the idea of categorizing people as either good or evil because it's an oversimplification. *I'm not one of those people*, he thinks.

His shoulders sink: a deep darkness in his chest, an

image of a black hole whirlpool bordering reality, circling around his heart.

His attention refocuses: bringing order to chaos, helping people in need, bringing happiness to others. His posture straightens itself, drawing back his shoulders, disappearing the weight of nothingness, opening his lungs, the darkness in his chest vanishing.

He doesn't know what to do regarding the radiation numbers. Maybe he should go against his instinct. Alarming Space-Bee with hypotheticals about her health might do more harm than good, especially since he's most likely wrong. He's trying his best to be self-aware through all this mental, emotional bullshit. He's weathered this familiar storm so many times before. It's frustrating being logically aware of emotions he can't control. Maybe he does need a lifetime of therapy and shouldn't try to "rationalize" himself out of it. Why can't he just be logical?

Scorcher looks up the technical journal article and the research data where the fungi radiation absorption rates were calculated. He has to pay for the journal article himself. One of the Earth's richest billionaires owns his company, but he still has to purchase technical articles related to his job with his own money.

It ends up being a simple math formula, which was curved-fitted to empirical test data, that is used to calculate the radiation. The problem is there are about thirty other environmental variables which affect the calculation, and thus the effectiveness of the fungi at absorbing the radiation, and all those variables are assumed to be either negligible or controlled. How accurate can these equations be for any arbitrary environment outside of a science lab?

After starting from scratch and running through the numbers it still doesn't make sense. Rocko and Commander

Ōtsuka have had extremely high exposures, and Space-Bee has been particularly hit. Most troubling, Scorcher reads through the peer-reviewed paper and finds a lot of unresolved questions and quite an extensive list of further research recommendations for future study. The authors don't recommend relying on their numbers because they had to arbitrarily pick and choose data points, unscientifically and non-objectively, to publish some sort of technical conclusion. The authors deemed most of the field experiment data taken outside of the lab as unusable. Excessive fungal loss was observed on the International Space Station, but details are not published. And ever since the International Space Station was retired and controllably crashed back into the ocean, the backup data from experiments is difficult to retrieve, if it even exists.

Scorcher recalls from overhearing Space-Bee and Rocko earlier that Seattle Trajectory directed Mission Control to not worry about avoiding the deadly radiation hot spots in the Van Allen belts, from which in theory the fungal shield should protect the astronauts. "A lot to hang one's hat on," Scorcher murmurs to himself aloud, worried that Seattle hasn't planned wisely.

During his chats with Space-Bee, he always has too much worrying going on in his head to be focused, and debates whether he should tell Space-Bee his concern or not. The decision is against, not wanting to sound too alarmist and have to deal with her possibly challenging him about his "paranoia." It's stressful when she's in one of her bulldog moods and wants to just argue against everything.

He must figure out how to get more information from Four-Leaf about the radiation sensors and calculations, someone who clearly doesn't trust him at this point. Scorcher does not want to stir the pot by asking Seattle

Medical directly, but he also wants to avoid some weird confrontation with the technical fellow. He decides it's best to not look like he's going behind his back. It is best—with keeping Space-Bee out of the loop, even though it clearly concerns her—to speak with him about it directly. He can do it after the tag-up meeting with Seattle.

*   *   *

The meeting seems drawn out for Scorcher; Seattle asks for status on all the tasks and improvements for which the technical fellow is responsible. Four-Leaf interjects at a steady pace, saying that Scorcher has some real vision on how to make things better, and he mutes the phone to remind Scorcher of how he's responsible for the team's long-term strategic priorities and vision. A burning knot forms in his stomach. Four-Leaf unmutes the phone and mentions that his colleague is doing a good job at keeping on top of things, which confuses the issue further since he does not get positive affirmation at any other time.

The meeting ends with a long list of action items for Scorcher, who needs to redo a bunch of project schedules, something that makes him die on the inside. Scorcher wonders if Four-Leaf takes any of this seriously or what goddamned game he's always playing. Four-Leaf puts everything on the back burner until it is a complete disaster. He only responds to putting out fires, proverbially and literally. This "boy from Belfast" absolutely needs that feeling of being just barely out of control to be motivated into doing anything. Like the way he drives the lunar vehicles around: he takes the most dangerous route and exhibits the most aggressive maneuvers, often almost flipping the vehicle. Why does he do that *every* trip out? From Scorcher's perspective, if a situation has not gotten to the point of being out of control, then Four-Leaf acts bored with it. And Scorcher is also bothered that when he does say that he is nervous or panicked, he behaves with eerie calm. Is this the stoic personality of an astronaut or the mind of a sociopath with a personality disorder? Scorcher looks up to realize that he's sitting quietly while maintaining a hard focus with his eyes on him. Realizing that he's caught, Four-Leaf looks down to grab his notebook.

"Do you have any more background on the radiation stuff?" Scorcher asks him as he's getting up. He stops mid-crouch to sit back down, looking back at the questioner.

"Have you fixed it yet, mate?"

"Well, no. I haven't fixed the scripts yet."

He responds, "You can maybe do some regression testing with our last operating system updates to see why it's not working."

Scorcher says, "Well, what I really meant was some more info on the calculations themselves and the sensors. Like how the system is supposed to work."

"Oh? I see." Four-Leaf folds his hands on the desk.

"When I re-run the numbers, it looks really bad. Like for all of us…like, well—"

"You always just do whatever you want, don't you? Aren't you drowning enough, mate?"

Scorcher responds, trying to make a mild joke to ease his anxiety, "Well, I hope to not be drowning in radiation." He chuckles slightly, like he always does when he's nervous.

Four-Leaf feigns a smile by grinning with his thin lips. "You always just work on whatever you want." He shakes his head.

Scorcher to himself: *Didn't he just say that for like the tenth time?*

"Well, if you want to play biology student on your own time, I obviously can't stop you."

Scorcher's mind goes blank, and he can't remember what specifically he wanted to get from Four-Leaf. He slightly panics and just starts rambling to fill in the silence before Four-Leaf gets up to leave. "The calculations are fairly straightforward. The technical journal article doesn't seem to be founded on very firm ground." Scorcher then gets more assertive and furrows his brows. "Does Seattle Medical really hang their hat on something so sketchy? Didn't they do any of their own research into coming up with an effective radiation shield before driving through the radiation hot spots in the Van Allen belts?"

"How did you know that?" Four-Leaf is caught off guard.

"I heard Rocko and Space-Bee talking about it," explains Scorcher.

"Since when does Space-Bee talk with Rocko without wanting to punch him? Well, you and I both know that Commander Ōtsuka is very experienced and wouldn't put the crew in danger."

"She could also be over trusting of Seattle Medical and her chain of command," Scorcher proposes.

"You think that, huh?" Four-Leaf tilts his head and leans in leading with his gaze.

Scorcher submits and dips his head slightly, looking at his own hands on the table, "Well, I'm just speculating. Everything is proprietary, and no information is publicly shared. So it's hard to know."

Sitting back a little bit and unfolding his fingers, he responds, "I know you are. Is there anything else you wanted to chat about?"

Scorcher feels awkward asking Four-Leaf a second time for the same information. Especially since he doesn't know what to ask for specifically. Shooting in the dark: "Well, that still doesn't answer the question. Is it—"

"I'm sorry about that. That's all outside my purview, mate." Four-Leaf gets up and exits the room. Scorcher turns off the projector.

A reply comes from a voice over the phone, which Scorcher thought he turned off. "Hey Scorcher?" said the male voice.

Scorcher jolts, "Yes, sir?"

"This is Ivan."

"Yes, of course. Sorry, I thought I logged off."

"No worries. I just briefly overheard you asking about the radiation exposure stuff. I wouldn't worry about it. We have a good team down here covering your butts. But just FYI, the sensor data is kind of tricky, so I'm not surprised you're struggling with it. We don't always get the best measurements, so we rely on data published from the Chinese and Russian sensors from their spacecraft and lunar surface instruments. Somehow, our medical team averages it all out to calculate a more realistic number to show us good."

He's seen this thousands of times before in his field. *Goddamn typical engineers, they don't even use the sensor data directly, they're just making shit up playing with the numbers until they're so far from the truth, they don't even know what's real anymore. Typical engineers playing these games to show things "good" for management.*

He replies to Ivan with another question after his internal rant. "What about the *Vegvisir*, though? I understand that for long term exposure, there is a lot of interference with structures, equipment, and whatnot. But is a stupid little Geiger counter really not that robust? I mean, come on. Why not just use that measurement directly to be conservative instead of trying to find some arbitrary way of showing the numbers good? It seems like it would be fairly reliable. It's not even that complicated to build a Geiger counter. And the *Vegvisir* goes directly through the Van Allen belts repeatedly and lunar based sensors don't help adjust or normalize the data to be more accurate. It whitewashes the numbers—"

"Um, I'm not totally sure about that, because Medical takes care of it. Don't forget, Scorcher, that even very simple pieces of equipment on Earth fail in space. That's why like half of the electric power drills we send up, even after extensive proof-testing on Earth, don't work in microgravity. And you know it's actually a little more complicated than a Geiger counter," Ivan defends. "We have both direct and indirect particle detectors, positioned at Central Lunar Mining where you are and from NASA and ESA sensors across the lunar surface—"

Scorcher ignores Ivan. "And the bulkhead panels which use the fungi's radiosynthesis to absorb radiation, I can't find any real solid published data where I can duplicate the results you would need in order to actually protect the crew aboard the spaceship. It seems a bit optimistic. It's easy to calculate the volume of fungi blanketing the ship and then using NASA's formulas to calculate the reduction in radiation. But even then, assuming worst case instead of best case," Scorcher just keeps going, "the radiation is high enough to suspect that the fungi isn't working at all."

Ivan laughs over the phone, but not from amusement. "OK, hold on for a damned minute. I'll touch base with Medical and make sure they're getting the data they need from you. If they need you to resend anything else, they'll let you know directly. The best I know is that this system was designed to be very robust and hands-off for the crew so y'all wouldn't have to worry about it. I've gotta run. Take care of yourself. Talk to you later, and we'll get back to you soon."

Scorcher goes to turn off the audio this time, but it already looks off. Maybe he turned it off subconsciously.

He mentally processes what he just heard. So the radiation data is not very reliable, or easy to calculate at least, so that's concerning to Scorcher. But maybe that's all right. Seattle probably knows what they are doing. But at the same time, the radiation readings wouldn't read too high, would they? As Scorcher is interpreting it, the crew aboard the *Vegvisir* are *over*exposed, not *under*exposed. The sensors would generally read too low, or underpredict the radiation due to structural, magnetic, and other interference. The sensors wouldn't erroneously overpredict radiation—at least, it's a lot less likely they would. And the fungal radiation shield, even though it's based on proprietary company technology, Scorcher wonders if the engineers really did know what they were doing when they designed this system, which is in fact a living organism in addition to it being mechanical. That's a whole other area that mechanical and rocket engineers, as brilliant as they might seem, don't know anything about. They already mess up what is *within* their field. Are they knowledgeable enough to figure out how to come up with a practical solution for a terrarium—a radiation shield that is good enough that people's lives can rely on it—when the NASA and university teams were not able to? After all the other shortcuts that Scorcher has seen on behalf of the Founder and his efforts to beat everyone else to the Moon, he has very little trust and faith in people when profit, pride, and ambition are in direct conflict with rigorous safety. It seems to Scorcher that, typical of engineers being pressured by management, they always have ways to artificially show via rigorous calculations that there isn't a radiation problem. And if anything goes wrong, they have these misleading numbers as defense, reinforced with non-disclosure agreements and liability waivers.

CHAPTER 23

Via instant messenger on his phone, Scorcher entreats Space-Bee to do an inspection of the radiation shield panels. He bluntly explains that his fear is that the fungi residing inside the boron-infused polyethylene 3-D printed panels is likely all dead—a failed terrarium. The radiation numbers add up too high. Any trust in company processes or procedures regarding safety is now defunct. He takes a deep breath to overcome his anxiety from the resolve to stop his passive tactics.

Scorcher turns on the audio receiver of his digital radio, "Yes?"

"Why don't you just call me directly? You're being so passive," Space-Bee says.

Am I? he questions angrily to himself. *Ironic, since she avoids human contact at all costs.*

"This is kind of a random request." She continues to vent.

Scorcher didn't expect this hostility. Nevertheless, he takes the time to explain that during his limited downtime, he's been re-calculating the radiation exposures of the *Vegvisir* crew and all the associated computational details. "I first became *really* concerned after talking to Seattle about it. This all started after I had issues weeks ago sending over the sensor data they requested."

Space-Bee is silent for a moment. "Why didn't you just tell me there was a concern? We chat every day."

"I'm not sure," he responds honestly, but wants to sidestep the confrontation. "But anyway, I think you can just do a couple of inspections to verify that there's nothing to be worried about. Aren't there borescope inspection holes?"

"There are. I'll take a detailed look after I'm done with some other stuff. I'm not sure what I'm looking for, though. What am I looking for, *Sam*?" she says, emphasizing his real name with sarcasm.

That's a good goddamned point, he scolds himself. *What exactly* should *she be looking for? Such an obvious point.* "I'm not sure. I have no idea what healthy fungi looks like. Probably not green."

"Probably not," she says impatiently. "But why would it be green anyway?"

"I'll look it up for you," he offers.

"That would be great. I've gotta run off to finish some other urgent things. You know how it is. I'm debating with myself if I should even bring this up to Commander Ōtsuka. I suppose I have to. She'll probably wonder why you didn't talk with her first, directly, or go through the appropriate chain of command."

Scorcher is stunned and frustrated he didn't think of that, either. Or did he think about that earlier, but just forgot? He's starting to lose faith in his ability to hang together.

"You send me those details, Scorcher, and I'll take a look. Don't worry about the Commander, I'll take care of it. Out." She cuts off the transmission.

*　　*　　*

Later, Space-Bee does the inspections per some tech orders that Rocko found in the digital maintenance manual before Scorcher could get back to them. She sends a note to Scorcher summarizing what they found, accompanied by extensive photos. And conclusively, via the inspection ports, everything looks sufficient. To the crew onboard the *Vegvisir*, this seems simple enough and as relieving as it could be. Commander Ōtsuka gets on the radio to personally thank Scorcher for taking the initiative to follow-up with them. However, this isn't enough to appease him.

"You're seriously contesting our inspection results to Seattle? With no evidence?" Space-Bee asks, the choppy digital radio transmission not filtering her annoyance.

"No way it's ever this simple," he justifies. "I just feel like there's more to this. Maybe you guys are all right, for now at least. But what about us down here?"

"You mean all the people on the Moon, deep underground, with perfect medical vitals?" she asks.

"Well, aren't you all experiencing nausea and sickness which might be from radiation?" he asks, attempting to persuade Space-Bee to be empathetic with his concerns.

Long silence.

"I'll admit it could also be something else," Scorcher replies to remedy the silence.

Space-Bee explains, "Seattle Medical believes it's bacteria and chemistry levels of the air on the *Vegvisir*. Or maybe outgassing of some of the equipment in microgravity. Nothing deadly, just an annoyance. And something that we're actively addressing with remedies."

Scorcher feels deflated by this response but refuses to back down. "It's not adding up from all angles," he justifies.

"It never does, Scorcher. Everything is a risk out here. That's just the way it is. I don't believe there's a conspiracy," she says surely.

"Well—"

"You've got a lot on your plate. I'm saying this as a friend. You need to focus on the day-to-day mayhem back at Central Lunar Mining to avoid another explosion. Now, I don't believe that it's a conspiracy or negligence like you do, but it doesn't matter. From what you've told me, you need to ramp up safety inspections and delay rushing ahead. And since Four-Leaf is supposedly countering you at every mere suggestion, let alone your decisions, then maybe just pick your battles. For the sake of your sanity and everyone's safety."

Scorcher can't accept compromise here. Especially after the recent dual air disasters where 346 innocent people…he can't even finish his thought.

"Scorcher, I know you're under a lot of stress. We all are. And Seattle is. And so is Four-Leaf, and the others living in turf houses minding their 'sheep.' We're all on the same team here. Let's not have any unnecessary distractions," Space-Bee concludes.

"Well, I guess that's it for now," Scorcher says. "When are you guys coming back to port?"

"I don't know. We'll chat later. If you start obsessing over this more, please just talk to me first," she requests.

"Roger. I guess I'll just try to see if I can get anything done." The obsession switches over to Shigley, with thoughts of the dead astronaut buried in the nearby ridge on the Moon.

CHAPTER 24

Scorcher studies his reflection in coffee brewed from stale, oxidized beans.

Oxygen loves ruining stuff, he thinks. Oxygen creates rust and weakens alloys; it damages cellular DNA and ages people; it teams with heat and fuel to scorch whatever it touches. He wonders if he himself isn't the real oxygen here, reacting to his environment such that his net accomplishments are destructive. Has he made CLM worse off?

He reconsiders this and suggests he hasn't had any impact at all—good or bad. Though he blames his ineffectiveness on corporate tyranny, as always; hierarchy isn't the right term here. He's supposed to be in charge at CLM, not some technical fellow babysitter.

Is this life?

He regrets how he's been playing too nice with Four-Leaf to maintain the peace—while still being judged by him as a rebel. A few minutes earlier on his stroll from the telemetry room to the coffee shop, he was intercepted by Four-Leaf who explained to him that he knows about all the time "wasted" on the radiation investigation. He said that he needed to stop doing whatever he wanted and just needed to do his job: set the agenda for making Central Lunar Mining more efficient, ensure it doesn't blow up, and actually keep to the schedule for once. As Scorcher stood there listening, Four-Leaf explained that Commander Ōtsuka complained about Space-Bee being directed by him to inspect one of the fungi panels, which ended up damaging the delicate panel which now needs repair. Scorcher didn't know about that last detail.

He is now sitting and replaying the conversation in his head, thinking about how he halfway tried to defend himself in the hallway by saying that if it was a good design in the first place it wouldn't have broken, but he didn't go as far as trying to refute Four-Leaf's claim about the commander's frustration. Four-Leaf only responded by reiterating that he should back off, *mate*.

Scorcher sits there, his mind feeling like mush, overworked and fuzzy-headed. He gets up and skips his work for the day, without feeling any guilt. He lies in the cot, turns out the light, and closes his eyes. Strangely enough, he sleeps. And sleeps for sixteen hours, not even getting up once to relieve himself of his coffee.

*　　*　　*

He feels the salt in the air, the sharp breeze, the smell of fish combined with the arctic smell of snow and ice. He looks down at the water under the edge of the bulkhead, seeing a pitch blackness which actually *does* have texture, which actually *does* have feeling and substance. He runs his fingers through the wave, like stroking the hair of a forgotten sensation, a forgotten love. Something one can only experience on Earth, a place so far away, it perhaps doesn't exist. The lack of comfort, the icy burn, the lack of uniformity and environmental control, the lack of design and predictability, are liberating. He just wants to go home. He's not home right now, and he wants to go home. To leave this nothingness where he currently exists, and live where there is natural pain, discomfort, and joy. Live where there is something, anything, instead nothing. All he wants is to go home. The profile in the water vaguely speaks to him. *Please, don't forget me. I feel nothing and desire anything. Take me.*

*   *   *

By a miracle, he wakes fully rested for the first time in months and lies in his cot without any emotions draining him. As emotionally neutral as a robot.

Well, maybe not any robot, he says to himself as he thinks about Stabby squealing away to avoid a good kick.

Scorcher wakes with a new resolve, as though his mind has spent the last sixteen unconscious hours reordering priorities and the emotional deck of cards that has been dropped and scattered over the course of the previous months. This is the first time in millennia that he hasn't woken feeling completely worthless, contemplating various paths to suicide or different ways of justifying his worthlessness and emotional torture. Something is different this morning. Not that he has any motivation to do his current assignments; he has a new motivation to commit himself to adding order to this chaos. He thinks about how Space-Bee gave him a little more attention than she needed to, like a friend who is committed to his well-being. Like a sponge lying in the desert, desperate for water, he absorbed the slight change in manner from Space-Bee, which became an emotional validation of himself, and his own existence. Like he is worthy of someone's empathetic connection.

"I came here to make a difference. I can fix this," Scorcher tells himself aloud. Empowerment flows through him. Even as the shadow starts creeping back over his heart, he doesn't let that stop him from his self-pep talk. Never again will he let something like that explosion, and maybe Shigley's death, or the *Vegvisir* crew's mysterious sickness, happen again. Because it can and will happen again, unless he takes action. This whole place is a mess, and he was hired and flown all the way out here to cut through the bullshit and fix it.

He gets up and makes his bed for the first time in months, thinking of a motivational speaker he once watched online who said people must first get up to make their bed. Discipline starts small.

Getting back his focus—seeing again through a proper lens—Scorcher dons his ambition and aims toward his two biggest unresolved obsessions. But to him, both are related and inseparable, even though he has no evidence of a link. He needs to first get to the bottom of the radiation issue. It frankly doesn't add up. Second, he wants to understand how Shigley, who apparently was the most experienced and respected astronaut in the lunar territory, perished.

During one conversation casually probing Ayubu on the topic of Shigley, it was repeated that he was Four-Leaf's boss and a well-respected technical fellow. It doesn't make sense that the loss of a prestigious crew member is essentially never discussed or memorialized more openly. The entire affair is bemusing.

But before he gets too far on worrying about Shigley, he sees an opportunity to significantly advance his investigation, free from interference, with the *Vegvisir* arriving in only thirty-six hours. That isn't much time to come up with a plan.

CHAPTER 25

Scorcher patiently studies the video surveillance feed of the space dock. He watches the crew of the *Vegvisir*—who have just landed moments before—disembark through the green snake-like umbilical that the Minister is responsible for attaching to the ship while in port. Various other systems are also linked, plugged, and locked, this time by Four-Leaf, who likely wants to use his presence to passive-aggressively annoy the Minister. "Power move," Scorcher says to himself, somewhat comically but also not impressed. Also in the background, Scorcher sees some of the sheep he's programmed to graze in the far distance. He's reminded of all the rumors he's heard, of legends, strong opinions, adages, and seemingly arbitrary beliefs about sheep and how to tend to them and their ailments. Always over abominable amounts of coffee every Stammtisch—the monthly get together.

"I'm going to miss something about those rare times we're all together," he says. "It was never boring arguing about sheep." The semi-nostalgia surprises himself. He supposes that when there is so little human interaction, any at all seems precious, especially around such eccentric people living in a quirky and isolated unknown island on the edge of existence.

For this landing, Four-Leaf has decided to give the crew

a tour of one of the Annies for the get together. This gives a rare opportunity to show off the establishment to the *Vegvisir* crew, who spend all their time onboard the ship. However, this port visit involves a painfully slow systems purge and software reboot—a perfect storm—that leaves the crew stranded on the Moon for a few days. Scorcher says he needs to stay behind and miss Stammtisch for indisputable safety reasons and to finish prepping the factory before getting the mining and processing operations back up and running at full scale. Ayubu and Keystone both volunteer to help, but Scorcher persuades them it is not necessary. Keystone is slightly offended, which Scorcher knows because he simply said so, but moves on in his normal fashion. Four-Leaf naturally looks suspicious but doesn't object. Space-Bee half-jokes to Scorcher to beware because Stabby knows all, to which Scorcher responds he has nothing to hide. Maybe she does know him too well now, he thinks. Four-Leaf reminds Scorcher that anything major requires technical oversight from a technical fellow and to be sure that Seattle has the latest schedules.

When they leave, Scorcher waits until they drive over the horizon on their sheep. After waiting a few more moments, drinking coffee and looking out of the café window, he turns around and exits, tipping the brim of an imaginary hat. He walks down the hallway toward the space dock. As he arrives at the pressure lock, he puts on a pressure suit— meant only for internal operations and not external spacewalks—and runs through the systems checks. Safety first.

After he's finished, Stabby rolls up, blinking his red lights, and nearly slices the suit open at the ankle. Scorcher shoos him away, and he obeys. As Scorcher climbs the umbilical, he is reminded of how awkward it is to squirm through. It was a lifetime ago when he was last onboard.

"This design has to be an afterthought."

He feels a vibration, and he stops. Did someone drive back? Would he have actually felt that? For a few moments, he freezes. If anyone has driven back, it will be obvious to them that he is in the umbilical, where he shouldn't be since permission has not been granted to him by Commander Ōtsuka to board the ship. The fear of getting caught intensifies his senses and imagination. With his heart racing to near panic levels, like a child who ditches class for the first time and stumbles upon a truancy officer, he rushes through the snake and gets to the hatch. It's locked.

He pauses for a moment to look at the wayfinder symbol of the *Vegvisir* painted on the hatch. Though Scorcher is no sorcerer, he accepts this symbol as fate leading him to the right path he should take, telling him not to be discouraged.

This hatch is totally different from the other hatch used for spacewalks. He failed to consider this. He doesn't know the procedure to open this type of door.

"Why did I not think of that?" he scolds himself, followed by curses. "But also, why wouldn't they use the same damned door?"

He reminds himself not to delay. He's had time to think about these types of details. He just assumed the hatch would be either open or a familiar design. These things are always overly complicated. There's no digital display panel on it telling him whether the pressure is equalized. It's just a plain hatch with a massive lever arm. He's never paid attention to it—or he forgot after bumping his head so many times.

Scorcher commits. He's just going to take the risk and manhandle the hatch open. After counting to three in his mind, he does just that, and the hatch swings to the side without a hitch. He horizontally crawls through the access hole and flops lightly down onto the deck. He shuts the hatch behind him. The pitch blackness touches his eyes. He turns on his flashlight.

He climbs up towards the airlock, which is kind of awkward with the Moon's gravity impacting how one can travel, and he approaches an area he knows has the easiest access to the bulkhead panels with the radiosynthesis fungi inside.

He pulls out his tools to carefully remove the face sheet on the panel, taking time to use trial-and-error to investigate the best way of doing so. Like many parts of the rocket, it is no trivial task, and it becomes an arduous attempt for forty-five frosty minutes. He knows that with aerospace structures, which are optimized for both weight and strength, they tend to be extremely strong, but also very delicate if handled improperly. It's not trivial. It's not impossible. Is he pulling too hard? Should it take this much force to remove a stuck plastic cover, or did he miss a bolt?

He finally removes the face sheet hiding the internal plastic honeycomb core inside of the panel. The terrarium is exposed. The honeycomb core provides both lightweight strength and convenient partitioned residences for the fungi. To his dismay and horror, something worse than damaging the panel occurs. He discovers, to the best of his understanding, that the fungi across the entire panel he's looking at are totally dead in all locations, except those cells right next to the borescope inspection ports. So during Space-Bee's inspection, she could have been misled into thinking everything was fine. He studies it closely and points his flashlight beam focused on one honeycomb cell at a time, using the light to pick at his findings. The homogeneity of death almost makes it look intended and uninteresting.

This, of course, directly contradicts the findings from Space-Bee, though she only looked through the borescope herself. "The lawn is dead except at just the damned borescope inspection locations," Scorcher says out loud, sitting himself down on the edge of a sideways-oriented control panel.

"Is it possible that the lawn was *over* exposed to radiation and the borescopes' locations had additional radiation protection? Or maybe the fungi aren't totally anaerobic and actually need oxygen exposure to fully support the radiosynthesis? Who knows?" he whispers. At the same time, it's difficult for him to tell for sure, and he has enough self-doubt to need to verify his finding. If anything, he wouldn't even trust himself to tell if a mushroom was alive back on Earth. And he never took a biology class at university, so a microscope would be useless anyways. He pretty much only does math and engineering—which is fine because he has an idea for an experiment to prove his suspicion; it just requires him to steal one of the panels off the ship for a bit.

CHAPTER 26

Scorcher completely removes the sandwich panel assembly as a single piece after carefully reattaching the outer face sheet. The technical term for this structural component is "sandwich panel" because it consists of two outer, thin face sheets and an inner honeycomb core that is nine centimeters thick, a structure commonly used in aerospace and perfected by the British for lightweight, high-strength applications in the 1950's. The entire panel dimensions are approximately one meter by one meter by nine centimeters. It won't be trivial getting it through the green umbilical. The risk of puncture from the panel's sharp corners, the risk of breaking the panel, the risk of getting stuck then unstuck.

He opens the hatch and goes partially nude by taking off his pressure suit to give him more flexibility and ease the struggle. From the far side of the umbilical, a faint tune can be heard from Stabby while he's vacuuming.

When he and the panel finally burst out of the far end of the glorified slinky and into CLM, Stabby halts vacuuming suddenly and turns to escape.

Scorcher needs hard evidence to verify his suspicion and prove—through scientific measurements taken from calibrated instrumentation, rigorously scrutinized—that the fungi panel is not absorbing deep space gamma radiation. He needs to prove that the panel is a dud, and the fungi are dead. And he needs to do so quickly. The goal is to show that radiation coming in from the top side of the panel simply passes through the thickness to the bottom side without being absorbed by the fungal meat. But this is nearly impossible—in such a short time frame—since radiation can come from all directions on the lunar surface, and he doesn't have a pristine lab environment to run his experiment.

Breathing easy from having not punctured the umbilical to the vacuum of space or having performed some other fatal action resulting in his own termination, Scorcher prepares for something which almost surely won't work. He takes the fungi-harboring panel and places it in a pressure-tight cargo container about three times too large. But the key is to have a container that can be hermetically sealed. He sets up a little experiment where the panel lays flat on top of one of the sheep. The sheep will drive it around outside, with a radiation sensor on the top and another on the bottom.

For his experiment to work, he needs radiation entering primarily from one side, then zooming through the thickness at lightspeed to exit the opposite side. If the fungi are working, the radiation will be high on top, and low on bottom. The problem is radiation can be randomly reflected by terrain (the Moon is actually brighter than the Sun if viewed through a gamma-ray telescope); he doesn't have time to figure out a good spot to run his experiment, so instead he's going to have the sheep drive it around with the hope that he can later sort out the good data from the bad. He can't waste time collecting data from a spot where radiation is not unidirectional. That would give a false negative that the fungi are dead. The other complication is that Scorcher can't decide if the measurements should be taken in sun, shade, or both.

Even though the sun is out, from the perspective of the South Pole, the shadows are almost equivalent to perpetual evening. On Earth, with the atmosphere present and acting as a light splitter, a shadow is just a dimmer version of what's not in the shade. On the Moon, everything is more extreme, more black and white, sometimes literally. A simple shadow is absolute black in the bright reflection of the out-of-shadow areas. And the angle of the sun is low on the South Pole horizon, making shadows meters long—if not kilometers—and difficult to avoid in this mining valley surrounded by countless ridges. Where can he get good and consistent direct exposure to the sun? On the other side of things, not all the deadly radiation is coming from the sun. Some of it originates from the dark blackness of space itself. In this blackness is a continuum of deep space radiation coming directly from above. So with some radiation coming from the horizon, and some from the zenith above, is it best to avoid the shadows, or stay in the them? How can he get good data if he doesn't have time to do both?

Driven by his scientific pessimism, Scorcher has doubts his radiation readings will work at all. He needs to drive the panel and collect data far away from the radiation scattering and noise that is caused by the Central Lunar Mining facility itself. The experiment must be conducted in the purest location possible, he just doesn't know where. But maybe having the sheep drive around aimlessly might work. Scorcher's fingers are crossed.

He takes a risk and programs the sheep to drive around for twelve hours, hitting both direct sun and deep shade, hoping that enough data is collected in both domains so he can separate out the sun/shade variable.

CHAPTER 27

He can't allow himself to wait patiently for twelve hours until the results come back. He has another critical task to accomplish. A mission driven by his need to know, which both terrifies and nauseates him. He knows he can no longer play reactionary to all the absurdness that occurs at Central Lunar Mining. He knows he can't just stand by anymore. Whether it's all related, he does not know for sure, but he's here to resolve something else that has been troubling him ever since the drunken meeting with the Minister months back.

It can't be found out. It would cause mass disgust and exile if he were ever discovered. But given the risk, weighed carefully and silently for the last few weeks in Scorcher's ethos, he decides to go on a journey for answers to the gravesite of Shigley—and farther.

He leaves the experiment to run autonomously, the sheep driving around to help normalize any radiation exposure and absorption. A panel lying in a single spot, and thus data collected in a single spot, may be prone to some sort of local geographic interference to the radiation which could skew results. This means his experiment with the fungi panel must mobilize to reckon environmental errors.

The low sun now fully hides the ridge in shade; Scorcher goes toward the darkness. He doesn't know if his senses are misleading or not, maybe because of the blackness, but it actually feels colder than normal, and he's shivering. The outside feels icy and damp, which he knows is impossible. His suit functions show nominal. He checks that his head-mounted camera is recording, and it is also reading nominal and operating; however, he won't know until he gets back to Central Lunar Mining if the video recording was successful. Cameras have dodgy reliability in these extreme temperature gradients.

Given that, he begins the journey. Scorcher goes to the hangar to get atop an outfitted sheep he steals from the Minister and rides to the location of the ridge where Shigley is buried. It's an unmarked location, other than the Minister's stacked rocks. But there are stacked rocks everywhere, and nothing is distinct even in daylight, let alone darkness. Scorcher has fitted a couple additional flashlights to his helmet and crudely sets an array of light emitting diodes around the sheep for additional illumination. With all this illumination, it may be more difficult to see, especially since the lights are bright white and lack any warmth to help add depth. Though on the Moon, warm light depth is moot anyways, he considers.

"First to find its location," Scorcher says to himself as the sheep accelerates him into the black vacuum.

*   *   *

He spends five exhausting and frustrating hours searching, depleting stamina, consuming precious oxygen—way too much time and much more resources than he obviously hoped to expend. A couple of times during the search, he stumbles or falls off the sheep. And since everything happens in slow motion, it takes an eternity to know whether his fall will land him on level ground or into a bottomless crevasse. He can't believe how long it is taking to find this grave. Looking back in the distance, he can see the lights of CLM.

Finally reaching his destination, he intentionally knocks over the carefully stacked rocks to vent his frustration and celebrate his victory at finding the grave, certain this isn't some other random pile of rocks placed there by meteorite or Moonquake.

He's wrong and, discovering this, panics.

He jumps on the vehicle and searches farther.

There is a small, abandoned Annie about fifty yards away. "Interesting," he says, surprised at the find. His oxygen is getting low, but he continues with the tedious effort anyways. He has to do this. This could be his only chance, with everyone gone and collected far away over the horizon.

Scorcher double-checks his arm panel, thinking maybe he's so lost that he somehow stumbled across Ayubu's Annie. However, his location shows he is nowhere near Ayubu's outpost, and this particular Annie doesn't show up on the infrastructure charts he's memorized. As Scorcher approaches it and studies the door, he finds it is in fact unpowered. "RIP" is written on the door. He opens it.

Paralysis strikes as he looks into the dark, unpowered room. He is both rigid and weak at a sight so black that it looks like a solid wall. He relies on his head-mounted flashlight to peer inside before stepping in. The far end clearly leads into a long lava tube. Scorcher enters.

There is a makeshift barrier of lightweight wall partitions at the back, standing two meters in height, or about halfway up towards the cave roof. Passage into the lava tube is possible by simply moving over one of the panels leaning against makeshift vertical posts. Scorcher feels he shouldn't be here but talks himself into continuing. He knows he must, but struggles, grasping for fortitude.

He gets his first audio warning that his oxygen supply is low.

Scorcher crosses the superficial border of the front room and is now in the next cave partition, the crypt. He wipes the dust from his head-mounted camera, which he prays is still recording properly. This is nothing like the simple, shallow grave and marker he assumed. It's unreal that this place is even here. His thoughts and surroundings have muted the deafening sound of the fans and pumps in his suit—his hearing is absent. There is only stillness and solitude, like standing in the center of a quiet, cold cathedral, alone and small, but not alone, encased and separated from the rest of reality. A dead man lies here; he doesn't have to see it to sense it. A former man with hopes and dreams, who was born to a mother who cared for him, who joked with his adolescent friends, suffered break-ups, had highs and lows, stomached embarrassments and achievements. Mentored Four-Leaf. Everything. And now it is all gone for him, his conscious universe ended, like it was never there, except for the frozen cells and tissues lying on the floor of this colder-than-frost cave, in a desert where not even the most robust are meant to exist.

Being next to the dead body has shaken him more than he expected. He stares blankly.

Is there even a point to anything?

Scorcher turns his head lamp to the corpse and stares.

He severs his uncertainty and answers: *There is a point.*

There must be. The idea of beginning and ending is an artificial construct—our lame understanding of time. A very one-dimensional, black-and-white understanding of what is here and what isn't here. Scorcher chooses to believe, while standing in this cave, that time is not the lens with which to view life, nor are life and death the metrics, and that everything and nothing must exist together at the same moment. And he must fight for justice for those whom he cannot touch and those who might not yet exist to him. But who all exist, nonetheless.

Scorcher settles to his knees and removes the tarp to begin the crude autopsy.

CHAPTER 28

He removes the tarp and exposes the body lying supine in the dirt, clothed in a spacesuit. The lifeless pressure suit is looking upwards, toward the ceiling of the lava tube, a black void in the transparent facemask shield. Scorcher is unable to see if there is a face in there, so he goes to lean forward. He proceeds until his eyes gain focus upon a head wrapped in cloth—a head he's somehow surprised to see. The cave seems to collapse on him, and he is unable to scream.

He starts to hyperventilate but then closes his eyes and manages to slow his breath. An audio warning in his suit goes off again, indicating that his oxygen supply is low. He slows his breathing further as he momentarily looks at the cave walls for reality reference, which of course haven't budged.

When he's ready, he checks the dead man's spacesuit to see if there is any electrical power available, and there appears to be enough to turn on the arm-mounted tablet. The pressure reading of the suit is zero pascals: the inside of the suit is a vacuum. Scorcher reaches his arms down around the neck and searches for a metallic protrusion. He grasps a shallow knob and uses all his weight to unlatch the helmet, which finally snaps free. He removes it as carefully as he can. The head and neck of the dead astronaut are completely frozen solid, rigid like steel. The living man removes the wrapping and exposes the dead man's head. All these actions, of course, take time and happen in complete silence, making them seem performative, fictitious.

The face looks completely blistered, but the skin is without decay. Signs of what Scorcher believes is vomit coat the inside part of the helmet but have been wiped from the transparent face shield. He gently glides his hand along the suit to look for the other release latches. All take much effort to break free, and he is forced to use a brick-sized rock from the lava tube to hammer the locking joints free. Scorcher reaches into the suit and is burnt by the iciness through his gloves.

With the body removed completely from the suit, he then proceeds to remove the long underwear, exposing the nude flesh. The underwear tears and peels off in pieces, though some of it remains on the frozen body. The unholiness of this action causes Scorcher's reptilian brain to emotionally black out and permanently block the imagery, of which he will never speak.

Refocusing on the autopsy, he tries to gain strength to proceed by leveraging logic.

What kind of accident was this? This doesn't look like a rapid decompression death. Shigley's entire body is covered in burns and blisters. He looks like he was burned alive, but his spacesuit is unharmed. How is this possible, unless it was radiation poisoning? Or how is this possible from *radiation poisoning?* Scorcher attempts deeper breathing to counter the confusion and calm his heart. *But with burns this severe, how was he still able to work? He would have been debilitated for at least a few days before reaching this point. None of this makes sense.*

An audio warning in his suit goes off, indicating that his

oxygen supply is low.

Scorcher frantically verifies that his head-mounted digital camera is still recording, which he takes a mental note not to forget later. The grotesqueness of the corpse is gagging his mind's eye; he needs the digital records to be his memory. For the first time in decades, Scorcher blesses himself with a sign of the cross: top, bottom, left, right. The scene on the far side of his mask is a dream. He must be grasping sea ice and not what his eyes are showing.

The artifact collection is complete.

He rushes to put the body back in order, re-wrap the head, rejoin the suit and helmet together, lay the suit, and replace the tarp. The man with the liquid blood stands.

Behind the body are some container boxes which must be some of Shigley's personal belongings. Scorcher quickly sorts through them, not finding anything useful except for a laptop, which he removes to bring back to base.

He starts to walk away but then drops Shigley's laptop down into a slit in the rocky floor next to the body. As he is hopping sideways to catch it, he slips in slow motion, and his helmet lodges between rocks. At the frightening sound of a pop, Scorcher freezes, scared to make the next move. A solution to this conundrum fails to resolve itself in his blank, non-responsive mind.

He has no idea how to get up. A mundane, simple action can lead to a very terminal consequence. He is completely inanimate in darkness. Warm liquid—probably blood—is pouring from his head, guided enough by gravity to prevent him from drowning.

Or will I? he wonders, nearly inverted. He doesn't have much luck in spacesuits.

An audio warning in his suit goes off again, reminding him that his oxygen supply is low.

Scorcher rashly throws his head out and waits for a few seconds: he isn't dead. He stands up, briskly looks around to set order to what he can, retrieves the laptop, and exits the crypt.

Exiting the Annie, he shuts the hatch with the crudely written message on it, thinking back about how it was ridiculous that he blessed himself moments ago. He doesn't know what to feel right now but is relieved that what's done is done. He scurries over to his sheep and scrambles back toward Central Lunar Mining.

Scorcher secures the laptop inside a container in the sheep, hoping that it is still functional after all this time at cryogenic temperatures.

His senses and vision clear on exiting the makeshift catacomb, like waking up well-rested from a dream. The fog in his mask is gone. He kicks the sheep, and they haul off. The sheep is pre-programmed to automatically take the quickest route back to the "barn," as the Minister calls it, where inactive sheep and industrial equipment reside at the far end of CLM.

The bumps on the ride blur the oxygen level readings on his wrist display. The numbers are obviously not looking great, but he probably won't suffocate.

Generally, in case of a mechanical breakdown or some other unforeseen mishap, which is par for the course, doubling the amount of oxygen expected to be used is best practice, similar to scuba diving. But holding one's breath for two minutes won't suffice in space where carbon dioxide poisoning and hypoxia are perhaps even more pernicious monsters than on Earth.

Scorcher and his sheep arrive back at Central Lunar Mining at about the right time for him to check on the radiation and fungi experiment. He heads to the barn to see if the sheep carrying the panel is back yet.

"I'm sure you fancy company in the barn anyway, sheep," he says to his ride.

Once at a complete stop, he disembarks. He reaches to push the gray and indistinct "return home" button on the side of the sheep, but then pauses right before his index finger reaches it. In the contrasting light of white and black, the gray button is almost an unfamiliar tone, more vibrant than a red rose on Earth. The gray rectangular button, large enough to fit the finger of a space glove, is vibrant in its non-black and non-whiteness. He shakes his head to snap his vision back into focus.

An expanded audio warning pierces his ears to assert that his oxygen supply is *critically* low, and his suit is automatically reducing flow to barely maintain vitals. The computer voice also tells him not to work too hard.

He pushes the sheep's button, feeling the satisfying click even without the noise, and the dirty white vehicle, which was bright yellow before the Moon dust painted it, drives itself and the laptop cargo into a miniature pressure lock going directly into the barn. The man hops over to the airlock and slams the door shut behind him.

The pressure equalizes sufficiently for Scorcher to override the cleaning process and take off his scraped up helmet and toss it to the ground. The pressure lock has another forty-five seconds before releasing him.

Instead of staring at the countdown timer, Scorcher looks down to stare at his gloves. The very same gloves that just handled Shigley's frozen corpse. His DNA is probably all over them.

After Scorcher is back inside Central Lunar Mining, he de-suits down to his thermal long underwear and goes back to take a shower, ignoring his appetite and dehydrated state. Walking down the hallway almost feels dreamlike, like in the cave. But here, it's the physical and emotional exhaustion combined with another inexplicable surrealness.

At his bunk, he sits down for a moment to chug water out of a bottle, letting his mind go blank.

A few moments later, he opens his eyes and sees Stabby in what he can only interpret as a complete panic, with blinking red lights and a swaying mini-sword. Scorcher takes in a slow deep breath and fills his lungs with the plentiful oxygen-rich air, though he has an eerie feeling and instinctively checks behind himself to see if he's being watched.

Without saying anything and already forgetting about his plans for a shower, Scorcher stands up to follow Stabby, who rotates around, turns the corner, and races down the hall. It's a familiar scene to Scorcher because he's done this before. Stabby reaches some stairs he can't get down and Scorcher, once again, picks Stabby up and sets him down like a pet. Since Scorcher needs to continue this way to the barn anyway, he follows along.

When they both reach the doorway into the barn, Scorcher is stunned. This makes no sense to him. The storage room with all the backup sheep is completely rummaged. The sheep have essentially been slaughtered — batteries violently pulled out, panels torn off and bent, countless bolts, nuts, and tools scattered. Some of the sheep innards drip from red-dyed transmission fluid that has sprayed about.

Disquieted, he simply stands there without moving for what must be minutes. Stabby is motionless behind him. He takes a step into the room and stops again. There is no explanation for this impossible scene. The sheep in the barn have been destroyed: tracks torn off, heads decapitated, side panels kicked in, wiring intestines shredded and scattered.

Every other human is fully accounted for, kilometers from here, and no one could have been here during the time he was gone.

CHAPTER 29

Scorcher walks over cautiously to see that two of the sheep, dirty with Moon dust but wholly intact, are near the miniature pressure lock giving access to the lunar surface: the one containing the fungi experiment and the other he saddled earlier. He has been in this room multiple times before his trip.

How is this fucking possible? he asks himself. *No one else is here!*

A rhythmic, repeating buzz impedes. He checks his smartphone: there is a message from Four-Leaf telling him to contact him right away. Scorcher doesn't know what to do and can't be bothered right now. The pool of chaos around him is unbearable and probably impossible to clean up before anyone gets back.

Is this sabotage? Is there someone else here? Paranoia permeates. The digital pressure-lock logs might tell him if anyone else came or left—or worse, just came and is still here.

But who could possibly do this? Scorcher thinks, taking shallow breaths. *How did this happen, and why were the sheep slaughtered?*

Scorcher runs back to the main control room and shuts the hatch. He tries to improvise a defensive weapon, but his brain is overwhelmed and not processing reality clearly. In fact, he doesn't even know what reality is right now. Maybe he dreamt this. He runs back to the barn at full sprint—after grabbing a fire extinguisher as a defensive blunt-object— and sees that the abomination is real, then runs back to the control room a second time in ninety seconds.

On the main computer, he remotely activates all the pressure hatches for an impromptu full lockdown and starts running diagnostics to ensure all systems are nominal. Environmental readings: atmospheric pressure, *check*; oxygen, *check*; water vapor, *check*; carbon monoxide, *check*; etc. Scorcher is manually verifying all environmental and systems readings, default settings, tolerance bands, even though the computer itself would highlight and bring attention to any abnormality. But given the circumstances, he trusts nothing.

Next, electrical systems. AC power stable at 400 Hz nominal…

Within about twenty minutes, he's able to verify that there are no anomalies. He checks the history logs for the pressure locks and doesn't see anything unexpected for the last few days.

There is a motion-activated camera in the barn that actively records when motion triggers it. However, the video only records him loading the sheep with the experiment, and then starts again when the sheep re-enters through the pressure lock. No recordings of what happened in between.

He receives another message from Four-Leaf telling him to contact them *immediately* at Ed's Annie.

"Hey, Four-Leaf," Scorcher says on video chat on his phone.

"Scorcher. We got an emergency message that life support was failing in one of the spacesuits. What's the status? I thought you weren't going out."

Scorcher punches his leg. When one of the spacesuits suffers critically low pressure levels or some other criticality, it gets logged and sends a warning to all other crew members as a safety precaution. He stares blankly past his phone after an epiphany. "That means that when Shigley's suit failed, there was a permanent log created of the event on every computer and smartphone at the time. It's been hidden in plain sight this whole time," Scorcher mumbles unintentionally aloud. "Maybe there is a computer out here somewhere that Seattle didn't wipe of the spacesuit error log, like what the Minister was claiming." Or at least that's what Scorcher thinks the Minister was saying. It's hard to remember, and there were a lot of Irish coffees that meeting.

"Buddy? Pal? Mate? Hello, Scorcher," Four-Leaf says sarcastically. "Can you hear us?"

"Yes, of course," Scorcher replies sullenly, turning his focus back to the screen.

"What were you doing spacewalking? You had us all nervous there…" Four-Leaf takes his camera and pans over to everyone tightly cramped in the Annie. They all either wave or give a thumbs up, except for Commander Ōtsuka, who is as stoic and firm as ever. But she is draped by more than stoicism—there is a vehemence peeking through, which reaches Scorcher.

"Well, I had to deal with an emergency," Scorcher lies, but then tries to tie it into something he can show for. "There was an incident in the barn with the sheep." With that comment, everyone is completely silent over the audio. Of course any mention of sheep would yield complete attention. "It looks like someone came in and trashed the place, scattered tools and whatnot. There must have been some kind of explosion or something."

"What are you talking about?" Keystone interrupts. "Isn't Stabby there? What did you do with Stabby?"

"Do with what?" Scorcher doesn't hear Keystone properly. There is a bunch of indistinct arguing picking up in the background. The video accidentally pans around the room wildly as Four-Leaf readjusts himself. Scorcher sees that the crew of the *Vegvisir*—Commander Ōtsuka, Rocko, and Space-Bee, arranged in a line like a three-piece matryoshka set, largest to smallest—are standing awkwardly in the corner, all holding coffee cups in their right hands.

"Shut up, Keystone," Four-Leaf interjects curtly. "Was there another explosion? What did you hear when it happened?"

Scorcher doesn't know how to answer because he was technically not even there at the time. "Um, I was asleep and didn't hear anything," he says.

Four-Leaf furls a brow. "Oh? Napping outside? And you forgot to bring oxygen?"

He continues babbling. "But I did a diagnostic check and there was nothing. No environmental anomalies, power anomalies, nor smoke detection, the pressure hatches didn't shut automatically—"

Four-Leaf looks down and to the left and murmurs, "Chinese."

"Wait, what?" Scorcher yells a little too loudly. He said the same ridiculous thing about the power outage on the *Vegvisir* when Scorcher first arrived. "No. That doesn't even make sense. There are no Chinese nationals even on the Moon right now. Remember the taikonauts left months ago?"

"It's because he hasn't been listening to Stabby, who has

probably been warning him, poor buddy," Keystone can be heard saying over the audio background. "This is no coincidence."

Four-Leaf asks, "Were the oxygen tank-ferrying sheep damaged? How about the bottle connection to refill those tanks? If those are damaged…"

He's right, thinks Scorcher, *the Minister has a hardline providing oxygen resupply to his detached structure, but the Annies need oxygen routinely shipped out to them. They might all have to come back to CLM.*

"You know, mate, Commander Ōtsuka also got an indication that the *Vegvisir* hatch was opened and shut a couple times. Is this related? Is the ship in one piece? Did you have something to do with that?" Four-Leaf's tone and investigative tilt of the head indicates to Scorcher he won't trust his response either way.

What's with all these goddamn auto-alerts? Scorcher curses. He realizes that Four-Leaf must be reading his facial expressions right now. "Um. I was checking everything, trying to figure out what was going on. Thought maybe the *Vegvisir* had an explosion or something." Before Four-Leaf can respond, Scorcher continues. "I know I should have contacted you right away. Sorry about that."

"Well, take lots of pictures and document everything unperturbed. If you want to start cleaning up after taking pictures, that's on you," says Four-Leaf. "We're going to head out and come back right away. I think the *Vegvisir* crew are homesick for their rocket anyway." Four-Leaf smiles. "Nothing was supposed to go wrong while you were alone."

"It never is," Scorcher says.

"Understood. Watch your back in the meantime, mate. Out." Four-Leaf disappears on screen.

This means that Scorcher doesn't have much time to reinstall the panel back on the *Vegvisir*, which means he'll have to enter the ship again, probably setting off some other alarm, but he'll just have to cross that bridge later. There is no other way around it. But then that's even less time to review the data and return the sheep back to its pre-experiment configuration. And grab Shigley's laptop. So much to do in such a short time.

Scorcher allows himself to quickly read a text message he just got from Space-Bee. She says that the mining technicians are stunned. They're working themselves up about this horrible crime against the sheep. It's a bad omen. But she also explains this apparently isn't the first "haunting," and the last time this happened there was no explanation, but something else tragic…

Scorcher ignores the rest of the text and can't tell if Space-Bee is buying into this nonsense or if she is just merely mocking them. "I don't have time for this," Scorcher says to himself. Then turns to Stabby, who has just driven in. "I don't have time for any of this shit right now." Stabby doesn't respond as Scorcher storms out of the control room.

He spends the next couple of hours painstakingly disassembling his experiment and bringing the flight hardware back onto the *Vegvisir*, where he encounters numerous difficulties reinstalling the panel. As precisely as he tries, he's unable to get the panel to fit back the same way it came off. To avoid having to uninstall even more structure—some of it being primary load-carrying structural elements which would be dangerous to mess with—he must force the panel back into place with the knife-edge sides cutting against the delicate, thin aluminum hull. He pulls the panel back off and places it to the side just to double check that he didn't damage anything.

Looking at the hull—the physical fine membrane between space's infinite harshness and a tolerable atmosphere inside the *Vegvisir*—Scorcher notices that there's a thermal protection system made of the same thermal blankets used on aircraft jet engine cowls and thrust reversers. It's another metallic honeycomb sandwich panel that acts as insulation. He's relieved.

It's non-structural. Who cares if I scratch it slightly?

He picks the panel back up for another re-installation attempt.

What could go wrong? he nervously jokes with himself.

There's a loud, strong scream—a nail on a chalkboard—followed by the panel popping back into its home.

He's confident it's just the non-structural thermal protection system taking one for the team. But he's out of time to investigate and estimates that the damage or scratch can't be too extreme and will likely be fine until the next inspection cycle, even if a crack develops and grows from thermal cycling. He acknowledges that he definitely left his mark.

Arriving back at the barn, he photographs and documents the inexplicable destruction. Maybe it was an airlock malfunction when he was rushing through, or some other sloppy action on his part. But it becomes less explainable to him with every digital photo he captures. The scene has no appearance of an explosion to him. It's like a poltergeist ran through and tore everything apart. Wires are torn out of machines, and circuit broads shattered like glass. Malignant and pestilential, if Scorcher didn't know any better.

CHAPTER 30

Sailing by a weak but pointed second wind, the engineer processes and organizes the experimental data as rapidly as his attention allows. He may be arched like a withered tree draping over the keyboard, but his mental focus is upright and invigorated. He sees himself as the stereotypical image of nerd rage, which oddly motivates him and reminds him of university.

The noise from typing halts as he studies the screen, not aware of his surroundings.

Stabby coasts by faster than normal and pierces Scorcher in the ankle, followed by frantic beeping. "Jesus Christ, Stabby!" He kicks the knife off the robot, using his boot to inflict violence back onto the naïve vacuum.

It's a clean cut that doesn't hurt because the blade is sharp, but it still feels deep based on the tug. "You little bastard. I'm bleeding. I'm going to need stitches—but what else is fucking new? I wish you died with the sheep." He considers destroying him in the vacuum of space, just barely stops himself. He pokes the wound with his dominant right hand. "God, that's deep." He stops withholding himself.

Scorcher picks up his improvised pipe weapon and bashes Stabby over the top, breaking off his knife-mount completely. Stabby drives off in sloppy retreat, barely missing a bulkhead.

Guilt splashes his heart, fueled by a reservoir of pent-up frustrations and unacknowledged emotions. The weight of chaos and disorder censor his sputtering, inconsistent energy drive. The real weight of imagined concrete holds down his tingly forearms. The room is foggy. The table slaps his cheek and he's awake again, looking down at his ankle.

He stumbles over to the first aid kit on the wall and bandages his ankle up. The immediate hope is to slow the bleeding and allow that bandage to absorb the blood. Another adrenaline rush strikes.

He starts pounding the metallic table with his fist while screaming profanities. He pulls a back muscle in the process, then takes a breather for a minute. He stops himself from sobbing to go back to his data reduction.

He sits silently for twenty minutes to clear his mind and let his emotions pass. He needs to get this done and manages to reengage after another slap on the cheek—this time with his own hand.

The data show that the radiation levels on both sides of the panel are about the same. This clearly indicates that either the fungi are dead, or the experimental results are completely garbage. Two very different outcomes, and even odds for both. He checks the magnitudes of the gamma radiation to verify that the radiation is about two-hundred times higher than what strikes a person on Earth. Or about ten times higher than on a subsonic commercial airliner. Scorcher notices there are significant spikes, peaks, and valleys, depending on time and location of data collected. But it's all independent of the placement of the sensor relative to which side of the panel it is on, meaning that from the perspective of the radiation, it was like the radiation shield wasn't even there. Next question: what to do with this finding and who to tell? He's already been shot down multiple times, and he needs to think of a way to get people to believe him.

He heads over to a first aid kit again to re-wrap his ankle. As he's doing so, he nearly gets a panic attack thinking about how the original spacesuit problem, with the coolant leak that nearly killed him months ago, is still unresolved. Why this just now pops into his head, he doesn't know. Then his horrible jerk of a mind piles on everything that has happened since then. It's a reminder of all the pitfalls and history he doesn't know about because people like Four-Leaf keep information from him, maybe as a control thing.

Scorcher talks himself down from a complete panic—or at least he thinks he does—knowing that he needs a clear functioning mind, especially now. His attempts aren't working, though. What he doesn't appreciate is that a panic attack is not something that is intellectually controlled. It is a bodily response, a physical response, just like any other emotion. It is an involuntary and innate survival mechanism that cannot be reasoned out of when, emotionally and spiritually, a person has been pressed too hard and for too long.

Next up, Scorcher tries Shigley's laptop since he is no longer able to focus on systems diagnostics and security camera feeds, especially since it is not getting him any closer to an answer. The laptop refuses to turn on, of course, even after plugging it in and warming it up above cryogenic temperatures. He needs to figure out how to mine through any existing hard drive data. But in the meantime, he gets an indication that someone is in the pressure lock now. Must be the first of the crew to come back. He has no instinct on whether the timing seems right. Scorcher sloppily places the laptop in a drawer in the control room and leaves it plugged in and charging with a wire hanging out of the drawer.

He intends to head down to greet whoever is at the pressure lock, but first he needs to digitally archive all his photographs and video from his earlier trip to Shigley's crypt. He feels sickened and disgusted by what he's done, especially the handling of the body, but then he reminds himself that the ends justify the means. He needs to get to the bottom of what's going on here and expose the company for what it is. Expose Four-Leaf for what he is—and isn't.

He accepts his tactics for what they are now but still doesn't have a long-term strategy. He can worry about that later, and the opportunity of getting hands on data to expose the crimes here couldn't wait for the convenience of a well-thought-out plan for what to do once the information was collected.

Once he's armed with the truth, maybe he can figure out how to handle it. He begs fate to allow for a couple of days' time to process everything he's learned. Or at least decide what it is that he has learned.

CHAPTER 31

Two days pass, and Central Lunar Mining is filled with more souls than it's used to, but the numbers are well within its design capacity. The three crew members of the *Vegvisir* are doing extensive routine maintenance and diagnostic checks on board their ship, plus upgrading software which requires exhaustive regression testing of all systems—not a trivial task. It's a full house at CLM, a full house on the *Vegvisir*, and a full house in the "winter house," yet another makeshift turf house disconnected from the main campus that Ed and Keystone threw together. It's essentially a storage shed—or another barn, as Keystone and Ed call it— that temporarily houses their sheep. One location where they can all fit and remain powered in standby mode. They don't want to abandon their sheep at their Annies. A makeshift collection of solar panels and batteries keeps them fed in the meantime.

It seems unusual to Scorcher that for two days there was almost no talk of the sheep slaughter. Four-Leaf himself quietly reviewed the video logs, noted the times that the space lock was in use, etc. However, he didn't react, didn't share anything with Scorcher. They've had no meetings on it whatsoever. The only outcome is that Scorcher has sent a report back to Seattle detailing the scope of damage to the sheep and equipment and the general mayhem as an unexplained industrial mishap. Four-Leaf's poker face has Scorcher on edge. And most worrisome of all, he just can't fathom what has happened. But he lists the possibilities, nonetheless, like uneven air pressure blowing open a hatch between rooms or a lithium-ion battery overheating. Or maybe some other intricate chain of events which are highly unlikely but obviously not impossible. Like a simultaneous Moonquake and battery explosion that left no clear evidence trail behind.

The crew of the *Vegvisir*, however, have disappeared to their ship. Meanwhile, the Minister inspects every corner and nook of the place without explaining what he's looking for. It is questionable that even he knows, in Scorcher's view. But he can't speculate on how everyone is feeling. He hasn't had the opportunity to connect with them. The Minister, to Scorcher's surprise, has been working smoothly with Four-Leaf, too. That really does seem out of character and makes him additionally uneasy and uncertain.

The three remaining mining technicians—Keystone, Ed, and Ayubu—are now bunking at CLM, as well. Four-Leaf demanded that they throw bodies at the problem to get Central Lunar Mining squared away and back up and running at full capacity. After the last series of mishaps, and especially now with this latest unsolved occurrence, Seattle is demanding with increased emphasis that everyone get their act together. They have even threatened "economic consequences" to everyone here, to which Scorcher rolls his eyes. His role in this, naturally, is setting a "vision" that will be ignored by Four-Leaf and defining schedules which will also be ignored except when Seattle smothers him with his own Gantt charts.

Scorcher walks into the coffee shop to feed his caffeine addiction and oral fixation—probably the only pleasure he has—and for the first time, the room is filled with a multitude of other humans—about four, which seems like so many to him that he can't even exactly count them without doubting himself. The crowd makes him anxious and self-conscious. He sits down and attempts a normal conversation with Space-Bee, but the knowledge of what he knows and has been up to forms an awkward barrier.

"How are you feeling?" he asks her with a more than subtle level of concern.

Space-Bee notices and responds in an agitated tone implying that Scorcher should back off. "I'm doing *good* Scorcher. Everything is *fine*."

"You mean you're doing *well*? Superheroes do good."

Space-Bee replies, "I said what I mean. I've noticed you're always correcting my grammar. Is that your superpower? Being a dick?"

Scorcher just sits there.

She tempers down. "Are *you* OK? You don't look very good," she says.

He laughs slightly, looking at his own hands resting on the table, and doesn't respond to her inquiry. His mind starts thinking about grammar. He forgets about his painful obsession with the truth for a short moment. "Grammar is so interesting, it's like equations, but the equations change with different languages, and they're always evolving." He thinks about this in silence for a while, then responds to his own internal train of thought, "But I'm just not all that great at linguistics, and it's not something I even knew about until later in life when I started studying random languages on smartphone apps. How do you think I learned basic phrases in Russian, French, and Swahili?"

Space-Bee: "What did you really want to be when you grow up? Why didn't you just become an English major?

You've mentioned this before."

Scorcher, overcoming the wedge still in his chest, says, "I wanted to study English literature, actually. I even won a high school poetry contest my senior year."

Space-Bee's eyebrows raise. "Oh, really? You? Why not, then? Why'd you go to grad school for aerospace engineering and rocket science?" She laughs.

"Well, I fundamentally disagreed with English professors. I felt like an outsider."

"Oh? That's not surprising." She chuckles again.

"Yeah, they tend to take a very critical look at things, and not in the way I liked. They encourage too much sympathy, which is destructive and not natural."

"Sympathy's not natural? Who told you that?" she says.

"No one told me that. Well, there is this self-help book…"

She rolls her eyes. "That's dangerous."

He ignores her. "The theory is that evolution has wired our brains such that empathy, and not sympathy, occurs the most naturally. Creation, not destruction. That viewpoint really struck a chord with me. And then I started to think about it even more. The fine arts at universities can train people to be overly judgmental, especially with politics. Maybe I'm wrong, but to me sympathy is like feeling sorry for someone, which is a judgment. Sympathy often leads to more violence, even well-intentioned sympathy.

"If people are empathic and connected, they naturally want to meet the needs of others. It's just human nature. And this eliminates violence and conflict.

"But long story short, I didn't trust majoring in English. I'd become too molded on sympathy, whereas I believe the truest way to experience art is through empathetic connection to the artist, without judgement."

"I don't believe you."

"What?" Scorcher leans back up.

She shakes her head, "First off, you obviously like some books better than others, so you judge, too. I mean, I can see some of your points. But when you were eighteen going to college, you didn't think that way. You were a kid, not someone who had spent years thinking about how biological evolution defines artistic expression. You said empathy not sympathy, right? You hadn't had years to be stuck in your own head yet." She sits up. "I might be reclusive and weird, but I pay attention, Scorcher. We talk a lot, and I hear a lot of the same stuff over and over from you."

Space-Bee's forwardness is like cold water to his face. She seems different to him. He can't tell if she is changing or if she's just opening up more and starting to act more naturally. The person he's sitting across from now is not the same person he sat across from during his first coffee here at CLM. He's all right with that but feels he needs to adjust in some way.

She continues. "What was the *real* reason you didn't become an English major? Why did you choose aviation? Did you just dream of being a pilot like every other boy?"

Space-Bee lumping him into the category of "every other boy" reminds him of how his teachers from primary and secondary school often treated him. He's no longer interested in this conversation, but answers with intellectual honesty the best he can. "I don't know."

CHAPTER 32

Scorcher's lying in his cot, looking up toward the ceiling. Not far from his bunk is Ayubu's cot, where he too is staring up at the ceiling. The air of a teenage sleepover permeates, probably from their discussion of unusual sightings and unexplained events at the Annies. Scorcher of course doesn't believe in ghosts and is troubled by how superstitious and unreasonable everyone else seems to be, except for maybe Four-Leaf who either doesn't believe or keeps it all hidden under his act. Amongst those on the Moon, talk of the barn being haunted is making a comeback, but each person has their own theory as to what this means. This might be a good sign for Scorcher, though, because people aren't blaming him publicly. However, he is troubled, nonetheless: why aren't they more accusatory, knowing that he was the only person here?

The consensus is that Stabby—who is clearly the "victim" of Scorcher's neglect—needs to be repaired and re-outfitted to symbolic guard duty. Stabby needs his knife reattached. With everyone present at CLM, Scorcher wouldn't admit missing Stabby for being out of service during his convalescence.

With Ayubu, the conversation of ghosts, or just a ghost singular, doesn't get very far. Ayubu seems to not take the topic very lightly and thinks it's bad luck to speculate about specters. "It's just not something people of my culture speak casually about," he explains to Scorcher half-jokingly but sincere. This seems as good an answer as any. "What was the deal with the spacesuit, Scorcher?" he asks, changing from one uncomfortable topic to another, though this one is clearly better for him.

A slight knot pulls Scorcher's stomach from knowing he must lie. "Well, you know, there's just so much going on with inspections and quality. You know how it is. There are basically no quality inspections, I mean, nothing worthwhile to ensure that whatever we 3-D print has a good service life. Or even that it doesn't have any cracks or defects in it."

"Yes, that is true. There basically is no quality assurance." A few moments of silence pass, and Ayubu rotates his head to look directly at Scorcher, who is still looking up at the ceiling. "So you were just checking stuff out? Anything I should be aware of? Usually you share these things."

"Well, I was looking at the landing pad for the *Vegvisir* resupply ship. And the exposed plumbing for the ice-to-propellant conversion systems. You know, just everything, I guess. I lost track of time. Totally overworked. You know how it is." Scorcher unconsciously grinds his teeth after noticing he keeps using the filler "you know."

"Yes. I know." Ayubu turns his head back toward the ceiling.

It's not entirely clear to either of them what they should be working on, or how it helps anything. They're just bodies thrown at the "problem" without foresight. Management in Seattle has been especially anxious, given the slow recovery to full volume operations in refining precious metals and shipping them back to Earth. They want to take advantage of political conflicts on Earth driving up the market value of rare earths. But even at full production, the bottom-line profit margins of the entire operation are moderately negative at best. And only that good because of the occasional lunar infrastructure grant the Founder can con out of NASA for "lunar investments" even though NASA will likely never use the facilities.

Ayubu continues, "I'm not really sure how I can help here right now. Though it is nice being around people for once. You get kind of crazy in solitary confinement like that, even though I often talk with you online about tasks. Funny—I am doing my normal tasks that I do at my remote Annie, except now remotely." He laughs. "This place is *wild*, man. You know that, Scorcher?"

"Oh, I do. Space is always trying to kill us."

"It is worse than that, friend," replies Ayubu. "Space is indifferent. We are nothing to it. It does not try."

Scorcher ponders that for a moment and then decides to ask something that, for some reason, he never really considered until now. "Your actual name is Ayubu, right? Why do some people here have callsigns or nicknames, but other people just go by their real name?"

"Hmm. Scorcher is not your real name, then. Good question, Scorcher, or Mr. Samuel Robertson," Ayubu says while grinning. "I am not sure. Maybe because we all come from different training or backgrounds. We are just kind of randomly stuck together. I went by 'Peace' during astronaut training in Iceland, but I was the only one to make it all the way through the program, so no one is around to remember. Then when I got here, no one asked."

"Interesting."

"I think Ed's actual name is Steve, but somehow he goes by Ed."

"That's random. I just thought he was actually an 'Ed,' and 'special' at that."

Ayubu smiles, "So what about you, Mr. Scorcher? Does something burn in your heart? Why they call you that?"

"Well, a couple reasons, I guess. Originally because I set off a fire alarm from a bag of microwave popcorn. I pushed an extra zero and walked away, forgetting about it. I was thoroughly judged for not just using the default 'Popcorn' button."

"I can see this, friend," Ayubu says, smirking.

"But also a genetic mutation I suppose," he mildly jokes.

"Oh?"

"My hair is dark, but my beard comes is red. Looks like my face is scorching."

"Ha! That is true!" Ayubu responds, pointing a finger at him. "Your face is fire. How unusual."

"It is," Scorcher admits. "People grabbed on to that jokingly, alongside the popcorn incident. The red beard probably came from my Canadian dad's Scotch-Irish side, if that's not a mouth full. My mom's multiracial but pretends she's not." He abruptly switches topic. "I agree with what you said earlier, Ayubu: this place is wild. But in a horrible way."

Ayubu, glancing to study Scorcher for a moment, simply nods. He turns back to look at Stabby circling back into the room, annoyingly loud to both. "What do you think of that one? He looks naked now." He lazily points with his long finger, palm up.

Scorcher looks down at the vacuum bot, "Why do you always keep circling back when I'm having a conversation? You're like a child who only wants attention if I'm talking with other adults or I'm on the phone. I swear, he just magically appears whenever I talk with others." He turns back towards Ayubu after spending a few minutes watching Stabby glide around. "Well, I'll be honest. I've been secretly wanting to reprogram him—or it. Whatever."

"Oh? For what?"

Scorcher smirks. "To dance, obviously. Look at those moves, Ayubu. He's constantly wiggling and twirling all unnecessarily. I think he just can't help himself. Those sheep are gonna be all over those moves. He has potential!"

Ayubu laughs. "I think if you are the one teaching Stabby to dance, you will have to do something with that knife strategy first. You know you have no business being a dance teacher. But I do not need to say that out loud."

He laughs back. "Yeah, well. Who knows?" Stabby disappears around the corner. Then the smile erodes. He repeats, "Who knows?"

"You know they think it is you, Scorcher. Not everyone, but some."

"I figured that."

"They are not saying it out loud, but you can guess who," he says, trying not to admit too much.

"Yeah. I see. What do you think?" Scorcher asks.

Ayubu looks like he instantly regrets saying what he needed to get off his chest. "I do not know. I am just always checking my back and counting the days to get out of here. I need real warm sunlight. Not that bright white LED above us half the time. I did not realize the sun would even be different here, friend. Back in Kenya, the sun is welcoming and yellow. Red at dawn or dusk. Here, it is like those annoying LED headlights on cars."

Scorcher risks probing again. "Yeah. But, I mean, what do you really think happened?"

"Rapid decompression blew the barn to pieces."

"I considered that too, Ayubu," Scorcher says. "But there

are no records of rapid decompression."

Ayubu carefully rolls his head to see Scorcher. "Ghosts," he says softly.

*   *   *

Later that day, Scorcher sets the team agenda and assigns actual jobs to the techs since Four-Leaf is just having them fiddle around on meaningless tasks, like reviewing the service logs of plumbing systems or cycling a series of auto shutoff valves and recording the response time.

How is all this data even going to be used? Scorcher complains in his head. *They're not even fixing anything. Why does Seattle management just go with the flow and never challenge Four-Leaf? Why are they so spineless with him?*

In the midst of the nonsense, the mining technicians are still doing their other full-time jobs, some getting more fatigued than others. The obviously uneven distribution of workload needs to be addressed in Scorcher's view. So he comes up with the idea of having a rotating focus or point of contact for odd jobs, instead of compartmentalized "subject matter experts" among the miners. This is to keep individuals from getting overloaded, or worst of all, bored and complacent. As a plus, the plan helps with cross training. For instance, it's not fair or sustainable to have Keystone work all the jobs replacing regolith filters in the environmental control system—because he helped build the system and understands it the best—while someone else only has to do their normal "nine-to-five" day job of tending sheep and surveying dirt. Though in fairness, all jobs here keep people busy fourteen hours a "day," night or shine.

Four-Leaf reacts quickly to the new team management strategy and demands a meeting with Scorcher, who complies begrudgingly. After everyone arrives, minus the Minister and the *Vegvisir* crew, Four-Leaf starts off faux-panicked and confrontational. He says, in front of the whole room and with Seattle listening over the phone, "What do you even do here, mate?"

Scorcher doesn't feel like taking his shit anymore. "I make sure you can breathe. And ensure enough propellant is processed to get off this goddamned rock when the time comes."

Four-Leaf: "If he's not going to respect me, I'm not working with him. Look how belligerent he becomes." His acting is poorly staged; his tone is strangely calm and contrary to his intended message.

Scorcher can't believe people are buying this.

One of the nameless managers in Seattle responds quickly, in a peacekeeping manner. "Ooookaay, ooookaay, guys, uh..." she says, taking in a long, shallow breath through her teeth, probably hoping everyone else does the same.

Scorcher rolls his eyes, and Four-Leaf notices with a subtle satisfaction.

"Soooo, Scorcher," the female voice continues, "we're going to redirect you and reprioritize your work. I think we'll all feel better about thaaaat."

After she oddly fades off and takes too long to continue, Four-Leaf starts up again, "We're going to need you to do a lot of external work until the sheep—"

"External?" Scorcher asks furrowing his brows.

The manager jumps back in, "—until the sheep get repaired. We have an urgent priority." She continues to explain that Scorcher is being redirected to literally dig ditches on behalf of the sheep until they get repaired by the other techs. The rest of the upgrades, repairs, maintenance, and so forth of the rare mineral refinement and mining factory, power plant, and water-to-propellant conversion facilities, will be managed by Four-Leaf directly and performed over the next couple weeks by all the mining technicians.

"What ditches, again?" Scorcher asks, offended and completely not following what this new "top priority" task actually does. "Why is there always so much beating around the bush with you people?"

"It's a new project to be started immediately…"

Yes, I already know it's being started immediately, Scorcher thinks, *even though everything is a complete shitshow as it is and starting something new makes no sense.*

He has no idea about this new project even though he's in charge of schedules and project management. But apparently Four-Leaf knew.

They continue to explain the plan to Scorcher without actually getting to the bottom line.

"You want me to install dozens of pressure hoses that spray regolith slurry?" Scorcher asks incredulously. "Let me get this right: first you want to be able to mix Moon dirt with some yet-to-be-determined cryogenic liquid to make a slurry. Second you want to take this slurry and spray it into the sky—like a massive Slip 'N Slide made of geysers."

"Exactly!" a random Seattle project engineer interrupts, excitedly. "It was Four-Leaf's idea, actually. He's been working on it tirelessly for months now. Helping us run the numbers and stuff. It's part of a bigger plan for improved efficiency and safety. But essentially, Scorcher, and everyone else who doesn't know yet," the cartoon-pitched male salesman continues, "the future of shipping minerals back to Earth is not with the *Vegvisir*. It's with unmanned cargo containers which will be launched from Earth en masse, land on the Moon, get loaded up with refined ore, blast themselves back off the Moon, re-enter the Earth's atmosphere, and parachute gently back to the Texas desert. Then repeat the cycle. The current process of using the *Vegvisir* has ended up being too inconsistent and costly in overhead. Which you probably already know. Eventually, we just want people focusing on science-y and touristy things and really expanding our footprint. As you know, the Founder's goal *is* thousands of people working and living on the Moon."

"Ok," says Scorcher, "I think I missed the punchline."

"Oh, no punchline!" he says enthusiastically, clearly missing or ignoring Scorcher's tone. "These containers will be reusable and have a small rocket motor to land on the Moon. However, the amount of fuel required to operate the motors for both landing *and* takeoff is too much. That means less payload for cargo. So Four-Leaf came up with the idea of spraying the sky with industrial hoses, spewing an endless supply of Moon dirt aimed directly at the containers on final approach. The hoses will be used to spray and slow down the containers. The rocket motors will only be used very minimally. The cargo containers will fly through the dirt and be slowed down by it, almost like parachutes."

"Except dirt?" Keystone asks, trying to visualize if this is plausible, but clearly less offended than Scorcher is that Four-Leaf has kept everyone out of the loop.

"Correct! Except with dirt. *Moon* dirt," the voice laughs obnoxiously. "This will save on precious weight to carry more cargo and less rocket fuel. Even though there is plenty of propellant available from the South Pole ice-water source. The dirt clouds we poof into the sky will act as drag to slow down the pods."

"Long story short, mate, we need some ditches dug for the equipment. And you seem like our man," Four-Leaf concludes with a slight smile, satisfied with his timing.

Scorcher is pissed on many levels; he can't let it go. "So I guess the whole bigger plan of having something like the *Vegvisir* as a continuously orbiting vehicle is a big fucking bust. What about the sales pitch you guys gave me a couple years ago? The *Vegvisir* was to make access to space affordable by decoupling launch windows and operations because it could supposedly act as the communications, power, and orbital transfer infrastructure on behalf of dozens of simultaneous projects. Essentially you guys are abandoning the prospect of expanding the *Vegvisir* to support space operations like commercial space stations in LEO and LLO, lunar mining, research labs, orbital industry parks, and tourism. The Highway to Space is getting canceled, just like most other fruitful space projects with any real meaning or potential. Except that you're keeping mining, of course, to deface the Moon."

"Well, something like the *Vegvisir* is overkill for how it's currently being used. You are correct. The *Vegvisir* was designed and sized for a much broader scope than what we have now. But that doesn't mean it's getting canceled," speaks the voice.

Scorcher circles back to how this impacts him. "And why do *I* need to manually dig ditches? Is any part of this whole operation ever planned ahead of time?"

"Well, it's more prepping the ground to lay foundations for the equipment. Plus, we'll eventually need large piles of regolith to be sucked and blasted. You can also help with piling the dirt. We also want to experiment with a new mixture of lunar-mix concrete."

And once I'm done with that, Scorcher thinks, *that's when I'll be put out to pasture like Shigley.*

"Am I the only one ignorant about this cargo container and spraying-the-sky-with-dirt plan?" Scorcher throws in.

"I only found out about it from social media," Ayubu says, but avoids eye contact. "You know how this industry is, friend. The employees are always the last to know."

Four-Leaf adds, "How strangely true that always has been, mate. The secrets people keep are always the things you really need to know in this industry."

Scorcher considers this might be the only time he agrees with Four-Leaf, but not without blame.

CHAPTER 33

After three weeks of solitude in planning, surveying, placing markers, manually digging holes, maybe refilling holes, and piling up dirt for future dirt-geyser ambitions, Scorcher's work comes to an unexpected halt. Everything seems to break or go wrong. His suit gets torn and needs repair; the one digger-modified sheep helping him goes haywire and wanders off randomly for the hills; drill bits break more than normal; the power goes out; a shovel breaks; his sock gets a hole. And all of this started to occur when he reached one apparently sacrosanct location.

Five days earlier, there was a particular mound of rocks which was unusual in appearance and needed to be dug through. These were located about five-hundred meters from Central Lunar Mining. What made them unusual, even to Scorcher who has no interest or eye for geology, was their color and texture. They were of a reddish color, bold, in fact, and not covered in dust, as though they'd been polished, which on the surface of the gray Moon made them stand out. The mercury-colored lubricant used by some tools would turn red and organically bleed from the rocks—something he hadn't witnessed before. No humans or sheep had ever tracked around this area of ground before; no footprints or vehicle tracks had disturbed this lunar patch. When he first encountered the rocks along his pioneering path of running plumbing and power to his seventh regolith slurry hose, he stood there, staring in awe. Staring at the beauty. Staring at the novelty—the hue. Maybe he somehow ended up on Mars.

Then staring up into the sky, wondering if Earth really exists. Wondering if the invisible *can* exist, and if the Earth isn't his delusion. He jokes with himself that he's losing the concept of object permanence he developed as an infant. If Earth does exist, however, that means there are probably millions suffering worse than him, and he tries to use that fact to comfort himself. Millions are unable to solve their life's problems—so at least he's not one of them, he justifies.

* * *

"Ed, I don't know what's happening out there. Everything is going wrong. Are you able to fix some of the tooling?" Scorcher asks, hesitantly, knowing Ed's reputation for often making things worse or more broken in a new, creative way.

"That's no problem, Scorcher, I'll take care of it." Ed looks side to side to verify that no one else is within hearing range.

"What is it, Ed?" Scorcher snaps.

"Well, the Minister would definitely have a theory about this, based on what you've told me," says Ed. "Don't want to say too much on it though."

Scorcher reluctantly goes for the bait. "What did he tell you this time?"

"Well, about the mound of rocks, of course. The rocks that are giving you trouble. The rusty ones that you say really stand out."

Scorcher corrects Ed. "Well, it's not the rocks that are giving me trouble, it's all the tooling and the fact we're in this goddamned wasteland. I just barely made it to the reddish rocks themselves. It's just a coincidence. Causation isn't—"

"That's not what the Minister would say. Or Keystone or Ayubu, for that matter."

"I've never known Ayubu to talk in fairy tales."

Ed looks at Scorcher with wide eyes and a crinkled forehead but continues nonetheless, poking a finger into the listener's chest. "Maybe even Stabby would say differently, if he could talk. It's just bad luck. You should dig around the rocks. Not test fate. Don't cut through those rocks."

"What are you talking about?" says Scorcher. The conversation is making the hole in his sock more annoying. "You don't actually believe in ghosts or Moon elves or anything."

"No, of course not," Ed laughs. "But there are things such as luck. And whatever causes that luck, you'll never know. Not even I'm smart enough to know for sure."

Scorcher takes a deep breath. "Well, either way, can you fix the tooling? I need it so I can continue working *around* the mound of 'unlucky' rocks."

"Just remember, you're the one who called them unlucky. I'm just giving you advice, tried and true out here."

"Fair enough," says Scorcher. "I'll work around the haunted rocks. No need to fight it. So, is that why the Minister keeps stacking rocks on the ridge for Shigley?"

Ed nearly jumps out of this skin at the mention.

Scorcher can't tell if he looks shocked because what he's asking is obvious, or if it's more bad luck he is inviting by mentioning it at all. Or maybe he has hit a nerve deeper than that, has challenged the man's superstitions too persistently. Living in an extreme environment with no possibility of reprieve, knowing that it may end at any moment, Scorcher considers that Ed must have no choice but to accept the unknown and embrace the fantastical. Maybe superstition is the most logical order to the universe out here. But that doesn't make it any less annoying.

Frustrated, Scorcher unsympathetically turns around and walks away, wondering if the Christian Minister hasn't gone pagan, too.

In the meantime, while waiting for Ed to repair his tooling, he gets a couple days' worth of non-EVA work back indoors at CLM. The silver lining of this purgatory is that he no longer has to do scheduling, which is such a relief that even hard labor at the lunar gulag seems like Disneyland. He even tells Space-Bee that he couldn't be happier.

She's skeptical, but the weight off his chest tells him he's right. That is until the topic comes up of how Scorcher's efforts are helping promote Four-Leaf up a notch in his career to *senior* technical fellow, assuming the regolith slurry hoses are a success. Rumor has it that that could also bump him up to chief engineer of the newly announced Green Mars Initiative. At that, the weight is back like it had never been relieved.

Regardless, the benefit of mindless labor for Scorcher is mental time. He can regroup on his investigation into the radiation poisoning and the plausibly related death of Shigley. He knows the suffocation of project scheduling and defending his team against management would otherwise make him lose perspective on what really matters. And for the first time in days, he's not either out in the field or constantly accompanied within the walls of CLM.

He identifies goals and sets targets. First, access Shigley's laptop and perform exploratory computer science surgery. Second, retrieve any backup log data that was deposited on other digital devices from the time when Shigley had spacesuit problems. This can determine if there was a decompression event that suffocated him, or some other sabotage. Some code monkey wrote the spacesuit software to log any emergencies to any available computer memory hardware throughout the network, not just on the suit, to cover a case where the suit might not be recoverable postmortem. Scorcher doesn't understand why a centralized network wasn't used for this, but he benefits nonetheless from this very unusual coding paradigm. He may never know the original thinking.

On the day of action, he wakes up early before everyone else and leaves his cot while attempting not to wake Ayubu. He goes to get a coffee and stands in silence looking out of the window, as though he hasn't already seen enough of the Moon. It's completely silent except for the low drum of the ventilation system pumping breathable air replenished by lunar ice byproduct.

Out of habit, Scorcher rubs his eyes, irritated from the Moon dirt. He picks up his phone and reads a message he received yesterday from Space-Bee. In the text, she states that Shigley's instant messenger profile has reappeared mysteriously. Scorcher forgets to breathe. This might be from Shigley's laptop reconnecting to the network, which he hadn't intended.

"Has his laptop been doing that for days now?" he frets.

Scorcher briskly finishes his coffee in a gulp and heads to the central control room. He checks the drawer that Shigley's laptop is supposed to be in, and it isn't there.

"Where the fuck is it?" He checks the next drawer down, and it's sitting there with the power cord unplugged. He's only half relieved at finding it.

"Did I put it in this drawer, or was it unintentionally moved by someone else? I thought the battery needed to be charged…"

Behind him, he hears a familiar sound: "So, so, so." He turns.

But he sees no one there. Stabby is vacuuming and sporting a new, more impressive, joust mount. He drives back over the floor grate, and his spinning bristles make the sound "so, so, so" over the vent vanes. It looks like one of the technicians, probably Keystone, 3-D printed a larger knife mount.

"No time for this now." Scorcher turns away from Stabby.

He opens the laptop, and the power is on. It must have been moved by one of the other technicians. Maybe he'll try to nonchalantly ask Ayubu about it later. Though he doesn't have much time, because Four-Leaf is sending Ayubu, Ed, and Keystone back out to their Annies very soon. Albeit Four-Leaf and the Minister are probably the only ones who would come in here. He can worry about this later, he decides.

Virtually navigating through Shigley's laptop, he accesses the directory where his personal logs should be, but they're missing. Either that or he just never kept a daily status report because it wasn't required at the time. However, Shigley did keep copies of his medical checkups: blood pressure, blood O2 level, any symptoms or irritations, all collected by Seattle monthly via quick interviews. He wonders if this was out of mundane habit or if Shigley had a particular reason to archive his own copies.

It looks like he had serious radiation symptoms. Symptoms that initiated for Shigley well before his death and built up over time but are now in line with Space-Bee's current struggles. Nausea, vomiting, diarrhea, headache, fever, dizziness, trouble focusing. It looks like the doomed man was just abandoned, left to die, isolated from the rest on purpose. Scorcher calms himself down and tries not to let his heart race physically or to snap conclusions.

What's still unusual is that if Shigley did die from radiation poisoning, he would have been immobile for days prior to dying. There's no way he would have been able to be out in the field working.

Something else peculiar is what the spacesuit itself was doing. Fortunately for Scorcher, these data were autosaved on Shigley's laptop so there is no need to hack the emergency log files from another computer location. Finally something works out with this totally oddball computer network configuration.

He steps over a cruising Stabby to avoid injury. "Ah, you missed, you rodent," he says, literally talking down to him.

The digital datafile gives contradictory information. Every warning bell possible must have been going off. Within a moment's notice, all the spacesuit sensors started reading null or invalid numbers. Shigley's breathing and heart rate accelerated as though he'd been running. Then his breathing stopped, and he had cardiac arrest…no, wait, he didn't have cardiac arrest until a few seconds later. It looks like he passed out from carbon dioxide poisoning and possibly hypoxia? It wouldn't have happened that quickly, though. Something's not adding up.

It looks like he suffocated, but *not* from depressurization, which goes against what Four-Leaf supposedly told the Minister. After Shigley died, the suit started working normally and everything seemed fine, except with a corpse in it.

The O2 tanks were full with no leaks evident. Scorcher continues to speculate, wondering if it is possible that Shigley was "worked to death," committed suicide, or was killed intentionally by a staged incident. He could see someone committing suicide if they were in as hopeless a scenario as Shigley, but it might not have been his personality. Though many people under extreme stress and total isolation do have extreme thoughts on how to stop their pain.

What was he doing out there? Scorcher asks himself for the hundredth time. He pulls up the last work order number appended to the spacesuit's history log. Every time someone goes out on a spacewalk, there must be a work order number associated with it. Granted, oftentimes the astronaut doesn't provide a meaningful work order number for an actual task like "repair fuel pump 39h." They'll just check out a new number and write "normal operations/ standard settings" or something else meaningless that doesn't explain why they went out there. But maybe it could be informative. Scorcher just needs to figure out where the hell all that information is archived on the server. That could take forever since the current computer servers and network didn't exist during the early days of CLM. The data might not even be accessible from here.

He types the work order number into his notes on his smartphone for later investigation.

He stops with that trail for now and pulls up Shigley's personal emails. He finds messages where Shigley was complaining about signing a health waiver so that the company would not be responsible for injury or death, even from company neglect. Scorcher remembers signing the same waivers, that they agreed as part of working here there would be no legal jurisdiction other than the company itself, essentially existing even outside of international waters.

Shigley had quite a bit of back and forth with Seattle and complained that his mental health was suffering from being isolated from everyone else (only Four-Leaf, the Minister, and Keystone at the time) who all remained back at the partially constructed Central Lunar Mining.

His must have been the first Annie structure where a technician lived and tended sheep remotely, he ponders. He'd like to know more about who this tortured guy was and why he was so desperate, so isolated from everyone else.

He finds the "corrected" radiation statistics: Scorcher nearly falls out of his chair. Apparently Shigley was starting to think that all this radiation business was a coverup himself and didn't appreciate Seattle Medical's stratagem. The numbers are based on the proprietary data that Scorcher knew the Seattle Medical team had but wouldn't share. It seems that Shigley essentially had the same job as Space-Bee before being stationed on the Moon. So Shigley used to travel extensively through the Van Allen radiation belts, like the *Vegvisir* currently does. This was probably back when they were scouting for a site location to build CLM.

He quickly emails the radiation data to Space-Bee, but in the same email lies to her, saying that someone from Medical gave it to him confidentially. He doesn't like being dishonest but buries his conscience. Working off Shigley's laptop means he's creating a new digital trail of his investigation that someone else could look up in the future to indict him. He accepts that there is ultimately no way to really cover up his investigation, which means that he's rolling the dice on how long until the wrong person finds out.

Radiation, poison, death: the numbers themselves aren't as bad as Scorcher calculated. That's at least solid now. But nonetheless, the radiation is deadly. So assuming that the same environmental conditions and trends exist for Space-

Bee on the *Vegvisir* as they did for Shigley on the same ship, the following is certain: Space-Bee's DNA is irreversibly damaged. But by how much?

CHAPTER 34

"That guy cracks me up," Rocko chuckles aloud. "I see that Keystone gave him a new knife."

"Yeah," Scorcher confirms.

Both men are sitting in the café as Rocko's eyes track Stabby cleaning the floor. Scorcher is trying to track as well, but not Stabby. His mind obsesses over the information he's accumulated.

Maybe it's all too far-fetched to be real, he thinks. *Maybe I'm totally delusional for thinking that all these people would allow astronauts to shamefully suffer and die for profit.* Then he remembers the preventable airliner accidents at his previous employer and the failings of FAA intervention.

Rocko starts speaking again but Scorcher only catches the end of it. "...that guy cracks me up."

Didn't he just say that? Scorcher asks himself, feeling confused. He tries to say something to avoid admitting he hasn't been listening. "Yeah. Keystone sure is interesting." A few moments of awkward silence pass. Or is it only awkward to Scorcher? "So, no one has ever really explained to me how Stabby got armed."

Rocko is silent. *Ironic that he's not talking now,* Scorcher thinks.

"Well, man, Stabby was—or *is,* I should say—a legacy of Shigley," Rocko says, quieter than normal. "It's hard to explain, but everyone has just gotten used to him being around. He's a sure thing around here. You probably feel the same way, what with something new going wrong every day. Nice to have good ol' Stabby patrolling the halls, keeping us safe from the gremlins always terrorizing us."

Scorcher pulls back a bit. He's never been a huge fan of becoming attached to pets. However, he has grown attached to the little Moon Roomba—he did save his life from being crushed to death under a tank. "Yeah. Stabby's good to have around."

Rocko laughs. "Ah, I knew you were a softy." He slurps his coffee. "I can never tell with you. Always causing trouble or plotting something. Now they got you digging ditches." Rocko looks at Scorcher, smiles, and slaps him on the shoulder. "I've been there, man, though more in my earlier days when I was enlisted, doing God's work for America and freedom."

"So, Keystone and Shigley?" Scorcher inquires, revisiting his first question.

Rocko seems unsure how to answer. "Well, I know there was an accident with Shigley. He was killed on the job. I'll just say it straight. He wasn't careful with his life support or something. Not that I have proof. Seattle is vague about it, saying he also had a mental illness. They claim he was suffering from being overworked and made a few mistakes."

There's no way he made more mistakes than Ed, and he's still alive, Scorcher rashly counters in his mind. "So Shigley wanted a mascot?"

"Well, not exactly that either. The Minister claims he was suffering from Third Man Factor. If you know what that is."

"Yeah, I think so," Scorcher recalls. "The Minister explained it to me awhile back. It's when someone in isolation—like a mountain climber or arctic explorer—starts imagining that there is another person with them."

"Yes, that's basically it, brother," Rocko says. "Happens all the time. Even with an old, lonely widow, still talking to her partner who has been gone for years. But she doesn't know better."

"Or does she?" Scorcher adds.

"Well, maybe sometimes, sometimes not," Rocko says.

"Who was here when Shigley was?"

"Only the Minister, Keystone, Four-Leaf, and I have been here long enough to have worked with Shigley. Seems like a different time then. Space-Bee, Ed, and Ayubu all came after him, just like you. And our flight commander. But things did get weird with him before the mishap. I haven't really spoken about this since then, but I'll be straight. Like I said, the Minister claims he was suffering from Third Man Factor or Syndrome or whatever. Guardian angels," Rocko says in a mock spooky voice with a smirk on his face.

Scorcher suppresses his annoyance.

"But anyways, Stabby is *his* child. Or he took CLM's Roomba experiment and turned him into Stabby. Though the paranoia started leading to 'gremlins' wrecking equipment, turning stuff off that should have been on, misplacing tools. Being alone out here can really make your imagination run wild. That's why I stick with a ship full of ladies. But Shigley was a great guy, and Keystone really respected him. Keystone claims the sheep slaughter in the barn has happened before—happened to Shigley, who got reprimanded for it. Then apparently Four-Leaf took the opportunity to position himself as 'Seattle's eyes and ears,' which fast tracked him to the Technical Fellowship. That effectively swapped Four-Leaf's and Shigley's job roles. Keystone claims Four-Leaf moved him out to the Annie for being 'naughty' and not listening. But that's all hearsay to me, man. Who knows if he's being totally truthful or just imagining it. Seems like a tank must have exploded or something—not Shigley's fault. These sheep are complicated machines—a lot of moving parts, let alone each one has its own personality. This was not the right type of job for Shigley. He should have stayed on the *Vegvisir* or gone back to Earth. He was too extraverted for this shit." He attempts to joke while exaggerating a smile. "Not a weirdo like you guys."

"So you left and went back to Earth. But now you're back?"

The smile fades. "Yeah, that's right. I'm not a figment of your imagination." Rocko jabs his finger into Scorcher. "I think Space-Bee actually has the most flight time now, even though she came up last. Just kind of worked out that way. She is a real workaholic. Always volunteering to put herself through the grinder. It'll catch up to her one way or another, I know it."

I know it, too, thinks Scorcher. "So she's had the most radiation exposure."

The statement from left field has Rocko resettle his posture. "I suppose that would be correct. Though it's kind of complicated. But yeah, now that I think about it, she's had the most deep-space time outside the Van Allen belts, more than all the rest of us. Commander and I have spent most of our time in LEO and have had more leave time going back to Earth."

A few moments of silence follow as Rocko reminisces, then he says, "It's kind of funny. At first, everyone hated Stabby because he would jab your ankles or get in the way. He actually isn't all that effective at helping with the regolith issue."

"You don't think so?" Scorcher asks.

"No, well, yeah. Stabby is helpful. But the regolith still makes its way everywhere, like into your lungs." Rocko stands up to look out of the window. "When Shigley left to go to whatever outpost or—Annie, is short for what?"

"Ancillary structure."

"Right. That and acronyms—I'm bad at them. Shigley was pissed when that old fart Minister told him not to take Stabby with him. Minister has regretted that ever since. Brought it up quite a few times, actually. 'Shoulda let the boy have his pet.'"

"I didn't realize that. Interesting."

"But then one day, long after Shigley's death, he broke down—Stabby broke down, that is—and Keystone and the Minister felt they couldn't just let him return back to his default factory setting."

"I didn't realize Keystone and the Minister talked. Everyone seems so isolated now," observes Scorcher.

"Well, believe it or not, we used to be a lot more social. A lot more optimistic. These people have just been down here for too long. At least I get to see Earth on a regular basis—puts things back into perspective. Probably why Four-Leaf desperately tries to keep everyone talking by holding Stammtisch monthly. So anyways, now Stabby's become like a mascot here, and no one dares to fuck with that. Four-Leaf seems somewhat indifferent, but he's hard to read."

"So how did Shigley end up by himself?"

"The whole time, Shigley was quite ill, but he was too prideful to say anything. We all just assumed he was having a bad reaction to the regolith. At least that's what Four-Leaf and Seattle claimed. So having Stabby around him constantly made sense as well. Eventually, he had a list of reasons for wanting to go to the Annie: his commute was too intense, he wanted to be left alone. Seattle went along with it since they wanted to start spreading people out anyways."

Scorcher shakes his head and interrupts. "Four-Leaf said Shigley had regolith reactions? Since when does Four-Leaf not just defer anything medical related back to Seattle? And Shigley wanted to be 'left alone?' I thought you just said he was super extraverted and Four-Leaf forced him out of CLM against his will."

Rocko checks his phone quickly. "Yeah, he started acting weird," he says. "Not really himself. And then that whole spacesuit malfunction."

Scorcher unintentionally speaks before thinking, "That's not what the Minister claimed happened to him."

"Oh, really? What does he claim?" Rocko asks.

"Nothing specific. Just that he thought there was more to it."

"Really? Hmm." Rocko checks his cell phone. "Well, man, who knows, I guess. Anyways, back to the grind it is. Sorry to cut out. Later, man."

*　　*　　*

Scorcher wakes up before his shift to sneak over to see if the EVA suit logs can be traced on the dead man's laptop. He creeps past the rest area of the *Vegvisir* crew.

"Can't sleep, huh?" says Commander Ōtsuka.

"Good morning, Commander," replies Scorcher, straightening his posture.

"You were quite the sleepy head when I first dropped you off about a year ago. At ease," the flight commander says, half joking. "Or has it been a year?"

"Yes, ma'am, over a year. Time flies when you're having fun."

"Heard you got ditch duty. Good luck with that. Anyway, we're heading out soon. Ships up and ready and we have a timeslot to get us back to LEO to rendezvous with the European Space Station. Need to run a little errand for them. Seattle sold off our services for a quick buck. They were having some trouble with one of their cislunar rockets and needed to get an experiment out to the Moon for scientific surveying sooner than later. Carry on," the commander concludes her choppy statements and walks off. Rocko follows behind, smiles at Scorcher, and shakes his hand as he passes. Space-Bee trails behind, lost in her own thoughts, but also distracted by something physical. Though she is not covered in dust, her skin is more like the color of the Moon than ever.

She quickly adds after passing, "I haven't read your email yet. Don't worry, I'll get to it."

Scorcher has a sick feeling in his gut. The anxiety of how she might react. He starts questioning whether he should have even emailed her about the radiation data. He knows how emails can come across a lot stronger than talking in-person.

But isn't this serious? Can it be too strong? These games are wrecking Scorcher.

He reaches the control room, and the Minister is there. *Of course,* Scorcher thinks, *someone needs to help with the ground support of the* Vegvisir *launch.*

"Here to lend a hand, lad?" the Minister asks.

"Sure."

"Good," the Minister replies. "Go suit up. You unhook the snake before she takes off. I've had enough years of that rubbish. That's all I ask as I live out my last few days in hell dealing with you lot."

CHAPTER 35

The completely silent and fiery white avalanche rushes towards his face shield. It's like a scene from a bad movie. He has never seen something so rapid and yet prolonged at the same time. Exhaust from the *Vegvisir*'s hydrogen powered rocket sandblasts Scorcher's spacesuit for his first lunar hurricane. He's standing way too close to the launch pad—the Minister didn't stop him.

After everything settles and Scorcher picks himself back up, he mentally pats himself on the back for surviving an experience he and the other techs always joke about. He figures experiences are all he has left anyway, even if it means destroying company spacesuit property. He knows Seattle will chew him out for this, but he grins at the thought.

After checking that his limbs are still intact, he starts laughing in the most absolute sense, with an intensity proportional to the detonation of endorphins. Making it back to the airlock, he is still laughing like a maniac. He wonders if he has completely lost it but doesn't really care for the moment.

He unexpectedly passes the Minister down the hall inside CLM, whose eyes—for the briefest moment—are clear. "We laugh at funerals and cry at weddings," he mumbles, then exists like he never existed.

After a sad protein-carbohydrate bar breakfast, Scorcher works an entire shift doing ditch duty. Luckily there's more planning and surveying than actual digging for today's shift, and most awesomely no project scheduling or dealing with Four-Leaf.

After this shift is done, he heads back to the pressure lock and re-enters CLM. Checking his phone, he notices that Space-Bee has sent him a series of messages. She needs his help and complains that her symptoms are becoming debilitating, and it keeps getting dismissed by Seattle. Commander Ōtsuka is not amused and is starting to demand some answers from Seattle Medical. The randomness of her language and thoughts concerns him.

The *Vegvisir* is currently sailing around the Moon in a parking orbit before performing a cislunar maneuver to head back to low Earth orbit. Scorcher heads to the control room by himself and sits at a computer station, not for any other reason than to converse with Space-Bee. Continuing the pattern of no restraint, he doesn't hold back and decides he won't quit until Space-Bee helps him expose the conspiracy for herself.

Scorcher writes: *You looked horrible earlier.*

Space-Bee writes: *I feel horrible. I can barely function. I'm nauseous.*

Scorcher writes: *Rip off one of those damned panels and tear it apart. Prove that the fungus is dead. I'll send you a picture of what the dead fungus looks like.*

Space-Bee writes: *Commander Ōtsuka is holding us off and keeping us in a lunar parking orbit. She's refusing to fly directly through a radiation hot spot in the Van Allen belts, which Seattle trajectory originally intended for us to do.*

Scorcher writes: *Understood. So what does she think?*

Scorcher doesn't hear back from Space-Bee for about

forty-five minutes. He's tempted to type another message, but she responds first.

Space-Bee writes: *We've torn off 4 of the panels against Seattle's order and disassembled them. The fungus is all dried out and totally dead. We doubt there is any radiation shielding.*

Scorcher writes: *Expose them! WTF!*

Space-Bee writes: *They've already responded. Seattle claims a Chinese-sponsored company has been attacking us, but they can't give many details at this time. Maybe an engineered virus that kills the fungus. Maybe a microwave attack, like at the embassies back on Earth.*

Scorcher writes: *You know that's absurd bullshit. Did they just make that up now? Who are you talking to?*

Space-Bee writes: *I'm too sick to argue that, Scorcher. But Commander isn't pursuing it further at this time, not in front of me at least. Maybe it's related to the previous unexplained issues like the one you had to repair on your cislunar spacewalk when we first met. I'm busy, gotta go.*

Scorcher writes: *Be careful.*

He knows it's a cover up by the Company, deflecting attention from the safety shortcuts they've taken and the failed fungal technology. It's complete incompetence and arrogance, not a viral attack by a foreign government. Does the Founder know? He must, Scorcher thinks. He's probably the one leveraging Sinophobia as a distraction, though he's such a social media cartoon character, who knows how the Founder is involved.

Either way, the cat is out of the bag, and the shit is going to hit the fan around here. Word is going to get out. This is going to disrupt everything and cause a general revolt from all the technicians here. Or at least he hopes it does. Where will Four-Leaf stand?

CHAPTER 36

A firm tap on the shoulder jolts him: Scorcher has been called into a meeting with Four-Leaf and the Seattle team to receive comments back on the technical and safety recommendations that he made his first days here. He's sitting in the tiny video-conference room—as usual, the video link isn't working—to discuss an agenda that isn't fully known to Scorcher. For someone who has mostly been cut off from important work, the promptness is troubling. This was all so many lifetimes ago that he's almost not certain that he ever submitted those recommendations himself.

A representative from Human Resources introduces herself saying that she'll be casually sitting in. Then another voice on the phone—a name that Scorcher can never remember—says, "Mr. Robertson, maybe bring us up to speed on the recommendations you made earlier?"

"You mean over a year ago? Sorry, my memory isn't that good. Too much head trauma from exploding pipes caused by corporate shortcuts," Scorcher says in a tone matching the words. "I mean, you did call this meeting. Don't you have an agenda?"

Seattle goes on mute for a few moments. Scorcher looks up to see Four-Leaf wearing his poker face, clearly not daydreaming of faraway places. Scorcher recalls how he once creepily told him not to give up so easily. Then, in a friendly manner, "You know, guys, I can summarize it for Jill and Bob, if you'd like."

Seattle unmutes, "Go ahead, Mr. O'Connor. Thank you."

"Certainly," Four-Leaf begins. "First, there was the matter of the 3-D printed build file for a structural fitting for the ammonia plumbing. The fitting detail that had a leak on the external bulkhead."

Scorcher thinks back to when he and Space-Bee watched the snow fall the first day he was here.

"There was apparently an issue with the build file, but I personally have not come across that issue before. It was probably just a random fluke or user error."

"Have you ever actually tried?" Scorcher says.

Four-Leaf continues without stopping, "Second was his assignments for the mining technicians to open up a lot of things that don't need to be disturbed for inspections, but this has all been handled by me recently after the incident in the barn."

"The barn?"

"Sorry, Jill. I mean the storage room that had inexplicable damage when Scorcher was alone."

"Oh, right. Thanks for clarifying."

Four-Leaf continues, "Opening things up for inspections can sometimes cause more harm than good. A lot of this equipment is quite delicate."

A random male voice on the phone replies, "Ah, yes. Thank you."

Scorcher adds under his breath, "If by 'delicate' you mean poorly built with no foresight considered."

"Lastly, there were some recommended upgrades to the EVA helmets that I, and you all, deemed superfluous, and frankly not practical," says Four-Leaf, leaning towards the speaker phone. "I believe we would void our life insurance warranty if we don't have our spacesuit supplier make the changes themselves."

"Ah, yes, good point," says the phone.

Good point for a bean counter, Scorcher thinks. *For them it's natural to be riskier with someone's life than with their insurance coverage.*

Getting past the outlandish life insurance argument being made by Four-Leaf and Seattle, Scorcher has to think about what exactly he recommended for spacesuit upgrades. He doesn't actually remember making any recommendations on the spacesuits, but he is uncertain. He thinks he just recommended inspections and not upgrades. Four-Leaf's generous imagination might just be throwing him under the bus.

Scorcher isn't paying attention, but some other meeting items are covered. Then they make their way back to Scorcher's recommendations.

"We agree with you, Mr. O'Connor. Those items from last year can be closed. Resolution: canceled. No further action required."

"Thank you," says Four-Leaf, straightening his posture.

Scorcher curls with more than a hint of defeat. Though he has no idea what Four-Leaf's victory actually is. Is it control? Is it territorial? Is it some petty power move? Is it that everyone thinks Scorcher is an idiot and Four-Leaf feels lifted by it?

Seattle directs him to follow Four-Leaf's lead from here on out and to stop any further side investigations he may be doing.

Scorcher stands up and asks rhetorically, "Why did you even send me here?" He walks out of the room without being excused and heads towards the control room out of muscle memory.

"I guess he's dismissed, then," he can hear Four-Leaf saying.

Moments later, he arrives in the control room but doesn't know why he chose to come here. That's what his leg muscles wanted, he supposes. He sits down at the desk and stares at the bulkhead for a moment, pondering what's expected of him. Digging ditches? Laying pipe? Is he even considered an engineer anymore? Probably not, he concludes, though no one has told him that explicitly. Maybe that's implied strongly enough since they've taken away all his responsibilities.

Scorcher stands up from the computer station and turns around. He flinches as he sees the Minister standing there, staring at him with eyes he doesn't think he's ever seen before: terror, confusion, disgust, anger. He looks down at what the Minister is holding, half hugging to his chest, and realizes his own actions have doomed him on a very personal level.

CHAPTER 37

Unable to speak, the Minister has frozen in place. It looks like he wants to speak, but the words don't come out, blocked by a newly formed aphasia. His posture is as upright as he can make it, but the result is still a slouch. Even though the minuscule gravity isn't strong enough to compress his spine, the old man has shrunk from years on the Moon.

Though taller, Scorcher feels he is looking up at the Minister.

"The rocks on the ridge were disturbed," the Minister spits out, which is curious to Scorcher since he doesn't first mention what he is holding. Albeit he may be pasting together a much bigger story. Scorcher knows he often doesn't jump straight to the punch line. He unwillingly focuses on a grotesque purple scar and wound refusing to heal on the Minister's hand.

"Last time I traveled past it, when coming back a few weeks ago, the stones were disordered, and I didn't have time to set it right and give my prayer of peace to him. At first, I thought the way I was placing the stones was wrong. I thought I was to blame for not making it right. For not making amends for the kid."

"Oh," Scorcher says stupidly.

The Minister's cheeks rise and his eyes squint, showing

his dentures like he's staring into the sun.

"Are you asking about the extra laptop I found?" Scorcher tries to lie and instantly regrets it.

The Minister jabs the edge of the laptop into Scorcher's chest. A random ill-timed thought comes to Scorcher's mind about how he doesn't remember the Minister's real name.

"And you tampered with his body for some reason. I didn't bury this laptop with the stacked stones, the stones on the ridge that should never be touched. I buried it with the poor guy, the one who you should never mention out of respect for him. Come clean with me, or I'll kill you right here! I swear on Shigley's grave I will—the grave you have defaced!" the Minister shouts.

Scorcher is unable to answer. The silence between them lasts for centuries. Scorcher hopes this magically ends somehow without him having to take the initiative.

"Answer me, boy," the interrogation continues. "I know whose this is." And this time he strikes Scorcher with it, hard enough to break it apart. Scorcher instinctively squats to protect himself. He now stands hunched over and turned away from the ancient man who has seen too much rubbish and abuse himself. Computer pieces scatter on the floor and tumble along in a way that would seem unnatural if they were in Earth's gravity.

The Minister spins the shamed man around, like a child who has committed an unforgivable crime and must be charged as an adult.

Scorcher speaks up, stammering, "I needed to know what happened to Shigley. I think whatever happened to him is happening to all of us. I think Seattle is lying about our radiation exposure and we're all slowly dying out here. I think Shigley's suit was sabotaged to depressurize so Seattle could hide that they've been incorrectly calculating our radiation exposure. I think this is corporate murder, and I suspect that is only the tip of the iceberg and this whole operation is a disaster waiting to—"

The Minister takes a step back, almost seeming appeased that Scorcher has finally spoken up. "What you did was wrong, boy. I cannot face you now. You have disturbed the dead. Never in my life—" the Minister stops there, turns around while weakly reaching for the door frame, and leaves the room unfocused, with only a small part of Shigley's keyboard in his hand, likely unaware he is still holding it. He slowly disappears around the corner, dragging his heavy feet.

"I ran an experiment with the radiosynthesizing panels from the *Vegvisir*," Scorcher yells after him. "It's all bullshit," Scorcher means to yell, but he has not been managing his breath and it comes out raspy and he starts coughing. The Minister doesn't hear him anyway. Stabby drives off after him, who Scorcher didn't even realize was there.

Scorcher considers that his action to investigate Shigley's death has gone too far: digging up the grave, stealing the radiation panel from the *Vegvisir*, playing all these games. How has he let this get so far?

He sits back down and ponders what the hell is going to happen next. Is he really in the wrong? he asks himself. Why does he feel like the villain in all of this?

In the surveillance video feed, he sees the Minister suiting up to go back over to his hangar where he can be safe again in his private cave, probably to go lie down and die. He wonders if he'll mention his discovery to anyone else. This leaves Scorcher alone with Four-Leaf at Central Lunar Mining, just the two of them now, plus Stabby. Scorcher is physically shaking from anxiety right now.

He rises from his seat and starts collecting the laptop debris, the last broken bits of a dead man, broken by his tenure on the Moon. Scorcher sees himself as Shigley now: someone who strove to push through to the heavens, but like the others, only found hell.

*　　*　　*

Four-Leaf sends out an email to everyone to inform them that the next Stammtisch is canceled in light of recent events, which he doesn't explain. However, Scorcher is unable to control himself and responds to the email, to everyone on the distribution, to make his case that there has been a conspiracy to cover up Shigley's death and justifies his actions for tampering with the grave. But he fails to provide a thorough context. He panics when he realizes the confusion he must have caused by defending a grave-digging incident that basically no one else even knew about.

He waits, but no one ever responds to his email.

After a few hours, Seattle holds a special meeting to discuss the "implications of recent events." They call Scorcher in.

His lungs seem unable to fully inflate as he walks from his cot to the meeting room. The skin on his arms and legs feels hot. He enters the room—déjà vu—to see Four-Leaf leaning over the speakerphone, Seattle obviously on the line.

"Mr. Robertson, we don't understand why you told the *Vegvisir* crew that Seattle Medical had given you radiation data when they had not," they start peppering immediately. "There is no conspiracy, so we're confused as to why you're making it out as one. Also, cyber security is going to conduct an investigation into how you invented this data, or if you inappropriately accessed confidential personal identifiable information. We expect your full cooperation."

Scorcher sits and takes a deep breath. "I need a breath first."

"Sure, check your O2," says a different unsympathetic voice through the speaker. Her name is a blank to him now.

They all sit in silence. Scorcher starts thinking about how they must know by now about the grave digging but are prioritizing asking about his crime of running numbers to double-check safety. Even with egregious acts like gravedigging, misuse of company resources, trespassing on launch vehicles, and unexplained mass destruction in the barn, Seattle interrogates him about undermining their official company line on radiation data. A year ago, this wouldn't have made sense to him.

Everything that Scorcher has calculated—either from sensor data, his sheep experiment, or data he stole from the now destroyed laptop—he knows now is superfluous ever since Space-Bee messaged him that the *Vegvisir* crew confirmed the radiosynthesis fungi had all died. It is impossible to know if the fungi ever worked as a shield in the first place. Or maybe not impossible, but the facts are concealed in inaccessible history, guarded by a bureaucracy engineered for self-preservation like any other organism.

These people are so out of touch with what's really important, Scorcher thinks. But then he corrects himself: what he thinks is important is not aligned with Company values—the *actual* Company values. He's a tool and a commodity, not the hero astronaut, but just like any other person in a corporation or government agency.

Knowing there is no chance at getting those on the phone to acknowledge that they are in the wrong and need to fundamentally reconsider everything they've done in their careers, he tells them to "fuck off" and leaves the room. Four-Leaf is completely silent with his arms folded, leaning back and sitting calmly.

*　　*　　*

Scorcher goes to his safe place to get coffee.

Then Four-Leaf strolls into the café, which seems strange to Scorcher because he hasn't seen him in this room for months. The café *was* a safe place—melancholy, but safe—until now. The technical fellow, the king of the Moon hill, pastes faux sympathy on his face. Scorcher stares back.

Four-Leaf initiates the dialog. "It's time to pack your bags, mate. The *Vegvisir* is coming back to get you. Seattle doesn't want you doing any more assignments."

No more ditch digging, Scorcher thinks.

"And your suit has been remotely deactivated. So you can't leave the main campus. If there's anything you need from the Minister, you'll have to go through me."

"Exactly how you like it." Scorcher hasn't even realized that the spacesuits could be deactivated remotely. He strongly suspects Four-Leaf is lying to him. He kind of wants to steal a spacesuit just to piss him off. How far can he go with it?

"But in the meantime, mate, you get to take a couple days off. You've been awarded the first lunar weekend in our history. So, really, you're coming out ahead, mate. You've won this round."

Scorcher feels the skin on his shins, calves, and forearms burning. They must be turning bright red. He's forgetting to breathe.

Four-Leaf continues. "But then let's meet up first thing at the beginning of your shift after your weekend. We still need your help doing scheduling, and maybe bringing my coffee. You have the most insight into both those things. And since your EVA pressure suit is deactivated, I might swap some parts with mine. There is a slight leak with one of the gloves. So until that gets repaired, I'll be staying full time with you at Central Lunar Mining."

They stand in awkward silence for a while. It's almost as though Four-Leaf is waiting for a reaction, but Scorcher is empty.

Before bailing to go back to his work—whatever the fuck it is that Four-Leaf does for work—Four-Leaf repeats something that Scorcher confidentially to Ayubu when no one else was around. "You'll have plenty of time to teach Stabby how to dance."

Scorcher is caught-off guard and feels exposed on a new level. All he does is stare at Four-Leaf, who reacts to Scorcher's facial expression by telling him, "You are your own worst antagonist."

CHAPTER 38

After Four-Leaf's snide comments, Scorcher bails on him—or is it that Four-Leaf left first? Scorcher is uncertain later. But the firestorm of recent events in his mind escapes through his arms as he pounds the desk with his fist. He slams his fist with all his force. Energy directed from his heart to his arms. He loses his senses and doesn't even know what room he is in or what desk he is pounding. He pulls a muscle in his back during the process, collapsing in pain and exhaustion.

Scorcher can't believe he has been duped in so many ways. He feels stupid for not realizing that Four-Leaf has been using Stabby to spy and audio record on him. There really is no winning here. This Moon labor camp and slave-colony is wholly governed by corporate pigs on Earth, managed by a sociopath as the sergeant, with minion technicians—the real sheep here—doing their bidding while only looking out for their own skin minute by minute. The only sense of control they get is from the molestations of their own robotic sheep.

I'm not the bad guy here, am I? Am I the fuck up? he asks.

He searches for any type of comfort and reassurance, any symbolic bedrock. Space-Bee's condition is too much to accept, so he mentally wanders to Ayubu's smile and friendliness. He'll always remember that first smile and warmth. He's going to really miss Ayubu, even though they had few off-hours time together in person. He is so smart and sociable, and so much better in so many ways, including surviving.

But Scorcher *knows* they are all getting poisoned from radiation. He *knows* they are all shamelessly lying to him. He *knows* this place is a ticking time bomb. He *knows* that they are all just numbers and assets balanced for tax and insurance purposes on spreadsheets. He *knows* that there will be another accident, but the end justifies their means. He *knows* nothing will change because of economic incentive. He *knows* the culture can't change and there is nothing he can do about it. He *knows* everyone else has sold their soul or gone to the dark side like Four-Leaf, who is futilely trying to make his own universe by being the chief pawn in a billionaire's game to outdo his other billionaire rivals.

He is beyond drained and directs all his hate towards his most visible threat and target of blame: Four-Leaf. In his fit of rage, Scorcher walks down the hall, past Stabby, whom he didn't realize he was developing an attachment to until learning of his betrayal. Who and what else has been spying on him? Is Space-Bee an informant, too?

He arrives at the staging room just before the pressure lock near the barn and contemplates just walking naked out into space. He sees his own spacesuit and Four-Leaf's, side-by-side.

Scorcher turns to walk into the barn. A tsunami passes through him again. His whole life he has been "freeze" or "flight." But in this environment, it is "freeze" or "burn." Black shadows, blinding white, day in and day out.

"Freeze and burn! And nothing in between!" Scorcher yells, unrecognizable to himself.

His mind has been cold-worked to a new state. It is now a weapon of higher strength and piercing power but mended to higher brittleness. Scorcher comes back from the barn.

He destroys Four-Leaf's spacesuit. Damage that cannot be remedied: smashes, slashes, and punctures. Torn wires and a broken face shield—not a trivial effort. The revenge doesn't provide any ease. It's just directed anger and directed insanity that needs to go to someone else. Like all life suffering, it must be transferred indiscriminately to both the evil and the innocent. It is the only way. It needs to be directed to targets. There is no choice for Scorcher. He has no free will, and his only escape is destruction. He lashes out further until he has spent every last ounce of energy. He is worn.

Calm washes the weight from his chest. He mentally respawns without any thoughts or drive; his mind is blank. Then, it turns inward.

He can now start his weekend with immediate regrets. Immediate regrets for the destruction he's just caused. Immediate regrets for losing control. Immediate regrets for any decision he's ever made. Immediate regrets for even being born, somehow justifying to himself that he is at fault for his own birth. He sleepwalks back to his bunk then lays on his cot. Breathing heavily, he closes his eyes.

*   *   *

On his first day off, he awakens and no longer has tunnel vision. He notices that people have a different attitude towards him when he pitifully tries to communicate with them via instant messenger. It's not until later in the day, after a lonely lunch, that he starts to recall how he sabotaged Four-Leaf's spacesuit. His heart drops upon this unexpected rediscovery. Was it a dream? He hopes for the best, hopes that he is mistaken and that it was only some confusion and delusion caused by stress. But he needs to find out for himself.

He walks past the room where Four-Leaf is chatting with the management in Seattle.

The technical fellow has been able to turn the mining technicians and Seattle Corporate against Scorcher, after his show-stopping behaviors of investigating Astronaut Shigley's death and challenging authority.

Scorcher returns to his room. His temporary hysteria yesterday is still not clear to him, but the results are real. His flashback was not a dream.

Scorcher lies on his cot with thoughts of saving himself through death. The simple solution to stop the pain. A simple and final act of passive-aggressive vengeance to those around him. A classic "they'll feel bad when I'm gone" sort of resolve. He gets up to create a makeshift curtain around his bunk. He pulls the curtain closed. It feels like a coffin.

In his mind, he goes over his failures—his failure of not being a pilot like his mom wanted for him, his falling short of being an adventurer, a lover, to have a purpose.

Miraculously, his death is postponed—his plot of suicide vanishes—due to someone else's premature death.

As Scorcher is researching on his smartphone about ways to kill himself, he gets news from an uncle he forgot about that his estranged cousin was recently found in an indistinct field in Ohio. Apparently, she fell into psychosis last night, coincidentally at the same time as Scorcher's delirium, her mind protecting itself from a lifetime of abuse and neglect. And she was found dead this morning.

His commitment to harm himself evaporates at this news. For many hours, he just lies there, in the dark, behind the curtain, without any thoughts, his mind holding the universe at bay until he's ready to exist again.

*   *   *

Through an unknown inspiration, he frantically gets up, turns on the light, and finds the only available physical paper and pen. He starts writing a letter to his cousin who has just passed away. It takes him all evening, crying and writing at the same time.

Is this what life is? Is this all there is?

Something writes through Scorcher without his direction: he writes to save her, he is out of his control, an intertwining of emotion and something invisible and greater than himself. His pen is driven by this force.

My Cousin J—,

Twenty-two years ago, I last spoke to you in person. A lifetime ago is an inaccurate description: another existence, a different story, a mismatched perception. The subsequent years since then don't appear as a straight and clean path when I look back. They appear more as an aged road. I see scattered cobblestone blocks in the general direction of the past, some turned over, some broken, some missing, some thrown to the side, some still neatly in place, or in some cases a piece chipped off and left in my pocket for sentimental purposes as I continue on my journey forward.

I sometimes forget those mementos are in my pocket at all. Or that I even have pockets, until something external reminds me. But it causes me to pause the world and the universe—just for a moment—when I accidentally find these chips, which are now worn and have become less sharp as I travel farther down the road.

As I look closely again, I realize my path is not solitary. It isn't a single path at all. But many paths intertwine and cross. It's covered in footprints originating from other paths, going back and forth. Everything crisscrossing, not so separated after all. Sometimes bricks are shared, and sometimes bricks are stolen from other roads.

When the clouds arrive, I can't see as distinctly. But when the clouds part, I do see more clearly, remembering that what I forgot, I haven't forgotten.

The cobblestones, crushed from anger and defeat, I grind into sand as a mortar. I use it to hold together the newly laid fresh bricks for my new fresh road, the road of now, in the present. The mortar is strong, stronger than it would be without the sand—the sand of pain, destruction, suffering. The sand of life. The more bricks that are destroyed in the past, the more mortar and cement I have to build the future, the stronger my road becomes, until I'm uniquely different from the rest. Living in the present, going forward, people admire the road that's laid, not realizing that my secret ingredient is the tears of my experience, and they are what makes my road most worth traveling. What a tragedy it would be to stop at this point.

This is the message I wrote for you, hoping that you can relate, at least in some way. I'm not sure what it means in its entirety, but in my heart I feel it is meant for you most surely, so I pass it on with full sincerity.

Your cousin Sam
The Moon

He takes the letter he just wrote and scorches it. It's in the past now, nothing but ashes.

Just like the rain, the wind, his home. All of it he ran from, and for what?

His cousin's wrists are inches from his eyes, shiny quicksilver dripping along the cuts.

He starts screaming, "All I want is to go home! I want my

home! I'm a fucking failure!" He wipes his face then says more quietly, "I tried to do what's right. Sacrifice myself for everyone else. And people like Four-Leaf still just shit all over me! And everyone lets it happen to boost their own career scorecards." His vision is blurred from the tears, from something other than a Lunarman's salt-burn. But he doesn't allow himself to cry, and through clenched teeth, he spits, "They all know I'm a fucking joke."

After a few moments of breathing, a clarity manages to reappear.

He knows the story of his cousin's death isn't a story of the deceased as much as it is a story of those still living. That's what he must fight for. Her death isn't some isolated event in a linear, stand-alone epic. He sees now we're an infinite volume of novellas, each one folded into the tragedies and triumphs of all others. All these stories have value and meaning, otherwise they couldn't exist. And from this he knows there is no single truth for time. As in the life and physics of the universe, all perspectives from any point of reference are valid, unable to contradict one another due to their mutual invariance and linking.

The thoughts of those on any frontier, so far from home, are shared, across all times: unchanged by any change, unaffected by any effect, but perhaps invisible to the observer, concealed by desires, feelings, intellect, or experience.

He rehydrates himself with the Moon's water and gives his mind a break for a moment. But then he can't help himself.

Staring at the walls, he wonders if there is any absurd meaning buried in the marks and scuffs from the wear and tear.

Space-Bee interrupts by reaching out to him.

CHAPTER 39

He hasn't realized yet that it's technically day two of his suspension because he hasn't slept yet. But Space-Bee's note brings him back to reality. She needs his help: a purpose is still slated for him. Scorcher reads her message three times to fully understand it.

Apparently Four-Leaf lied to him: Space-Bee confirms that the *Vegvisir* is not coming to take Scorcher back to Earth. At least as far as she knows, and there aren't many secrets on that spacecraft. In addition to that, she claims to not have any real insight into the drama that Scorcher has been living with the Minister, Four-Leaf, and the other technicians. Other than the fact he broke into some old shack and rebooted an old laptop he happened to find. But she doesn't admit to any knowledge of gravedigging. To his relief, the crew of the *Vegvisir* is ignorant of his actions and struggles, as they have their own, which is enough to spare him a speck of dignity.

Space-Bee is panicked. The crew is on edge. And frankly they don't really give a shit what's happening on the Moon right now. He wonders if all this Moon drama isn't just petty, his self-pity overblown. Perspective is everything, and it's impossible to maintain when living in solitary confinement. From what he can tell, Space-Bee and the *Vegvisir* are going to do course corrections to head straight back to low Earth orbit, with instructions to switch out the crew. The *entire* crew. Not the normal rotation where one person leaves, two people stay, and a single new replacement arrives. Originally, Rocko was going to trade out with a new replacement, Space-Bee was going to train the replacement, and Space-Bee was going to be prepped by Commander Ōtsuka to take over command. But none of that is happening now. They are to bring the ship back to 450 kilometers altitude over Earth, which is a relatively high LEO, then use the escape capsule to return to civilization. This means leaving the *Vegvisir* on autopilot and in the hands of Seattle control after sealing all the internal pressure hatches and disembarking. Commander Ōtsuka is not amused, to say the least, at Seattle's urgency and the lack of information about why. The backup crew will be arriving to board the *Vegvisir* at an undetermined date. No further explanation provided. As Space-Bee continues to explain, they are now avoiding the Van Allen belt radiation hot spots, but their trajectory coming back to Earth is going to be quite "aggressive."

She confesses it is unknown to everyone how long the *Vegvisir* will be empty and dormant, floating silently in a vacuum. Two weeks? Two months? Two years? What does this mean for basic support of the crew on the Moon? Is this another secret Four-Leaf keeps? The *Vegvisir* was the closest thing to an evacuation plan or lifeboat in case things on the Moon became unsustainable or not livable. Scorcher draws the analogy of an underwater diver going so far into a cave that if there is trouble with the oxygen tank, there is no way to make it back safely to the surface in time via such a serpentine path. Was the *Vegvisir* ever really that accessible to begin with in the event of a real emergency? Either way, not having a crewed supply ship continuously circling between here and Earth feels different to Scorcher. The drawbridge is not up, it's gone.

Scorcher doesn't know what to do about the fact the Four-Leaf lied to him and instructed him to pack his bags. Should he still play along? It's going to be an awkward Monday morning.

After reading her surprisingly concise message countless times, to miss no details for his distracted mind, he heads to the café. He selfishly notices that he might really suffer by not having the *Vegvisir* come back in a while: the coffee supply is low. In the meantime, however, until they get the trajectories recalculated, Scorcher can look up in the sky and see the sun's reflection off the *Vegvisir* as it flies overhead. Now that the shadow of the Moon is upon him, the *Vegvisir* is the brightest object in the sky.

CHAPTER 40

Scorcher wakes to complete silence and darkness. He wonders if he's dead. He opens his eyes and sees only red light. He wonders if he's in hell. Then he comes to more fully. CLM is shut down: the silence woke him. Panic strikes him like a hot blade slicing through his brain, as though he's having a stroke: the emotional scab is torn off his neurological trauma center once again—more vulnerable each time.

Scorcher sprints to the control room via hallways illuminated with red flood lights.

What could it possibly be now?

Four-Leaf is pushing buttons firm enough to break fingernails, if his weren't partially missing. "Seattle, CLM, do you copy?" He makes another attempt over the cislunar frequency. "*Vegvisir*, this is CLM, are you hearing us, mates?"

There were no explosions this time, at least none that Scorcher felt. For about two minutes, Four-Leaf completely ignores Scorcher until finally his persistence succeeds into a microsecond of down time. He responds, "There's a network error on all wireless and hardline communication systems routing through us."

Scorcher isn't quite sure what that even means. *Error with which network?*

"Life support systems nominal," he says.

Stabby is aimlessly rushing the halls, arbitrarily swinging the knife around.

"Is that on the Microsoft Windows side or the Linux side?" Scorcher asks. The CLM systems were originally divided such that half the network ran on Windows and the other half on Linux. Not so much on purpose, but it happened that way. Scorcher has been slowly migrating network functions to Linux for improved reliability, with the goal of sunsetting the ancient Windows Operating System.

"It's the Windows side. It's a planned network outage."

"Then why the panic?"

Four-Leaf stops typing for a moment and squints his eyes shut. "It's not a panic," he says clenching his jaw. "During the security patch update and the planned network outage, it unexpectedly broke a lot of our legacy computer processes that should have been unrelated and unaffected. We need to run through the code and figure out how to fix it for the short term."

Another Band-Aid fix.

"Most importantly, we need to make sure mining isn't affected, which I don't think it is."

Most importantly, Scorcher curses in his head. "But we can't talk to anyone?"

"We lost communication with Seattle and all the Annies."

"Even the Annies?"

"The backup quantum internet and QEC is only working at 10% fidelity." Four-Leaf turns to run through checklists.

Scorcher stands there not knowing what to do. "Where's the *Vegvisir*? Are they overhead? We can probably just bounce a signal off them." Scorcher is tempted to run to the break room and peek out the window.

Four-Leaf looks at his watch. "They should be overhead now." In lieu of using the headset, which seems to have been misplaced, he grabs the hand mic, which hasn't been used in years. He blows off the dust and tries over the radio.

Every word that Four-Leaf speaks attacks Scorcher with unease, given all the circumstances up until this point. He can't stand hearing Four-Leaf's voice but knows he needs to stay to help. It's tempting to bail and leave Four-Leaf to figure it out, but his concerns for Space-Bee, Ayubu, and the others are an anchor to keep him from turning around and escaping under the bed covers.

Communication is finally established with the *Vegvisir* when there is a direct line-of-sight from their transitory lunar parking orbit.

"Hey, man, glad to hear from you," Rocko says over the intercom. Scorcher wonders why Rocko is the one who sounds surprised and relieved.

Four-Leaf explains that their planned network outage on the Windows side has backfired and basic communication is down, which normally isn't the end of the world, but the problem seems propagated.

"This is just our backup ham radio. I'm glad my jury-rigged wiring got it to work. I think it's the first time I've ever tuned to a frequency with an analog dial." Rocko continues to explain that they had the same unexpected blue-screen-of-death from an update he was doing. But to be frank, he's quite baffled at what's going on, especially since telemetry that would allow them to land in case of an emergency isn't working.

To Scorcher, this is reminiscent of the failed crew capsule docking to the International Space Station back in 2019, which was caused by software mishaps.

"Will you be 'good to go' by your next pass?" Four-Leaf asks.

"Negative, boss," says the radio. "I can't totally reboot the local network because life support, navigation, communication, everything is on one network system instead of being parallel and independent. So, it's tricky to partially reload and repair the corrupted operating system. I don't even know what's going on, man."

"So they have *no* communication with Seattle," Scorcher states incredulously.

Four-Leaf doesn't react.

Rocko continues over the radio waves, "It's going to take about eight hours to fix all this up here, I'm guessing. So, multiply that by three to be realistic. One of the critical computer scripts is stuck in an infinite loop since the blue screen popped up, locking up unrelated functions. I want to be careful exiting the loop."

Scorcher starts a rant. "So first, they broke NASA coding protocol by using while-loops with no upper bound, dynamic memory allocation after initialization, and recursive coding like what developer weenies use for dorky cell phone apps. NASA programming is very specialized and hardly anyone is proficient at doing it anymore. Once again, the Company took cost shortcuts by removing the requirements for robust NASA-STD-8739 coding…"

Without acknowledging his soapbox, Four-Leaf directs Scorcher to focus on checking secondary systems, like bathroom lighting. "As far as I'm concerned, you're on shift now. All hands on deck if you want to make it out alive." Four-Leaf continues to think out loud, saying that he's going to attempt the slow piecewise approach to get CLM fully back up and running, however telemetry assistance to the *Vegvisir* is a low priority for now. A lot of his movements seem unintentional.

There must be something I don't know, Scorcher thinks. *Or is he just finally breaking, after all these years?*

A realization snaps into Scorcher's mind that explains how it is that the troubles in orbit have accumulated to this. Years ago, when they prototype tested the *Vegvisir* avionics for fault tolerance, known as hardware-in-the-loop or HIL testing, the current network and communication systems didn't exist yet. That means that as the *Vegvisir* has been updated over time, it's never been fully stress tested in its exact current configuration. At least there is no record of that ever occurring at CLM, the only ground station where that could have happened. Why hasn't he heard about this from his technical fellow before? "The current avionics configuration on the *Vegvisir* was never HIL tested prior to being put into service, was it?" His voice elevates, "Is this your doing, too? Yet another short cut?" *Jesus Christ,* he thinks to himself.

"I have nothing to do with the bloody HIL," Four-Leaf says without looking at Scorcher. Then he transmits over the radio, "*Vegvisir*, CLM, I'd like to try to bounce communication off of you back to Seattle, once you get a chance."

Rocko radios back, sounding out of breath and exhausted. "You got it, boss." Scorcher can sense him shaking his head in frustration as he speaks. "I know you guys are literally in the dark down there. We'll get this tin can up and running in no time," he says with forced confidence over the analog static. "And we...that other problem that we talked about an hour ago? Commander Ōtsuka and Space-Bee are investigating it now, and I might have to jump over to lend a hand. They have the fungi panels removed to inspect the damage. There appears to be damage on the TPS, maybe a quality issue from factory installation. If you don't hear from me, I got pulled—"

Break.

Silence. Scorcher runs the abbreviation TPS in his head: thermal protection system.

"*Vegvisir*, you dropped after 'got pulled.' Repeat."

Rocko comes back, "—yeah, we're totally going to put on our pressure suits now."

"For a network outage?" Four-Leaf asks, apparently before thinking based on his eyeroll toward his own words.

"Negative. We're losing air volume faster now. Commander doesn't like it. The ECS is still holding cabin pressure for now, but it's struggling. Using our static ports to map the cabin pressure all around, it shows it's somewhere in the mid-cabin section of the ship. The delta pressure is just high enough to throw a warning. But we don't know the source entirely."

"Copy," replies Four-Leaf.

"That sucks because if we have to seal off the mid-section, it'll split the ship in half. Commander and I will stay in the forward section, Space-Bee in the aft. We won't be able to move freely back and forth without depressurizing the whole ship."

The mid-cabin section is where Scorcher removed the fungi panel. He knows that all pressurized spacecraft and aircraft leak a very slight amount of air over time. It's impossible to avoid. But if the loss rate is too high, that's indicative of a crack or hull damage.

Four-Leaf suggests to Rocko, "Micro-meteor impact?"

Scorcher has a flashback of the loud nail-screeching noise of the TPS when he reinstalled the fungi panel and all the pounding he had to do to get it back in place. His heart drops.

"Nah," Rocko replies. "I mean, negative on that. There were no indications of something like that from our accelerometer data. No hull vibrations representing an impact. Hold for a moment while I chat with Space-Bee. She might have found something."

A few moments of agony pass.

Rocko is back on. "It actually looks like a TPS clip attaching to the hull skin got bent somehow. The backup structure that the clip attaches to is really flimsy, so not surprising it got damaged."

The blood leaves Scorcher's legs from all this new information and his possible connection to *Vegvisir* pressure leak: he needs to sit. The only other chair is next to Four-Leaf, so he floats down to the floor. *That stupid clip should have been installed on the rigid frame instead of just the thin sheet metal*, he thinks. But poor designs like this—where some wire, tube, or bracket is weakly mounted on flimsy backup structure—sneak their way onto every aircraft and spacecraft. This is often an error of an inexperienced design engineer, the subsequent schedule constraints restricting anyone from going back to redesign and fix it, and management pressuring to sign off on something that is "good enough for government work."

"There was enough leverage on the clip to almost pull the bolt out entirely. The sheet metal skin around the bolt is dimpled when it shouldn't be. There might be a small crack there, but it's basically impossible to see because it's so cramped. Maybe from the outside—" The radio cuts out again.

The two at CLM are silently trapped in their own thoughts. Scorcher thinks of what horror can come from all this, particularly in their environment. As the external hull of the *Vegvisir* travels from sun to shade and back, repeated thousands of times as they orbit, the structure will thermally expand and contract—by a gross amount—and cause residual stresses to build and release around the crack tip. Over time, these thermal cycles will increase the crack tip a microscopic amount each iteration. Once the crack reaches a critical length, it will grow rapidly and without control, leading to absolute structural collapse in microseconds. Since different structures attached together will have different coefficients of thermal expansion, and things never heat up evenly, a battle occurs between these structural components. It becomes a race between the time it takes to discover and repair the crack, and a fatal explosion.

Scorcher thinks back to the thermal fatigue issues from his aircraft days between the titanium wing ribs and carbon fiber reinforced plastic of the wing skin being so severe that the structure was constantly having to be redesigned from in-service cracking, sometimes causing fuel leaks on a tarmac. *In other words, warranty costs*, he thinks ironically. And the thermal environment of an aircraft is much less extreme than a spaceship. He can only imagine how high the residual stress must be that is attacking the crack right now. To make things worse, at the extreme cryogenic temperatures of shade in outer space, the material becomes extremely brittle around the crack tip despite the surrounding virgin material becoming statically stronger. The net holistic result is a more fragile structural system.

When at the training facility in northern Iceland, Scorcher recalls seeing a tiny crack on the windshield of his truck, maybe half a centimeter long. He turned on the windshield defroster to max heat and power. The battle between the arctic cold and the trucks volcanic defroster air was lost by the window. The heat from the defroster smacking the below freezing window caused the tiny crack to snap across the entire windshield instantly. The same happens to cryogenic metal.

The good news is that if they depressurize the *Vegvisir* cabin and relax the pressure strain on the ship's hull, any crack growth will slow to practically zero if minor enough. But has the damage gotten so bad that they could have structural collapse when landing?

They might survive a landing…

All he and Four-Leaf can do now is work out the software issues and hopefully get telemetry navigation back online so the *Vegvisir* can safely come back to port at CLM soon. The alternative is to have Rocko spend days messing around with getting the software working again with the laser-enabled LIDAR sensors the *Vegvisir* uses for close-proximity navigation. Scorcher knows that CLM can help the *Vegvisir* with trajectory tracking and get them down much sooner than it would take Rocko to recalibrate sensors and run stress tests. The ship repairs are needed sooner than later.

He interrogates the technical fellow, "Did you not coordinate and stage the network outages so that we won't lose our backups? We lost control of everything here but need to help get the *Vegvisir* back here as soon as possible."

"We haven't lost control," Four-Leaf insists in a loud tone. "I need you to check that all the hallway and toilet lights are functioning."

Huh? "My question still stands."

"What question is that?" Four-Leaf asks, frantically typing away and studying the screen.

"Were you doing network upgrades in parallel with what's happening on their ship? Was it not coordinated?"

"No. When you were getting your beauty sleep feeling

sorry for yourself, I wasn't touching anything on the network or operating system. The *Vegvisir's* updates shouldn't have had any effect on us. I'm not sure yet why whatever that screwball Rocko was doing affected us down here," says Four-Leaf.

Scorcher doesn't believe him. "I see. So, I'm supposed to waste time and check light bulbs around toilets. That's the priority."

"Do that and get back here immediately when you're done. Check if the pressure locks are working for the sheep. And get them ready."

"The sheep?" Scorcher questions.

"We might have to send them out to the Minister and our miners at the Annies. They can be our carrier pigeons."

Scorcher is not at all surprised that it might come down to that. He just hopes they aren't all just a bunch of Shigleys by now.

"Let me help with communication and telemetry."

"No," Four-Leaf replies.

He ignores him and starts trying to reach Space-Bee through instant messenger and email on his smartphone. "Curious that instant messenger is working. I thought that everything was down."

"Everything *is* down."

"Or is it?" Scorcher challenges.

"You always just do whatever the fuck you want," the Irishman says without looking up.

"I see IM on your screen working."

Four-Leaf turns around. "Look, mate. We're all going to be fucking dead if you don't listen to me. I don't have time to explain, but the toilet lights are connected on the same line as the auxiliary carbon dioxide converter, and I'm showing a fault ahead of both. I need you to check the bloody toilet lights to see if that's true because that should only take five seconds without crawling through ducts. Now stop being a tosspot, or I'll gag you. Aye?"

The force from Four-Leaf's eyes jolts Scorcher back. Not knowing what to believe, he turns towards the toilets to check the lights.

When he gets back, Four-Leaf provides a list of all the code that Scorcher needs to tediously isolate and debug. By his estimation, it's probably days or weeks of effort. Instead of objecting, he goes with the plan until he can think of something better. There's no way this is the quickest way to get the *Vegvisir* back to port. What's Four-Leaf's motive?

CHAPTER 41

A couple of hours pass: this means lifetimes for the *Vegvisir* crew, but it feels like mere seconds to Scorcher. There seems to be a dozen showstoppers in his queue right now, and he can't manage a single one.

Scorcher clicks away at his computer, uncomfortably close to Four-Leaf, yet emotionally numb from his role in dooming the *Vegvisir*. He knows he's supposed to be doing something productive but instead he's just scrolling through random code. He doesn't even remember what system he's looking at. All that's circling his mind now are flashbacks to when he reinstalled the fungi panel, over and over, trying to make sense of what he could have done differently. If he wasn't so dissociated, he'd collapse from the weight that what he's done so far is criminal manslaughter.

Is this how it happens to people? He wonders how he became instigator, martyr, and victim all in one. He starts to feel sorrier for himself than for the others.

He sits up; his mind jumps to an invigorated state. He can't believe what he's just found. He's searching through one of the archive folders where data from the old network was saved, and he's found an endless bunch of text files with "WO" in the name. That could stand for "work order."

He double-clicks to open one of the text files and

confirms that's exactly what it is: a work order for a spacewalk dating back to Shigley's time. The directory was probably created when they switched from the old network to the new.

Under the table below Four-Leaf's field of view, he slips out his smartphone and retrieves the work order number that he wrote down previously before Shigley's laptop was destroyed. He types in the number and all that comes up is: "Seattle directed to not wait for sheep. Proceed with manual operations. See W.O. 00002457."

What the hell does that mean? Scorcher searches work order 00002457. A lot more comes up.

Scorcher immediately recognizes that Seattle ordered Shigley to manually tap an ice well, something that should have only been performed by a sheep since the ice patch was in a permanent shadow region. Based on the notes, the ice would not yet have been electrically neutralized and would have had an extremely high voltage caused by the nearly horizontal sun's solar wind dropping negatively charged electrons into the crater while the positively charged ions stayed on course and passed by. There were literally millions of years of static electricity built up in the crater Shigley was ordered into. A voltage strong enough to discharge and kill an astronaut if they weren't careful, especially if an astronaut's feet accidently touched ice in the permanent shadow but still had their helmet high enough to be in direct sunlight. Their body would become a medium like someone rubbing their feet on a carpet and getting shocked by a metal doorknob. Except this would be a bolt of lightning discharging an entire ice lake in microseconds.

Scorcher leans back, not carrying what he looks like in front of Four-Leaf.

This *must* be the way Shigley died. Seattle ordered him to manually drill and tap ice water in a statically charged polar crater when it was too dangerous to do so. And they knew better. Everyone knew better. Four-Leaf knew better. That explains the burns on his body that weren't present on the spacesuit. Maybe if he'd had time to check closer or clean off the spacesuit, he would've seen damage on the spacesuit itself.

Shigley was electrocuted to death, and Four-Leaf obviously knew about it since he recovered the body. Four-Leaf must have known Shigley had been told to do something he shouldn't have been told to do, and then he helped the Company cover up the accident.

He jumps at the sound of a firm female voice over the radio, "CLM, *Vegvisir*. You copy?" It's Commander Lucy "Siren" Ōtsuka.

Four-Leaf picks up the handset. "We copy you, Siren." Scorcher doesn't recall the flight commander and the technical fellow directly addressing each other before. He readies himself for what might come over the radio waves.

She continues, "We need CLM to establish a link to share terminal navigation data. Rocko is standing by. I'd like to test the connection as we pass over for a couple orbits, then proceed with a max dive landing. Rocko has gotten the flight computers and avionics functional and set up for a deorbit-to-land except for the terminal sensors. Space-Bee is in the aft cabin doing crosschecks for depressurization of the mid cabin. Rocko and I are staying forward. Do you copy?"

Four-Leaf sits for a moment staring at the floor to comprehend their situation and what the *Vegvisir* desperately needs from them. His head pops up. He casually turns around and completely ignores her. "Any word back from the pensioner?" he asks him.

Scorcher's mouth drops. "What? I don't understand. Aren't you going to respond?" His imagination goes to Space-Bee's body getting sucked through a small hole. A deafening and violent event followed by infinite silence and cold, extinguishing life. What the hell is Four-Leaf thinking about if not the exact same thing?

"Have you heard from the Minister, mate?" he clarifies in a nearly friendly tone.

Did he not hear Commander Ōtsuka? Scorcher asks himself. *Am I losing it?*

"CLM, did you copy?" she asks clearly.

In the fog of confusion, Scorcher answers honestly, "Uh, yeah, I was able to contact the Minister via hard line." The Minister told Scorcher two hours earlier that he's preparing for the inevitable surrender to God's judgment for what they've all done, followed by some other rambling about blood on their hands. But Scorcher keeps it simple, dizzy from what is playing out right now. "He's hanging in there."

They're interrupted again. "CLM, *Vegvisir*, did you copy?" Scorcher estimates they're on the very edge of direct line-of-sight right now and will soon lose communication with the *Vegvisir* for the nearly two-hour blackout before they reappear over the opposite horizon.

"Should we respond before they hit the blackout window?"

"That's not what I asked," Four-Leaf clarifies.

Scorcher's skin on his forearms and shins gets red hot. "The factory is up and running. Nothing from the Annies. Oxygen and life support at CLM are good. And field operations are on standby waiting for sheep."

Four-Leaf responds with a simple nod. He turns back to

one of his monitors and starts typing awkwardly with the index digits of his misshaped fingers.

Aside from the *Vegvisir*, Scorcher is growing more concerned for the remote Annie inhabitants. At some point, oxygen must be shipped out to them using tanks strapped to sheep. But the wireless network is no longer functional and isn't talking to the sheep.

"Ah, bloody hell," Four-Leaf curses, then laughs briefly. "The damned network restart has reset all the sheep. They're all lined up and coming back to us blank slates."

Scorcher spins around to his own computer and frantically pulls up the security video feed, hoping that he's wrong. The sheep coming back is a blessing in one sense, but it'll take days to reload all of them and program them to head back out to the Annies. He spies all the sheep—coming in from CLM and surrounding Annies—lined up outside the CLM barn.

He bails on Four-Leaf and sprints down the long halls to meet the sheep. Four-Leaf yells something behind him, but he disregards it, thinking of how Four-Leaf ignored the *Vegvisir*. When he arrives at the barn, the sheep have already started to enter indoors via their mini-pressure lock, one by one.

He checks around in a tool cabinet to find a voltmeter-sized handheld diagnostic tool with dangling USB cable. He plugs it into the first sheep and scans the software version. His concern is validated: everything is wiped clean to factory reset. It barely knows it's a sheep.

He runs back over to the control room with Four-Leaf, who ignores his return.

Scorcher searches for the latest software needed to reload the sheep but doesn't find what he expects. He quickly skims the readme file of the new install and discovers some significant changes. The sheep reset doesn't appear to be an accident from Four-Leaf resetting the network; it appears to be intentional.

The latest software patches are further automating the sheep to eliminate the need for people to be physically present to maintain them. Is that what Four-Leaf has been working on? Additional functions such as self-diagnostic software features have been added. Remote access links are to be turned on so that everything can be directly managed by Seattle. But obviously this can only happen after the Moon's communication gets re-established. Did any of the miners know this was happening? And why keep it in the dark? His only guess is that all Four-Leaf cares about is getting CLM to the state that Seattle wants it, and if anyone gets hurt, they knew the risks coming out here and signed the liability waivers.

Scorcher changes his focus. He needs to get in contact with the Annies. But his lack of proficiency in coding in five different computer languages, including the ancient Fortran77 in which no one else below retirement age is proficient, is daunting. He blames Four-Leaf for this chaos for allowing everyone to write code in whatever language they were most proficient in instead of commonizing. Like most things here, it was to do things as quickly as possible with everything else second.

Why is there so much shit going on right now?

He exits to the hall to pace back and forth away from Four-Leaf. He needs to figure out a solution to re-establish communication with the miners. Maybe something unconventional. If he had access to his spacesuit he could manually navigate out there.

But wait: what about Space-Bee, Commander, and Rocko?

Scorcher hears Four-Leaf talking. There are long moments of silence followed by short bursts of terse verbiage, then back to silence and waiting. Scorcher's mind is rushing so fast it all sounds like gibberish. Then he starts to understand.

"Just breathe," says Four-Leaf with a smirk on his face toward Scorcher, his hand on his chest while he mocks taking deep breaths. "Things have gotten a little worse for us, but it'll be fine. Commander Ōtsuka has decided to land and dock on the Moon immediately instead of holding in orbit a couple rounds. They aren't going to wait for a link-up with our terminal sensors. I figured that would happen. That lady doesn't know her own ship all that well. She's too emotional, naturally." He pauses. "If they evacuate back to Earth, they have to abandon the *Vegvisir* and possibly lose it. But if they land back on the Moon, then we can at least repair it and be the hero once again for these clowns."

They hear Rocko's voice over the radio. "If we can, we might wait two more orbits before the emergency landing so we can prep the ship correctly. I'm going to close the visor on my light pressure suit until we can chat again, so I might not hear you on the ham radio."

Four-Leaf turns back. "Copy 'might not hear you.' Godspeed, mates. Out."

Scorcher bails once again, sprinting towards the café for a visual on the *Vegvisir*. The shooting star drops over the horizon on its 119-minute orbit. He waits anxiously, without any coffee available. Between the fight or flight responses, he defaults to freeze again.

After endless moments of watching a blank sky, he notices the reappearing ship.

Hasn't it only been a few seconds? He then admits that it must have been two hours in actuality.

But clearly the reappearing ship is neither landing at CLM nor going around in orbit again. It zooms by quickly in the sky and looks like a larger shooting star now, too far for its outline to be resolved. Except that he can also see the thrusters burning sporadically, beautiful rainbow clouds of gas reflected by sunlight.

It's sunny up there, he thinks.

The *Vegvisir* is obviously landing, but not where it should.

He continues watching the craft as it lowers in the sky. Without effective depth perception, it's impossible to tell if its height above the ground is decreasing rapidly or if it's simply on a trajectory that will miss striking the ground before reaching the horizon. He's expecting the worst.

The light in the sky rapidly drops behind a distant mountain. To his relief, he doesn't see an explosion.

He runs back down to the control room. Four-Leaf is sitting dumbly at the console, then turns toward Scorcher who says, "They went down, didn't they? Why did they miss us?"

"I don't know," Four-Leaf answers plainly, his posture weak. "It's difficult to tell from my viewpoint. Their deorbit burn was either too early or too late, depending on how you view it. This is probably where they ditched," he points to a crater on a map on the computer screen.

Scorcher pleads, "We have to save them! I'm begging you to reactivate my spacesuit. I can go reach them. Or maybe get help from one of the other technicians."

"You don't even know where they've landed," Four-Leaf shoots back, his shoulders straight and his arms gaining strength once more. "They're already dead, mate. It's impossible to reach them. And even if you do somehow, it's a suicide mission. You need to accept the fact that they're already dead and we've already lost enough people. You stay here and get communication working with our techs at the Annies. Don't get distracted from what's important. I might need to go out to ferry the miners back if we can get CLM booted up."

"We can't let them die on the *Vegvisir*! I need to save them." If the crash is due to a rapid decompression caused by Scorcher's own negligence, he won't be able to live with himself. But he needs to know, and he needs to save them.

"Well, like always, you just do whatever the *fuck* you want anyway, *right*?" The veins in Four-Leaf's hands and neck look ready to bulge from his body—like they could reach and strangle Scorcher before the rest of his body could catch up.

"I fucking tried to fix this place and was fought with resistance the whole time! It's people like you who fight making any improvements. You caused all this yourself, you goddamned fraud. The heroes aren't the ones who save the day, they're the ones who do the mundane tasks with foresight and proper planning. You are no hero!"

Four-Leaf laughs ironically. "You're saying I, the firefighter who has to constantly clean up everyone else's shit, am not the hero?"

Scorcher lowers his voice in a misleading calm fueled by adrenaline. He repeats an analogy he once heard, because Four-Leaf *needs* to understand this. "People are quick to give an award to a firefighter who gives CPR to a man who fell off a cliff. But the engineer who has the foresight to install a railing at the top of the cliff to prevent the fall in the first place, will never get any praise. But they're the true hero."

The technical fellow shakes his head. "You dug up a fucking grave. Get out of your own head, mate. And fuck off. We all have skin in the game, especially me. Stay out of my way." He gets up from his seat to leave.

Scorcher runs over to see the coordinates of the crash site. The direction seems right—it's aligned with the mountain peak he saw briefly illuminated by the ship's lights. If anything, Scorcher can use that distinct landmark as a compass. But how should he get there? Steal a sheep? A whole herd, to bring survivors back—or bodies? What spacesuit can he use?

Four-Leaf comes storming back into the room, irate. "You sabotaged my spacesuit, you twat," he tells him. "Irish justice would be me blowing out your knees." Four-Leaf punches out Scorcher.

Nothingness.

CHAPTER 42

Scorcher wakes to his head throbbing at the same pulse as Stabby's flashing red light, his knife en garde toward Scorcher's face.

God, this is pathetic, he thinks.

Slowly rolling to a seated posture on the freezing floor, he sees that some of his blood froze to the surface. *At least it brings color to the room.* The couple patches of his skin that were in direct contact with the floor but not shielded by his thermal underwear feel like rings of fire orbiting numbness. The direct cold exposure is more intense than anything his skin has felt (or been numbed by) in a couple years. He wonders if the environmental control system has failed.

Could have at least placed me in the cot, whoever did this. He shakes his head. *Was it me who did this?*

The decrepit starfish he sees sliding on the floor transforms into his veiny hand pushing down for support. His mind keeps going back and forth into which world he is in right now.

After he remembers that the hand belongs to him, he asks, *Have I lost weight since lying here?*

He gets up, a small but empowering victory to accompany improving consciousness.

Stumbling with lunar finesse towards the door, he finds it locked. The digital access pad flashes red at each attempt to open. Stabby is yelling threatening beeps at him from behind. Scorcher goes to sit back down.

After resting for fifteen minutes, he turns around and limps towards the troublemaker. He casually disables Stabby's computer and removes the blade. But that's just the first step in the trick to escape.

Pulling out his smartphone, he links to Stabby's computer, which is on but in standby mode. He hacks into the source code and has Stabby tell the door to unlock itself, a feature that he questioned the logic of earlier but is now forever grateful.

Without any real plan, he tracks down the long hall toward the pressure lock. He sees Four-Leaf there, staring at Scorcher's spacesuit like he's trying to figure something out. Scorcher tries to gain composure and strength.

The excessive white noise from the air duct allows Scorcher to steal up from behind, albeit sloppily, and try to knock out Four-Leaf by grabbing a wrench off the floor. Scorcher falls short in strength and doesn't strike with sufficient impact on his target's head, and Four-Leaf spins about, disoriented and stumbling instead of being knocked out cold. Scorcher panics from adrenaline and starts striking Four-Leaf's face, causing blood to spray back from his nose and mouth. Over and over again, seemingly countless strikes, nothing powerful enough to finish the job. Four-Leaf falls screaming. He still isn't unconscious. Scorcher panics. "Why isn't this fucking working? It only took one punch to knock *me* out!"

Scorcher, terrified at the violence he is causing, instinctively goes to run away instead of following through. In the Moon's weak gravity, he gets his boot caught on Four-Leaf, and his body arcs over the technical fellow like a yo-yo being swung over someone's head. Scorcher slams into the floor and strikes his own head quite hard. "Goddamn it!"

He struggles to get back up, flipping his feet like a scuba diver trying to get his boot free and out of the grasp of an angry injured shark. After a few moments—three seconds or ten years, who knows—Scorcher realizes his boots are free. He does one last, strong heel kick for good measure and feels his knee overextend when he hits nothing but air.

He crawls along the floor, mimicking a man climbing a ladder, towards the pressure hatch. When he gets there, he looks back. He doesn't even recognize Four-Leaf's face. Scorcher traps Four-Leaf inside and leaves him next to the only available spacesuit. Four-Leaf is swirling around like a leaking hose spurting blood.

"What the fuck am I doing?" But he feels like he must follow through to maintain control. Didn't the technical fellow swing first? he tries justifying, but at the same time knows better. He then thinks of how Space-Bee would judge him, followed by how the damage he caused on the *Vegvisir* might have doomed her. If anything at all, he must fix what he did. No time to repent.

Scorcher partially depressurizes the room to one-fifth atmospheres to knock out Four-Leaf, but hopefully not kill him. Watching Four-Leaf stumble then go limp nauseates him.

After a couple minutes, he goes to grab some wire to tie up the unconscious man, but first re-pressurizes the pressure lock. The calculator-sized pressure equalizer vent pops open. Scorcher's ears pop, and his throbbing head starts pounding harder.

Scorcher quickly approaches an unconscious Four-Leaf. He needs to deal with him.

As he is tying him up, he notices that his breathing and

heart pumping are exaggerated, and his skin is like a frozen corpse. Scorcher just now remembers that when you depressurize the atmosphere, the temperature drops significantly. It must have dropped to near cryogenic temperatures, maybe giving Four-Leaf frostbite over his entire body. Scorcher panics at the thought that he might have executed him unintentionally via freeze-drying.

"'Irish justice.' Fuck me." But after a few moments of observation, he becomes optimistic that he hasn't killed him.

He drags his limp body to the nearest room with a cot and wraps him warmly. The benefit of low gravity is really paying off right now.

Scorcher quickly exits but then returns just as fast. He places food and water next to Four-Leaf like a dog, then unties him enough so he'll be able to access it, assuming he'll make it that far.

He checks again and Four-Leaf is unconscious but breathing more steadily now. Scorcher cleans off the blood, then bandages him quickly. He feels disgusted touching him with his bare hands but powers through it.

As he abandons Four-Leaf for good this time, he hears a slight moaning from the lump of technical fellow laying there and prays to the Moon's ghosts to watch over him properly as he locks him in the room.

CHAPTER 43

Scorcher quickly continues with the false appearance of someone with a thought-out plan, someone who isn't just acting rashly. No longer considering what just transpired, he redirects toward Space-Bee and her crew: he can't abandon those on the *Vegvisir*. Not given the circumstances: he's responsible for them now and must save them. He's already gone so far as possible manslaughter over his impulsive suicide mission to reach the *Vegvisir*. He has nothing to lose for himself now but the others. Fueled by adrenaline and quest, he leverages all his focus and problem-solving skills to his new purpose. But how can he reach them without a vehicle? A spacesuit alone isn't enough, assuming he can even hack it. And all the sheep are essentially useless newborns after the factory reset.

He slaps his forehead. "Not all the sheep have gone through factory reset," he says. He recalls disabling the network cards of a couple sheep undergoing maintenance: they were shielded from the factory reset and should still be functional.

He starts rapidly tapping his finger to think of a plan, one that optimistically assumes he can get the hardware he needs.

First step is to trace back the location of the crash site as best he can. He tries to go through Four-Leaf's chicken scratch left on the desk in the control room but can't really make sense of the numbers. Scorcher recalls the flight path that the *Vegvisir* should have been taking under nominal conditions. When he checks this against a topographic map of the lunar south pole, he verifies that when he saw the *Vegvisir* drop behind the highest peak on the horizon it was off trajectory. They must have shifted course and changed heading. But how sharply had they turned? And for how long were they traveling off course? What was their altitude and sink rate? The answers to these questions are needed for him to better estimate where they most likely ditched. But realizing that he can't precisely answer these orienteering issues, he drops it and goes with his gut. With time pressing, he's hopeful there will be lights on the space vehicle or something else to help guide him.

But there definitely won't be a flaming, fiery mess in the vacuum of space, Scorcher thinks to himself morbidly. If this were a crash on Earth, he could follow the plume of smoke during the day or the flashes of fire at night.

Where the *Vegvisir* has most likely crashed is far outside the territorial claims of the Company and Founder, and much farther than where any sheep has traveled previously. Scorcher suspects that it is even farther than the unoccupied Chinese science station, called "Panda Station." After doing quick hand calculations of how much life support he needs and how much battery power the sheep are going to hog, he realizes he has just barely enough to make it there, if he's lucky. Which means that in practice, he won't be able to make it. In all likelihood, he's going to get lost, injured, or in some other way delayed. He needs more.

He exhales a breath of frustration, leans back in his chair, and looks up at the ceiling to ponder how to make this work. He knows they're out there this very moment.

The best bet might be to stop by at Panda Station and pirate their supplies, he thinks.

The trip needs life support and medical supply provisioning balanced with the logistics required for transportation and navigation. He can do without food for a couple days, so he decides to skip on that and instead bring backup oxygen containers for any survivors. But by then the sheep's battery will be dead, and they'll have to walk back. The dune buggy has an even shorter range, and the benefits of its solar panel chargers are moot without sun.

Scorcher puts all his gambling chips on the Chinese outpost and hopes to score big. If he turns up empty-handed at Panda Station, he might have the battery power and oxygen to make it back to CLM alone, but then what's the point? Though Panda Station must have some sort of communication system where he can tell people on Earth, outside of Seattle headquarters, all about what has happened. That alone is enough enticement for the suicide mission.

He makes a mental note to himself to eat a protein bar but then forgets immediately. His mind is focused on the more important details of the rescue mission and the calls for justice he wants.

Then a certain recollection hits him hard enough to nearly knock him off his feet: Seattle remotely disabled his spacesuit, and he sabotaged Four-Leaf's. Scorcher just stands there frozen, trying to come up with a solution to the predicament he caused.

There's got to be a way to hack into my EVA suit and unlock it.

*   *   *

Four precious hours later, he's come up with nothing. Scrolling through the object-oriented C++ computer scripts of the suit, he discovers a mess of a few hundred thousand lines of code. "How the fuck does the suit even turn itself on?" he yells, frustrated he can't find that portion of code. Maybe he can reload all the software on the suit as a factory reset? But how? And does the suit ping some server somewhere for security access after a complete reset, negating the effort?

Scorcher attempts to put the suit on just to verify for a fact that it doesn't work. This takes about fifteen minutes, and he nearly overheats and suffocates since the environmental control pumps are digitally disabled. This system is too complicated for him to figure this all out now. He needs another plan, but he doesn't know what.

He runs over to try contacting the others at the remote Annies but comes back empty handed to face off with the spacesuit again.

The vacuum-turned-spy comes rolling in without his blade. "What do you think, bud?" he asks his former pet who betrayed him. "No point in hiding anything now, I suppose." Scorcher continues to think aloud. "What if I just swap suit computers between mine and dipshit's? God, how long would that take though?" He's tapping the untrimmed, brittle nail of his index finger to the nail of his thumb. "What if…" He approaches Stabby, who turns around trying to escape. "Stop there!"

*   *   *

Thirty more precious minutes later, Stabby is inverted and plugged into a computer on his back as Scorcher queries through the computer scripts stored on the vacuum's local hard drive. Scorcher finally finds it.

Previously, Scorcher had been quite dismayed by whomever developed Stabby's computer code because the little critter can lock and unlock pressure hatches. But this also happens to use the same code libraries and programming superclass scripts as that of the spacesuit. In other words, Stabby can reactivate Scorcher's spacesuit—it's the exact same lines of code.

Scorcher picks Stabby up, rolls him over, kisses him on the top of his head, then begins to plead. "I don't need you to do something for me. I need you to do something for your friends and the others. The ones you've been protecting need your help now more than ever." Scorcher pretends in his mind that Stabby understands.

Regardless of whether he does, Scorcher is successful at getting Stabby to activate the locked spacesuit. The victory energizes him higher than at any point in his life; he can't help but do an end zone dance.

But there is one final question: should he rig one sheep or two?

Using one sheep is risky because if it breaks down he's screwed. Taking two sheep, however, means there is twice the likelihood of one getting stuck in a rut, and he'll not have the ability or the time, in the vacuum of Moon space, to move the limited supplies from the stuck sheep to the free one. He treats it like betting on both black and red on a roulette table: one is for sure going to fail, which means the mission will fail. And he can't double the supplies up: not enough exist, naturally. And with "0" and "00", it could mean complete failure. But if all bets are on either red or black—not both—then there is almost a 50% chance of success.

"Who gets to be the lucky sheep?" he asks the two still-functioning vehicles in the hangar. Scorcher sees the first sheep is covered in a reddish dust, not unlike the stubborn pile of mystery rocks that stood in the way of his earlier purgatory. Another sheep is covered in grayish dust: that's the black one, obviously. A third one has "00" printed on the side for the ID. He chooses this one.

His sheep-mule is packed. Two days earlier, neither he nor the sheep had any idea they'd be here now, setting out to traverse land that no one has ever touched before. He gets to realize his dream of being a true frontiersman, and it means nothing to him now.

The sheep goes through its pressure lock, and he nervously watches as the haphazardly attached supplies scrape through the door frame.

He yells at it to squeeze through until it's done. Then it's Scorcher's time, and he finally makes it outside in his own spacesuit.

The external lights normally on around Central Lunar Mining are off. Without going two meters, he's already lost trying to find the sheep in total blackness. He thought his head mounted flashlight would be more helpful, but the blackness is too vast.

Through sheer determination, he arrives just outside the external pressure hatches to find his ride, and he awkwardly saddles up, trying to figure out how to contort his body around the supplies.

As satisfied as he'll ever be, Scorcher drives the sheep forward and off they race, but not in the direction of the *Vegvisir*.

CHAPTER 44

Scorcher rolls up at maximum speed toward what he thinks is the gravesite. The sheep being pushed to its limit kicks up clouds of the infamous Moon dust known for jamming spacesuit bearings and embrittling its fabric. In the vacuum of space, the clouds of dust rise and collapse much more rapidly than in an atmosphere, one of the few scenarios where something appears in fast-forward on the Moon.

Scorcher's actions are weakened and imprecise from hunger and dehydration—he wonders how either he, his suit, or the sheep have made it this far. As the sheep starts slowing down, he turns on his head lamp.

"It's a shame there isn't a windshield wiper on my face screen," he says to the sheep. He tries to wipe off the stubborn, statically charged dust but gives up and turns back to the task at hand.

It is impossible for him to do the actual navigating himself: he's simply relying on the pre-programmed coordinates he gave to the sheep before departing. The rugged sheep has its multiple LIDAR sensors and some other obsolete technology to keep on track and avoid obstacles in the blackness.

The sheep's tank-like tracks instantly stop, throwing Scorcher forward into the sky. The lack of any depth perception and the sluggish falling action from the weak gravity terrify him with thoughts of being thrown off into deep space. For a split second he thinks of how Alan Shepard was able to hit a golf ball over the horizon during Apollo 14.

The dust quietly collapses, and he can see the stars again. He's on his back somehow, even though he expected to be on his face.

Vertigo strikes and the infinite sea of stars makes him feel like he's lost in deep space. Terror washes over him. It takes all his strength not to panic.

"Come on, I've been out here for well over a year now. I'm used to this!" he yells. He can't ignore the fact that he's more alone than he ever has been, but the desperate mission keeps him going. He corrects his crooked headlamp and tilts it back, then scurries up. He knows that his pitstop puts everything at risk, but his goal is the opposite.

He's here to rebuild the rocks at Shigley's grave, which he knows—as stupid as it sounds—is something that must be done. He doesn't know how, but the fate of the whole crew is intertwined with this rash detour. Scanning around, it all just looks like a bunch of random rocks. How can he tell if he's even in the right place?

"What the fuck am I doing here?" he scorns himself. "Where's the sheep again? How have I lost you? I just saw you." And to his astonishment, after spinning around three times, the sheep miraculously appears right in front of him. "Ah, thank God. But where the hell are we?" He looks up toward the still unfamiliar stars of the Southern Hemisphere and nearly breaks under the sight of constellations washed out by the oppressive quantity of distant suns. All he sees is chaos and disorder.

"Keep looking, you're near it now."

"Are you sure?"

He scans left and finds what looks like a rock stack. Then the door to the abandoned Annie materializes in front of him. "There we go. Thanks. Hopefully it's the right Annie."

"Which else could it be?"

"My thoughts exactly."

Scorcher reaches down and starts to rebuild the crude stone monument he previously destroyed; he's repenting and returning order from the chaos he created on the ridge. The red rocks that once haunted him while he dug ditches also reappear and start to vaguely form along the entire horizon. He ignores it and places the last of the Minister's original stones for Shigley.

After finishing the final touches, he then adds his own benefaction to the stack with the hope that making the monument taller than it was initially will offend no one and maybe buy redemption. If not for superstition and luck, then for Shigley, who to Scorcher is alive invariant to time.

He scrambles to remount the sheep and orders it to the next waypoint: Panda Station. Hopefully his good deed has bought him some luck at finding usable Chinese supplies.

As the sheep's tracks take off spinning in the soft dust, the left one momentarily jams on a rut. Scorcher immediately slides off and the sheep departs without him; it vanishes immediately into the blackness.

As he soars down into a black hole, his head lamp goes off. This time when he impacts the ground, however, he doesn't see the stars. His mask is buried deep in the Moon's soft powder. He frantically jumps up and, after falling a couple more times, starts sprinting. He strikes his shin on yet another rock and falls. His headlamp is back on after a few attempts. He stumbles and falls again. He notices a blinking light, but it's not the sheep: it's something from his own suit.

He jolts forward in the dark and dumbly picks a random direction to run with the hope of catching up. He falls again and his transparent face shield smacks against a sharp metallic corner of the sheep he didn't even know was there, stuck and spinning its tracks while wedged in an awkward crevice, not budging. Scorcher is absolutely shocked his face shield didn't crack open.

He holds there for a moment to see if his face shield explodes off, though if it does, he'll probably never realize it.

He gets up and halts the sheep's spinning tracks by smacking the emergency stop button, nearly losing a finger. He wonders if that's how Four-Leaf lost his fingertips.

He sluggishly moves around to shovel an escape path with his hands to free the sheep; it isn't the first time. It doesn't take long for his body to start perspiring excessively. He starts paddling more rapidly until his muscles are strained to the breaking point from the repetitive action combined with his dehydration. His body's natural kinematic mobility fights against the kinematic limitations of the spacesuit. He anticipates blisters forming on his wrists and shoulders. Unable to readjust to a more comfortable motion, he starts to bleed but disregards it out of urgency.

Twenty minutes later, he's able to move enough dirt out to provide a path for the sheep's escape. This time, however, it's not escaping without him. Scorcher ensures that he is firmly tied and strapped to the sheep so this doesn't happen again; he might have just spent all his luck.

He switches the headlamp back off to save battery power and the duo bump and rock onward to China's Moon.

*   *   *

After a few millennia of terrifying monotony beat down

his spirit and galvanize his new blisters, his head is forced downward from the sheep-guide slowing down. They change heading by turning about ninety degrees to the right, for fate knows what reason. Then the Moon morphs under them; they start to traverse in soft powder.

The new surface is like riding on fluffy snow. The sheep is really trekking it, and even without any visual reference, it feels fast to Scorcher. He can almost imagine a breeze. But as it continues to trek, the terrain starts to feel mushy, slushy, and sticky, like skiing on spring snow.

The sheep slows to a halt to turn back to the left about ninety degrees, this time sinking into the Moon's surface like quicksand. The sheep seems to panic as it starts riding back and forth like a mechanical bull, but eventually it gets them free. This terrifying sequence occurs three or four more times before the terrain finally hardens beneath them and Scorcher feels the traction catch like car tires on an icy road finally gripping a dry spot.

It's a steep incline now, like riding a rocket into a field of stars. But instead of heaven Scorcher reencounters vertigo from the jolty, unpredictable motions. Scorcher knows his weight is going to tip the sheep back and it'll crush him.

"Hang on, brother."

"I am!"

Now he feels the arching freefall. The painful, forcing sensation of gravity is momentarily gone. The trio go skyborne over the top of the sheer cliff.

Scorcher exclaims from whiplash on impact. At the soonest opportunity—when he isn't too scared to release his grip—he turns on his lamp. By this time the sheep beast has clearly proven its ability to parkour miniature cliffs and starts traversing flat again.

Scorcher can't believe his eyes. It looks like they're on

some dirt road, a path just big enough for a single-lane road and elevated by approximately two meters from the surrounding Moon. This highway *must* be an illusion.

"I think this is the road the sheep was looking for."

"You think?"

"Certainly."

The sheep apparently knows where it's going, and it's exploiting this road-like feature. Scorcher is astonished at how naive he is about such an infrastructure—if it is in fact infrastructure and not some coincidental naturally formed feature. Not that the road is paved, it is primitive. But it mimics a constructed road, to which Scorcher plays Devil's advocate and starts to doubt that this is actually a highway. "How come no one ever mentioned it?" He spends a lot of time worrying about this. If only he had studied the auto-selected route in more detail and kept it to memory, but he didn't have time. The crew of the *Vegvisir* are waiting for him; he knows it.

As they continue to speed across this path, Scorcher leaves his lamp on like a child's nightlight.

More zooming across the landscape through a monotonous cartoon background loop.

And still more.

Looking forward, he sees a ring of violet smudge define the outline of a tunnel, a tunnel he feels he is traveling through. The headlamp lights the most immediate ground and the dust being kicked up. He considers that he must be facing backwards if he can see the dust but is aware enough to admit his confusion. His brain is painting images on the walls of a tunnel that aren't there, onto a tunnel he knows isn't there.

"Those look like trees," he states in astonishment. The fear of driving into a tree becomes his new focus. They're not in the center of his vision but on the periphery where he can see faint gray images of tree stumps zooming past him. Every time he turns his eyes to look at a specific tree, though, it disappears. It's a competition between gray tree stumps and violet smudge walls.

Just as the spacesuit gives its first indication that the oxygen reserve is low, he feels the sheep skidding. It tips over more quickly than Scorcher thought possible, and it slams him into the ground. Lower gravity doesn't mean lower momentum.

"I'm leaking blood," he shouts. His entire right side is aching. In fact, he doesn't even know what pain to focus on. It's all over. And he's restricted in his pressure suit and can't flex enough to soothe muscle cramps. He's struggling for movement by pressing against the edges of his suit, only making the sensation and cramping worse.

"Don't just stand there, jerk! Help me up!" His neck is killing him. "Help me up, goddamn it! Help me! Help!" Scorcher's breathing is out of control, and the female computer voice in his suit tells him to pace his breathing. After a few moments, he obeys the voice.

Realizing that his partner is not going to save him, his adrenaline temporarily turns off the pain and he's able to get himself unstuck. While standing up, he gets a sharp cramp in his back that he can't stretch far enough to relieve. The muscle just pulls tight. He cries out and waits for the pain to become bearable for a few moments.

Looking around, he sees where he is: Panda Station! He pushes past his cramps and bruises; nothing's holding him back.

A forest of solar panels surrounds him, and a single door leading into a mound of Moon welcomes him. Scorcher pathetically struggles the last ten meters toward the reflective yellow, green, and orange-striped hatch. Much more brilliant in color than the dull gray and customary metallic structures composing Central Lunar Mining and the Annies.

He sees a violet button and an orange button. He takes a breath.

"Uh, purple?" Nothing happens. "Orange?"

The hatch opens, and LED lights brightly illuminate the interior of the cramped pressure lock, forcing Scorcher to squint.

"That was surprisingly easy. I guess I don't need a key. A small victory." Not that CLM is locked either, but he'd been expecting that for some reason.

He has trouble squeezing in. "Come on…" He latches the door behind him, and he can see water vapor coming in from the vents. "That's weird. Air should be transparent," he says numbly.

Green lights illuminate on the panel near the interior pressure door, located on a rectangular shoebox-sized metallic box mounted to the wall. Green: a more familiar color indicator for Scorcher than violet or orange. A cute cartoon panda with a spacesuit helmet is waving to him on the display screen. *Another small victory*, he considers.

A short laugh escapes him.

CHAPTER 45

It's vast and empty like a deserted shopping mall, reminding Scorcher of Shanghai's vacant Pudong district. Panda Station is essentially absent of anything usable, but regardless, this empty shell has massive potential compared to anything the Americans or Europeans have in place.

Why are the Chinese so able to build massive infrastructure even on the Moon? he asks. One thing he can't tell is if it's been stripped or if it's never been filled.

After verifying the atmospheric pressure and chemical content with the pinhole-sized static pressure port sensor built into his suit's exterior, Scorcher halts his oxygen supply and opens his face shield.

Ears pop.

What he really forgot to check was the temperature. The arctic cold is a complete shock to his face, then body, as it pours into his suit and ice crystals form on his nose hairs. The sensation makes him want to pick his nose, but he can't with his gloved hands. The blood on his skin and the moisture in his adult diaper start to freeze. A thermal alarm goes off on his suit.

"When does the glorious part of being an astronaut happen?" he asks himself.

The whole facility is inundated with wide-open storage rooms and countless pressure hatches. This place is absolutely massive, and it is well lit and clean. Absolutely spotless other than incomplete wiring and some skeleton walls missing panels. He's ashamed he brought in so much dirt.

"Someone would definitely know that I was here."

A Chinese vacuum bot comes out. Maybe not.

"Oh, God. The Chinese got one, too?" he says disdainfully, thinking of his ankles. Except this one has propellers to hover as a drone. Maybe it has other uses, too.

Scorcher refocuses his exhausted brain to the mission. The sheep needs a charged battery, and he needs pressurized oxygen tanks topped off. If both supplies even exist, maybe the Chinese used NASA and ESA international space standards to build their electrical power connections for electrical and fluid systems equipment—but he can only hope.

As Scorcher scrambles around the mall to find a room that isn't bare of anything useful, he is kicking himself for learning Russian but not National Chinese. There are plenty of signs everywhere, but he doesn't understand them.

"Was this whole facility just built to store signs?"

The endless corridors are blindingly lit; there's probably a small nuclear reactor powering all of this. Scorcher wonders if CLM is just kept overly dim with its hydrogen power. But after spending an eternity hopping about, it becomes too physically painful, and Scorcher needs a break. He estimates that he's only checked a fraction of the total acreage before burning out.

He accepts that the worst possible outcome is the most likely: either he goes back to CLM empty-handed, or he goes on a suicide mission to die while futilely attempting to save the crew. A crew whose location he doesn't know exactly and who might not even be alive.

Scorcher does a mental estimate of the battery life for the sheep and his suit, but he's pessimistic that by the time he finds his invisible colleagues in the total darkness of the Moon's midnight desert, that he'll even have enough to make it back to Panda Station. Or maybe not even enough to survive past the solar farm...

In terms of life support and medical supplies, he decides to roll the dice and not think about it. He closes his helmet and reheats his suit. Scorcher walks to the screen with the waving panda cartoon and pushes buttons until he can re-vacuum and exit the station, disillusioned and delusional. He wasted so much going out of his way for Shigley's grave and Panda Station.

After a few minutes outside, the weight of the stars start to smother him again.

"How are you doing, buddy? You got enough oxygen? You can have mine if you'd like," Scorcher offers to his ghost friend.

Scorcher, standing in the darkness next to his sheep with his headlamp on, attempts to remove his oxygen supply and give it to his fictitious partner. Immediately, the spacesuit starts to set off alarms and prevents him from the unintentional suicide. He sits down on the sheep, defeated, and starts to cry for not being able to give oxygen to his mirage.

When he looks up, he thinks he sees a shooting star, but it's moving much too slow.

*   *   *

Time passes somehow. Or does it? Is time done?

Scorcher is standing outside trying to orient himself. His frozen skin is starting to burn as his suit is quickly heating up to just above freezing. He hears a "low power" warning from his suit, and to remedy it, he goes to plug it into the battery supply on the sheep.

He looks around for the sheep but can't find it. He sees its light blinking far on the horizon.

Wasn't I just right next to it?

The sheep with all of his supplies has wandered off, heading back in the direction of CLM. The sheep takes all the supplies: battery power, oxygen, water, and medical.

Scorcher is too exhausted and disoriented to care.

He notices his bloody parts and the diaper starting to unfreeze and become itchy in a new way. Then he asks himself a very serious question about how he wants to die. Does he want to be well lit and have some Chinese nationals eventually find him? It'll probably scare the shit out of them, he considers. Will his body rot?

Or should he run after the motorized mule—the goddamned traitor—that has left him here to die? He could adjust his suit atmosphere to induce hypoxia which would eventually lead to cardiac arrest.

He sits down on a Chinese telecommunications box next to a solar panel.

I wonder how Stabby is doing? "Is that a sunrise on the horizon?" he asks himself out loud. A sunrise isn't due for quite some time. Is it possible to see a sun that is below the horizon when there is no atmosphere to light up?

"What are you looking at, Scorcher?"

"I spy with my little eye, I spy the color—sunrise," he responds, in a delusional childish voice.

"There are no pre-dawn sunrises here."

In an almost drunk state, he yells back, "You don't know that, and aren't you hungry? Let me feed you."

"Don't be ridiculous, those are your friends over there. That's an oxygen tank with a small flame smoldering from a leak."

"I thought you don't have fire in space."

"You also thought I needed more oxygen."

"Well, fuck it then, let's go. And fuck you!" Scorcher gives the finger towards the nearest solar panel then stands up and wobbles. He sees his target now: a kindling on the horizon. The light is not behind the ridge, it's on the near side of the mountain. Whether it's one-hundred meters away or ten kilometers, he has no idea. But this is sufficient for him. Dying is boring anyways, assuming he hasn't already done so already.

All he needs is a direction to focus on to overcome his physical and mental pain, some incremental waypoint that won't overburden him by thinking too far ahead. He doesn't need to see the bridges he'll eventually have to cross. So he proceeds on a course with his focus only on the most immediate task. He embarks on the impossible.

CHAPTER 46

Hypothermia is fooling Scorcher into thinking his skin is burning, while also plummeting his judgment. If he could, he would strip naked to relieve the false fire. And he might have even attempted taking his suit off if it weren't for his callsign in fiery letters reappearing and vanishing around his periphery, giving him enough distraction to keep walking.

He stops for a moment to re-saturate his lungs with oxygen and remind himself of what he's doing.

Think about the crew of the Vegvisir *and how the name was chosen because of its origin as an Icelandic symbol of wayfinding.*

Kicking through the shin deep powder reminds him of fresh snow. Then it reminds him of the knee-deep red volcanic ash he once trekked through while on an adventurous hike up a summertime volcano, Fuji-San.

Breathe in. Step. Pause. Breathe out. Repeat.

Snow begins to kiss him. The flakes are completely silent in the surreal light of the head lamp. His childhood swathes through his mind and people who have long been dead welcome him.

When he looks straight up, it gives the impression of traveling light speed. He can no longer tell where he is, or why he is struggling, but his body still knows it has a direction and purpose, so it continues.

Scorcher starts to imagine himself as a Viking crossing the arctic tundra, futilely trying to survive so he can avenge wrongs. And he is half-convinced that he is one, running to his family, on a mission of revenge. His outer flesh at this very moment is both fire and ice.

The snow stops and he's lost in the weightlessness of deep space.

The snow begins again.

He curses himself at the all too familiar sight: leaking ammonia. The infinitesimal amount of clarity is enough to bring him back from the edge of life. The leak is coming from the crash site: he's there. He can't exactly see its origin, but he must be close. His helmet-mounted light isn't powerful enough, and his eyes are having trouble focusing, but he knows he is near, and that's enough inspiration to partially sober him.

In the abstract lighting, he can't tell if he is looking down into a valley or upward toward a mountain peak. He must really focus and think. "OK, I'm leaning my head back, so I must be at the bottom of the cliff. I'm hoping this is just a big rock, but it's probably a fucking mountain." He laughs at the idea of these being his last words.

The burning light from the crash site is no longer visible, but he concludes that that is because he's at the bottom of a sheer cliff and has lost the line of sight.

"Well, we can't go straight up, so let's go right." His left ankle starts to hurt while walking lopsided with his left foot on higher ground. He looks up again and sees a part of the spacecraft above him over a ledge. Scorcher tries to bring the object into focus and believes he can make it out. It's one of the personnel entry hatches from the ship. On it, he can make out the circular symbol of the *Vegvisir* compass, rotated such that North is pointing to the left.

"How about left instead." He takes the symbol's advice and switches direction.

After about ten minutes he's grateful for the gods telling him to switch directions: his ankle feels less horrible traversing left instead of right. Scorcher exploits the light gravity as much as he can, which is all his body knows now.

The cliff disappears above him, and he finds himself on what he's guessing is a plateau or butte. His intuitive sense of direction and mission both vanish and feel omnidirectional all at once. He trips into a cavern and slams into a door. It's creepily familiar.

He struggles but wields open the outer pressure hatch of the Annie using the all too familiar process and finds himself inside of a pressure lock. But this untrodden Annie is a bit different. It's obviously hidden quite well and has less of an appearance of a mound-shaped Norse turf house and is more like a cellar. The control pad also seems like an older version; or maybe newer?

He's too exhausted to be shocked, confused, or philosophical about the current situation, or to tell whether he's just hallucinating. Maybe he's just hallucinating. But he plays nicely and goes through the muscle memory of initiating the pressurization process and trusts that his brain wouldn't use the image of a sad Annie as a hopeful mirage. He notices there's no cleaning procedure to rid him of Moon dust but frankly doesn't care.

After waiting for too many minutes, he realizes he didn't get the normal visual indicator light that the pressurization is complete and he can proceed inward. Maybe if he goes through the door, it just leads back outside into the open Moonscape or into the depths of a cave. Or maybe not even a cave, but an open pit, which is basically just as bad as the bare Moonscape.

He shakes the ideas out of his head; there's no point speculating. He reaches for the handle.

CHAPTER 47

The room is barely lit. Half expecting coconuts and palms, something even more stunning appears behind the interior pressure hatch.

As he falls through, he is caught by Space-Bee—which he mistakes as an embrace—who is standing tattered and half dressed, covered in bruises and scrapes. The pain and distress initially on her face disappear instantly from around her immutable eyes, which are the same stoic dark he's always known.

"Holy shit!" Scorcher starts coughing and grasps Space-Bee as best he can. He is unable to hug properly and instead grabs her greasy hair too firmly. She doesn't stop him.

The roundness of an actual human voice startles his ears. Naturally, she starts with, "You smell horrible."

"Did it blow up? Did I kill you?" his strained voice gargles out.

She tilts her head and furrows one brow. "What's that?"

"Did the rapid decompression knock you out of orbit? Did I kill you?" he asks again, shivering. The dam has broken, and his strength is flowing away.

"Oh, what? No." She explains, "There was no explosion. I mean, we did depressurize the mid cabin, and we were successful at that. The cold gas thruster kept us on track, but then jammed. The thruster locked open and depleted all its fuel. It knocked us so far out that all we could do was de-orbit and land anywhere possible in the polar region. We couldn't risk trying to find a stable orbit, so we came down. The only option was to ditch, based on our trajectory."

"I broke the thruster?"

She shakes her head and squints. "What? No, Scorcher. The nitrogen thruster jammed open."

"So, you crashed because the depressurization knocked you out of orbit?" He can't stop thinking of the fungi panel that screeched across the haul after he snuck onboard the *Vegvisir* to reinstall it.

She grabs both of his shoulders as though to shake him, but his dead weight doesn't let her. Her eyes seem to hypnotize him for a moment. "Stop trying to think, Scorcher. Forget the stupid depressurization. That didn't knock us out of orbit. It was the malfunctioning cold gas thruster which would have otherwise probably jammed while landing at CLM." She looks up to think, then back, "If we had come to land normally and never used the thruster during depressurization, the thruster malfunction would have occurred at a critical time during routine landing. It would have blown us straight into the factory at the last moment, probably killing all of you there. We lucked out that it jammed in parking orbit because that specific thruster is normally only used during terminal descent. It's a weird coincidence, if anything." She studies him to see if he gets it.

Scorcher collapses at the relief of knowing he is not to blame. It's almost impossible for him to believe it was an unrelated thruster malfunction — that would have occurred, nonetheless. But Space-Bee's glare makes the unhelpful loop in his psyche stop.

She sets him on the floor on his back and disappears as

though she was never there.

Was I really talking to her? Where are the rest?

She reappears with water and sits down cross legged. She then rolls him over to attempt hydration and uses her lap as a pillow for him. It takes longer than he expected to be able to swallow the water, taking all his focus to overcome his stubborn throat.

He hears a familiar musical beep that his sheep's Bluetooth is within range. "Is that my sheep that just rolled up?" he asks, forgetting to ask how she herself got here.

"It came here on its own two hours ago then ran off before I could grab the oxygen bottles. I guess it only likes you. I saw your headlamp bouncing and failing its way up the cliff while I was outside. I'm nearly out of pressurized oxygen, so I was unable to get you." Then she jokes, "I would have gone to save you but figured you knew what you were doing."

"I guess that's why you looked less surprised than me. So the sheep went up the cliff? How did it know to come here?"

"No, it probably went the smart way to avoid the cliff," she explains.

"Well, I brought you air," he says.

"Oh? Just for me, huh."

She removes Scorcher from his spacesuit and lays him to sleep on the empty cot, then wraps him in her own clothes at her own expense in the cold.

*   *   *

When he awakes, Space-Bee is sitting on the floor with her back leaning against the wall. Her eyes are closed and the skin on her fingertips is raw from where she's been nervously picking.

"Do you have the strength to tell me what happened?"

Scorcher asks, trying to think of the best way to phrase the question.

"Yes," she responds neutrally. "Instead of going around, we decided to ditch at an old landing site we had once surveyed but thought wasn't worth maintaining."

"I didn't know this place was here," Scorcher says.

"It wasn't a secret, obviously, that Seattle has surveyed multiple sites. But yeah, not something that was ever published in detail since the results of the survey are proprietary," she explains.

"So are there other sites like these?"

"Yes," she replies simply. Her eyes open but stare blankly forward.

"And?" Scorcher pursues.

Space-Bee is confused, "And what?"

"Where are they? Are any of those also being used as catacombs?"

She closes her eyes again. "Come on, Scorcher."

He takes a moment before replying. "So, you knew about this landing site and went for it." He then asks the tough question. "Where are the others?"

"Dead," she answers directly. "We missed the landing site in all the chaos. Commander Ōtsuka and Rocko likely died of cardiac arrest from carbon dioxide poisoning a while ago," she states monotonously.

Scorcher isn't surprised by her awkwardly precise language; he can tell what her mind has been obsessing about while he slept. "But you lived," Scorcher says.

"Apparently."

"I came here to save you, but you saved me," he says to her.

Space-Bee laughs weakly, "Maybe."

Scorcher thinks about it for a second. "Only you had a

spacesuit. They only had their IVA pressure garments meant for pressure loss inside the ship, but which wouldn't let them travel a far distance outside because their oxygen supply is tethered directly to the ship. They physically couldn't leave the ship to escape."

"The forward cabin depressurized quite violently when we landed and tore open. They were barely conscious and quite bloodied. I tried to offer the EVA to Ōtsuka or Rocko, which was stupid because how would we have done that. But the Commander answered and ordered me to go to this base and come back with anything that could help."

Scorcher interrupts impatiently. "They're there now?"

"They are both there, but…" she trails off. She mumbles for a few seconds, but Scorcher can't follow. Still, the result is clear: the other two are lost, and she was unable to help them.

An excessive-nitrogen warning from Scorcher's limp spacesuit pierces his ears, catching him off guard. Then Space-Bee's suit sounds off with the same repeated high-low, two-note tune. "You're sabotaging the air in the Annie before I got here."

"I forgot," she mumbles. She starts humming the theme song to the movie *Home Alone* since the warning coincidently mimics the first two notes.

"You were committing suicide."

"I was the only one who could fit in the EVA. She ordered me, even though I'm dying from radiation poisoning anyway. I'm such a waste. Rocko should be here."

"That fat donkey definitely would not have fit in your EVA, Space-Bee," he replies.

"That's all he was to you, a fat donkey?" she asks, more as an accusation than a question.

"Jesus Christ, don't take me so literally right now. I can't even think straight." Scorcher rubs his temples and squints—Rocko used to joke and call himself a fat donkey, he justifies to himself. "And the O2 canister attachments for the spacesuit do not match what's on the IVA," he remembers.

"Yes," Space-Bee says, "but it's more complicated than that anyways. I told them a couple years ago to make them common hardware in case of an emergency, but way too much money and testing had already gone into those suits. The engineers on the EVA team didn't talk with the IVA team."

"Right," Scorcher sighs. Though it makes sense that there wouldn't be much overlap between an EVA spacesuit designed for external activities versus an IVA pressure garment never meant to leave a ship. They're both technically pressure suits, but very different.

Space-Bee changes the topic, "I know I should eat, but I can't right now."

"Oh yeah. Food. I didn't bring any," Scorcher discloses.

"I have a couple protein bars I accidently took—you should have one, Scorcher. Take mine."

"I'm going to fix the nitrogen setting, if you don't mind?" Scorcher tells more than asks while stumbling over to the computer.

"Sure."

When Scorcher returns to sit on the cot, he invites Space-Bee to sit next to him. He puts his arm around her, not knowing where to go from here. She allows herself to lean on him for once. "I can't just die peacefully," he says.

"Is that why you smell so horrible? Is that the opposite of peaceful?" she asks.

"Possibly. But the point is they did this to us. They did

this to Rocko and Ōtsuka and Shigley, whom I've never met, but I know I'm connected to."

"They?" she says unconvinced.

"Yes, the whole goddamned system and the individuals who enable it," says Scorcher.

"They," she repeats. "*We* are the individuals, Scorcher. Is that why you came to get me? Who are you even going after? The Founder? Four-Leaf? What's the point of anything?"

"I came here for you all."

"I'm dying, Scorcher, not you. I feel fucking horrible all the time. Why not just let me die in peace?" she pleads.

"We need to take our friends home, Space-Bee. They deserve it," he says softly but with conviction. "We can't let this culture be what sets the foundation of the future. This can't be the future. We need to do what's right for everyone who will come after us. People will keep coming here, but it's got to start with the right people and in the right way."

"So, your mid-life crisis is at war with our Moon culture?" she asks without enough energy to fully show her skepticism.

"This isn't about a fucking mid-life crisis."

"It's not? What is it, then?"

"It's about how I've spent too much time fighting small problems that only represent the symptoms. The symptoms like leaking pipes, mild explosions, people dying of radiation poisoning or abuse, the sociopaths like Four-Leaf who are attracted to this madness. I never had any real chance of fixing Central Lunar Mining or fighting Seattle or the Founder. But that doesn't mean I should surrender." Looking at her irises, he can't tell where she stands, but she's clearly not very moved by it. "I don't know where this is taking me, but I know we need to fight. We need to first take care of our friends and do what's right for them. Then we need to take care of you—you deserve it."

"I don't feel like I deserve anything," she says. Then, tearing up, she hugs Scorcher's damaged body. "I'm scared, Scorcher. I'm dying, and it's really scary."

"I know," he says, trying not to reveal too strong of an emotional reaction. "But I'm going to take care of you, so you don't have to worry."

After a few moments, she lifts her head back up to wipe away the tears. "I'm sorry, but this is all just so much right now, and I hadn't expected to actually ever see another living person again. I don't actually want to die here either."

"We won't. And please don't be sorry. If anything, I'm sorry. I've always just ended up turning everything into a shit show. I imprisoned Four-Leaf, for God's sake," he chuckles ironically.

"I know you are stubborn and only wanted to do the right thing this whole time. Trust me, I get that. I just never really knew how I felt about it." She pauses.

"I want to be straight with you. I think Shigley was murdered by the Company to coverup that he was suffering from radiation poisoning. They needed him to do something really dangerous. And then Four-Leaf either got in on it or knew the entire time. Shigley died when Seattle ordered him into a permanent shadow region to tap an ice well without following the appropriate precautions."

"You mean the ones they warn us about in training that have enough static electricity to kill? He would've known better. Why would he voluntarily do that?"

"You don't know what type of pressure he was under. And it is technically possible to do it manually under very specific conditions. But Seattle must have sent him in anyway. And Four-Leaf recovered the body, with a sheep, according to the Minister."

"The Minister knew?"

"Well, not totally. I remember the first time he mentioned Shigley, he said Four-Leaf retrieved his body with a sheep, thought that his suit failed by depressurizing. But I don't believe that."

"Who would have done that intentionally? The Founder? Four-Leaf? Seattle Medical? You seriously think this is some stupid conspiracy? This very easily could have been an accident."

"Either way, even if it's just manslaughter, we have to expose these people for who they are. I need to fight for justice. Not just for Shigley, for all of us and those who will come after us." He sees Space-Bee pulling away and decides there's no point in pursing this any further. Neither of them has the energy for it.

He thinks back to the victims instead. "I want to bring our friends home. We can't leave them here. Even if I have to drag them all the way back from this hell."

"How are we going to do that?" she asks, but at the same time, Scorcher can tell Space-Bee is trying to think of a serious plan, something he knows she's a master at.

"Well, first and foremost, in the first-aid kits I brought there should be something to wipe all the piss, shit, and blood off my body," Scorcher proposes, with Space-Bee nodding lightly, rubbing dust out of her itchy eyes. "Then after we force-feed ourselves, we go to recover our friends." Speaking their names out loud is too much. "Hopefully, if we can charge up the sheep—"

"We can't—this place is empty. The 400 Hz power outlets for charging aren't even installed."

Scorcher admits defeat. "Having me code the charging scripts would likely cause a fire during battery charge with our highly volatile lithium-ion batteries. Is the crash site on the plateau?"

"Yes."

Scorcher sees that Space-Bee is thinking. He gives her time to organize her thoughts so she doesn't miss something.

She continues, "We can use the sheep to ferry the bodies across the plateau and down the ridge. Then we'll just have to catch up with it wherever the sheep runs out of battery power."

For the first time Scorcher is not impressed by her planning. "Are you prepared for what that means to us, Space-Bee?" Scorcher asks. He studies her face and her injuries and wonders how much there is that he can't see.

"Scorcher, why is it only you? Why did the others not come? Where are they?"

"They're literally stranded. I didn't have time to go after both them and you. But it's not looking good because all their sheep were lining up at CLM without them. Somehow, they've been reset, their software wiped clean and set back to factory defaults. It's going to take days to update them and send them back out. The guys are left at their Annies, as far as I know. On top of that, I couldn't radio any of them, so I have no idea what their statuses are." He secretly hopes the Minister took the initiative to work on this while he was gone.

"I don't understand why you didn't go after them instead of us. What were you thinking? If they're in trouble, you could have saved them much more easily. Why did you waste your time coming out here?"

"They probably have enough ingenuity to make it back to CLM on their own. And anyways, if I could only have time to save one person, who would you have expected me to choose?" he asks.

"Not the sickest person here," she complains.

"Why does that matter?"

Space-Bee doesn't answer the question and stands up like she's done. She heads over to the first aid kit that wasn't there before to get out alcohol wipes. Apparently the sheep didn't run away this time; she must have donned on her EVA suit while he was sleeping. "There is a second Chinese outpost that we know about but weren't allowed to discuss, even though we flew over it all the time. It might—"

"You're shivering," Scorcher says, noticing her goosebumps.

"I'll turn the heat on high for my suit." She comes back to sit down on the cot. She uses her hand to rotate Scorcher so that his back is facing her. "I'll clean your disgusting back, then you do the rest. Somehow, you got regolith mixed in with the dried blood—looks gray and shiny like liquid quicksilver."

"Yeah, I'm not sure how that got there."

"I'm not sure how *you* got *here*," she counters.

"Me neither. Lucky, I guess."

She shakes her head. "I wouldn't call this lucky. Where are Four-Leaf and the Minister, again? Weren't you together?"

"I don't know. I got in a fight with Four-Leaf. I might have tied him to a cot. But I at least left him with food and water," he says. He doubts he needs to explain that he wasn't sent by Seattle.

"Jesus Christ, Scorcher."

Before long, and before completing the task of cleaning his back, Space-Bee starts to cough uncontrollably and can hardly catch herself. Scorcher holds her as she bends over in a fetal position and is unable to take breaths between coughs, turning violet. It takes all his strength not to completely lose himself at seeing such a pathetic sight.

*   *   *

After attaching the crew member bodies in their disconnected IVA suits onto the sheep, Scorcher hits the "Eco Route" and "Home" button on the digital touchscreen on the sheep's side. It then heads off into the distance, leaving them behind.

Scorcher and Space-Bee—Samuel and Samantha—watch as the sheep vanishes beyond the limits of their headlamps, their backs to the *Vegvisir* crash, never to look at it again. They both know that they don't have enough oxygen, electrical power, or physical endurance to make it all the way back to Central Lunar Mining. But Scorcher feels a miracle will happen between then and now. And all they need to do is try their best to survive by reaching the uncharted Chinese outpost. All they need to focus on is the next waypoint. There is nothing left for them here anyway; they must go.

Just then, Space-Bee grabs Scorcher's arm and points at a bright celestial object in the distance. Scorcher has the unrealistic hope that it's a ship coming to rescue them. As they both stare at it, the ultra-bright star grows to take a triangular shape.

The other stars start to disappear as the eyes of both astronauts adjust. The triangular shape grows into the shape of a mountain peak, floating in the sky amongst a beautiful blackness and the invisible horizon between Moon and sky. To Scorcher, it looks like a snow-covered island or iceberg floating in deep space—like a dream. Dawn has arrived on the Moon and the long darkness is over.

It is unspoken but understood that the bright peak,

blinding out the stars and the mostly shadowed geography, is their beacon. For Space-Bee, it guides her to the end and comfort. For Scorcher, it guides him to justice and purpose. The peak is a reminder that they are not alone in the blackness; there is still a universe and a path for them to struggle on. And beyond that, maybe even a fragile white and blue marble, whose own mere existence is also impossible.

"There couldn't be a more intense visual contrast between light and dark," Scorcher says.

Space-Bee responds by tugging his arm to signal that they should start going, and they do just that.

They walk off in the direction of the lighted peak, holding each other's hands like children, ghosts crossing the frozen desert, into the unknown.

Who will share their thoughts?

ABOUT THE AUTHOR

J. R. Cygal is a senior structural analysis engineer with over two decades' experience in aerospace. He's lived across the U.S. but now resides in the Pacific Northwest. In winter he often alpine skis or attempts snowboarding at Crystal Mountain or Stevens Pass. Some of the authors who have inspired him include Ursula K. Le Guin, Robert A. Heinlein, Mikhail Bulgakov, Jón Kalman Stefánsson, and Dmitry Glukhovsky.

He sincerely hopes that this novel—for the first time in fiction—shows the struggles that so many in aerospace experience when fighting for what's right.

ACKNOWLEDGMENTS

The author couldn't be more humbled to share his debut novel in speculative fiction with readers. He feels he owes everything to his beta readers, editors, and friends who over four years taught him so much. This includes Brianna, John, Liljana, Decillis, Cousin Mathew, Nathaniel, Vanessa, Julia, Durlav, and others.

Special kudos to Emily Poole at Midnight Owls Editors for providing magnificent line editing and copy-editing services. Any proofreading errors present in this manuscript can be blamed solely on the author.